Olive's Boys

Joseph Canning

By the same author:

Once Upon An Island

The right of Joseph Canning to be identified as the author
of this work is hereby asserted.

British Library Cataloguing In Publication Data
A Record of this Publication is available
from the British Library

ISBN 1846853850
978-1-84685-385-2

First Published 2006 by

Exposure Publishing, an imprint of Diggory Press,
Three Rivers, Minions, Liskeard, Cornwall, PL14 5LE, UK
WWW.DIGGORYPRESS.COM

To Carol

ONE

OLIVE CULLEN awoke to find herself staring up at the pale blue-grey of the sky: behind her, the early morning sun was slanting down through a hole in the ceiling to form an elongated oval on the opposite wall: around the hole, a section of plaster the size of a small tabletop was missing: directly above, there was another hole where the roof tiles should have been.

'Something must have come through in the night,' Olive thought vaguely, yawning and blinking as she struggled to throw off the weight of drowsiness which follows a long, deep sleep.

She was lying at the foot of the bed still wearing her red overcoat: looking about her, she saw the brown linoleum around the bed was covered in a layer of white dust and small pieces of plaster: then she realised that her face, her hair and her coat were all covered in the same white dust: so was the eiderdown upon which she lay.

When she sat up, still in a daze, a lump of plaster the size of a saucer slipped off her arm: several other pieces were strewn across the floor: one larger piece had hit a leg of the washstand before fracturing into three. Scattered amongst all of this on the rag-clipping rug beside the bed were a dozen or so chunks of broken brick and shards of broken chimney pot: lying on its side on the floor was the small black-cased alarm clock which normally stood on the washstand: wearily, Olive picked it up: it was showing just after six o'clock.

'The bricks must have come from the chimney,' she thought, but without at first comprehending why a section of the chimney should have come crashing through the roof and ceiling into the top-floor flat: it was then she remembered: and it was then, too, that she remembered the babies.

A shriek was already rising in her throat as she twisted round to look towards the head of the iron-framed double bed: for it was there, nine hours previously, precisely at a quarter-to-nine the night before, she had placed the two youngest of her children, eighteen-month-old Michael and six-month-old Joseph.

Olive's half-stifled wail turned to an outright sob of relief when she saw the children lying just as she had left them, their heads up against the bolster, still wedged by the pillows she had placed either side to prevent them rolling on to the floor: and, miraculously, both were untouched except for a coating of dust on their clothing and some small pieces of plaster lying between them and on the pillows either side.

Michael, thumb in his mouth, was still sleeping peacefully, twisted half to one side, his chest slowly rising and falling: baby Joseph, wide awake, attracted by the movement of his mother, was gurgling happily to himself, both feet curled up before him and pulling at the toes of his pale blue woollen leggings.

Even as Olive took in the tranquil scene, her very breath seemed to freeze within her: balanced directly above the bolster against which the heads of the two children were resting was a lump of masonry from the fallen chimney: three pieces of brick, still welded together by their mortar, had plummeted down on to the curved brass rail of the bedstead directly above the children's heads. By good fortune, the bed was some six or nine inches away from the wall and, after denting the rail, the bricks had tipped backwards, away from the sleeping infants and now were wedged in the small gap: had they tipped the other way, both the children's heads would have been crushed.

Even in her exhausted, sleepy state, Olive moved swiftly, seizing the baby Joseph and then the sleeping Michael and placing them together in the dust-free patch at the foot of the bed where she herself had been lying: it was then that the sickening awfulness of what might have happened swept over her.

'Oh, my God!' she sobbed to herself, a sudden desperate shame overcoming her. 'I must have fallen asleep! I must have slept through it all.'

Gathering up the tiny bundle of the fidgeting Joseph in one arm and laying the sleeping Michael over her other shoulder so that his head nestled against her neck, she picked her way carefully across the fallen rubble of bricks and plaster to the bedroom door, forcing it open with her foot. Fortunately, the door leading from the living room of the two-room flat out on to the landing was still ajar, just as she had left it the previous night, and, despite the blacked-out skylight, there was just enough early morning light on the unlit stairs for her to pick her way carefully down the three flights to the ground-floor, tug open the front door and step out into Rupert Road.

Rubble lay everywhere: in the street, on the pavements, on the steps leading up to the front doors of the four-storey houses which made up Rupert Road, even down in the dark wells of the basement flats: broken brick, fractured tile, shattered glass, splintered wood, all overlaid with a thick covering of brown dust. The smell of burning filled the air: one end, the northern end, of Rupert Road's soot-coated length was obscured by a hanging pall of blue-grey smoke as though a dense mist had risen off the river during the night, drifted into that part and was refusing to disperse. Halfway down, in the middle of a shimmering lake of water, a dark green fire engine was parked askew, blocking the road: from it, hosepipes snaked in all directions, overlaying each other like the tangled roots of some great tree. Beyond were more fire engines, half-hidden by the curtain of smoke, and moving among them the scurrying black figures of shouting, gesticulating firemen, appearing out of the haze one second and vanishing back into it the next. One fireman, hurrying along the pavement on some mission away from the others, halted, stupefied, unable to believe his eyes as Olive emerged from the doorway of number forty-two carrying the two children.

'Good God, woman! What the bloody hell are you doing in there?' he cried, running up.

'I fell asleep,' Olive told him angrily, picking her way down the steps and crunching fragments of glass underfoot. 'I just fell asleep. All right?'

It was not all right, but the fireman could not bring himself to say so: Olive's fierceness deterred him. 'Fell asleep! God, woman!' was all he could say again, 'Fell asleep! Fell asleep!' and stare after her as she made her way towards the top end of Rupert Road, where the High Road runs and where the late September sun was climbing pale and chill above damp, glistening rooftops.

Far off in the distance, the long, steady, wail of the 'all clear' siren was sounding: Olive Cullen and the other residents of Rupert Road had just endured their twenty-first successive night of bombing: the London Blitz was at its height. That was why Olive was hurrying along the pavement with Michael draped over one shoulder, snuggled against her neck, and the baby Joseph cradled in her other arm, a fearful look upon her face. Rupert Road south had its own communal shelter, a squat, utilitarian, biscuit-brick building with a foot-thick, reinforced concrete roof and sandbagged entrance, partly sunk underground, built on the site of a former timber yard a hundred yards farther along the street. There, nine hours earlier, she had left two of her other children, the three-year-old twins, John and Thomas, and she wanted to know if it were still there and they were safe!

TWO

FOR Olive and the other Londoners, it had all begun late one sunny Saturday in September, the seventh: she had spent the afternoon sitting in the warm sunshine in the small park a mile or so along the High Road from its junction with Rupert Road, watching the twins and Michael playing with other children in the sandpit while occasionally rocking Joseph in the cumbersome, double-hooded pram in which she conveyed her two youngest. Then, with the twins hanging on to the sides of the pram and bemoaning every step they took, they had begun the weary trudge home just before four o'clock.

At that precise moment, a hundred or so miles to the south the bloated figure of Reichmarshall Hermann Goering and a gathering of Luftwaffe officers were standing on the French cliffs at Cap Gris Nez and smiling to themselves: a massive air fleet was passing overhead: three-hundred and fifty bombers, Heinkel 111s, Dornier 17s and Junkers 88s, escorted by six-hundred weaving Bf 109s and 110s, extending for mile after mile, all heading north westwards, across the Channel, towards England, towards London.

Plotters in Kent, using the new radio direction finder tubes, spotted the aircraft gathering in their carefully stacked formations over the Pas de Calais soon after four o'clock: Royal Air Force fighters were scrambled from Biggin Hill, Tangmere, North Weald, Middle Wallop and, north of the river Thames, Hornchurch. The Hurricanes and Spitfires met the bomber formations over the rolling hop fields of Kent and as they flew westward up the Thames estuary following the wind of the river: but, caught by surprise and not concentrated, the defending fighters were brushed aside by the sheer mass of the enemy.

Olive was preparing the children's tea of bread and butter and jam sandwiches, with the wireless turned on when the air raid sirens began to wail: she had just heated Joseph's milk and tipped it into his bottle to cool and was waiting for him to awaken from his nap, at the same time humming to the brass band music on the wireless. Like many of her neighbours, she crossed to the window and peered out to see what was happening: Olive could see nothing, though below in the street people were looking up and pointing. Amongst them, a helmeted air raid warden was shouting and blowing his whistle and, somewhat futilely, trying to usher them farther along the road: but no one seemed to be taking any notice: some people even stepped into the road to avoid his waving arms: all continued to look up and to point: distant to the east, Olive heard a dull booming sound. Then a policeman arrived, threw down his bicycle and roughly began pushing people towards the end of the road where the Rupert Road south air raid shelter was located: only then did Olive realise what was happening: an air raid had started! The people in the street realised it, too: after that, everyone began to hurry, mothers with children, fathers carrying other children, old people, youths and girls: they all suddenly appeared as if from nowhere, all hurrying towards the shelter and all looking up as if in fear.

On the various landings of forty-two Rupert Road, doors were being banged shut and feet were clattering down the uncarpeted stairs towards the street as people vacated the lower flats: everywhere there was a sense of panic and desperation: women were shouting to women: mothers were screaming at children: children were crying, frustrated by the urgency demanded of them by adults which they could not match. Even as she stood at the window looking out, Olive suddenly became aware that someone was hammering on the door: it was her neighbour from across the landing, Old Ma Parrett.

'Olive! Olive! Open the door! Come on, girl! Open up! Open the door!' the old woman was shouting in a voice near to hysterical. 'The sirens are going. We've got to get the children down to the shelter. Come on, girl, open this door! Hurry up, for Gawd's sake!' The last words were spoken even as Olive pulled open the door and her neighbour pushed her way into the flat, followed by her wheezing, cancerous husband, Walter, a shriven husk of a man, fading away towards death, so Olive thought, like sunlight vanishing off the face of the earth when clouds drift across the sun.

Ma Parrett was a heavy-set, grey-haired, West Country woman in her mid-sixties, who still spoke with the distinctive burr of that region: she and her husband were long-term residents of the flats, having been at forty-two Rupert Road since just after the First War: previously, they had had a bigger flat on the second floor, but circumstances had relegated them to the cheaper and smaller, top-floor flats. They had come up from Somerset in Nineteen-Twenty, he to drive the trolley buses, she to work as a clippie: Ma Parrett was used, therefore, to ordering people about. 'You can carry Joey in the baby bag. I'll take Michael and the gas masks,' she announced, making immediately for the table and seizing a startled and wide-eyed Michael from his chair and hooking the three small children's gasmask boxes over her free arm. 'Walter, you get the twins. Come on, hurry up, or the bloody Germans will be here!'

That was how it all began for Olive: with a panic-stricken rush back into the bedroom to snatch up Joseph from the 'cot' she had improvised from a drawer, a pillow and a blanket. Such was the terror and hysteria which gripped her at that moment that she expected at any second to hear bombs exploding outside and for the house to disintegrate in a blinding flash all around her. In her desperation, she accidentally banged the sleeping Joseph's head with her elbow as she fitted the anti-gas helmet over his head and upper torso. Immediately, the child cried out, whether from pain or from being awakened she was not sure and, worse, realised she did not care: at any other time, the tiny face peering out through the perspex window wet with tears and visibly reddening with frustration and rage, would have caused her to pick up the squalling infant, to cradle him and to comfort him: but there was no time for that, not at that moment.

Ma Parrett was becoming more insistent. 'Come on, Olive, get a move on!' she was exhorting, at the same time pushing her shuffling husband and the open-mouthed twins through the door. There was just time for Olive to snatch up two towelling nappies drying on the fireguard as she passed them: the baby's milk, the children's sandwiches, Michael's boiled egg, her own untouched cup of tea were left on the table: for outside, the siren was continuing to wail.

By the time Olive reached the landing, Ma Parrett was already on her way down the first flight of the dim-lit stairs, clutching the bemused Michael against one pinafored shoulder with one hand while clinging to the bannister with the other: ahead of her, the stooped and shuffling Walter was attempting to usher down the twins.

'Come on, boys, down you go, down you go,' he was urging, touching them on their shoulders as if that alone would move them downwards: but the poor man, given only the pillows and blankets to carry by his shrewish wife because he was too weak and infirm to be entrusted with anything else, was having difficulty in persuading them: on each step, they paused to look back with anxious eyes, unwilling to go any farther without their mother.

'God, man! Get a move on! They'll be here before we get halfway if you don't shift yourself!' Ma Parrett was shouting as Olive hurried along the landing to join them, clutching the still-wailing Joseph in his anti-gas helmet and almost weeping in her panic and anger: anger because her husband, Robert, was not there to help her: anger because he was a hundred and fifty miles away down in Plymouth with his two brothers, Brendan and Gerry, and more than likely standing at the bar of some locked pub at that exact moment, having spent the whole afternoon there.

To herself she cried: 'That bloody husband of mine, he's never around when you need him! Trust him to be away at a time like this! Trust him!' She had to rail against someone and the absent Robert was a natural victim.

Aloud, however, to her children, she just shouted: 'I'm coming, I'm coming!' Her words were enough to reassure the twins waiting on the landing below to continue their slow, careful, moody descent towards the ground floor. Consequently, they were the last of the families to leave the flats: by the time they reached the wide hallway where the prams were kept under the stairs, the house was deserted.

Along Rupert Road itself, a steady stream of people was heading for the south shelter on the waste land of the old timber yard: Olive and the Parretts reached the sandbagged entrance just as the despairing wail of the siren died: as they entered, Olive took one last look back: small dark puffs of smoke were appearing as if out of nowhere above, below and amongst a great flock of birds approaching along the river. Except, they were not birds: they were Junkers 88s and the small puffs of dark smoke were exploding shells from the guns firing at them: Operation 'Loge,' the much-vaunted air assault on London, was about to begin: it was exactly five o'clock.

The Rupert Road south shelter, one of two erected at either end of the street, had been built to accommodate only three hundred or so adults and children from the forty houses which comprised the roll at that end: in effect, it was more of an overflow shelter for its much larger northern brother, which could hold upwards of seven hundred. That afternoon the south shelter was packed with many than it should have been and it was a squeeze to get inside: many of those there that teatime were strangers from other streets nearby and not on the shelter roll: the attack had taken everyone by surprise while they were out shopping along the High Road and they had made for the first place of safety. Even as Olive and Ma Parrett pushed their way in, other breathless latecomers came surging in behind them, stumbling in to people and almost knocking the twins over: among them were several boys and girls still in their pre-teen years who had just left the Embassy Cinema, a half-mile along the High Road, after the afternoon film show and had been directed there by the angry policeman. The girls were white-faced and trembling and several were crying: the boys, as boys will, were putting on a show of bravado, laughing and sniggering at the snivelling girls: everyone knew they should not even have been in London: they should have been safe in the country, but no one said so: then was not the time.

Once inside, it was a matter of pushing in and finding what bunks and space one could: Olive and her brood and the Parretts found themselves next to a haughty woman in a black fur overcoat who seemed more concerned with what might happen to her three cats when the bombs fell than what might happen to the company around her. 'Oh, I do hope they will be all right,' she whined. 'They're all I've got since my husband died.'

The blatant selfishness of it incensed Ma Parrett. 'Bugger you and your cats!' she told the woman angrily. 'There's kiddies in here. You should think about them. We've got more to worry about than your bloody cats!'

They had: overhead, the first of the enemy formations, Junkers 88s, which had formed up at fifteen-hundred feet over St Omer and had followed the railway north of Sevenoaks towards their target, were opening their bomb doors as the great smoky haze of London loomed on the horizon ahead of them. Eighteen-hundred feet above the rolling hop fields of Kent, the Heinkels, which an hour earlier had assembled over St Pol, were droning north over Westerham. The target of both was the great area of docklands in the East End, Silvertown, Deptford, Woolwich and Millwall, and the vast basins filled with shipping, the miles of quays and the colossal warehouses. Through the great docks, the West India, the Millwall, the Royal Victoria, the Albert and the Surrey Commercial on the south side of the river, passed every commodity imaginable from all over the world: chilled meats, marble, rubber, fruit, spices, perfume, ivory, tea, tobacco, timber, wool and wheat.

In the next hour, the great air fleet crossed and recrossed the area on their bombing runs virtually unimpeded, dropping high-explosive bombs and magnesium-cased incendiaries which exploded on impact and burned with a heat fierce enough to melt steel amongst the warehouses, factories, streets of terraced houses, shops, hospitals and schools.

THREE

THE FIRST 'all clear' was sounded at ten minutes past six: for an hour Olive and the four hundred others who had crowded into the Rupert Road south shelter had listened to the steady drone of aircraft overhead and had prayed silently to themselves as the bombs screeched and whistled down: they had heard the far off crump of explosions and had felt the concrete floor vibrate underfoot, but they had remained untouched: now they were able to leave. When they emerged, shaken and blinking into the early evening sunlight, they could scarcely believe what they saw: some just stood on the pavement, looking: awed, unable to move: others spread themselves into the middle of the junction where Rupert Road joined the High Road and gaped in open-mouthed horror. Over the river to the distant east, pillars of black smoke were billowing and spiralling up thousands of feet into a clear blue sky: everywhere on the wind, there was the acrid smell of burning: it seemed as if the whole of the East End was on fire.

'Oh my Gawd! Those poor people, those poor people,' someone cried aloud, voicing all their thoughts, knowing the maze of streets and terraced houses which lay beyond the spreading wall of angry, red flames spurting above the rooftops in between. Even as they stood there, a fire engine came clanging along the High Road, forcing those in the centre of the road to part, to be followed almost immediately by a second and then a third, all heading eastwards as fire crews from across London raced to answer the call.

In the East End, a mere four miles or so across the rooftops from where they stood at the top of Rupert Road, other shaken survivors were emerging from whatever shelter they had managed to find to discover themselves surrounded by flames and falling buildings. The docks were a blazing inferno: Silvertown was ringed by fire and the only escape from it was by water: the whole of the one-and-a-half miles between the North Woolwich Road and the Thames had been virtually destroyed. Scores of terraced houses, the back-to-back homes of dockers and factory workers for almost a century, had been destroyed: and those not destroyed had been badly damaged: hundreds had died or were dying even as they watched.

In the warehouses along the river, barrels of rum were exploding in 'whooshing' fireballs: great columns of thick, choking, black smoke rose from thousands of burning bales of rubber: in buildings alongside, fifty-gallon drums of paint burned with an uncontrollable fury, while in other warehouses stacked wooden chests of Indian and Chinese tea and great mounds of American grain burned to add their own searing heat to the conflagration: all around, walls collapsed, roofs caved in, glass shattered and water jets from the fire hoses turned uselessly to scalding steam in mid-air. At the quaysides, ships and barges burned: the Thames was literally aglow with blazing barges: rivers of melted rubber and liquefied sugar flowed in cataracts of fire over the dockside and spread in fiery sheets over the surface of the water. In the Surrey Commercial docks on the south bank, two hundred acres of timber blazed, giving off a heat so intense it blistered the paintwork of the fireboats futilely hosing the burning riverside warehouses on the opposite bank.

Olive and the Parretts stood among the silent, sombre crowd for a few more minutes watching the distant inferno: not through any ghoulishness, but simply because they, like others, felt they needed to record the scene with their own eyes so as to be able always to remember it: to have turned away too soon for whatever reason would somehow have seemed a slight upon those struggling in the midst of it all. Eventually, some people on the edge of the crowd did begin to drift away: Olive, wanting to get back to the flat, for the sake of the twins, was glad when their persistent whining gave her the excuse to leave: the horror of what they had just witnessed had stunned them all. Was this to be the new war, the way all wars were to be fought in future?

'Those bloody Germans! Those bloody Germans!' Olive found herself repeating again and again: it was all she could think to say.

'They need shooting, the lot of them! Bloody Nazi bastards!' Old Man Parrett declared bitterly for all and anyone to hear. 'We had enough of those buggers in the last lot. We ain't going to have to go through that all again, are we?'

For once, the normally opinionated Ma Parrett could find nothing to say: her face was ashen and she was brushing away tears as she followed Olive up the dark stairs to the fourth-floor landing, carrying Michael: she was still trembling visibly when she handed him back to Olive at the door of the flat. 'All those people,' she finally managed to say. 'All those people.'

Two hours later, at eight o'clock, the sirens wailed again: this time, Olive was standing at the sink in one corner of the living room washing the children's clothing in an enamel bowl.

'Oh my God, not again! Not again!' Angrily, she flung the washing on to the draining board and made for the landing: the tears of rage and frustration just came welling up: she just could not keep them down.

'Mrs. Parrett! Mrs. Parrett,' a desperate Olive called: already on the landings below, she could hear people heading down, banging doors and shouting to each other: they, too, were saying the same thing: 'Not again! Not again!'

The older woman was pulling on her coat even as she came out of her door. 'Don't worry, we're with you, girl,' she announced as the panicking Olive ran back into the bedroom. 'The buggers ain't here yet.' She seemed calmer and more composed than she had been after the trauma of the afternoon: but there was a bitterness about her which she had never shown before. 'Bloody Germans,' she cried, 'dropping bombs on kids! What kind of people are they? I hope we're giving them what they're giving us. I hope we're bombing them flat, so help me.' Behind her the shuffling, skeletal, toothless Walter, a bundle of pillow cases and blankets under one arm and his wife's shopping bag in the other, grinned in macabre agreement.

It took Olive and Ma Parrett almost a minute to shake the twins awake: then, while Olive once again hurriedly fitted the anti-gas helmet over Joseph's head and checked to ensure the bellows pump was still attached and the respirator was clear, her neighbour lifted the still sleeping Michael on to her shoulder. The twins' pitiful protest began as soon as they were hustled out on to the landing and realised they were being forced from their warm bed into the cold night air: but, such was the desperation of their mother, they received no sympathy and were chivvied down in the same urgent manner as before.

'How long is all this going to go on for?' Olive cried out, more to herself than the old couple, as they made their way down. 'I hope this is not going to go on for too long.'

Olive did not know it at the time, but it was to be the first of fifty-six successive nights on which London was to be bombed from dusk till dawn: the raid that night began at nine and lasted eight hours: the fiery glow of a burning London was all that was needed to guide the approaching bombers. This time they cruised across Battersea, Hammersmith and Paddington, unloading their high explosive and incendiaries at will: by three in the morning the planes circled over a raging inferno. When dawn broke and the last of them headed back to France, more than fifty major blazes and a thousand smaller conflagrations were burning: they burned on through the whole of Sunday into the Monday: two thousand Londoners in the densely packed East End dock area lay dead and injured: three mainline railway terminals were out of action and hundreds of homes, public houses, shops and hospitals had been destroyed or damaged.

And so began a nightly ritual for Olive and her children: each evening for the next twenty nights in succession, as soon as the first siren sounded, she and the children, helped by the Parretts, joined the scurrying panic of all the others at that end of Rupert Road to the south shelter. Some, fearful of being caught out, even took up their places as soon after their evening meal as possible, others as soon as dusk started to fall, hustling their children and husbands down the stairs, those who still had husbands at home, eager to claim their usual places on the bunks, as far from the doorway as possible in case a bomb dropped too near and well away from it, too, so that they and their children, with luck, would be settled and asleep when the cacophony started up outside.

Even going early, Olive and Ma Parrett still found themselves having to argue for bunks sometimes, though not for themselves: overcrowding was becoming more acute and already the system of allocating places and ticking off people's names as residents of Rupert Road when they entered had broken down completely: it was now first come, first served. Some of those there were complete strangers who had come up from the devastated East End: hoping to find any place which would put distance between them and the docks, even if it were only four miles as the crow flew, like Rupert Road: it was safer, they reckoned, than where they were. One woman told Olive that some of the blazes around them were still burning four days after the raid which had started them: the firemen, she said bitterly, had left them to burn themselves out and so at night they had become an obvious beacon for the bombers coming up from the south and east: and she was not going to stay there and become a sitting duck for Hitler's bombers! So there!

Olive could only sympathise with her: it was not her fault that there always seemed to be far more people in the shelter than the number for which it was built: the houses in Rupert Road were all converted into flats, from basements to top storeys, most of them occupied by families: in some houses, there were six or eight flats and, consequently, a teeming bedlam of noise and argument. What was happening was that many from the bottom end of Rupert Road were traipsing the threequarters-of-a-mile to the smaller south shelter simply out of fear that the northern one was too near a sprawling engineering factory and some prominent goods warehouses: they much preferred the smaller, more compact southern shelter because it was well away from what, in their view, was a certain target.

Worryingly, too, for Olive and the other Rupert Road mothers, was that by the second week some of the newcomers were starting to take up permanent residence in the shelter, venturing out during the day only to buy or to queue for whatever they needed, while leaving their little encampment in the charge of some older relative. With many of the schools closed by government order and others destroyed, groups of children were beginning to play directly outside the shelter itself during the day, ready to dash inside when the sirens sounded: hopscotch chalk marks had appeared on the pavement, one of the swings in the little park along the High Road had already been broken by them and a public toilet, no more than two buckets and two sacking screens, had had to be set up on waste ground near the shelter as the ones in the shelter itself, now augmented by pails and coal scuttles, were frequently overflowing.

It was noticeable, too, to Olive how tired looking some of the men still at home and accompanying their wives to the shelter had become since the bombing had begun, though there were few of them: mostly, they were older men and those in deferred occupations who had not been called up for service and had somehow escaped air raid duties: they seemed to think it their duty to remain awake all night to calm their children just by their presence and apparent lack of concern when, if the truth be known, they were as worried as anyone. Olive liked to think Robert might have been like that had he been there, staying awake so that, if the children were disturbed at all during the night by nearby bombing, he would be able to smile and to comfort them and resettle them while she tried to sleep.

Another thing she had noticed was how nervous some of the older women, who should have known better, were becoming as the ring of anti-aircraft batteries hurriedly established around London to the north, south and east opened up, to be followed almost immediately by bright, violent flashes in the sky as their shells exploded futilely among the droning aircraft. Their lack of resilience was having its effect on the morale of the younger ones and some were talking about joining the trek westward being made nightly by the many from the shattered docklands areas: in families and neighbourly groups, they were decamping to the West End well before the sirens sounded, feeling that they were less likely to be bombed there. Some were even moving on to Paddington station: small groups lugging suitcases could be seen daily waiting on the concourse there for a train to anywhere: Wales, Cornwall, the West, it did not matter so long as they could get away from the bombs and could sleep at night.

Others were beginning to occupy the Tube stations: the authorities had foolishly resisted calls to allow these natural deep shelters to be used, but the tired and fed-up Londoners, contemptuous of bureaucracy, had taken matters into their own hands and, in a mass outbreak of civil disobedience, were pouring into them in their thousands every night to sleep on the platforms and on the escalators and stairs: at least, there they knew they were safe.

FOUR

THE APPARENT ease with which the German bombers roamed the skies above the capital in the first few nights of bombing was a cause for much bitterness among the many hundreds of thousands who nightly crowded into their shelters, whether they be some sturdy concrete-roofed construction holding three-hundred or more such as that to which Olive and the children went each evening, or a corrugated, curved-steel-roofed Anderson dug three feet into the soft clay of a back garden and covered with eighteen inches of earth, refuge for a family of six, or simply a cupboard under the stairs into which all the family crawled as soon as the siren sounded.

That the people were unhappy would have been clear to anyone eavesdropping upon the agitated conversations conducted in the Rupert Road south shelter: though a few bombers had been brought down by anti-aircraft fire since the raids had begun and pictures of the crashed aircraft had been published in the newspapers, it did not happen often enough for most people: now they were voicing their opinions out loud.

'The buggers keep on getting through, don't they?' was the repeated gripe of one man. 'Why? I'll tell you, why! Because there ain't enough guns around London to shoot 'em all down, that's why. There ain't enough guns, I say. That or the people firing them can't shoot for toffee!'

Olive, who was trying to calm a fidgeting Thomas, recovering him with the blanket each time he kicked it off, was ready to agree with him when unexpectedly Old Ma Parrett, sitting alongside her, rounded on the man.

'They're doing their best!' she snapped. 'They're bringing in guns from all over the country to help protect us, same as they've got firemen coming in from all over the country to help put out the fires. A woman who was over at Paddington station today to see her daughter and her children off said there were scores of guns being unloaded on to the platform. Scores of them. Some from as far away as Wales and Cornwall, so there! The army's doing its best and they don't need jeremiahs like you telling it different. If you don't like it, why don't you get out there and help them shoot!'

'I'll believe it when I see it for myself!' the grumbler sneered in reply.

'You may get your chance,' a man standing by the canvas gas screen called out, almost gleefully. 'There's a hell of a racket going on out there. Something's happening. They're giving them hell tonight by the sounds of it! Crikey! Listen to that!'

Suddenly people were crowding near the entrance to listen: outside the noise of the guns seemed to be much louder than usual and more continuous: the men and the youths were smiling at each other: some were even laughing aloud: it was the cheeriest thing Olive had seen in all her nights in the shelter. That night, gun sites all along the inner action zone, from Hackney Marshes to the City, were blazing away into the night sky to throw up a veritable wall of fire to meet the incoming bombers. The gunners had been told they no longer needed to worry whether they hit any of the planes: that night they were to put up as many airbursts as they could: that night the thirty-five guns of the inner action zone fired thousand of rounds of heavy anti-aircraft ammunition and succeeded in forcing the enemy planes to a higher altitude so as to make bombing more difficult: and, of course, the sheer volume of their fire was enough to hearten the population.

Except Olive: to her the noise of the guns was the sole reason why Thomas was so fitful: he was hearing them in his sleep. Fortunately, the one common agreement among the mothers was that children had priority on the bunks: if one were taken by some lounging young male, especially if he were from the northern end of Rupert Road, or even one of the docklands youths whom they did not know, a waspish 'Come on, you, off there! Scarper!' from a thin-faced, headscarved mother, backed up by a phalanx of similarly headscarved and becurlered women, was enough to send the surly interloper muttering to the far end of the shelter to seek another place.

Neither did the mothers want their offspring to be awakened by inconsiderate latecomers: they felt they had enough to contend with the Germans trying to bomb them without being disturbed by the hearty souls who thought it more prudent to begin the early part of the evening by obtaining 'Dutch courage' in the Duke of Wellington on the corner or the Queen's Arms and the Marlborough farther along the High Road and said rather too jovially for one or two of the complaining women, 'Well, you never know where we'll be tomorrow, girls! This might be our last chance to have a drink!'

Olive herself had flown at one of the fools who came lurching down between the bunks and banged against the one on which the twins were sleeping, waking both John and Thomas just as there was a particularly loud explosion a half-mile or so away: a parachute-mine or something like it, someone guessed. It had made the whole shelter shake: showers of grit and dust cascaded down from the foot-thick slab of steel-reinforced concrete overhead to mingle with heavy clouds of blue tobacco smoke in a brief, choking fog. The twins howled with fright and she never did get them back to sleep again: the fool of a man retreated rather rapidly after what Olive said to him. That is why she did not like the shelter: hated it, in fact: neither she nor the children slept well in the fetid, smoky atmosphere and some nights she did not sleep at all and the children slept only intermittently. That meant long days of weariness followed, days of washing the children's clothes, the never-ending round of changing Joseph's nappies, feeding him every four hours, feeding the fractious Michael almost on demand, separating the squabbling twins, getting their dinners, sometimes spending whole afternoons in one or other of the ration queues: queues for bacon, queues for eggs, queues for meat, for sausages, for sugar: standing in the cold and the rain with the two youngest in the double-hooded pram: then back to the flat to get the twins from Ma Parrett's flat, get them their teas and prepare them for another night in the shelter even before the sirens began wailing.

Then had come the hours of waiting: waiting in the dim-lit shelter as the burgeoning smell of sweat from close-packed, unwashed bodies mingled in the warm, stale air with the creeping stench of splashed urine from the curtained-off chemical lavatory: waiting, too, as the bomb-laden German aeroplanes sped down the runways of captured aerodromes in northern France and Belgium, climbed slowly into the darkening sky and then, guided by direction beams, droned north and north westwards in their hundreds towards London. For Olive and her four, it had been night after night of trying to sleep through the continual banging of the guns: and night after night, too, of dull, crumping explosions as the bombs rained down, some far off, but others near enough to Rupert Road now for them to think the Germans were aiming specifically at their street and especially the accursed engineering works and warehouses at the north end.

'One – two – three – four – five – ' Those in the south shelter would count as each of the bombs making up the stick came nearer: half-dozing mothers slumped on the hard wooden benches beside their restless children would look up in alarm and cigarette-smoking men would freeze in mid-exhalation the nearer each bomb came. The ground would shudder beneath their feet like the beginnings of a small earthquake: then the aircraft would be over them, the sixth bomb would fall, the heavy canvas gas curtain over the entrance flap would jerk violently from the blast as if it were being punched by an invisible assailant, but it would be past them! And those awake in the shelter would look at each other as if to say, 'We've survived that one,' and breathe sighs of relief.

To help the children to sleep, Olive, like most of the women, had from the start taken pillows and blankets to the shelter: to hasten their descent each evening, she and Ma Parrett had got into the habit of dropping their rolled bundles down the stairwell with cries of 'Look out below!' and 'Coming down!' so that when they reached the hallway it was a simple matter to gather them up, put baby Joseph and Michael in the double-hooded pram kept under the stairs and wheel it to the shelter.

In twenty successive nights, the old couple had not missed: but on the twenty-first night, they did miss.

FIVE

WHEN, on the twenty-first night, a Friday, the siren sounded, Olive was dozing in the single armchair beside the gas fire: the other residents of forty-two Rupert Road had long since gone clumping down the stairs with their rolls of blankets and pillows tucked under their arms and their flasks of tea and cocoa and little packets of sandwiches stowed in their shopping bags. A weary Olive had just listened to them go: the children were all abed and asleep, she was comfortable in the armchair, the wireless was on, the fire was warm: and while she had dozed, the clock had ticked on...

That day, too, Old Ma Parrett and her yellow-skinned husband had had a late afternoon appointment at an X-ray clinic two bus rides away: the old man's chest was getting worse: he had a pain under his ribcage, he was coughing more and more and there was blood mixed in with his spittle. 'Get them kids down there early, Olive, we might not be back in time,' Ma Parrett had warned before she left.

Why Olive delayed, she did not herself know: perhaps it was through sheer tiredness: or perhaps it was because she knew that night she would have to take the children alone and could not summon the energy: or perhaps it was because she hoped that night the bombers would not come: after three weeks of continual bombing, surely they would give up sometime?

After tea, she had pottied the twins on the chipped and rusting blue-rimmed enamel bowl she used for that purpose, changed a dozing Michael and later Joseph and put them all on the iron-framed double bed, John and Thomas at the foot, the babies at the head, with the pillows separating them, their heads against the bolster. If by some miracle the air raid sirens did not sound that night, if for once the German bombers did not come, then she and the children would all have a good night's sleep: she would leave them on the double bed and try to make a bed for herself on the floor alongside: the twins' single bed was too rickety for her to sleep on. And, while she waited, she would do some knitting.

A week before she had unravelled the green wool from one of her own cardigans and now she was sitting in the armchair before the gas fire in the living room, struggling to follow the pattern for a small jacket she was knitting for Joseph which she had kept from one of her women's magazines: but she could not keep her eyes open: her eyelids kept closing and several times she had to jerk herself awake. It was the heat of the fire, not weariness, Olive reassured herself: that and the lulling music on the wireless and the boredom of being by herself with no one to whom she could talk. She desperately needed Robert there, not only for his comfort, but for someone to whom she could talk, even if he did often sit at the table smelling of drink, having first called at the Queen's Arms on his way home and spent half the night there. He was her husband and she felt he ought to have been there: she needed him there, not a hundred and fifty miles away working in the docks at Plymouth, laying concrete with his two brothers. He had not been home for more than two months, though that was nothing unusual with Robert: nor had he written, except to send a postal order at the end of July for ten pounds, ten shillings: now it was late September and the money was running out and she was having to draw on her post office savings just to pay the rent man and buy what food she needed. Sometimes she grew angry just thinking about Robert's long absences: sometimes she suspected he did not want to come home: she did not suspect another woman, more that he was enjoying his freedom away from his family, and her, and doubtless was spending his time in pubs, drinking. Since the three of them had all gone down to Plymouth, his brothers, Brendan and Gerry, had been home regularly to see their wives, Martha and Muriel, but not Robert: the last time he had arrived home had been at the end of June, nine weeks before the bombing began.

When that started, she had expected that he would rush back, as most men would, to find out if his wife and children were safe: but nearly three weeks had passed and there had been neither sight of him nor word from him, by letter or by telegram, or message through his brothers. Curiously, there had been nothing from them either: or from their wives, Martha and Muriel, all of which puzzled Olive: as soon as she was able, if Robert had not made contact by then, she determined that she would take the Tube to where they lived and find out why.

In the meantime, she needed to know where he was, what he was doing: she needed him there, with her: in bed, playing with the children in the living room-cum-kitchen, just standing at the sink on a Sunday morning shaving, even just sitting at the table smelling of beer: she would not have minded, so long as he was there! She was still thinking about him when she drifted off into a deep sleep: it was the high-pitched wailing of the siren which roused her.

She had no idea how long she had slept: an hour perhaps, an hour-and-a-half even: the next thing she knew someone was banging at the door: a voice was calling out to her: 'Olive! Olive! Are you in there, girl? The air-raid siren, Olive! You ought to be in the shelter, for goodness sake!'

'Oh God! Not again?' Olive cried, jerking awake and rubbing at her eyes. 'Not again! Not another bloody air raid! How many more? How many more?'

Ma Parrett, a torch in one hand, two pillows and a folded blanket under one arm, was leaning against the door frame, perspiring and breathing heavily. 'I saw your light,' she gasped. 'Good lord, girl, whatever are you doing still here? I only came back for our pillows and blankets. We've only just got back to the shelter ourselves. We had to wait hours at the clinic because the hospital was hit last week and everything's all over the place. Gracious, girl! I didn't realise you were still here till I saw a chink of light under your door. I've been banging for two minutes at least. You must have been well away, gal, well away.'

'Oh my God, I didn't realise! I must have dropped off,' a yawning, Olive cried, aghast as the realisation of the situation struck her: she was still fumbling for her coat on the hook behind the door when Ma Parrett pushed past and made for the bedroom.

'Come on, girl, get a move on,' the older woman cried, exasperated. 'We've got to get these kiddies down to the shelter and there's only the two of us to do it!'

Outside the blood-chilling wail of the siren rose and fell: it was as Ma Parrett tugged the eiderdown off the four sleeping children that Olive realised the foolishness of her delay. When she tried to awaken the elder twin, John, he whimpered aloud, wriggled in protest before pushing her away and curling up again in a foetal position: when she lifted Thomas and stood him on the bed, hoping he would open his eyes, he simply flopped back down as though he had rubber legs, refusing to be awakened: in the comfort of a warm, soft bed, those twenty past nights had taken their toll on the children, too.

It was then the two women realised they would have to carry them down: but they could not carry all four at once, not down four flights of a darkened stairway, and then a hundred yards along the street to the shelter. And there was another problem.

'We've no pram to put the little ones in!' wailed a distraught Olive, now fully awake. 'A bloody wheel came off this afternoon on the way back from the shops. I haven't had time to mend it.'

There were tears in her eyes as she said it, the kind women shed when they realise their helplessness in the face of a situation with which a man could have dealt without trouble or panic: she was angry at herself for not having gone to the shelter earlier: and angry, too, at having to make a decision which, if Robert had been there, she might not have had to make at all.

Ma Parrett settled the dilemma: dropping the blanket, she tucked the pillows under one arm, scooped up the three small gasmask boxes beside the bed, then bent to pick up the sleeping Thomas and laid him over one shoulder the way she normally did with Michael. 'I'll take him and these, you just take John and the nappies. Leave the babies for now!' she ordered.

As a startled Olive turned to protest, the older woman rapped out a stern: 'It's the only way, girl! We haven't got time to argue. I reckon we've just got time to get these two down to the shelter and for you to come back for the babies. You're much faster on your feet than I am at my age and you can carry them both. Come on, Olive, let's get moving. The sooner we get there the sooner you can come back.'

Even as her neighbour made for the door with Thomas snuggled against her shoulder and the gasmasks bouncing against her wide hips, the wail of the siren seemed to grow louder and more insistent. Olive knew the older woman was right: there was nothing else for it but to leave the babies and come back for them. To the south, the yellow beams of the searchlights were already probing the growing darkness and all the while the German bombers were droning ever nearer: with luck, she would have time to dash back to the house, grab the two youngest and be back in the shelter well before the first bombs fell: so she hoped!

For a brief instant, Olive wondered whether she should put the baby in the anti-gas helmet before she left, but a shout from Ma Parrett, already on the landing with the torch, decided her against it: she would be back in five minutes anyway. With a last anxious look at the two tiny figures resting against the bolster, blissfully unaware of the drama being played out around them, Olive hurried after the older woman, cradling the sleeping John, her stomach churning. Ma Parrett led the way down the darkened stairwell of the blacked-out building, shining her torch on each step so that they reached the hallway three landings below without mishap.

Out in the street, the eerie, discordant wail of the siren was even louder and more threatening: a helmeted air raid warden, red-faced and angry, came rushing up. 'What the bloody hell are you ladies doing out here?' he shouted above the continuing wail of the siren. 'You ought to have been in the shelter hours ago. Your kids ought to be asleep in there not out in the bloody road! Come on, get a move on! Bloody Jerry'll be here before you get there if you don't hurry up!'

'We got held up,' snapped a furious Olive, angered by the man's hectoring tone. 'Some of us have got children to get ready, not like some – '

But the warden was already hurrying away, shouting at someone else.

SIX

THE warden ushering in the latecomers, of which there were about a dozen, was a chubby, bespectacled man whom Olive disliked intensely: he knew her husband was away for long periods and he always gave her a smile: Olive knew why and she blatantly refused to reciprocate: she was not letting that fat little fool into her bed! What she did know was that he had a habit of patting the women as they passed, especially the younger women and the girls when he gave his 'Come on, girls!' call: and he did not pat them on the arms either: always on the bottom. Olive shivered involuntarily as she saw him and had the satisfaction of seeing Thomas's dangling foot catch him the ribcage as Ma Parrett pushed her way roughly past into the L-shaped entrance.

The shelter was packed: again there were more in there than there should have been: and the early arrivals had long ago taken the lower bunks where the dust falling from the ceiling during the nearer bomb blasts would not disturb them. Fifty or so children of various ages, from babes-in-arms to thirteen-year-olds, children who should have been safe in the country (who had once *been* safe in the country but had returned home) were sprawled on them asleep, many two to a bunk, some covered in blankets, others with coats draped over their sleeping forms. Around them, smoking, talking, drinking tea or bottled beer, sat and stood about three hundred and more adults, many of them younger women of Olive's age, about sixty from the various flats, but with a sprinkling of grey-haired, false-toothed older women, a few nonchalant youths and anxious-looking girls in their early adolescence: the nightly cursing was already under way.

'Bloody Hitler! They should chop off his other ball when they catch him!' from an out-of-breath, grey-moustached, old man in a cloth cap and brown herring-bone overcoat, who came shuffling into the shelter in carpet slippers, shirtless and wearing only his longjohns: thinking himself safe that night, or just hoping himself safe, he had been undressing in front of the gas fire and about to take a wash in his tin bath when the sirens had sounded: he had not even waited to pull on his trousers as he made for the stairs.

'Ought to string him up by them, that'd teach the bugger!' from a puffy-faced, perspiring woman in her fifties seated on one of the hard wooden benches, curlers in her hair, a smouldering cigarette clamped in her mouth, her fingers curled round a dark unopened bottle of stout.

'How much longer is all this going to go on for? That's what I'd like to know,' plaintively echoing Olive's earlier cry, from a white-faced, headscarved mother in her mid-twenties, who was always one of the first into the shelter each evening with her four-child brood, mercifully all already asleep.

Olive and Ma Parrett were in too much of a hurry to bother with such sentiments: with a brusque command to her yellow-skinned husband to 'Move!' the older woman pushed the poor man along the bench he had taken and laid the sleeping Thomas on a coat, before turning to take the heavier John from Olive's aching arms. That done, she gave her husband a curt 'Watch 'em!' command and then was physically pushing Olive through those crowding the gangway towards the exit. 'Go on, get going, girl!' shouted Ma Parrett. 'Leave the twins with us. They'll be all right. Get your little ones. And, here take my torch, you'll need it.'

But as Olive hurried out of the doorway, she felt two hands grip her arm, pulling her back. 'Hey! Where the bleedin' heck do you think you're going, missus?' a voice said. 'You can't go out there! Bloody bombing's started! Do you want to get killed?' It was the chubby air raid warden with the roving hands.

For a second Olive looked at him, unable to comprehend what he was saying: her mind was thinking of the time it would take her to cover the hundred yards back to the house, then climb the three flights of stairs, snatch up the babies along with Joseph's respirator and make the return journey: outside, far off to the southeast, she could already hear the sound of guns and the crump of bombs.

'I've got to get my babies,' Olive pleaded, trying to wrench her arm free. 'My two youngest are still in the house. We couldn't bring them with the others. I had to leave them. We couldn't carry them all. We had enough to carry with the twins and there was no one else to help us. I had to leave two of them on the bed – '

The man stared at her, incredulous. 'What! You left your kids on the bed in the middle of a bleedin' air raid? Are you mad, woman?'

'I've got to go and get them!' Olive shouted shrilly as something rattled on a roof opposite and fell into the road: she knew what it was – shrapnel from the guns. 'They're both babies. One's only six months old, the other's eighteen months. You don't expect them to walk here, do you? Have sense do, man!'

The attempt at sarcasm failed miserably on the chubby warden: if anything he tightened his grip on her arm: he was not going to let her go. More shrapnel from the guns bounced on to the road with a metallic clink. 'You can't go out there, woman, you'll get hit,' the chubby man bellowed above a growing din of guns and bombs seeming to come ever nearer. 'If that stuff clonks you on the head, it'll kill you stone dead. Them's solid bits of steel coming down. I'm sorry, but I can't let you go out there, missus.'

'I have to go,' cried Olive, starting to wriggle, her fury rising even more when his grip did not slacken. She just did not like the man holding her the way he did: his arms were encircling her now from behind, squeezing her across her breasts and he was pushing his groin up against her buttocks, one leg hooked in front of her so she could not move forward.

A second air raid warden came darting into the entrance, dropping the canvas curtain behind him, eager to get under cover now that the rain of shrapnel was beginning to fall: it was the angry man she had seen earlier.

'She's trying to leave the shelter!' the chubby man cried out as Olive began to wriggle even more fiercely. The second man also took hold of her.

'You can't go out there, missus,' he declared, breathing heavily. 'It's too bloody dangerous. The guns are firing straight up over us. Everything's coming down. I only just made it myself.'

'I've got to get my babies! They're still in the house!' Olive was screaming now, almost hysterical in her desperation to struggle free, her voice so shrill and piercing it made even the air raid wardens flinch. And she was not just wriggling: she was fighting to get free of them, beating at the arms encircling arms, lunging forwards and back, twisting and ducking, an eight-stone woman against two thirteen-stone men.

Behind her she could hear other voices, mostly from the women, Ma Parrett's among them, shouting: 'Let her go! She's goin' for her babies, you bloody lunatics!' and 'Bloody little Hitlers! Let her go! It ain't your job to stop her! Let her go! Let her go!'

Whether it was the rising anger of the mothers against them or the violence of Olive's struggle and the desperation contained in her shrieks which made them loosen their grip, she did not know: but the instant the chubby man relaxed his hold when she backheeled him on the shin, she had wrenched herself free and was plunging through the curtain out into the road.

She heard shouts behind her, shouts from the two men and shouts from the women in the entrance behind them: the men's voices were harsh and angry, though what they actually said was lost in the cacophony all about her: the women's shriller voices seemed almost to be cheering, willing her on, urging her to get the babies.

As she ran, head down, half-stooping, one arm raised protectively, Olive was aware of flash after flash, an unending series of them behind the rooftops across the road, lighting up the horizon to the south and east as the anti-aircraft guns blasted skyward. Like millions of Londoners who heard the nightly banging of the guns, she was as comforted by the sound as she was by the broad rotating beams of the searchlights piercing the fire-reddened dark, believing, as all did, that the nightly wall of exploding steel put up against the approaching bombers would keep them at bay. None then knew the truth of the futility of that barrage and that the droning bombers continued to roam almost at will in the night skies above them.

Beneath her feet, Olive could feel the pavement reverberating to each bomb blast: suddenly, a mile or so to the east, across the other side of the park, where some warehouses stood, there was a blinding flash: a great orange ball of fire sprouted hundreds of feet skyward, lighting up the undersides of the sparse clouds, almost touching them, it seemed to Olive: all around the sky was turning a lurid red and orange: more bits of metal clattered on to the road and rattled on nearby rooftops, before rolling noisily down the tiles on to doorsteps below. Towards the middle of Rupert Road, past number forty-two, Olive saw an incendiary bounce off the roof of one of the houses and fall almost in slow motion into the road where it burned with a sudden fierce white heat. Already a wind was beginning to swirl, stirred up by the blasts of the closer bombs: dust and debris were blowing everywhere along the length of the whole street, getting in her eyes, up her nose and in her mouth.

She had run no more than fifty yards when suddenly she felt herself assailed by a violent compression which squeezed her whole body, rippling the loose skin of her cheeks and eyelids, at the same time spinning her round and throwing her violently against the low wall and railings of number twenty-four so that all the breath was knocked out of her: it was as though some unseen giant had first hit her, then picked her up and tossed her aside. Almost immediately, this was followed by the suction from the blast: in the next instant the same invisible hands wrenched her violently sideways and bowled her across the pavement into the gutter: Ma Parrett's torch went spinning into the road. Fortunately, Olive had managed to clamp her eyes tight shut as the first shock wave hit her, but even then there was a momentary panic as she felt as if her eyeballs were being sucked out of their sockets by the vacuum of the blast.

A five-hundred-kilogram, high-explosive parachute mine had exploded on impact a hundred-and-fifty yards to one side of her, at the top end of Ducie Street, the next road over, just where it met the High Road, and part of its rippling blast had been funnelled along an alleyway between two blocks of Rupert

Road's tall terraces just as Olive was passing. Scarcely able to breathe, she somehow crawled back on to the steps to the lower flat of number twenty-four to seek the protection of the low wall just as a rain of metal and debris came clattering down in the centre of the road and bounced against the pavement kerb where she had been lying: glass tinkled as shrapnel went through a sky-light, to be followed by a sharp crack as another piece shattered Ansell's butcher's shop window on the corner fifty yards away.

It took a minute or so before she could summon the courage to go on: she waited for a pause in the maelstrom and then ran, ran for dear life, in a whimpering, breathless panic with her arms flailing. She did not even pause to catch her breath when she reached the front door of number forty-two, but quickly inserted the key and stumbled inside: clawing at the bannister rail for guidance in the darkness, she raced up the stairs.

By the time Olive reached the fourth floor, her chest was heaving and her lungs felt as if they were about to burst: but she could not, would not, stop and rushed into the bedroom, fearful of what she might find.

Michael and Joseph were still sleeping peacefully between the two pillows, oblivious to the noise of explosions going on all around them: Olive did not lift the two immediately, but slumped down on the bed to rest and to catch her breath: the mere sight of such innocence amid the madness brought tears welling up into her eyes. Before she could help herself, she found she was trembling uncontrollably and the tears were rolling down her cheeks in a flood, leaving a bitter, salty taste where they touched the corners of her mouth.

She knew this was not the time to dissolve into tears and was angry with herself for having given way: she was just sitting there, resting, brushing at her wet eyes and cheeks when, unexpectedly, a great weariness came over her: it was as if someone were pressing down upon her shoulders, preventing her from rising. The noise of the guns and the falling bombs began to recede as if the sound were being drawn away down a long tunnel: without thinking, Olive lay back on the eiderdown and closed her eyes, relishing the give of the mattress as it eased the aches of her bruised back and arms: she just needed to rest for a moment, to forget her weariness and her worries ...

And that is when she fell asleep and slept the sleep of the exhausted.

SEVEN

'GAWD, Olive, where've you been? We thought you'd had it, girl! I ain't slept all night worrying about you!' Old Ma Parrett, stooping to hold a sullen-faced John's hand and carrying her own bundles as well as the twins' and Michael's gas masks, was smiling with relief as she came along the street away from the shelter with the throng of others: behind her, a morose and sullen Thomas, held the hand of her husband, Walter.

When the twins saw their mother, their faces lit up into bright smiles and they broke away from the old couple's grip and ran eagerly towards her, raising their arms to be lifted up. But, seeing their mother was clasping their younger brothers and could not lift them, they settled for a glad hug around her thighs. The bespectacled John, bottom lip pouting, buried his face in the folds of her coat, embarrassed by the tears which had stained his grimed face: he alone, it seemed, had realised the import of his mother's failure to return after the first raid ended. He had awoken soon after the third raid began at about three-thirty in the morning and had remained awake, sitting on the edge of a form as near to the shelter doorway as he was allowed, anxiously waiting for the canvas gas curtain to be lifted which would herald her return. Ma Parrett and the other mothers who were still awake tried to reassure him that she would return and tried to get him to go back to sleep and to move farther back into the shelter, but he had remained obstinately in his place, regarding the adults who surrounded him with a cold-eyed suspicion and steadfastly refusing to do either: he would remain where he was and wait and find out for himself. Only when the 'all clear' had sounded and his mother still had not returned did his spirit sink: he had seen the faces of the other adults, the grimness showing in their eyes as they exchanged glances and, head down, he had started to cry, snuffling quietly, wiping his nose with his sleeve, as boys do. Now his mother was safe!

'See, I told you she'd be all right,' Ma Parrett declared in an attempt to soothe him: but the still snuffling John simply buried his face deeper into the folds of his mother's coat and made no reply.

'I just fell asleep,' said Olive wearily and a little sheepishly. 'I just got up there, sat on the bed for a moment and fell asleep. I didn't even know I was doing it!'

Ma Parrett just raised one eyebrow and looked at her askance as she relieved her of the weight of Michael: there was no sense in condemning her neighbour: Olive was safe, her children were safe: everyone was safe: and she had not 'gone missing' deliberately. She was just exhausted, that was all: one of the thousands upon thousands of bleary-eyed, troglodyte Londoners, who, at that precise moment all over the sprawling city, were emerging from their air-raid shelters into the unexpected brightness of the early morning sunlight, glad to be alive, marvelling at their survival amid the destruction and devastation wrought all around them.

Tired and grumbling, stiff-limbed and shivering in the chill dawn air, yawning and stretching through lack of proper sleep, they came up from the cellars of houses, up from the basements of buildings, out from cupboards under stairs and out, too, thousands upon thousands of them, from corrugated-iron

Anderson shelters sunk in countless back gardens of long terraced rows of houses and heaped over with earth. Some came from overcrowded, unsanitary, brick, steel and concrete communal shelters, hastily erected by the authorities in parks, on playing fields, at the ends of streets, in school yards, or upon whatever spare ground was available, like those in Rupert Road: others emerged from a night spent under dank and draughty railway arches, huddled inside overcoats or whatever layers of clothing were to hand, lying on hard ground covered by blankets speckled with frost, desperate only for the comfort of a warm fireside, a hot drink of sweet tea and a soft bed to restore their spirits. At the sound of the 'all clear' siren, thousands more wearily climbed the steep escalators from the bowels of the Underground to emerge into the smoke-tainted, dust-shrouded light of another dawn after a night packed on the hard concrete of the platforms, often unable to sleep and as ready to complain about those who had kept them awake as they were to curse the enemy which had driven them there.

Hundreds more came from their nightly refuge in the ancient chalk tunnels at Chislehurst, southeast of London, trudging out into the cold light of yet another dawn carrying their bedrolls and empty flasks and as red-eyed, short-tempered and yawning as the rest, while a seething mass, some said sixteen thousand on a bad night, gladly left the filthy conditions of the subterranean Tilbury goods yard in Stepney, the very heart of the East End. On the heaths to the north and south of London, in the woods to the south, east and west, and amid the thickets and undergrowth of Epping Forest to the north, hundreds upon hundreds of makeshift tents dotted the ground under the trees as the people set up camp in any place where they felt they would be safe from the nightly rain of bombs, but most of all where they might sleep in peace.

Some returned to their small terraced houses over mounds of still-smoking rubble, picking their way along streets carpeted by the broken bricks and splintered slates of a score of homes and the shattered glass of a hundred windows, past tottering walls and the gaping innards of frontless buildings. Others returned to find the entrance to their street or the route to their home blocked by a solid mound of still-smoking rubble where the front and top floors of a three-storey or four-storey building had crashed into the road: it might once have been the local Sainsbury's grocery store, or the King's Head tavern at which they drank at weekends, or the Duke of Wellington with the young barmaid or the old Queen's Head with the grumpy landlord, or perhaps the butcher's, the fishmonger's, the wool shop, the newsagent and tobacconist's, the pawnbroker's, the haberdashery shop, or a hundred other kinds of business. Some returned to streets cratered and impassable, taped off, where a helmeted policeman stood guard at one end refusing to let anyone enter and the whole walls of buildings leaned crazily outward over the road yet somehow remained standing: or where the rear end of a trolley bus projected upwards from a deep hole amid a tangle of power cables and telephone lines, where the smell of gas escaping from fractured pipes was everywhere and columns of water gushed skyward from burst mains. In others, conflagrations might still be burning and, if they ignored the shouts and warnings of desperate firemen, they would have to step over scores of firehoses snaking down narrow alleyways where warehouses burned and flames roared a hundred feet into the morning sky and every now and again walls crashed down amid volcanic showers of sparks. There the heat could be so fierce at times that no one could get within a hundred yards of the blaze and the firefighters shut off their hoses to save water and stood back and watched them burn, knowing that all attempts to save them would be futile. And over it all great cloud-touching pillars of black and grey smoke rose, blotting out the sun.

In some areas, those who returned found whole districts had gone: everything they held dear obliterated overnight: shops, houses, churches, schools, businesses, public houses, whole streets vanished: in other areas, it might be just a small group of houses which had gone, two, three or four in a terrace, say, which had received a direct hit and been reduced to a heap of smouldering rubble: and such is the indiscriminate nature of bombs dropped randomly from three or four thousand feet that others left their shelters to find the houses on one side of their street obliterated, while those on the other side remained untouched.

In one street, where a dust-covered car or lorry might be parked, dented and battered by flying rubble, a half-dozen ambulances would be seen waiting in line, their drivers sitting on the running boards of their vehicles, smoking, or standing in a small group, chatting, while grim-faced gangs of helmeted, boiler-suited men and uniformed soldiers dug with picks and shovels at smouldering mounds of what had once been a row of terraced houses. Blackened, glowing timbers were heaved aside and small lorry-mounted cranes backed up to lift chunks of masonry the size of a car's bonnet: every now and again, a stern voice would cry out for 'Quiet!' and all would freeze and angrily hush anyone who did not. Sometimes a grateful, gasping, dust-covered figure, in clothes rent and scorched by the bomb blast, would be lifted gingerly out and carried away by smiling rescuers: but too often it would be a body that was lifted up and placed on one of the waiting stretchers, a blanket draped over to shroud the face and a loose, dangling arm tucked discreetly out of sight: a woman's arm, perhaps: or, sometimes, the thin milk white limb of a child.

And if you were working among it, you would know that, in that house over there five people were killed, a woman and three girls sheltering under the stairs: not a mark on them: all killed by the blast as though they had just gone to sleep. Over there, six were killed when their Anderson shelter took a direct hit: not much left of them: mother and father, three kids and their grandmother: just bits and pieces collected up from the garden. In that house, the one with the front blown off, an old man and woman had died lying asleep together in their beds, either too old, too infirm or too stubborn to go down to the shelter. And then, of course, six streets away, up near the gas works, or down by the garages, the communal shelter in the infants' school playground had taken a direct hit: fifty dead there who should have been safe with a foot-thick, reinforced concrete roof over their heads: twelve of them kids, they say, the youngest just six months old, four from one family who had come back from the country only that summer because their mother was fed up with being away from her home and friends: all dead now.

Rupert Road had again been luckier than most that night: only one house, number seventy-nine, on the opposite side of the street from where Olive lived and about sixty yards along, had been destroyed to add to the other two hit during raids the previous week: five in all now. As they stood there, a warden came hurrying up to talk to the policeman. 'Top end of Ducie Street's copped it,' he said. 'Bloody land mine. More than a dozen dead. It's a right mess! Couple of dozen houses gone. The front of the Co-op's down right across the Compton Road. Everything's blocked. Can't get anything past, trolley buses, fire engines, ambulances, nothing! Bloody Jerries!'

The bomb which destroyed number seventy-nine had fallen in the small backyard during the second of the four raids that night, at about five o'clock, gouging a crater seven or eight-feet deep. Number seventy-nine, the same kind of four-storey flats with basement in which Olive lived, now had no front or back: the first and second-storey rear wall had been blasted right through into the bedrooms and parlours of the flats on the same level, while most of the lower front of the house had exploded outwards and was now strewn across the road. Two of the doors had been blown across the street to embed themselves in the bay window of the second-floor flat opposite, number seventy-eight. Those doors on the third and fourth-floors which had not been torn from their hinges were hanging over an abyss where part of the house front on those two floors had collapsed. In one flat, a double iron-framed bed dangled crazily over the edge of jagged floorboards, while behind a couple of pictures hung askew: in another, a darkwood wardrobe lay on its side, also projecting out into space: both the beds in that room were mangled wrecks poking up through the rubble below where most of the ceiling had crashed down on to the furniture in the flat below: the whole block was tilting crazily.

The wardens had already roped off the house and one woman was wailing in the arms of some neighbours, while a grim-faced man talked quietly to a warden in a white helmet, a shocked, stunned expression on his face. Outright curiosity took Olive, the Parretts and children past the steps of number forty-two to join the throng of onlookers gathered in a semi-circle across the road farther down where a steel-helmeted policeman was holding them back: they needed to know as much as anyone else.

'Anyone hurt?' Olive asked, biting her lip as she saw the extent of the damage.

'No, thank the Lord,' a woman standing next to a teenage girl answered. 'Everyone was in the shelter at the top end.' Olive did not know the woman, but information of that kind – that the occupants had escaped unharmed – was readily passed on: everyone needed to know it to keep up their own morale.

Ma Parrett made the point without being asked. 'Another fifty yards and that could have been you, girl,' she said soberly, giving Olive a knowing look.

Walter, her husband, was looking back towards their own building. 'We've got a hole in our front roof by the looks of things,' he said, adding almost absentmindedly: 'Shrapnel, I expect.'

'Some bricks off the chimney came through into my flat,' Olive admitted, cautiously. 'The room's covered in plaster and bits of brick.' She felt embarrassed at having to make the disclosure, but felt that she ought: they would find out soon enough, anyway: as soon as they got back to the top floor: and she would have to tell the landlord, though the best she could hope from him in such straitened times and with shortages of everything, especially building materials, was a temporary repair, just a make-good piece of tarpaulin stretched across the hole and nailed down, neither use nor ornament, in Olive's opinion.

'Come on, girl.' Ma Parrett took Olive's arm and steered her away from the gawping crowd. 'I don't know about you, but I need a cup of tea. And these children need their breakfast. And one or two need changing,' she added with a sniff, pulling a face as she moved the sleepy-eyed Michael from one arm to the other.

EIGHT

UP in the flat, a grim-faced Ma Parrett surveyed the scene in the bedroom. 'Good Gawd, girl! You could all have been killed,' she cried angrily when she saw the bricks balanced on the head rail of the bed, 'you and the babies.'

Below them the street door was being banged shut as other tenants of the flats returned from viewing the demolished house: there were the usual echoing shouts of children's voices, the clatter of scurrying feet on the uncarpeted stairs and the weary rather than cheery goodbyes of the women as they each retired to their own flats: they had survived another night and were at least thankful for that.

A wheezing old man Parrett, meanwhile, having delivered his young charges to the door and having piggy-backed Thomas up the last two flights of stairs, despite Olive's protestations and his wife's chiding, went off to his own flat to make sure all was secure there: and to have his usual hour-long coughing fit. His wife watched him go, listened for a few moments as his coughing began and shook her head with a long sigh. 'He won't give up his cigarettes, though, will he?' she said in disgust. 'He'll stick to those till the bloody end, won't he?' Clearly, she was thinking he was not long for this world.

Olive thought it wiser to say nothing in reply: death was a maudlin enough subject as it was and she did not want to discuss it: she was still young, thirty-three: death was a long, long way off, she hoped. Instead, she concentrated on putting a brave face on her near miss, as much as to convince herself as to forestall criticism from her neighbour: and when it came to criticism, Ma Parrett never shirked her right to give it.

Friends though they had become, especially since the start of the bombing, that friendship had had an inauspicious start: within a day of Olive and her brood moving into flat ten at number forty-two just over nine months before, the two women had had a falling out. Olive knew it was down more to her own shortness of temper than to what she was to discover was her neighbour's sometimes caustic disposition, but it had created a period of unease and tension between two who, by virtue of being the only occupants of the top-floor flats, should have welcomed each other's company. A tart remark, made as much in jest as anything, by Ma Parrett, had sparked it: on the second day, the couple had caught up with the heavily pregnant Olive wearily climbing the stairs ahead of them, holding Michael, then just a year old, on one arm, carrying her shopping bag in the other and shepherding the then two-year-old twins up each step, all the time exhorting them to be careful or they would fall through the gaps in the rickety bannisters. 'Gawd, girl, I should have thought you had enough to contend with without having another!' Ma Parrett had exclaimed.

Normally Olive might have smiled, acknowledging that it was simply an instance of an older woman taking the liberty of remarking wittily and sympathetically upon a younger woman's condition: the use of 'girl' should have told her that: but that day Olive was hot, tired and angry. She had run out of money, she had been unable to buy what she wanted at the grocer's and she was desperately missing Robert: she had also waited an hour in the freezing

January cold at the butcher's for some mincemeat, all that was left by the time she reached the counter, and was in no mood for small talk or criticism. 'I'll have as many as I want,' she had snapped, deliberately turning her back on the older woman. 'They're my children. What I do with my life is my business and no one else's.' She had gone into the flat, slamming the door behind her, leaving her new neighbours standing on the landing and wincing at the acerbity of the newcomer.

Joseph's arrival a month later had brought them briefly together again, if not in actual friendship, at least in interest and admiration for the baby: the older woman had genuinely welcomed the child's birth, but even that had soured somewhat when in the weeks which followed his crying had begun to disturb the old man's afternoon naps, especially as his nighttime sleeping was too often interrupted by his own coughing. After that, relations had been cordial, almost formal, but never overly friendly: they passed each other with a 'Good morning' or a 'Good afternoon,' but little else was spoken between them. The start of the bombing had changed everything.

When the sirens had sounded for the first time that September Saturday afternoon, it had been Ma Parrett alone among the flat-dwellers who had realised that Olive would need help to get her children down to the Rupert Road south shelter: she alone had hurried to Olive's flat to volunteer her own and her frail husband's services, almost as though their two clashes had never occurred. It had surprised Olive at the time, but she had not said so: it had probably surprised Ma Parrett that she had even done it: it was as if at that moment, both faced with the same danger, the same threat of annihilation, they had realised they had a common purpose, to ensure the children reached safety at all costs. As they had gone down the stairs that first time, the two had even smiled at each other, silently acknowledging the triviality of their earlier quarrel. In the ensuing weeks, Olive had become totally dependant upon Ma Parrett and her husband in getting to the shelter: and, once in the shelter, of course, the old couple, childless themselves, would help to bed the children down and would sit with them, quietly calming them if they were awakened by the banging of the guns or the crump of distant bombs. Yes, Ma Parrett could be caustic at times and something of a busybody, Olive acknowledged, but she was generally well-intentioned and behind her brusqueness she was as friendly and caring as anyone: a good neighbour, in fact.

A strident call to the twins, 'Do either of you need the bucket?' was enough to start a scuffle as the two boys, suddenly realising their need, bumped each other to see who would pee first into the galvanized bucket in the corner of the bedroom: the more forceful John won, 'man-weeing,' as he called it, while a sulky Thomas waited impatiently. Olive, meanwhile, had put Joseph on the rag rug in front of the fireguard in the living room-cum-kitchen as soon as she had entered the flat and, returning to him, now was busy unbuttoning his leggings. She should have changed his nappy before she left the flat after her night's sleep, but she had been so anxious to get to the shelter and recover the twins she had not given it a thought: now he was long overdue: so was Michael.

'Let me give you a hand, Olive,' the perspiring Ma Parrett offered as Olive pulled the soiled towelling away, grimaced and gagged at the sight and the smell and hurriedly dropped it into the pail of water she kept for just that purpose by the unlit gas fire. Expertly for one who had never had children of her own, the older woman upended Michael on the same rug and, while the eighteen-month-old busied himself studying the intricacies of opening a matchbox and tipping the few live matches in it on to his chest, she performed the same distasteful task. She had done it frequently in the shelter and Olive was thankful for her to take over: the first time she had offered, seeing Olive's surprised look, she had laughed and declared: 'My sister had four of her own. I used to change them. I'd be some woman if I couldn't change a baby's nappy now, wouldn't I?' No more than that.

Cleaned, wiped, dried, powdered and changed, Joseph kicked lustily on the rug and sucked at his dummy, while Michael crawled off into the bedroom, where the twins, having discovered the hole in the ceiling, were standing amid the rubble, squinting up at the patch of pale grey-blue sky with a mixture of wide-eyed wonderment and amusement.

'Did a bomb really do that?' an awed Thomas asked. 'Look, I can see the sky through it.'

Soon after there was a sound of high-pitched shrieks from the bedroom: the two had found a new game, kicking the bits of broken brick about the room and jumping on the pieces of plaster till they cracked and powdered.

'Stop that! Look at the mess you are making,' scolded Olive, but it took a sharp command and an expression of anger from Ma Parrett actually to cow the twins into stopping their game. 'You'll have to get that fixed sharpish,' she informed, or, more like, ordered Olive, the way older women sometimes do. 'You don't want it raining down on the kiddies while they're sleep, do you?'

'If only they *could* sleep,' a weary Olive thought to herself. 'If only we *all* could sleep!'

As if to divert the adults' wrath, Thomas suddenly whined aloud: 'I'm hungry, Mum. I want something to eat.' A cry immediately taken up by John.

'I'm getting it! I'm getting it. I've only got one pair of hands,' snapped Olive angrily and instantly regretted it: the events of the previous night had left their mark on her after all: she was nervous and irritable: she had come close to death and she knew it.

'Do you give them porridge?' Ma Parrett queried, reaching up to take the oatmeal box off the small kitchen shelf: Olive nodded and turned the tap to fill the kettle: instead of a gush, there was just a trickle of discoloured water. 'This stuff's brown,' she cried. 'We can't drink this!'

'Run it for a few minutes,' her older companion advised. 'It should clear then. They could have hit the main or the fire brigade might have used it all up.' Olive sighed her understanding.

The gas, too, was low when she lit the small ring in the corner on which she cooked: the ring was a fixture of the flat: when she had taken it, sight unseen, glad to get it, she had hoped for a proper gas cooker, but there had been only the ring and, on the money Robert sent her, she had no hope of being able to buy even a second or third-hand gas cooker herself, let alone get it installed.

After Olive had run the tap for a minute or so, the water cleared somewhat, though there was still a brownish tinge to it.

'So long as we can boil a kettle, girl, and have a hot cup of tea, we'll be all right,' a patient Ma Parrett declared stoically. 'The bloody Jerries can go to the devil for all I care, though I do say so myself, and me a good Christian, too. So long as I've got a hot cup of tea inside me, I don't give a damn. Not any more.'

Meanwhile, with the gas fire also now lit, though it, too, burned low, Ma Parrett settled herself in the sole armchair and toasted the slices of bread which Olive had cut: eventually, the kettle boiled and the two women made their tea, sipping at it slowly with sighs of satisfaction and relief, relishing its restorative powers. 'Better than having the old man on yer, a good, hot cup of tea!' exclaimed Ma Parrett, giving a deep sigh and laughing.

Olive had to smile with her. 'Company's what I miss most,' she said, 'especially with him being away so much. When he does come home, he and his brothers are always in the pub. No sooner has he had his tea than he's off out. When he does come back, he's reeking of beer. Ugh! I hate that. I'd ban beer if I had my way.'

'Well, I'm partial to a drop of Mackeson myself,' said Ma Parrett quietly, simply to state her own position and in no way to disagree with Olive's viewpoint. 'As for the other, it ain't all that it's cracked up to be, is it? Me, at my age, I'd sooner have a good cup of tea and listen to the wireless.'

Olive was laughing now, keeping one eye on the boys while they ate, for Michael was chewing his toast with obvious qualms: he was carefully inspecting each piece before putting it in his mouth, then taking it out again to inspect it a second time after he had started chewing.

'Put it back in your mouth, it's nice toast,' Olive said, but unconvincingly, the way mothers do when they hope to persuade their reluctant children to eat whatever is in front of them: the child eyed her for a second or so, then decided to trust her and slipped the toast back into his mouth and chewed away.

'Down in Plymouth still, is he?' Ma Parrett asked: not in a nosey fashion, just a question to keep the conversation going.

Olive nodded. 'Yes, still down there, working on the docks.'

'How long has he been down there then?'

'Since the start of the year. I wouldn't mind, but he gave up our other flat, the one with two bedrooms, when he went. I could kill him for that, honestly I could!'

'He doesn't come home often then, does he? We don't see a lot of him.'

'He came up when the baby was born. After that, it was once a month if I was lucky. Said they couldn't spare him, that they'd got too much work to do. Lately, I haven't heard from him for two nearly months. Not since the end of July. I'm beginning to get worried, not only about that but because I'm starting to run short of money as well and I've got kiddies to feed and the rent to pay! I'm having to dip into my post office savings. Most times, I can manage in between the postal orders and what he gives me when he does come home. He gets good money – they pay well for what he's doing. Mind you, we'd all have a lot more if he didn't spend half of what he earned in the pub!'

'Well, that's men all over for you, ain't it, gal?' said Ma Parrett, solemnly shaking her head.

The porridge now had heated and, while the children ate that, seated at the table in the corner, with Michael in his high chair and John and Thomas kneeling on cushions on their chairs, the two women sipped their tea and talked, Olive seated on the fourth-hand small stool which the children regularly fought over when they wanted to sit near the fire, the older woman in the armchair. Olive was suddenly grateful she was there: after the experience of the previous evening, she needed someone to whom she could talk in the way she could not talk to Robert on the few times he came home: she also felt the older woman was wanting to say something to her: sometimes Olive sensed those things and she sensed it then: so she let the conversation take its course and waited.

It was typical of Ma Parrett that she should make the obvious point in her usual direct way. 'You can't go on like this, Olive, can you?' she said quietly and bluntly. 'You've got the children to think of, haven't you, girl? They come before anything. They ought to be in the country, out of harm's way. Not here. You could have lost both your little ones last night. You realise that, don't you?'

'Yes,' replied Olive reluctantly, 'I realise it, but what can I do about it?'

NINE

OLIVE well knew that she should not even have been there to have witnessed any of it: she should have been safe in Thurstone, safe in a hostel with her three other sons, nine-year-old James, or Jimmy, eight-year-old Patrick, and six-year-old Jack. In the first panic of impending war at the beginning of September the previous year, Olive, then three months' pregnant with Joseph and with Michael a nine-month-old babe in arms, had been evacuated with all of her six children to the perceived safety of the south Midlands town along with the whole of the Rupert Road infants' and junior school and three other nearby schools and kindergartens. At the same time all over London, hundreds of thousands of children were being taken off to the safety of the countryside or smaller towns: anywhere, so long as it was away from the capital, away from the threat of bombs and, more particularly, away from the threat of gas attacks, which even then people expected daily.

Robert had visited Olive and the children in Thurstone only twice in those first four months, both times travelling up on the Saturday morning, not arriving until midday, and leaving again on the Sunday afternoon train. True, the first time in the November, he had played with the boys, wrestled with Jimmy and Patrick on the floor of their hostel, which was separate from where Olive and the little ones stayed, and gone for a walk with them in the riverside park which had become their playground: and when he had visited Olive and the twins and Michael in their hostel, he had cradled Michael in his arms and tossed the squealing, delighted twins into the air in turn before catching them. But at the station, as he took leave of them, Olive had sensed that he was glad to get away, glad to get back to London.

Then, on his second visit in the bitter cold of January and one of the worst winters for a decade, Robert had dropped his bombshell: in future, he told her, his visits would be even more infrequent: he was going down to Plymouth to start work in the naval dockyards with his brothers, Brendan and Gerry, who were already working down there. Olive was angry, not only about his failure to visit her and the children more often, but also because it would put another hundred and fifty miles between them: consequently, they had argued bitterly: it felt to her that he was not wanting to make the trip from Plymouth to Thurstone at all: that he was deserting her and the children!

He was also giving up the two-bedroom flat at number sixty-seven Rupert Road, he told her: if he were working down in Plymouth with his brothers, he would not need the flat and it would be a waste of money paying rent. That fact more than any other had determined Olive to leave Thurstone: with no flat in London to which she could return, she feared she would be trapped in the smoky industrial town, stuck in a hostel with all the other grumbling mothers. There and then, she had decided she would go back to Rupert Road and make sure that she at least had the flat: there at least, she reasoned, she would halve the distance between them so he would have no excuse not to visit her and the children.

So, two days after Robert had gone back, she had followed him: after breakfast one morning, and seven months pregnant with Joseph, she had defiantly walked out of the hostel into a blizzard and had caught one of the few trains running back to London, taking with her just the three youngest, the twins, John and Thomas, and Michael, and leaving the three elder boys, Jimmy, Patrick and Jack, in their different hostels. To her consternation, she returned to number sixty-seven to find the two-bedroom flat had already been given up: another returnee family of five had moved in and they were not going to leave either: the one-bedroom, top-floor flat at number forty-two was all she was able to get.

'Perhaps you ought not to have come back from Thurstone?' suggested Ma Parrett, raising a querying eyebrow.

'I wasn't going to stay up there!' exclaimed Olive, the protest sounding more harsh than she intended. 'I spent four months on my own up in Thurstone, living in a hostel after we were evacuated at the beginning of September. And he hardly ever sent any money, a sixteen-shilling postal order once a fortnight. That is, if he remembered, or if he had any left over after a night in the pub drinking. Spent more money in the pub on beer than he ever spent on me and the kids! Always did. Before the war, if it didn't go over the bar of a pub, it went into a bookie's hands at the dog track or the race track. Best thing they ever did was to shut down the race tracks when the war started. Before this lot started, he spent half his money gambling, him and his brothers. Always going to win big one day, weren't they? Except "one day" never came, did it? The rest, what they had left, went on drink. When he was home in our other flat, I used to have to go through his pockets on a Friday night and take what I could find. Up in Thurstone, I was always waiting for a postal order to come – if he remembered to send it – and having to borrow if one didn't. People in the hostel couldn't lend you, they were in the same boat as me. No money either. And the people running the hostel were no help, too quick to fuss around you, telling you what you could and couldn't do all the time.' Here her voice changed to a hectoring whine, mimicking those whom she detested so much, the overly officious who too often seek to take charge of other people's lives. ' "You can't do that! You must do it this way!" Women who had never had children, who knew nothing, telling me what to do with my own kids. Pah! I didn't want that! I do things my way. I'm not having other people telling me what I can and can't do!'

'Besides,' added Olive, her voice resuming a more even tone, 'I had to come back to have the baby, didn't I? I wasn't going to have the baby up there among strangers. Doctor Kingston's always been my doctor and she was in London. She knows me and I know her. The best hospitals are in London, anyway. Proper hospitals, proper doctors and nurses. If I was going to have a baby, I wanted to have it where I chose, not them. I may have been the first in that hostel to leave and come back, but I wasn't the only one. Several others come back, too.' As she said it, she began to laugh, smiling at a memory. 'Started a real exodus, I did. People were fed up with being treated like fools. You should have seen the look on their faces when I told them.' Again the mimicked whining voice. ' "You ought not to be going back, Mrs. Cullen, it might not be safe!" Huh! I came anyway.' The last was spoken with the smugness of someone who had defied authority.

Olive took another sip of tea. 'If the truth be told,' she said, almost disdainfully, 'I just wanted to get back down here to be nearer to him, I suppose. I thought it would be all right.'

'Can't say I blame you, girl,' Ma Parrett interrupted with a laugh. 'I saw him briefly the two times he come up. He's a good looking bloke, your Robert.'

'Aye,' said Olive with a half smile, 'I'll give him that. That's about all, though. When I came back there weren't nothing happening then, was there? I thought I'd be all right. I'd be in the flat with the three youngest, have the baby and he'd be able to visit when he could. And maybe, sooner or later, he'd come home for good. Didn't turn out like that, though, did it? When I got here, he'd already given up flat. I had to go over to his brother's to stay the night. He was there and he wasn't too happy when I turned up with the twins and Michael. Told me to go back to Thurstone and not to be so silly. I told him where to go. There was no way I was going back to live in one of those hostels. I'd sooner have jumped in the river and drowned myself!' She seemed oblivious of the theatricality of the statement. 'Like living in a prison, it was. I'd rather stay here and risk getting killed than go back up there living on my own again So I got this place. It was the best I could manage. I hoped I would see more of him, even if he was working away, being nearer. More fool me since I haven't hardly seen him since. Oh, he came up the weekend Joey was born in the February. That was all right. His brothers came up, too, to wet the baby's head in the pub all night. They did that all right. He came up a few times after that – when you saw him – '

She paused, puzzlement furrowing her brow. 'You'd have thought a man would come up and see his wife and kids when the bombing started, wouldn't you?' she said, half to herself. 'Three weeks we've had of it and I still haven't heard from him. His brothers are no better. I would have expected at least one of them to have come over and seen me – to tell me why he couldn't get back – but I haven't heard a peep out of either of them or my sisters-in-law since it all started. Even then, he could have written a letter, couldn't he? That's not asking too much, is it, a letter? Or he could have sent a telegram, couldn't he? He knows what a post office is, I suppose? As far as I am concerned, if he wants me to go back to Thurstone, he can come up here and tell me himself, and he can bloody well come with me or I am not bloody going. I'm here and I'm stopping – ' She gave a little smile at her own audacity. ' – I don't know how long this war is going to go on – no one does. But one thing's for sure, I'm not going to spend the next two years living on my own in some bloody awful hostel while he's spending all his money drinking in pubs. That I'm not! If he wants me to go anywhere, he can come up here and tell me himself. I ain't living on my own again.'

'You're living on your own here, girl,' Mrs. Parrett gently reminded her. 'And it ain't about you getting killed, is it? It's about you and the children, putting them in danger. All those people that got killed the other day in the East End when the school was hit, some of them were evacuees who'd come back like you. We've had a month of this so far and God knows how many more still to come and you're just about at the end of your tether. You're cracking up, girl. Sleeping through the bombing, this 'ere blitz thing, or whatever they call it, is a sign things aren't right.'

'And where would I go?' demanded Olive petulantly. It irked her that the older woman was making such good sense.

'Ain't you got anywhere you can go, nowhere at all?' Ma Parrett enquired, raising one eyebrow disbelievingly. 'If things get any worse, me and Walter have already decided. We'll be going back down to Somerset, to where we come from, a little village near the Mendips. We'll go and live with my sister. There's room now her husband's gone and her family have all grown up.' The old woman paused here and Olive waited, knowing almost by instinct what she was going to say.

'Mine ain't got long as it is, as you've probably guessed,' she said with a catch in her voice, her lip trembling. 'So I'd want him to be there rather than here when it happens. Better for him and better for me. I'll have my sister. The doctor says he's got six months at the most. He may not even see out the winter. I'd like to take him back to where we used to live, let him live out what time he's got left there.'

'I'm sorry to hear that, Mrs. Parrett,' Olive sympathised. 'Does he know?'

'No.' Ma Parrett almost scoffed. 'He just thinks he's got bad lungs through too much smoking. He has, but it ain't what he thinks. He's got cancer of the lungs and it's spread elsewhere. He's riddled with it, so the doctor told me. Told me not to tell him. That's why we went to the clinic yesterday. Another check-up. Once the cancer reaches his brain, he'll go under. I don't want him suffering. I tell you, girl, if it gets too bad for him, I'm going to ask the doctor to put him down. You know, help him on his way, if you understand my meaning? I don't want him to suffer. If the doctor won't do it, I'll bloody do it myself!' the old woman said with an unexpected passion.

Olive was suddenly aware that the children at the table were casting concerned glances towards them: the fierceness of Ma Parrett's outburst had worried them.

'I mean it,' said Ma Parrett wilfully, her spirit seemingly bolstered by the mere act of announcing it. 'I won't have him suffering and unable to do anything about it, that I won't.'

'At least you've got somewhere to go,' said Olive, with a sigh. 'Mine's from Ireland, as you know, and he won't go back there for love or money. Says there's nothing there. They had a hard enough time trying to get away from it without wanting to go back. No work, nothing to live on. Out in the wilds of Donegal. I ain't never been over, but I've heard enough about it from all of them, him and his brothers. One field between the five of them and the old man and woman. A field won't keep five brothers and their families, will it?'

'You come from a village, don't you?' Ma Parrett enquired quietly. 'A village in East Anglia, isn't it?'

Olive began to laugh. 'Ha, I wouldn't want to go back there,' she declared. 'I'm not so sure I'd be welcome, not with my lot. Where would I live? I couldn't live in my parents' old house. My father and my younger sister and my two older brothers live there and I couldn't live with them, not with my brothers, anyway. There isn't the room, not for me and four kids and them all under one roof.'

'What about your mother?'

'She died,' answered Olive flatly. 'Died the year I come up to London. That's why I left. She died April the twentieth, Nineteen Twenty-Six, two weeks after my nineteenth birthday, and I come up to London the day after the funeral. I wasn't staying in that house to become a skivvy to my father and my brothers. I was the eldest of three girls, me, Theresa and Alice. With my mother gone, they thought I was going to be the skivvy and cook and clean for them, at least my brothers Percy and Hubert did. I told them different and left. My sister Theresa – she's a year younger than me – she told me to go and not to come back. "You go, girl," she said, "and don't you come back and good luck to you." She'd have come with me if she hadn't been courting a local boy, Alf Braybrook. So I left. I haven't been back since neither. I've written to my sisters now and again, mostly to Theresa, but I don't write to my father or my brothers and they don't write to me. Neither of my brothers is married, no one'll have them!' The latter was spoken with a contemptuous laugh.

'Still, you could go back if you wanted to,' Ma Parrett suggested. 'It'd be safer than here. You've got your sisters. Wouldn't they be able to help you?'

'I doubt it,' Olive replied, almost matter-of-factly. 'They've got their own problems, I dare say. I wouldn't expect to get much help from either of them.'

'It's somewhere to think about going if things get worse here,' Ma Parrett persisted.

'Maybe,' Olive acknowledged reluctantly. 'I won't promise anything, but I'll give it a thought.' She said it in the way people do when they have no intention of doing what they promise.

The two had finished their tea and now got up, just as the commotion at the table had begun to grow again.

Olive had no idea why she said it, but she suddenly heard herself saying: 'I'd only go if something drastic happened here to make me go.'

TEN

THE POLICEMEN burst through the door the moment Olive started to open it: a large, black boot was thrust through to prevent her closing it again and she found herself being propelled backwards as the door was pushed roughly open: a burly, silver-haired inspector in a peak-cap followed by two lanky, steel-helmeted constables entered. The inspector was carrying a revolver with a lanyard and the constables were carrying rifles: it was still early morning, three days after the talk with Ma Parrett and also after another wearying night in the Rupert Road shelter.

'Robert Cullen, is he here?' demanded the inspector, positioning himself in the centre of the room and pointing the revolver straight at Olive: the rifles were pointed at the closed door of the bedroom: on the landing, stood two other armed constables, feet astride, gripping their rifles, blocking the doorway to prevent any sudden attempt at an escape.

'No, he's not!' declared an indignant Olive, as shocked by the suddenness of their action as by the sight of the guns they carried. 'What do you want him for?'

She had the sleeping Joseph in her arms and had only just managed to hold on to him as she had stumbled backwards, almost falling over a fearful and wide-eyed Michael seated on the old chipped and rusting enamel bowl in which the children frequently did their 'business.' The child, on the brink of tears, was staring up at the policemen and the revolver, petrified.

'We've been looking for him for some time,' said the inspector, looking about him and ignoring Olive's question. 'We just missed him at his last place. He went out through the back window.'

'Well you won't find him here,' retorted a puzzled Olive.

The silver-haired inspector eyed Olive closely as though trying ascertain whether she was being truthful: she could see him running his tongue over his teeth the way some people do while they weigh up things.

A nod from him and the two armed constables, one a gangling, six-foot-six giant whose steel helmet almost scraped the low ceiling, made straight for the bedroom: they thrust open the door with a bang, immediately pointing in their rifles as if ready to shoot.

'Hey! There are children in there!' a panicking Olive shrieked: she had not expected the policemen to act that way, yet all she could think to add was: 'Don't you wake them up! I've just got them to sleep!'

She had indeed just put the twins down at either end of the single bed, without even giving them breakfast: they had all just returned from the twenty-fourth successive night in the shelter: the Parretts had been gone less than an hour: that was one blessing, that they were not in the flat to see the policemen burst in: they had also had a poor night in the shelter and were probably catching up on their sleep. It had not been a good night in the shelter: several bombs had fallen close by and on surrounding streets and the nearness of the explosions, the clanging of firebells as fire engines raced to the scene of the latest conflagration and the continual banging of the guns had also kept Olive and the twins awake most of the night. Indeed, had Michael not wanted to do his 'business' in the rusting enamel bowl, which made it easier to carry the contents down to the lavatory on the floor below, Olive would have been asleep herself in the double bed alongside Michael, with Joseph in his padded drawer: she had been settling Joseph and waiting for Michael to finish when the policemen's knock came.

Michael's eyes darted from the policemen and their guns to his mother and back to the policemen: the inspector, still in the centre of the room, still pointing his revolver at Olive, peered down at the child's screwed-up face, unmoved.

In the bedroom, the gangling policeman had poked his gun under both the double bed and the single bed in which the twins were sleeping: he cast an eye up at the ceiling where three strips of glued brown paper now covered the hole the crashing piece of chimney had made and, for a second, he seemed to contemplate whether that was an escape route, but then thought better of it.

Fortunately, Olive had cleared up the mess of bricks and plaster, swept the floor and taken the debris down to the dustbin in the yard in a pail: on the Saturday morning the rent collector had called and the day previous he had been able to get some workmen from the council to climb up on to the roof and fix a tarpaulin over the hole, one of the hundreds of such tarpaulins which normally covered farm hayricks, straw stacks and loads of peas and cabbages, but which had been requisitioned for just such a purpose and were by then adorning damaged roofs all over the capital.

'No one in here, inspector,' the tallest policeman called out, before going over to the window and looking out into the road: he gave the lower window a wrench to lift it and pulled a face when he realised it was painted shut and immovable.

Guns or no guns, Olive was not going to be intimidated by policemen. 'Why don't you go down to Plymouth and talk to him there?' she declared. It was bluster: what could Robert possibly have done to warrant them bursting into the flat in such a forceful manner?

'Because he's not there,' said the inspector coldly. 'He ain't been there for six or seven weeks. We've only just tracked him down to here. Last address we had was farther down the street, number sixty-seven.'

'Not there?' Olive was even more puzzled. 'He's in Plymouth, as far as I know.' She said it with as much contempt in her voice as she dared. 'He's been working down there since the beginning of January. In the dockyard. Laying concrete. You go down there and ask them if you don't believe me.' The last remark was a deliberate challenge to them not to question her honesty.

As if to make sure that she was telling the truth and that no one was hiding there, the second constable flicked aside the curtain under the sink and draining board in one corner with the barrel of his rifle.

'No one,' he said matter-of-factly, turning back to the inspector.

'So where is he then, missus?' the inspector demanded, giving Olive a steely-eyed stare.

She ignored the question and the revolver pointing at her, carefully laid Joseph on the rag mat in front of the fire and bent to lift the petrified Michael off the bowl so that its contents could be clearly seen and smelled.

'You can wait for an answer,' she thought to herself as she turned her back on the inspector and busied herself with wiping the child's bottom with a piece of newspaper, then throwing the paper back into the bowl.

'If he's not here, when did you last see him?' the inspector tried again, screwing up his face and stepping a pace back as the smell assailed him. 'Your own husband, you must know where he is?' Again the cold, suspicious stare as if to say, 'Don't lie to me, woman. I shall know if you try. Just tell us where he is.'

'I've not seen him for a couple of months myself,' declared Olive truthfully, pulling up Michael's nappy and refastening the safety pins. 'I only see him when he comes home and he only does that every now and again when it suits him and when he needs something, like all men. Last I heard he was down in Plymouth with his brothers, working in the docks.'

'We know where he's been working, missus,' said the inspector with the hint of a sneer. 'We've been to his place of work and to his lodgings, but he left them and the job a couple of months ago. Went out through the back window when the local police called on him, so he's not likely to go back there if he knows we're looking for him, is he? He's somewhere else and we want to know where.'

Olive was so startled by being told Robert had left his job and his lodgings and was 'missing' that it was several seconds before she finally blurted out: 'Well, I don't know where he is. If he's not down there, I'd like to know where he is myself. You've come to the wrong place if you want to find him because he's not here. What do you want him for anyway? What's he done that you should come bursting in here after him?'

'All you need to know, missus, is that he's gone on the run and we want him, one way or another,' said the inspector, waggling the revolver to make his point. 'A warrant's been issued for his arrest. We've had a communication from Plymouth to pick him up and to go armed when we did it. We were told to search this address. I dare say there'll be other places where we'll be looking. I have to tell you, missus, when they tell us to go armed to pick up a man, it means we have to be prepared to shoot if we have to, especially if there's a likelihood he'll offer armed resistance.' There was enough of a menace about his tone for Olive to realise he was probably telling her the truth and trying to impress upon her the seriousness of Robert's crime, whatever that was.

'Armed resistance! Whatever would he want to offer armed resistance for?' an incredulous Olive demanded as she picked up Joseph again from under the inspector's feet: her tone was contemptuous, disbelieving. 'He don't carry a gun, he don't even carry a penknife.'

The inspector ignored the outburst. 'No doubt he's gone into hiding somewhere,' he said, 'like the others. Well, he can't hide forever. He's got to come out into the daylight sometime and when he does we'll take him.' He paused and eyed Olive closely again. 'You don't sound Irish. You're not Irish, are you?'

'No, I bloody well am not!' retorted an angry Olive. 'I'm English. I'm as English as you are!'

The inspector nodded at that and retreated to the door after the gangling constable. 'Well, if he does come here for whatever reason, I hope you'll have the good sense to tell him to turn himself in to us as soon as he can,' he said with another sniff. 'The nearest police station will do. It's the only thing he can do in the circumstances. The consequences could be worse, much worse for him, if he doesn't.'

With that, he pulled the door shut: Olive could only stand and glower at the closed door through which she could hear the policemen clumping down the stairs.

Five armed policemen charging up the stairs obviously would not go unnoticed by others there and did not: on the landings below, there was a silence as the policemen descended: then the front door was slammed shut and the mur-

muring began. Olive well knew the kinds of comments the other women would be making and it angered her that she should have become the subject of their gossip: almost before she realised what she was doing, she had wrenched open the door and was standing defiantly at the top of the stairs: two landings below three women, a chain-smoking mother of four named Gates, an older head-scarved gossip called O'Brien and another woman named Plowden, looked up, startled.

'And what the bloody hell are you all staring at?' an angry Olive demanded. 'I dare say you've all had the police in your flats at sometime or other! Well, they didn't come for me. I'm still here. So you can gossip all you like, it's not me they're after.' The three women melted back into the shadows, but their murmurings would go on, Olive knew.

Ma Parrett was at her door looking out as Olive returned along the landing. 'Trouble, Olive?' she queried.

'No more than usual,' Olive replied, heaving a great sigh, though her answer sounded unconvincing. 'I'll tell you later. It's him they want, not me. God knows what he's done this time? God knows! The silly bloody man! The silly bloody man!'

Back in the flat she sat slumped at the table, her mind in a whirl: what had Robert done that armed police should come looking for him at the flat? Five of them! Robbed a bank? And what was he planning to do by running away, flee to Ireland? He would never get out of the country, she thought, not with soldiers guarding all the ports. Good gracious he could get himself shot! She had a sudden mind's eye picture of Robert running across a dockyard towards the gangplank of a boat: suddenly a soldier steps out of the shadows with a lev-elled rifle. 'Halt!' he shouts and fires: Robert flings up his arms and pitches forward on to his face. It was like a scene from a film: it felt so real, she almost heard the bang of the gun and shivered with fear.

Never mind 'What had he done?' The question was: if Robert was not in Plymouth, where was he?

ELEVEN

OLIVE spent a fitful morning dozing in the armchair just to catch up on her sleep while the children played and slept in the bedroom: after lunch, she determined, she would confront her sisters-in-law, Martha, who was married to Brendan, the eldest of the Cullen brothers, and Muriel, wife of Gerry, a year older than Robert.

Both lived a good four miles from Rupert Road, in similar second-floor flats in the same street of the next borough. Once, before the war, the three sisters-in-law had met monthly at one or other of the flats to gossip and to drink tea: but, though they had tried to resume the practice after Olive's return from Thurstone, through circumstance, they had not met since the June. Olive had missed the subsequent meetings, in July and August, first, because the twins had developed heat rashes, which at the time she had feared were chicken pox, and then because Michael and the baby had contracted summer colds and she had not wanted to take them on a trolley bus or on the Tube coughing over everyone and with their noses streaming. The start of the bombing had prevented a planned further meeting in September: they had been due to meet on the second Wednesday, the eleventh, but the bombing had started on the Saturday before and Olive had not had the courage to venture so far from the shelter, not with four children to worry about: and besides, by then she was already too tired, too weary and too drained.

But now she was anxious to talk to her sisters-in-law: their husbands, Brendan and Gerry, might well have told them something about why Robert was wanted by the police, and armed police at that! What one did not know, the other might, Olive reasoned: between them, they might be able to solve the mystery and, if not actually to end her anxiety, at least to ease it: they might even be able to tell her where he had gone after jumping out of a window to avoid the law! And why!

What troubled Olive as she pushed the cumbersome, double-hooded pram along the uneven pavement towards Grove Road, where Martha and Muriel had their flats, was the argument she had had with Robert back in the August of the previous year when war was looming. Robert had shocked her with his vehemence: she had always known his leanings, ever since she had first met him at the dance hall in Hammersmith and he had repeated them often enough in the nine years of their marriage: but she had dismissed them as simply male bombast: it had not entered her head that they would ever become the cause of a major argument between them. There he was, shouting loud enough for all the neighbours to hear: 'If there is a war, there's no bloody way I'm going to fight for the King and Queen of England! I'm buggered if I will!'

'You mean you wouldn't fight for your own children?' a disgusted Olive had cried: it was a Friday evening and Robert had returned from his labouring on the building site in a bad mood because of what he perceived was a discrepancy in his pay: he had been pieceworking, concreting, and felt he had somehow lost two hours of his money. 'They must have docked you for the time you spent in the pub at dinnertimes,' a sarcastic Olive had told him as he sat at the table eating his tea: his temper was such that night it was enough to deter Olive from telling him that she was pregnant again, with Joseph.

'I'd take them to bloody Ireland first,' Robert had declared. 'You won't catch me fighting with the bloody British Army, that you won't. Murdering bloody British bastards! The whole bloody country can go hang before I'll shoulder a rifle to save it and risk my life for one square foot of it.'

Robert was no pacifist: he had had enough fights in the public houses around the district to disprove that: he was known for his hot-headedness: if he thought the argument were going against him, he would strike out without warning: fists rather than words settled his arguments. He was just vehemently anti-British, that was all, and always had been: sometimes when he spoke out, he seemed to forget, even to ignore, that Olive was English.

'I'm bloody British and proud of it,' declared Olive, whirling round on him, a washed plate which she was about to dry in her hand. 'What kind of a man are you who wouldn't fight to save his own children? Your children are English – British – even if you aren't. They were born here so they're English, even if you don't like it.'

Robert was not having that. 'They're bloody not, they're Irish,' he said sharply. 'They take after their father. I'm Irish, they've got my blood in their veins, so they're Irish. And I would fight to save my kids if they were in danger, so don't you come that one with me, woman. Fighting for the lives of your kids is one thing. Fighting for the bloody King and Queen of England is another. I'd fight for my kids, I'd fight for my country – Ireland – but I'm buggered if I'm going to fight for yours!'

'You were born under the Crown,' Olive scathingly reminded him. 'You were a subject of the King when Ireland was part of the United Kingdom so you're as much British as your kids are!'

Robert simply repeated his sneer: 'Am I buggery!'

His anger against the British, bad enough before, had got worse over the past year, especially after the hanging of the two Irish Republican Army bombers in Birmingham gaol in the January. It was this incident which had sparked Olive's own detestation of the IRA: explosives hidden in the pump of a parked bicycle in Coventry had killed two innocent passers-by: until then, she had regarded them as a laughable force, especially as her husband had once been one of them, no matter how briefly.

'Oh, don't go on about you and the bloody IRA,' she scoffed. 'You were only in for a day when you were fifteen. Brendan told me all about you and the IRA. He said you joined in the morning and your old man went down in the evening and bought you out. Gave them money to let you go.'

'Brendan doesn't know anything,' sulked Robert. 'He was with the National Army at the time. He didn't know what was going on.' He well remembered the half-dozen cuffs about his ears he had received from his enraged father as he had dragged him out of the drill hall in front of several of his school friends, who had also just joined the Brotherhood, as it then was, during the Troubles of Twenty and Twenty-One. His father was a life-long friend of the father of the local commander and the two had gone down to the church hall together to buy Robert out. 'I'm not having my bloody sons gallivanting around Ireland shooting off guns at people they don't even know,' Old Man Cullen had declared. 'You've got work enough to do at home, boy.' It had been a sore point with Robert ever since and the other brothers, when they wanted to upset Robert, would often tease him about it.

Robert was almost beside himself with bitterness over the Birmingham hangings when he had visited Olive in Thurstone. 'The bloody rotten murdering bastards! Those men died martyrs. They died for their country. We won't forget what the bastard English did to them. The Irish people don't forget '

He went on like that for almost a minute: indeed, his venom built up to such a passionate and hateful crescendo that Olive finally rounded on him. 'For Christ's sake, shut up about the bloody IRA or the kids'll hear!' she ordered. 'You can keep your bloody opinions to yourself. I don't want to hear them and I don't want the kids to hear them either.'

'I don't care a sod if they do,' Robert had snarled back.

'Well, I do,' declared Olive. 'They're my kids, too, and I'm English and I'm not having them listening to all that Irish rubbish you spout. If you love bloody Ireland so much, why don't you go back and live there? You bloody Irish make me sick! You come over here, take people's jobs, live in England and earn your money here, but all you ever do is run the country down. Well, I'm sick of it. Sick of you and your brothers, always spouting off. If you don't like it here, bugger off back to Ireland, the lot of you, and leave us in peace! See how far that gets you.'

The last was a jibe which she knew would wound: she well knew the story of the five Cullen brothers living in a remote tiny hamlet in County Donegal miles from anywhere: Brendan was the eldest, George and James, the second and third eldest, then Gerry and Robert, the fourth and fifth.

As the brothers told it, their father, George senior, was a man of fearful temper, especially when drunk, who farmed a couple of fields and expected his five sons to do likewise in addition to finding other regular work in the nearby town twelve miles away. According to Robert, the brothers hatched a plot to get away from the old man – and Ireland – simply because they did not want to spend their lives following the plough and digging peat. As Robert told it, he and Gerry, then fifteen and sixteen, took the night mail train down to Dublin, ostensibly to spend a day visiting the various martyr sites from the Easter Rising, the General Post Office, Jacob's biscuit factory, St Stephen's Green, The Four Courts, Mountjoy Prison and Phoenix Park, before returning on the evening train. Their father was deliberately not told they had gone until they were missed the following morning, simply because he would have hauled them back, physically if needs be. By the time he learned of it, the two were on the ferry to Stranraer in Scotland, heading for Greenock, where they had arranged by letter to meet a friend's brother, who said he would help them to get labouring work in the docks: but when they arrived in Glasgow, cold and hungry, with nowhere to sleep, there was no sign of their friend's brother. While standing outside the station early the next morning, starved and miserable after a night sleeping rough, and not caring over much for 'the bloody English,' even if they were Scots, they stole two apples and a handful of plums off a fruit barrow. They were spotted, chased and to escape, they said, jumped aboard the first train about to go out: it turned out to be the London-bound express. According to the story Robert told Olive, they stole the tickets off another traveller and his wife, from the top pocket of the man's jacket hanging in a compartment, and so by their third day in Britain had reached London, where their troubles began all over again: eventually they obtained work and fifteen years later were still there in the capital and married with children.

Back in Ireland, meanwhile, the story went, when the two youngest did not return after a week, the old man took up the suggestion of his eldest son, Brendan, that the next two sons, George and James, should be sent to Dublin to fetch them back: but once in Dublin, George and James crossed on the same ferry to Stranraer and went on to Greenock themselves, expecting to find their two younger brothers there. They did not, of course, but, in time, found labouring work themselves, stayed, eventually married and were still there. Finally, when George and James, too, failed to return, the mystified and somewhat subdued father sent the eldest, Brendan, trusting that he at least would return to inherit the family's fields: but Brendan, too, crossed to Scotland, linked up with George and James and eventually found work on the railways as a restaurant car waiter: one morning, pulling into Euston Station on the overnight run from Glasgow, he came upon Gerry and Robert portering on the platform and decided to join them in London.

That at least was the tale which Robert told Olive when they first met: the detail of the story in Scotland was true, but Olive had heard a different account of why they all left Ireland from Martha: when Robert alluded to his tale, which he did frequently, she had to be careful to keep from him what she knew: Martha's story was altogether more harsh, and more poignant.

During the civil war in Ireland, which followed the signing of the 1921 Anglo-Irish Treaty effectively partitioning the country, the twenty-one-year-old Brendan had been conscripted into the Irish National Army in Nineteen Twenty-Two and billeted in a town no more than ten miles from his home: one morning, his squad and another had been loaded on to lorries and driven back to the very hamlet where he and his brothers used to walk the two miles to school and back. There they were driven along a track beside a wood and a river valley into a field: three posts had been set up in front of the slope of a hill: behind were three open graves: they were to form an execution squad for three members of the Irish Republican Brotherhood, who had assassinated a Government senator.

When the condemned were brought up, two youths of about eighteen and a girl of about twenty, Brendan recognised one of the youths as having been at the self-same school as himself and his brothers: indeed he had sat behind his brother George: worse, he was tied to the post directly in front of where Brendan stood in the line. In his consternation, Brendan stepped forward, grounded his rifle and informed the officer in charge that he knew the condemned youth from his schooldays and could not be expected to fire his rifle at him: the officer simply took out his own revolver, pointed it at Brendan's head and bluntly told him, 'You will fire your rifle, Cullen, because, if you do not, you will bloody join him!' He also refused Brendan permission to change his position in the line so that he could fire at someone else, even at the girl. 'No, damn you, Cullen, no!' the officer had stormed. 'You will stand where you are and fire when I give the command. They're Brotherhood scum. They've been tried and condemned and we're going to shoot the buggers here and now. So get on with it.'

The saddest part is that the condemned youth seemed almost pleased to see someone he knew among the firing party: he smiled on recognising Brendan and his eyes were on Brendan as they tied the blindfold: having a friendly face there among so many strangers on the day he departed this life was more of a comfort to him in his last moments than all the mumblings of the priest before him: someone he knew would at least know what happened to him.

When the command came, Brendan fired at the white label pinned upon the youth's chest the same as the others alongside him, hoping that, by some miracle, he alone had been given the blank: he was never to know, of course. He saw the expression upon the youth's face at the impact of the bullets, saw

him slump down and hang forward from his post like a collapsed doll: when
Brendan left the field, he was, like most of the men, trembling and as near to
tears as he could allow himself in the company of the others.

From that day forwards, Brendan felt himself a watched man, more so
when Michael Collins, who had signed the treaty, was assassinated. By then,
Brendan had been demobilised and had returned home: but it was not long
before the story followed him and the whispering began. One day his mother
found herself shunned when she walked to the village shop: national senti-
ment had changed sides! When they entered the church for mass on the Sunday, locals who had sat beside the family for years moved away from them:
even the priest deigned to speak to them and deliberately bypassed them at
the offering of the sacrament. When on the following Saturday evening, Brendan walked the three miles to the local bar for his usual drinking, he was refused entry: the same thing happened to James and George when they went
with him a week later: all three were turned away and Brendan was spat at by
one woman.

One night one of Brendan's old army pals, who had not been on the firing
party and who had himself 'crossed over' since being demobilised, called at the
house and advised Brendan to leave Ireland as there was talk among his new
friends, particularly among the dead youth's relatives, of taking revenge. So
Brendan left, secretly in the night, the first to go, saying he would make for
Greenock: but revenge was still in the air a month later and the same warning
came for the two middle brothers, George and James: 'Leave Ireland or else.'
So they, too, slipped away to join their older brother in Greenock.

Gerry and Robert, being much younger, appeared to be under no threat at
first, until Brendan's old army friend called a third time late one night with
another friendly warning. Even then, the staunch republican Robert insisted
they tour the martyr sites in Dublin before they left for Scotland: then they
took the ferry to Stranraer, stayed a night in Greenock with their brothers and
then, in the manner described, jumped on the express to London while running from the police after stealing from the fruit barrow: the theft from the
barrow was the truest part of the story!

The first tale was simply a way of avoiding the shame of the second: a family of republican sympathisers exiled from the land of their birth by their own
kind: that is what Robert railed against: the injustice of it. He did not blame
his eldest brother for having been in the National Army or for making up the
execution squad which had shot three of the Brotherhood: there was nothing
he could have done – like refusing to obey an order – not with a gun pointed at
his own head no matter what bravado fools might say otherwise. As a result of
all this, Robert alone among them had become more vehement in his out-
bursts: when the others talked about Ireland, they did it with a wistful smile,
almost with a shrug or resignation explicit in their words. Robert could not do
that: his words had to be harsher than the rest: with him the position was crys-
tal clear: the English were bastards and they and they alone were the cause of
all the problems in Ireland: if it had not been for them, there would never have
been a civil war and Irishman would never have fought Irishman! None of it
made much sense to Olive: they had got their country back, she reasoned, or
most of it, so why did they just not get on with living in it?

TWELVE

'WE KNOW where ours are! In the bloody Glasshouse in Aldershot, that's where! They've been there since August and hardly any money sent to us! But we don't know where yours is. Not with them, that's for sure.'

The speaker was Martha, Brendan's wife: Olive, Martha and Muriel, Gerry's wife, were sitting at the table in the small living room of Muriel's Grove Road flat, while the twins and Michael played with her two daughters, nine-year-old Anne and eight-year-old Jean, in one of the two bedrooms and Joseph slept on some cushions in the other alongside Muriel's baby, Peter. The three-room flat was much bigger than Olive's and better furnished, the upper of only two in the house: and, as there was a Tube station at the bottom of the street – indeed a feature of the flat was that there was a constant rumbling of trains passing through the tunnels underneath – Olive knew that she would be able to get back to Rupert Road and get the children their tea and then go down to the shelter well before the nightly trauma began.

'Ours went missing two months ago the same as yours,' went on Martha bitterly, taking a sip of her tea, 'but we've only just found out where they are! We've just heard this week. I got a letter from Brendan on Monday and Muriel got one from Gerry yesterday. They're in the same Glasshouse together. Neither of them is allowed to come home. All three – Robert included – got called for a medical back in the summer. Our two went and got passed A2, but your Robert didn't bother going. Just refused point blank. Our two would have been all right, but they ignored the call-up letter at their lodgings, didn't they, the fools! Stayed where they were, working. The MPs had to go to their workplace in Plymouth to get them. Apparently they didn't go willingly. Had to be handcuffed. They got put on a charge straight away as soon as they entered the barracks and ended up in the Glasshouse. They're in for the duration now, so Brendan says. They daren't risk not doing it or else they might get shot. Can't get out of it. He reckons they'll be put in the Pioneer Corps along with all the other foreigners they've rounded up.'

Here Muriel and Martha exchanged knowing glances. 'I hate to tell you this, Olive,' said Muriel quietly, 'but Gerry doesn't think that just missing the medical and then dodging the call-up is why they want your Robert. They would have just sent the MPs for that, like they did for our two, not armed police like they did. The police who went to Robert's lodgings were carrying guns. I hate to tell you this, girl, but there's talk that your Robert might have got involved in something else.'

'Involved? Involved in what?'

The two women again exchanged glances as if neither was prepared to go on: it was the blunt Martha who enlightened Olive.

'There was an armed robbery in Plymouth while they were all down there working,' she said, grim-faced. 'Some men held up the Navy's payroll van carrying the money for the sailors. Tried to rob it in the street a couple of months ago. Rammed it with a car just as it was turning into the docks road and tried to open the doors to get at the money. They didn't succeed because there were two armed sailors inside. Shots were fired and one of the sailors was injured, so Brendan heard. They reckon it was the IRA, especially as their accents were all Irish − ' She paused here to bite her lip. ' − There was talk Robert might have been involved somehow. Him and some of the people he drank with. They were − ' Another hesitation. ' − they were that way inclined.'

Olive was stunned by what her sisters-in-law were telling her: a haze seemed to rise up from the floor and to mask her eyes like a red mist: she felt giddy and would have toppled sideways off the chair in a faint had not Muriel reached out and taken her by the shoulder: several seconds passed before she was able to speak.

'An armed robbery! God help me! Tell me he wouldn't be so bloody daft as to do something like that! Tell me!' Olive pleaded. 'Not an armed robbery! Whyever would he want to do a daft thing like that? Why? He could spend his life in gaol if he did anything as daft as that!'

'We're not saying he did take part in the actual robbery,' Martha hastily interrupted to calm Olive's rising anxiety. 'It's just what Brendan wrote from Aldershot, that's all, Olive. I'm not saying your Robert was one of the gang − just that he knew some of those the police suspect might have done it. There has to be something in that. After all, the police did go to his lodgings armed with guns and they wouldn't do that just for someone dodging the call-up, would they? And your Robert has disappeared. Gone on the run. That's what's worrying Brendan. I only wish he were here himself to tell you himself. He knows much more about it than I do.'

'Robert said nothing about having to have a medical for the army when I last saw him,' said Olive, perplexed. 'What would they want to take a man with seven children for? I know he's the youngest, but why would they want to take him?'

'They're taking all the under-thirty-fives and your Robert's only twenty-nine,' interjected Martha.

'Thirty,' corrected Olive involuntarily. 'I was twenty-three when we married. He was nearly twenty-one.'

'He's young enough to serve then,' declared Martha. 'Brendan and Gerry are the older ones.'

'We can only tell you what Gerry and Brendan told us,' Muriel said, sympathetically, taking up the theme again. 'When I spoke to Gerry the last time he came home − just before they took him in -- he did say your Robert had got mixed up in some shady characters down there and they were worried about it. Nothing Gerry could put his finger on − just that there were some who Gerry said he wouldn't trust with passing the collection plate from one to another at mass. You know the kind, the ones who'd put in a button and take out two shillings! It seems he was proved right, by all accounts.'

'Brendan said they were straight from the bogs of Ireland,' Martha interrupted again, as keen as her sister-in-law to tell Olive what she knew. 'Brought over by the Government to work in the shipyard at Devonport down there. Big drinkers with old opinions, always going on about things back in Ireland. Still living in the past, twenty years ago. You know, us and them and De Velera and the Easter Rising, Black and Tans and all that stuff, but glad to come over here and take our money. He said both he and Gerry tried to warn Robert that he would be better staying away from them, keeping with them, but, well, you know, what a hothead your Robert is. Brendan said Robert and his so-called new friends got involved in a fight with some sailors who came into the pub. Men who'd just come back from Dunkirk. Tried to take the mickey. A lot of name calling went on and a fight started. Brendan and Gerry tried to drag

Robert away, but he refused. He said there was no way he was going to retreat from "the bloody English." Same old stuff we've all been hearing for the past ten years or more – ' She laughed to herself at the absurdity of the mental picture: Olive nodded her understanding. ' – Anyway, they told Robert he ought not to get mixed up in such company, but he wouldn't take any notice. As far as he was concerned, his new friends shared his views and that was all that mattered. You know he takes things far more seriously than either Brendan or Gerry. Brendan won't say much about anything these days unless he's asked. The hangings shook him, yes, but at least he respects me and won't talk about things in front of me. I'll give him that.'

'Gerry don't talk about Ireland much either,' said Muriel. 'He didn't like the hangings in January no more than anyone else. It shook him that we actually did it. But, if you mention Ireland to him, he just shrugs and says, "Well there ain't much I can do about it over here or want to." It's Robert who mouths off, Olive, if you don't mind me saying so. Good Lord, girl! You've been married to him for all these years, you know what he's like! He's still fighting the bloody Troubles!'

Olive had to admit she was right: to her it seemed as if Robert were bent on righting the wrongs against his homeland singlehanded, as if that way and that way alone he could re-establish his republican credentials.

After that, the talk turned to Muriel's and Martha's husbands: the women were worried about how they were coping.

'You know what a weak chest Gerry's got,' said Muriel. 'They still passed him A2, though. It seems they're calling up anybody now – anybody under thirty-five. They need the men, I suppose. I didn't think they'd be that desperate as to take Gerry. I could have done with him here when the bombing started. Still could. I'm hoping they'll let him home once he's out of the Glass-house and completed his six weeks of square-bashing.'

'Couldn't we all,' agreed her two sisters-in-law silently.

'You know Brendan tried to get out of it by pretending he was hard of hearing when he went for his medical.' said Martha with a little laugh. 'He pretended he couldn't hear what they said to him. He thought he had got away with it until he got up to go. The crafty blighters waited till he got to the door, then called out, "Oh, Mr. Cullen, one more thing!" The daft fool turned round, didn't he? They knew he could hear and that he was only trying to fool them.' The women all laughed together at that.

'You would think, that with Brendan and Gerry being in Aldershot, an hour's train journey away, they would let the both of them home just once to see if their wives and families are all right, wouldn't you?' Muriel complained bitterly. 'Compassionate leave for just one weekend. That ain't asking too much, is it? Bloody army. At least, once they've done their training, we're hoping they'll be able to get home easy enough, if they'll let them, if we're still here.' She began to laugh to herself.

The clock had ticked round to a quarter to four and Olive was anxious to leave: she wanted to return early because she did not want to be caught out again in the open during one of the sneak daylight raids which the Germans had suddenly started to send over in an attempt to unsettle the Londoners even further and to give them no respite, night or day. Only the afternoon previously, Olive had been standing in a queue of women at the butcher's at which she had registered on the High Road: as the siren sounded, the women had all looked at each other, none wanting to lose their place in the queue: then someone had broken and they had all rushed for the shelter in Rupert Road, a charge of women along the uneven pavements of the High Street, clutching their shopping bags, their children hanging on grimly to the various flying prams. The raid, by sixty-plus bombers and fighters, lasted less than fifteen minutes and, an hour after they had left it, the women were all back in the same queue, squabbling over who was in what place: three hours later they were back in the shelter listening to the sirens sound as the first of four night raids began.

Muriel and her two girls, Anne and Jean, walked with Olive and the children to the Tube station at the end of the street: Anne and Jean were happy to carry their twin cousins, while a smiling Michael rode happily at one end of Olive's pram and Joseph slept at the other. With Muriel wheeling her own pram, in which Peter, too, was asleep, it reminded them of the walks they used to take together before the war when the two used to meet regularly at one or other of the various parks in the district and the children all played together on the swings, seesaws and roundabouts or in the sandpit. The smell of burning in the air, the smoky haze that overlaid everything, the bomb-blasted buildings in several of the nearby streets, the shattered and cardboarded windows of many of the houses were all cruel reminders that the old days of peacetime were long gone and no one knew the future.

Muriel and Olive had known each other ever since Olive had first come up to London as a nineteen-year-old the year of the General Strike in Twenty-Six: Muriel had been the maid at the house of a well-to-do Middlesex gentleman county cricketer in Highgate when Olive arrived to take up the position of assistant to the cook or, as it turned out, drudge-of-all-work for the cook.

Being of roughly the same age, the two girls had quickly become firm friends, laughing and giggling together in the kitchen, playing tricks on the fat, sweaty cook, going out together on their Sundays off, spending much of their leisure time at the cinema: even going down to the West End once specifically to go to theatre to see a show, even though they could barely afford the price of the tickets on the meagre wage they were paid. They went only because they felt that, since they were living and working in London, they ought to go to a real theatre at least once, something they could only have dreamed of doing if they had remained in their villages, Olive in her tiny East Anglian village, Muriel in her village in Hertfordshire.

It was through Muriel that Olive had met Robert: Muriel had agreed to go to the Hammersmith Palais with a young Irishman named Gerry whom she had encountered while sitting in the park one Sunday when Olive had been kept behind by the cook to perform some menial tasks that the old harridan considered were necessary to retain favour with the mistress of the house. Olive had gone along as the blind date for her friend's brother and the much younger Robert had turned up.

'I just never thought he'd do anything so daft as jumping out of a window to avoid talking to the police,' Olive sighed in exasperation as the two walked along, pushing their prams, with the children ahead of them. 'You can't dodge the police forever. He should know that. They'll find you sooner or later. Where's he going to sleep? That's what I'd like to know. He's got to sleep somewhere. And where's he going to work? The police don't give up, do they? They always keep looking. I just can't believe he would do anything so daft as to get mixed up in an armed robbery. They check all the time. Anyone going for a job these days has to have an identity card and people ask them who they are and where they live, don't they? How's he going to get round that?'

'Don't worry, girl, I'm sure it will all sort itself out,' Muriel commiserated as they reached the entrance to the Tube and she and the girls prepared to turn back. 'I can't see Robert doing anything so daft as taking part in a robbery!'

But Olive could not help but worry: if Robert were on the run, it meant she would not be receiving any more postal orders from him: irregular as they had been previously, she had survived, able to pay the rent most weeks and keep herself and the children in food, light and heat by drawing on her post office savings. Though things were going on ration and it meant that she would get the same as everyone else, that was true only if she had the money to pay for them: and her savings were dwindling fast. 'I just wish I knew where he was and what he's doing,' she sighed. 'I don't know when I'll hear from him again.'

'He'll get in touch somehow, sooner or later, I'm sure,' said her sister-in-law. 'If they haven't got anything on him, there's no need for him to go on the run, is there?'

Olive almost wished it was the old days in their first flat: then, whenever Robert went 'missing,' usually he would be found in one of the half-dozen pubs along the High Road, invariably with Gerry, for they always drank together, sometimes with Brendan as well. Olive had found out early in their marriage that Robert liked to drink, always too much: and always, too, he would come home in a bad temper, bemoaning this or that, cursing this or that, and then would begin the round of his beery breath on her face, the insistence upon his rights, an awkward few minutes, his long sigh of relief as he rolled off her, then a deep slumber during which, like most men, he snored oblivious to all who might hear him. It was not what Olive had dreamed marriage would be like in her girlish days: she had wanted a house, with a back garden where she could sit and watch her children play on sunny days. Instead, all marriage had had brought her were seven children in nine years: living first in a cold third-floor flat at number sixty-seven Rupert Road, with just a living room, a curtained-off kitchen, two bedrooms with a double bed in one and three single beds in the other.

That was before the war, before she had gone up to Thurstone: she had only six children then and Michael was the youngest: he had slept in the main bedroom in a drawer she had pulled out of the chest of drawers and padded with folded blankets, the same kind in which the baby Joseph now slept: the twins slept in one single bed in the other bedroom, Patrick and Jack shared either end of another and only Jimmy had a bed of his own.

That was the flat which Robert had given up while she was in Thurstone: on her return, all Olive had been able to get was the smaller, single-bedroom, fourth-floor flat at forty-two Rupert Road, partly furnished, with a communal lavatory and bathroom on the floor below: she had cursed Robert for that, but then curses had been a part of the marriage right from the start. She had fallen in love with Robert almost immediately she had met him on that blind date because he had an easy, smiling charm, even though he was four years younger than her: when she had become pregnant six months later, he had not been too bothered about getting married, but had gone along with it to keep her happy, paying no attention at all to the details of the occasion, unlike Gerry who had been sounded out thoroughly by Muriel.

Olive and Robert had married in a joint ceremony with Gerry and Muriel at Our Lady's Church of the Immaculatae in the same borough in which Muriel now lived: it had been Muriel's idea, to cut down on the cost so they could all go back to the one room in the public house they had booked and cut a joint cake and eat a joint buffet so as to reduce the expenses. Olive sent invitations to her family as a matter of courtesy, but none had attended: the Depression was at its height and her father and her brothers had claimed they could not afford the fare up to London from the village in such straitened times: her father had also refused to let Alice take the fare for herself out of the housekeeping as she had no money of her own. The final blow came when Theresa, whom Olive wanted as a maid-of-honour, wrote back to say that she and her new husband, Alf Braybrook, would not be able to attend either. Olive knew the reason why Alf did not want Theresa to attend: because Olive had never got on with him when he was one of the youths milling about the village's streets. It was the absence of Alice and Theresa which saddened Olive the most: she wanted her sisters to see her wed, to be there, especially as, since her six-month pregnancy showed so much, she could not send them a photograph for fear her father and her brothers would see it. Her father would rail against her, she knew, and her brothers would laugh: so she agreed only to the one photograph of herself and Robert being taken together that day and only then as part of a group outside the church, with herself half-hidden on Robert's arm and her own and Muriel's bouquets carefully positioned to mask her circumstances: of course, she had not married in white.

For Olive, the refusal of her father, sisters and brothers to attend was only a momentary concern: she was marrying the man she loved and there were enough people from Robert's, Brendan's and Gerry's circle to make the wedding buffet and drinking session in the public house enough of an occasion to remember. The two other brothers, James and George, had come down from Glasgow with their two young ladies, confusing and similarly named Mary McDonalds. The only sour note was when Robert's parents had turned up at the church from Ireland: for the old man was wearing a hideous green suit: 'Green with mould!' Olive had declared at the time: it had been a bone of contention between her and Robert ever since.

James, or Jimmy, their eldest, had been born in the May of Thirty-One, then Patrick in the June of Thirty-Two, Jack in the July of Thirty-Four. Then, mercifully for Olive, there had been a break of two years when she had not got pregnant: but that was remedied in the November of Thirty-Six when she conceived the twins, John and Thomas: carrying the twins had been the worst for her, especially as, after their birth in the August of Thirty-Seven, the more delicate Thomas had remained in the cottage hospital for more than a month: his breathing had been so poor Robert had sent for the priest to christen him within an hour of the birth as he was not expected to live until the morning. Olive simply assumed it was something to do with a family curse: the same affliction which had struck down one of Robert's girl cousins in Ireland when she was just eighteen, just before the brothers had all left for England: she had dropped dead in church one day for no apparent reason, so Robert had told her, although she had always been frail. But Thomas had pulled through and, with the extra care of the family's general practitioner, Doctor Kingston, Olive had been able to bring him home after a month and now he was a three-year-old running ahead of her as she lifted the heavy double-hooded pram up the steps of forty-two Rupert Road into the hallway.

The twins were not even a year old when she fell pregnant with Michael, who was born in the January of Thirty-Nine, and when the war was looming in the September she was three months gone with Joseph.

THIRTEEN

WHEN Olive reached the fourth-floor landing, she discovered she had another unwelcome visitor: Miss Grogan, one of the children's officers from the borough council's health department, a tall, bespectacled, sharp-faced, middle-aged spinster, who kept her hair tied in a bun, wore flat-heeled brogues, thick stockings and a brown herring-bone tweed suit and looked always to be stooping. She was waiting on the landing as Olive came up the stairs with Joseph cradled in one arm, Michael on reins and the twins scampering ahead of her: it was not Miss Grogan's first visit to the flat: she had been several times over the past year, always with a brown leather briefcase tucked under her arm in the same way some women would carry a handbag: somehow Olive sensed it was trouble: it usually was of some kind or another when Miss Grogan visited.

To Olive, Helen Grogan was the epitome of the sour, university-educated, condescending, spinster do-gooder, who knew nothing about bringing up children and who frowned upon any and all practices which ordinary mothers adopted, disagreeing with how they fed their children, disciplined them, treated them, washed them, spoke to them, everything, in fact, about which she herself had had no experience, but who considered she knew best and confidently expected others to acknowledge it by word and deed.

Olive had first come across her a year earlier when the children from Rupert Road and the nearby schools and kindergartens had been evacuated on the very Friday before the war began. When it became obvious that war was imminent, letters had gone to all the mothers to tell them their children would be leaving the next morning 'for the safety of the countryside': on the appointed day, the mothers had all gathered at the school gates and there was much weeping and wailing as well as waving goodbye as the children were being formed up ready to be marched out of the school gates, hand in hand in pairs, to be walked to the Tube station a half-mile away and then by the Underground to the mainline station. Olive was lucky, or so she considered herself at the time: because Michael was just nine months of age and she was three months' pregnant with Joseph, she was able to travel with her six on the evacuation train along with several other mothers in a similar condition: but all those mothers not going with their children found themselves held back at the school gates by two policemen. When Olive reached the school playground with Michael and the twins, the children were already formed into lines, two-year-olds, three-year-olds and four-year-olds in one, five to seven-year-olds in another, and eight-year-olds and upwards in a third, all with their string-tied gas mask boxes hanging round their necks and brown luggage labels tied to their lapels. Thin-lipped, efficient and meticulous, Helen Grogan was going along one of the lines methodically checking the label attached to each child's coat and ensuring that each had a small packed lunch of some kind and some warm, clean and dry clothing for the journey. Her loud hectoring tone towards any of the children, of whatever age, who strayed out of line or who had not brought a lunch or who wanted to go to the lavatory irritated Olive, especially as it reduced several of them to tears: but it was Miss Grogan's utter lack of sympathy and understanding for the sad-faced mothers being held back at the gate which had infuriated her the most.

While among that crowd of desperate women, there were many trying not to cry too openly and even managing to force a smile and give a feeble wave, there were others for whom the actual moment of parting was akin almost to losing a child to the grave: some were near to hysteria when the lines of trusting, yet bewildered, children were marched past them out of the gate and across the road towards the Tube station where they would travel to the mainline station. It was at this point that order broke down: shouts more akin to wails and calls more akin to sobbing passed between mothers and children: some of the mothers, as if suddenly realising that they might not be seeing their children again for months or years, attempted to walk with the crocodile and even to dart into it to give their child or children one last farewell hug and kiss: these poor, misguided women, Helen Grogan curtly ordered aside. And when some, quite naturally, tried to follow the crocodile down into the Tube station entrance, there was Miss Grogan standing at the top of the stairs barring their way.

'There is no need for you to follow,' the foolish woman had informed the distraught mothers, spreading her arms, and thus only adding to their general distress. 'They will be all right with us. Let us take them now. Please, ladies, please!'

The consequence, of course, was that most of the mothers had simply ignored her, pushed her aside and streamed down after their children, determined that they would remain in sight of them until the last was packed into the Underground train and it had disappeared into the tunnel, even to riding in the same train as the children, some. It was as if Miss Grogan considered that, once the children were in her care, the mothers had given up their rights: they were no longer to be considered: nothing was to be allowed to impede her efficiency: she had been given the task of organising the evacuation of three-hundred-and-twenty children between the ages of three and ten and she was going to do it as efficiently and as speedily as possible and no one was going to stand in her way!

It was even worse at the mainline station where some mothers of children from other schools had managed to follow their little ones right on to the concourse, anxious to keep them in view until the very moment they boarded the trains going to where few knew and for how long none knew. The prim, authoritarian, spinster had ordered the phalanx of policemen and railway men to ensure the anxious mothers, and even some fathers who by then had rushed there from their work, were kept well back behind the barriers almost out of sight. When several women, overcome with remorse perhaps and regretting their decision to let their children go, had tried to break through on to the platform itself to take back their wailing offspring, they had been seized and pushed back physically by the policemen. Helen Grogan herself had hurried up at that precise moment, briefcase under her arm, clipboard in hand, to push one struggling mother back behind the barrier.

'Ladies, ladies, ladies!' she had coldly admonished the wet-faced women. 'Control yourselves! Please! You will only upset the children further if you behave like this and it will only make our task all the more difficult.'

So the tearful mothers, suitably chastised, had obediently stood back and watched the long column of children pass from sight along the platform leading to the waiting train, still in twos, holding hands, repeatedly turning their heads to look back and wondering why their mothers were no longer following: and all the time Miss Grogan was hovering near the barrier with her briefcase and her clipboard entreating the mothers to be brave as their children were herded on to a train to go off without them and none knowing whether they would ever see them again.

On the train, Olive had found the overly officious spinster as equally lacking in compassion towards the children as she had been towards the mothers, chastising tearful three-year-olds in compartment after compartment with the words, 'Dry your eyes do, child!' and 'Come on, buck up! There is nothing to cry about now!' and 'Why are you making that awful racket? Stop it this instant.'

Now waiting on the fourth-floor landing watching Olive struggle up the last few steps, Miss Grogan gave her that same condescending smile that she had given to all mothers on that fateful day just over a year previously.

'Ah, Mrs. Cullen, at last,' she said through pursed, thin lips. 'I've been waiting almost half-an-hour for you. I wonder if I could see you for a moment?'

She made no move to assist Olive as she fumbled with the key in the lock, neither to take the baby from her nor to take Michael's hand, but merely stepped aside as the door was pushed open, as if she did not want to be touched by the grubby twins. Miss Grogan was the type of woman who, by reason of her own self-importance, considered she should always be first to enter a room and seemed taken aback when the twins rushed in ahead of her and went scurrying off into the bedroom to play with two cotton reel 'tanks' made by one of the men in the shelter the previous night, unaware and uncaring that the cold-faced woman's sharp exclamation of surprise was directed after them. Little Michael also tottered in after them, eyeing the curious, tall, middle-aged woman with obvious suspicion and sought safety behind the armchair from which he continued to stare out at her while chewing on his straps: he would come out when she had gone.

Unfortunately, the twins did not close the bedroom door when they rushed in and the poorly patched ceiling was all too visible: Miss Grogan eyed the brown paper patch with the same disdain as had the policemen.

'I heard about your mishap, Mrs. Cullen,' she said, giving Olive a look which she could interpret only as 'You wouldn't be in this fix if you had stayed in Thurstone, you know.'

'I don't mind so long as it stays dry,' said Olive with a shrug, a manner which she had adopted as a procession of neighbours had visited to view the hole with gasps and 'oohs' and other useless expressions of awe and sympathy.

'Yes, quite,' acknowledged Miss Grogan, brushing some imaginary dust off the seat of the backless wooden chair to sit at the table. Then, producing a cardboard folder from her briefcase, she sat, lips pursed again, hands clasped, waiting while Olive placed her shopping bag down by the corner sink, laid the sleeping Joseph on the rug in front of the fireguard, told Michael off for chewing his straps, ordered the twins to make less noise in the bedroom and then returned to stand with one hand on the mantelpiece.

'We have had a telephone call from Thurstone,' said Miss Grogan slowly, as if choosing her words carefully so as not to alarm Olive. 'It's about Patrick. He's the seven-year-old, isn't he?'

'Eight now,' corrected Olive, perplexed, feeling a little pang of discomfort even at the mention of his name.

'It's not good news,' went on Miss Grogan. 'It's bad news, I'm afraid.'

FOURTEEN

'WHAT kind of bad news?' The indirectness of the woman's approach annoyed Olive: in her opinion, if people had something to say, they should say it.

'I'm afraid, he has run away from the hostel,' said Miss Grogan with a slight cough.

'Oh my God! When?'

'Two nights ago.'

'Two nights ago!' Olive was horrified. 'What in this weather.' It had been cold and rainy for the past two days.

'It's all right,' Miss Grogan reassured her, somewhat belatedly. 'He has been found and he is all right, unharmed, they say. Some workmen found him wandering along the main railway line. They discovered him in one of their little huts by the side of the track. He was asleep, sheltering from the rain. Apparently, he was following the main railway line back to London. He was more than twenty miles from the town going south, the authorities at Thurstone say, so he had obviously been walking for the whole of the previous day and most of the night, following the main railway line. The transport police have taken him back. He is safely back in the hostel. There is no need to be alarmed, though he has a bit of a chill. Why I have come to see you is that the matron has asked us to ask you if there is any way you can go up there and talk to him, please? They are at their wits end what to do about him.'

'What do you mean?' Olive asked, defensively. 'Boys do run away. He's not the first. I don't suppose he'll be the last. They get daft ideas in their heads.' Then a festering wound reopened. 'They should never have split them up. They were fine when they were all in the same hostel together in Queen Eleanor Road, but they split them up. Put Jimmy in Allotts Gardens away from Patrick and Jack, then moved Patrick away as well. They should never have split them up.'

Miss Grogan traced a figure on the greasy surface of the table: she was slightly embarrassed when she spoke and presaged her remarks by clearing her throat.

'I am afraid it is not as simple as that, Mrs. Cullen,' she said. 'You see, according to the authorities, this is not the first time your Patrick has run away.'

'It's the first I know of,' said Olive flatly, which was true. 'Boys do that kind of thing, don't they? But they never go far. They get to the end of the road, then come back. Patrick's only eight years of age. Where would he run away to? I ask you.'

Miss Grogan gave a weary sigh. 'We have it on good authority from the director in charge of the evacuees in Thurstone,' she said calmly and with emphasis, 'that Patrick had run away eight times previously since the beginning of January, which, I understand, is about the time you came back to London to be with your husband. This is the ninth time he has run away.'

'The ninth!' Olive was aghast. She had not dreamed Patrick was that desperate to get back to her: suddenly tears were welling up in her eyes: she had a sudden mental picture of her second eldest trudging forlornly along the shiny rails of the railway track in his grey short-trousers and bomber jacket, heading south, heading home, his scrawny frame hunched against the cold, hair plastered to his scalp by rain, coat collar turned up, face set, perhaps creeping cold and shivering into the railwaymen's hut and falling asleep on some sacking, hungry but determined. 'Good lord! What if the workmen had not found him? He might have died there and no one would have known.' The thought horrified her: but she had to defend herself, she knew that, especially against know-all types like Helen Grogan.

'Whatever are they doing letting a boy of eight run away nine times?' she exploded, only tempering her anger when she saw the wide-eyed Michael looking wonderingly at her from his refuge behind the armchair. 'What kind of people are they that they can't even look after an eight-year-old boy? These people are supposed to be professionals. They're supposed to know what they're doing! They haven't got a clue about kids, none of them! You need to have kids to know about them!'

Miss Grogan, somewhat taken aback by the fierceness of Olive's remarks, blanched at the latter part: the attack on her spinsterhood. 'The authorities are of the opinion, Mrs. Cullen,' she began, fixing Olive with a stern, beady-eyed stare, 'that it is your return here which has induced Patrick to run away from the hostel so many times. Each time he has headed in one direction only, south, towards London, which is where you are. Patrick obviously wants to get back to you.'

A surge of motherly pride came over Olive: at the same time her cheeks flushed with embarrassment: she almost felt proud of her son for what he had done, despite the danger in which he put himself. 'I am his mother,' she exclaimed. 'Where else would he go? His home's here.'

'Precisely,' said Miss Grogan and then repeated it. 'Precisely. We cannot help but come to the conclusion he would not have run away were you still with him in Thurstone. Patrick is only trying to reach you because you are not there in Thurstone with him, Mrs. Cullen. You are here and he is up there. It is quite natural that a boy of his young age wishes to be with his mother, to have his mother near him.'

There was a pause while the health department officer pursed her lips once more and sheafed through the folder of papers which she lay before her on the table. She extracted something and pushed it across to Olive: it was an official headed letter from the borough council's senior health officer, asking the railway to provide a second-class return railway ticket from Kings Cross to Thurstone for one Olive Mary Cullen, of Flat 10, forty-two Rupert Road.

There was a hint of pleading in Miss Grogan's voice. 'If we give you this and arrange for you to stay at accommodation which we will provide, will you go up there and talk to your son? Convince him that it is better to stay there where it is safe – away from the bombs – away from London? You will be able to see your other children while you are there. We will give you time with them.'

'You know,' she added after a further pause, 'I cannot help but think you would be better off up there yourself, Mrs. Cullen.'

Olive had known exactly what Miss Grogan was about to say and had her answer ready. 'I'm not going back and you can't make me,' she declared, emphatically. 'I didn't like the place when I was there before and I am not going back to it. I'm staying here. You can whistle before I'll do that, you and the whole borough council. I'll go up and talk to Patrick and to see the other two, but I won't stay up there a minute longer than I have to!'

'These are difficult times for all of us,' Miss Grogan tried.

'More difficult for some than others,' Olive thought, but did not say so aloud. Instead, she flatly declared again: 'I'm not going back and that's that. My husband's here – ' she began, then added sarcastically, more for her own amusement than information for Miss Grogan, ' – that is, when he's here at all. So you can tell them at the council offices that I am not going back. They'll have to bomb me out before I'll move anywhere!'

'There is a war on and we have to do what is best for the children,' Miss Grogan said lamely and rather unwisely.

'I know there's a bloody war on!' rapped Olive. 'I've just spent the past month trying to sleep in the air-raid shelter at the end of the road! Me and my kids! We know there's a war on down here even if others don't.'

'I urge you to think about it, Mrs. Cullen,' said Miss Grogan, trying to maintain what authority, and thus dignity, she could still muster in the face of a stubborn adversary. 'Will you at least go up to Thurstone this weekend?'

It was nice to hear the woman say 'please,' thought Olive. 'I'll have to take the others with me,' she suddenly realised. 'I'm not leaving them behind. I'll have to take them with me.'

Much as she felt it would have been easier to have left the twins behind with one or other of her sisters-in-law, Olive had to admit that it would be nice to see the boys again: she had not seen them since January when she had caught the train south. Would they be pleased to see her? She had a sudden doubt: she had always felt guilty about leaving them in Thurstone: she wished somehow she had been as adamant as her two sisters-in-law. Martha had refused to allow her two girls, Maureen, twelve, and Doreen, eleven, to be evacuated and, taking her cue from her, Muriel had kept back her two, Anne and Jean. There had been trouble and endless persuasive attempts by their borough council, but Martha and Muriel had stuck to their guns. The only real difficulty had been in getting the girls into another school since theirs, like the one in Rupert Road and most other schools, was closed. Eventually, until the bombing had interrupted them, all four girls had travelled each day on the trolley bus into another borough where a small school had been set up for the children of the 'backsliders,' as Miss Grogan called them: those who refused to break up their families and were willing to risk the wrath of their councils rather than send them away, plus other 'backsliders' who had sneaked back during the early summer, before Dunkirk, before the Battle of Britain, before the fear of invasion and before the Blitz had begun. It was Martha's and Muriel's defiance which had first put the idea into Olive's head to defy the wisdom of the authorities and return from Thurstone: if they could do it, why could she not do it also?

The Phoney War was at its height then: she half-hoped Hitler would come to his senses, or Prime Minister Chamberlain would, and they would make peace and the soldiers would return home and people could get on with living a normal life. People had enough troubles without a war, too! After all, the Royal Air Force was just dropping leaflets over Germany then, not bombs, and the army had not actually fired a shot that she knew about: it was all phoney, like they said in the papers. Only the Royal Navy had been engaged in fighting of any kind: there was a rumour about a thousand sailors who had been drowned up in Scapa Flo right at the start of the war, but that was just a rumour: probably true, but still just a rumour then. True, too, warships had shelled each other off the coast of South America and the Royal Navy had scored a great victory over one of Hitler's pocket battleships, the Graf Spee, in the South Atlantic: and, one had to admit that cargo ships were being sunk crossing between the United States and Great Britain and, undoubtedly, sailors had lost their lives: everyone knew that: but there had been no all-out war, had there? Nothing that could not be smoothed over: but for the Royal Navy, no one was serious about another war actually being fought between the two, not after the last lot, not after all those dead soldiers in France and all the one-legged and one-armed ex-servicemen one could see about the streets: no one except that loudmouth Churchill: he wanted a war, him and Anthony Eden, but no one else did. Olive had had no worries until Churchill had become Prime Minister: the war seemed to have started properly as soon as he had taken over. Before that, under Chamberlain, Hitler had 'missed the bus': Chamberlain had said so! There had been only a half-hearted attack in Norway which had led to Chamberlain's downfall: to Olive's blinkered political mind-set, no sooner had Chamberlain gone than the Germans had attacked – on the very day Churchill took office! It was silly, of course, but Olive believed it! First there had been the retreat from Belgium, then the evacuation at Dunkirk and then the air battles had begun over Kent and Sussex and the other southern counties: that was when she first had realised the war could drag on and on: when the planes were shooting each other down and people were saying we can beat this bloody bastard Hitler and his gang of Nazi thugs! Churchillian rhetoric and the end of all hope of peace!

Robert had made his feelings known from the outset of her return from Thurstone that he would have preferred her to have stayed where she was: the matter was still a bone of contention between them months later. When he had last been home in the July, she had stood at the sink on the Saturday evening, washing the pots, her back to him so he would not see her crying: she just could not bring herself to tell him the truth, the whole truth, not in the mood he was in: that she had come back to be with him because she loved him, because she needed him, missed him, needed his company, needed to escape the loneliness she had felt up there in Thurstone, the endless walks around the park and along the bank of the sluggish river, the dreary nights she had spent sitting in the hostel. For three months she had withstood it, all the time aware of her growing pregnancy, till she could stand it no longer: she needed to see her husband, to be with him. Instead, with tears streaming down her face, she just told him what she now told everyone else: 'I came back to have the baby. I wanted my own doctor, Doctor Kingston. She's always been my doctor, ever since I got married. She knows me. I didn't want someone I didn't know messing me about. That's why I came back, not for anything else.' She ended with a defiant toss of her head, which said, 'There, now you know!'

They had argued so fiercely that Robert had gone fuming out of the flat to spend another inevitable evening drinking in the pubs along the High Road: when he had returned from the pub crawl, tipsy as usual and looking for an argument, Olive had stood her ground, defied him.

Strangely, it had not exactly been about the safety of the children which had concerned him: more that, if she and they were in London, he would have to come up to London to visit them: and London could well be bombed! God almighty, woman, he had cried, there had been enough talk before the war about cities being the targets for bombs in the next war, and likely gas attacks! It had been in all the papers at one time or another and talks on the wireless: everyone knew what was likely to happen if a war started and, now it had, he did not fancy getting gassed or killed in a bomb raid in a war between 'the damned English and the bloody Germans!' That was what he seemed to object to most.

The argument had ended with her shouting at him: 'I am not going back, so there! If you don't want to come up again, don't! You can do what you bloody well like for all I care! I'm staying here!' She had done it out of pure defiance: the next day, the Sunday, Robert had caught the morning train back to Plymouth, without even saying goodbye to her or the children.

FIFTEEN

OLIVE saw the sleeping figure on the double bed almost as soon as she entered the flat: it was Robert, her husband: the twins saw their father almost at the same time and ran squealing with delight into the bedroom and were upon him, shaking him awake, before Olive could stop them. She and the children had just spent their twenty-seventh consecutive night in the Rupert Road shelter, the same as always, while the raids went on overhead: Olive had managed to sleep through part of the night: she had lain awake all during the first raid, which had ended at midnight, had slept fitfully during the second, which ended at two o'clock, but had been awakened at four o'clock by the flashes and bangs of the third. It was raining when at seven o'clock she ushered the boys out into the chill morning air and they had come straight home, not bothering even to join some of the others who were hurrying to the far end again where another house, number ninety-seven, it looked like, had been hit: the Germans, so the locals were convinced, had made yet another attempt to bomb the engineering factory and warehouses at the far end of Rupert Road and had missed again. That morning, too, as usual, the Parretts helped Olive and the children up the stairs, old man Parrett wheezing and coughing as usual, his wife snapping at him all the way up.

'These stairs are getting too much for him,' Ma Parrett confided in a whisper to Olive as the two climbed well ahead of the old man and the twins. 'Oh, what I'd give to spend one night in my own bed! Just one night! The both of us.'

'Me, too,' agreed Olive wearily. 'I could sleep for a week sometimes.'

Fortunately, when they reached the landing, Olive was able to take her own pillows and blankets from the old man and the Parretts went into their own flat, where the coughing continued.

Robert was lying there in his work clothes: a brown paper parcel tied with string, containing his only suit, was lying at the foot of the bed: he was unshaven and decidedly unkempt. His face and thick brown hair were grimed, his clothes muddy, damp and crumpled: his cheeks seemed more hollow and his cheekbones more prominent and he looked altogether more gaunt and thinner than she remembered him, like he had not been eating properly for some time. She had not locked the door when she had gone to the shelter, just pulled it shut, so she assumed he must have let himself into the flat, lain upon the bed in a state of exhaustion and fallen soundly asleep on the quilt without even removing his mud-spattered boots.

Robert sat up, stretched and yawned as the squealing twins rolled all over him: he tried unsuccessfully to fend them off as John's feet went painfully close to his groin, but not with much success. 'Steady there, boys, steady!' he cried, sitting up. 'That's enough now, that's enough. Come on, John, and you, Thomas, off! Off now!'

The twins, as all children will, blithely ignored him and went on tumbling across his legs, hanging off his neck and trying to climb upon his shoulders, vying with each other for the highest position. Michael, seeing his brothers hugging a strange man, who seemed not to mind overmuch, forgot his usual shyness and attempted to climb on to the bed to join them, but was unable to do so because of his smallness until his father lifted him up and sat him protectively between his knees.

Robert Cullen made no attempt to greet his wife by name, or to smile: no term of endearment was offered: instead, he scratched at his tousled hair, stared up at Olive standing just inside the door and growled in a low, surly voice: 'Christ, woman, I was hoping you would have taken this lot back to bloody Thurstone by now.'

'If I wasn't still here, you wouldn't be able to come here to sleep, would you?' Olive scoffed defiantly. 'I'm here because I want to be. I told you that the last time. It'll take more than Hitler and his bloody bombs to make me go back to a hostel in Thurstone, I can tell you!'

'You might not have a bloody choice if a bomb lands on the house while you're all in it!' said Robert, equally as angry. 'For God's sake, woman, you can't stay here with bombs raining down all over the place every bloody night. I've seen the street outside. The kids come first, don't they?'

'What would you know about it?' Olive demanded, letting out a snort and throwing the pillows and blankets she had brought back from the shelter on to the bed beside him: it was not how she had imagined his homecoming would be, but it was not unexpected: from the moment she had seen Robert's prone form lying on the bed, she had steeled herself for the inevitable: he had not disappointed: within seconds of their meeting, the old gulf of pride and obstinacy had opened up between them.

'You haven't been here,' went on Olive. 'You've been down in bloody Plymouth, safe in the nearest pub no doubt. You haven't been through what I've been through. I've survived – we've survived – and we'll go on surviving. It's my decision, my choice. They're my children, too. I'm their mother. If you were so worried about us, why didn't you come up when all the bombing started to make sure we were all right? You must be the only man in London who never bothered to find out whether his wife and children were still alive in the middle of all the bombing.'

'I couldn't come up,' said Robert grumpily, giving Olive a cold glare. 'I had other things on my mind.'

Olive decided it was not the moment to tell him what she already knew: instead she resorted to a girlish petulance: 'Then don't come back here trying to tell me what to do. I'm not going back, so there!'

Her actual concern at that moment was less for herself and her children than it was for him: after all, she and the children had just spent another dismal night in the shelter and had returned safely to their home: it was not her and the children who were in danger, but Robert.

'Never mind about me and the kids,' she cried. 'What about you? Don't you know the police have been here looking for you? Armed police! Why would police with guns come bursting into this flat looking for you, ready to shoot anybody and everybody, frightening the children, turning everything upside down?' There was a sneer in her voice as she added: 'It's not you and your damned politics again, is it?'

A sudden thought came to her. 'Good God! The police could be watching this place right now!' she exclaimed in alarm, crossing to the window to look down: but in the street below there was no one leaning against a lamp-post or loitering against the railings opposite reading a newspaper, which is how Olive supposed anyone watching the flat would pass the time: the only people to be seen were some women, carrying pillows and blankets, trudging wearily along the pavement towards their own homes, and some children playing up by the air raid shelter.

'I've been dodging the coppers for a couple of months or more so I suppose I should have expected the English bastards would come looking for me here sooner or later,' said Robert blithely. 'It's not me they're after so much as some people I know, some people I met in Plymouth. It's them they're after, not me.'

Olive gave another of her huffy sniffs, which to her husband could have meant almost anything – disbelief, disdain or disgust – and came back into the middle of the room: she lifted Michael from between Robert's knees, carried him back into the living room and placed him beside a happily kicking Joseph on the rug in front of the unlit gas fire.

'Why are they after you then?' she demanded as she pulled back the fireguard and applied a match to the gas. 'Are they the ones who tried to rob the sailors?'

Robert looked up in surprise: he had not expected that his wife would have known about the attempted robbery in a town so far away.

Olive revelled in his discomfort. 'Martha and Muriel told me,' she informed him, unable to keep the sarcasm and jubilation out of her voice. 'Brendan and Gerry told them all about it. And about you! At least they had enough sense not to get mixed up with the crowd you did.'

'I wasn't in on the robbery attempt,' Robert quickly retorted, swinging his legs off the bed and pushing the twins away with a sharp, 'Not now, boys' before he went on: 'I just used to talk to them in the pub, that was all. They were friends. I didn't know they were going to try a wages snatch, did I? I just used to have a few drinks with them.'

The twin were looking concerned: they had detected the clear hostility between their father and their mother and now they sat upon the bed side by side, their legs dangling, watching and wondering, the light glinting on John's round, wire-rimmed glasses.

Rather than answer her husband immediately, Olive crossed to the sink under the window in the living room-cum-kitchen so that she was out of his line of vision and busied herself filling the blackened tin kettle: the water pressure was low and it took her some time and that added to her growing anger. 'You must have known something about what they were up to,' she finally accused, banging the filled kettle down upon the gas ring in a display of noisy annoyance. 'You can't have been that blind and stupid. Brendan and Gerry saw through them, clear as day. Why couldn't you?'

'Because I didn't,' was all an equally angry Robert could wearily reply, coming forward from the bedroom to lean against the doorpost so that he could better argue with his wife, who was putting a match to the gas. 'Maybe I didn't want to. Anyway, I was working in Plymouth docks the day they tried it. I wasn't involved! Good God, woman, they were from Ireland, they were Irishmen! Why shouldn't I drink with them, my own bloody countrymen? Better than drinking with the bloody English anyway! Tight-fisted bastards, they are!'

Robert's denial that he had not himself taken a part in any robbery should have cooled Olive's anger, but it did not: she was almost as angry that he had got himself mixed up in such a situation as she would have been had he actually taken part in the robbery attempt itself.

Olive emptied the previous evening's tea leaves into the sink and turned to face her husband: there was still one question to be answered: she knew the answer to the question before she asked it, but asked it anyway. 'Who were these people you were drinking with then? Some of your republican friends, were they? IRA?' she scoffed. 'The same people who've been planting bombs all over the place trying to kill people? As if we didn't have enough with the Germans trying to bomb us every night, we have to worry about your friends trying to kill and maim us.'

'What if they were?' a defiant Robert shouted angrily back: then, after a pause, as if collecting himself, he added with a disdainful shrug: 'I suppose the police must have been watching them and they saw me with them. They must have thought I was one of them. I don't know. Maybe someone told them I was part of it or maybe they just thought I was because two of them were staying at the same lodgings as me and I used to walk to work with them. That's how I got to know them. I was on a different shift at times from Brendan and Gerry. They were someone to talk to. I haven't taken part in any armed robberies and I haven't planted any bombs.' He was exasperated himself now and there was open defiance in his tone when he added: 'The police don't bother me. I can dodge those flatfoots any time.'

'Huh! Some people are too smart for their own good!' Olive countered as she spooned fresh tea leaves into the pot.

'I've dodged them once, I can dodge them again,' declared Robert, coming forward now to slump upon one of the dilapidated chairs at the table. 'I did it down there and I can do it here. I've been doing it for the past couple of months and I can go on doing it. The dumb sods down there hadn't enough sense even to put a man round the back of the lodging house when they came for us. We all went out the back window as they came in the front door.' His smile had returned and there was an arrogance about his manner which infuriated Olive.

While waiting for the kettle to boil, she took a loaf of bread from the bin and began sawing at it with the bread knife. 'Well, if you ran away with them and the police want them, it's no wonder they are looking for you as well,' she said, the knife poised in mid-air. 'If you had nothing to hide, you should have stayed where you were and let them arrest you. Then they would have known you weren't involved, wouldn't they? Guilty people don't run away, do they? The worst thing you could have done is to run away. It's the worst thing anybody can do.'

Robert dismissed her argument with the same disdain as he had dismissed the others. 'The English police wouldn't have believed me, an Irishman,' he snorted. 'A sailor got shot, someone tried to rob their pay wagon. It stands to reason, woman, if they couldn't find the ones who actually did it, they would take the next best thing – the first Irishman they came across! Me, the one who used to stand there drinking with them in a pub! And I'm supposed to sit there and let them take me, am I? No bloody way! I don't know whether the sailor who got shot is dead or alive – I don't bloody care either – but, if he has died or dies, I am not going to risk getting hanged for what someone else did. Even if he doesn't die, they could try me for treason or whatever – armed rebellion against His Imperial Bloody Majesty's forces in a time of war or some such. Trying to rob the Royal Navy of its wages – even if I didn't do it. It's the first thing the police would do – frame me just to get someone. Any Irishman will do, as far as they're concerned. I was not having that. That's why I went on the run! I didn't know what those blokes were going to do. They didn't tell me and they didn't ask me to join them so I didn't. I went on the run because I don't intend to fight and risk my life for no King and Country, especially if it's an English King and Country! I'm just dodging the army. I was supposed to go for a medical like Brendan and Gerry just before the robbery. I got a letter at the lodgings back in the summer, but I didn't bother going. That's all they've got on me – nothing else.'

'You think you're so clever,' sneered Olive as she scraped out the last of the marmalade in the jar: but the sneer was more to cover her own anxiety rather than to reprimand him: her concern was that Robert had done the very last thing an innocent man would have done: he had jumped out of a window and fled: he had turned himself into a hunted man, a fugitive.

What worried her also was that his two brothers, Brendan and Gerry, the only likely restraining influence upon his wilder actions, could no longer exercise that restraint: could no longer give counsel, tell him he was making a mistake, tell him he was a fool: prevent him from committing some stupid act as they had done before. They had been removed into the army and now there was no one to act as a calming influence upon him, no one to reason with him.

Olive knew, as many others did not, that if Robert were not checked by either brother's common sense, their reasoning, he would become headstrong, defiant and even more arrogant: and then anything could happen. Anything.

SIXTEEN

THE NEXT few minutes passed in a frosty silence: Olive did not speak because past experience of her husband's quickness to temper deterred her from pressing him too long on any subject, especially if she were pointing out the folly of something he had done.

Robert did not speak because he knew that he would only worry his wife further if he were to tell her he had spent the past two months in hiding, moving from rooming house to rooming house, usually one step ahead of the police, relying on Irish friends to let him sleep on the floors of their rooms: and when unable to do that, he had spent a half-dozen nights sleeping in a disused warehouse, sneaking out each day to one of those self-same friends for some food. Neither could he tell her that it was because he had tired of that he had risked everything by returning to Rupert Road and his wife and children, knowing full well that the police might be there waiting for him, but still willing to take the risk to see them.

The kettle having boiled and tea made, she put on a saucepan of porridge on the gas ring and then Olive busied herself with taking the cracked and chipped plates, the handleless cups and the bent and stained spoons and forks from the drawer of a small cupboard which stood alongside the sink and banging them down upon the table with a loud clatter: just to make a noise: they comprised the family's sole dishes and cutlery, all she had been able to assemble since her return from Thurstone, and a measure of her poverty.

The sound of the utensils banging on to the table brought the twins out of the bedroom to join their father and younger brother Michael seated at the table, but all three children were clearly aware of the hostility still existing between their parents and so kept their heads bowed as if in a sulk, only now and again raising them to gaze alternately from one to the other with worried frowns upon their faces.

Robert contented himself with munching on his marmalade sandwich. 'How's the baby?' he asked eventually, simply to break the silence, at the same time leaning forward in his chair to encourage the gurgling child lying on the rag rug in front of the gas fire to grip one of his tobacco-stained fingers and deriving much pleasure from it when he did so.

'He's fine. He's put on weight. He's sixteen pounds now. He's healthy,' Olive recounted with a shrug, not of indifference, simply as if to ask, 'What did you expect him to be like?'

No matter how much she busied herself, Olive could not rid herself of her anxiety: the sound of a slamming door somewhere on a landing below only accentuated that nervousness: she kept glancing towards the door to the landing as if she expected at any moment to hear the clump of boots upon the stairs and to see the silver-haired inspector come bursting through again with his revolver at the ready.

Robert followed her glances towards the door and it irritated him: it jarred with his calm demeanour: it also affected his pride: it was as if his wife did not trust his judgment. 'For goodness sake, stop worrying, woman!' he cried at last when another door slammed and Olive flinched yet again. 'No one even knows I'm here. I came through the park while the bombing was on. No one saw me because there was no one about to see me. It wouldn't matter if they had. The local ARP don't know about me, do they? They don't know who I am. So it's unlikely they'll be on the lookout for me, especially as they don't even know I'm here. They were all tucked up in their little shelters keeping well out of the way of the bombing when I let myself in.' He was smiling to himself, pleased by his own success.

'It's nothing to smile about,' an agitated Olive chided. 'What about the bits of metal falling, all that shrapnel? People have been killed by falling shrapnel. You could have been killed by it. It's not safe to be out on the street when the guns are firing.'

Robert's obvious lack of concern horrified Olive: she had quite forgotten her own mad dash through it all a few days before.

'Well, none of it hit me,' Robert assured her, with a wearied sigh, this time giving the twins a wink, which brought smiles to their faces to replace the frowns of earlier. 'Besides there wasn't much firing anyway, not while I was about. Just some gun banging away in the park further along the High Road, just firing for the sake of it, it seemed to me. Didn't seem to be doing much good, anyway, from what I could tell. A waste of shells. The planes still kept dropping their bombs.'

His criticism annoyed Olive. 'We don't mind how long the guns fire or how loud so long as it keeps the Germans away,' she declared huffily. 'The more shells they send up, the better and the more likely they are to shoot them down, so there!'

The porridge had heated by this time and she came forward to the table to spoon it out: it was as good a time as any to ask, Olive thought to herself. 'Have you got any money you can give me?'

'Didn't you get the money I sent you?' Robert enquired, as if surprised his wife should ask.

'Yes, I got it, what little you sent,' Olive answered, the old sarcasm returning. 'That was over eight weeks ago. I've had to draw money out of the post office to survive since. I'm nearly broke. How you expect me to feed four kiddies on what you send me and what little I have in the post office, I don't know. Couldn't you have sent something since then? Money goes nowhere now, especially in wartime.'

'I sent you what I could afford and when I had it,' Robert protested grumpily. 'I haven't been earning since I had to skip out of the lodgings window, not regularly. I lost a week's pay because of that as it was. What I had, I needed for myself.'

'And what about your children?' Olive demanded, with the emphasis very much on the 'your.' 'Don't they deserve something? Have you given up feeding your own children?'

It was the angry look upon his wife's face which forced the husband to reach into his pockets and empty some coins on to the table, before adding three ten-shilling notes and a pound note from his wallet. 'There's three quid. It's all I can spare,' he said, grudgingly, spooning some of the hot porridge into his mouth, 'I've got to keep some for myself.'

'For drinking most like,' said Olive tartly, quickly scooping up the coins and notes and retiring from the table. 'I've got rent to pay,' she reminded him, 'and food to buy.'

Later, with all four children asleep, Joseph in his drawer, and the twins and Michael on the single bed behind an improvised blanket curtain, they lay together on the double bed, their arguing over, their tempers cooled, his anxiety soothed: it was then that he asked the question which Olive felt he should have asked long before: 'So how bad has it been then?'

'Bad enough,' was Olive's ambiguous reply as she slipped off the bed and rebuttoned her dress. 'Having to go to the shelter every night is the worst. You have to take everything with you. If it hadn't been for Old Ma Parrett and her husband along the landing, I wouldn't have got there half the time. Not with four to take, blankets pillows, the baby's things and everything. Sleeping's difficult at times. Sometimes I don't get to sleep at all, sometimes I just doze. If the bombs don't keep you awake, the guns will. The children sleep all right most nights, but they do get disturbed by the noise at times. I try to get them down before it all starts. Most mothers do. Trouble is there's not much chance to catch up when you come out. You have to spend half the day queuing. If you're not standing hours waiting in a bloody queue for something, you're having to go back into the shelter because now they're coming over in daylight, as if bombing us all night wasn't enough. Sneak raids, they call them, in the middle of the afternoon or at teatime.'

'Well, you know the answer to that one, don't you?' Robert said, with a sly smile, at the same time reaching for his cigarettes.

Olive pretended not to hear and so did not answer, but went into the living room to prepare a bottle of powdered milk for Joseph and to crunch some soup cubes into a saucepan for the other children's lunch: they, meanwhile, all slept blissfully behind the temporary curtain on the single bed.

SEVENTEEN

MERCIFULLY, that afternoon there had been no sneak raid: at least Olive had not heard the siren sound, though one ear had remained permanently cocked, listening for its wail: soon, she knew, she must give the children their tea and prepare to go down to the shelter. Robert had already told her he would not be joining her – as a precaution, he said, in case he was seen by a policeman – and Olive had already gathered everything, the gas masks, the baby's anti-gas helmet, the pillows and the blankets by the door to the landing: so that when Ma Parrett and her sickly husband came knocking, he could retreat into the bedroom to hide and she could just usher the children out and close the door behind her.

She knew, too, that she would have to ask the question sooner or later, just as she would have to tell Robert about Patrick and the trip she was planning to make the very next day: she waited and chose her moment when Robert came out of the bedroom and stretched himself in the armchair before the gas fire: she sat opposite him on the broken-backed chair, giving a fractious Joseph his bottle, having woken the sleeping baby for just that purpose.

'How long are you going to stay?' Olive asked, hoping he would say just the one night, yet really wanting him to stay even longer.

'Till Sunday night at least, if the coppers don't come charging up the stairs first,' Robert replied with a nonchalant shrug. 'After that, I don't know. There's a chap I'm going to see who, I'm told, can help me. I need to get a job somehow. I need to earn if I can. You need money for the kids and I need money for myself. Someone gave me the name of this chap he knows who'll fit you out with a false identity card. A real one. No forgeries, so I'm told. He works in the food office at the local council somewhere. You just slip him a couple quid and it's yours. Put a different name on it and you're home and dry. I'm not the first to do it. There's loads of blokes out there doing it. Half the fellahs on the last job I was on were on the dodge from something, the wife, the army, the taxman. Not one of them was working under his real name. It shouldn't be any trouble.'

'And what about your ration book?' Olive asked, more in the hope of tripping him up than anything else: perhaps that was something about which he had not thought.

'Same,' he said with a faint smile, raising one eyebrow mockingly. 'Once you've got an identity card, a ration book's no problem. People lose ration books, don't they? You just tell the powers-that-be you lost yours in a bombing raid. Pick a house that's been bombed in case they check up, put that address on your identity card, say you were lodging there and you've lost the lot. No trouble. You can do it in London. London's a bigger place than Plymouth. You can get lost up here and that's what I intend to do, disappear. For a while, at least. I can get work more easily up here than I ever could down there and not so many questions asked either and without the local constabulary breathing down my neck.' Seeing the hurt look on Olive's face, he laughed and said: 'Don't worry, old girl, I'll keep in touch. I'll see you whenever I can.'

She would have liked to have disbelieved Robert's story, but she knew it was quite likely to be true: there were people out there, the spivs and the black marketeers, who would cheat and lie and steal and do anything for money and to hell with everybody else! To hell with people who worked for a living and stood in queues half the day waiting for their meagre rations!

'It's not right,' she exclaimed, indignant and meaning it, 'people fighting and dying and getting bombed, ordinary decent people, and there's these people making a profit out of the war and you helping them do it. It's not right? If I knew who it was, I'd shop them as soon as look at him. Bloody racketeers, they all want shooting.'

Robert laughed at her outburst. 'I didn't start the bloody war!' he protested. 'Blame your famous Mr. Chamberlain for that. It was him who started the bloody war. My country's neutral. Perhaps they should have shot him like they shot that bloody traitor, Michael Collins.'

Olive did not rise to the bait: she did not want another political discussion with her husband and have him haranguing her with his views for the next half-hour: besides, she had nearly finished feeding the baby and needed to wake the other three.

'Well, you'll have the place to yourself this weekend because I shan't be here. This'll tell you why,' she announced in a petulant voice, handing him Miss Grogan's letter from the pocket of her pinafore.

'You wanted me to go to Thurstone, well, I'm going, but I'm not staying,' she said as he read it, frowning hard: it amused her that she had scored a point over her husband.

'Nine bloody times!' exploded Robert, sitting up. 'The poor little bugger! It's no wonder he keeps running away with you down here and him and the others up there. You should have bloody stayed up there with the kids like I told you to, woman. You're his mother, for Jesus's sake!'

'And you're his father!' Olive retorted.

The old arguments surfaced again and the mood of both after that was sullen: Robert had the expected temper of an Irishman, one that flared suddenly without warning at the slightest cause and which subsided just as quickly at times, especially when he wanted to get round her at bedtime. For herself, she knew that her sarcastic manner and her continual questioning of him, as much as her repeatedly stated disbelief of the many things which he considered gospel or sacrosanct, were surefire ways of infuriating him: that was why she did it: to get her own back for the long hours of loneliness she was forced to spend while he was out drinking with his brothers: they were the only weapons she had.

The iciness was still there an hour later: she had fed the children and so was ready and waiting by the door when Ma Parrett and her husband called: she went down to the shelter without a backward glance, fearful that one of the twins might ask whether his father was coming, too? Neither did and so Olive passed her twenty-eighth consecutive night in the Rupert Road south shelter, listening to the bombs falling and the guns banging away, while Robert remained in the flat in the dark with the blackout up. Strangely, for all their quarrelling, Olive found it comforting to know that he was close by and hearing the self-same noises as she was hearing: and he would be there when she and the children went back out in the morning, yawning and shivering in the cold, smoke-laden air, wondering what new buildings had been blown to pieces during the night. She had missed Robert as much as the children had missed him: but too often, she knew, their quarrels did not allow her to show it. The one good thing was that Robert had promised he would be at the mainline station in the morning to see her and the children off.

EIGHTEEN

OLIVE took the mid-morning train to Thurstone.

'I envy you, girl, getting away from here. At least you should get a good night's sleep for a change,' said a yawning, red-eyed Ma Parrett as they slowly climbed the stairs together, returning from yet another long night in the shelter: she was carrying Michael as usual along with some of the gasmasks and blankets: Olive was carrying Joseph in the anti-gas helmet and respirator: and Old Man Parrett was just about managing to usher the twins up the stairs ahead of himself.

Robert had gone when Olive pushed open the flat door, though the remains of an early breakfast would have been apparent to anyone who had looked closely enough: if Old Ma Parrett had known he was there or had noticed he had been there, she made no comment to Olive, but wearily and thankfully set down Michael at the door, handed Olive the gas masks and blankets, and turned to help her breathless, sagging shell of a husband back to their own flat. Olive caught her eye as she went: there was a sad finality about the shake of the head she gave and a grim, thin-lipped determination was showing on her face as she took his arm and guided him to their door: the poor man, it seemed, had scarcely strength to let out a wheeze, let alone draw in breath: it was as if there were no air at all in his black, mucus-clogged lungs.

Once they had all breakfasted on porridge, lukewarm tea and bread and dripping, Olive stood the twins and Michael on the table to wash and dress them ready for the journey in what passed for their better clothes – those less darned and less patched and less crumpled than the others: then she changed Joseph, packed what she would need into the old, battered, brown suitcase and a shopping bag and set off back down the stairs to the street, ushering the three elder children ahead of her once more and carrying Joseph and his respirator, both of which, thankfully this time, she was able to deposit in the spacious well of the pram. From there, it was a walk of no more than a half-mile to the trolley-bus stop and a twenty-minute journey to reach the mainline station, where they would catch the train to Thurstone: the worst thing for Olive was manoeuvring the double-hooded pram on to the trolley-bus platform after the children had scrambled aboard, especially as the conductor made no move to assist her, but impatiently waited to ring the bell: that was, until a struggling Olive rebuked him. 'Don't help then!' she cried: then he did.

At the station, the suspicious clerk at the ticket window seemed to take an interminable time reading the letter before issuing the second-class tickets: as though questioning why a woman with so many children should be travelling at all on such a warrant. While she waited for the gate to the platform to be opened, Olive kept a lookout for Robert: he had promised he would be there: she could only suppose he had slipped away from the house as soon as the 'all clear' had sounded in case the police returned: clearly, no police had been to the house to arrest him, which was a relief to Olive, so it was with some hope that she scanned the thronged concourse: the twins, more observant than their younger brother Michael, could not understand why their mother was forever glancing about her.

'Typical man!' Olive huffed to herself when there was no sign of Robert: all the time she was waiting, she felt her heart skip a beat each time a helmeted policeman strolled past: to her, it seemed they were keeping her under watch in the hope of catching Robert and each one that passed, in her frantic mind, seemed to regard her with more suspicion than anyone else: so nervous was she that it was as though she feared half the metropolitan police of London were waiting to leap out of hiding and haul Robert off.

A cautious Robert did not show himself until the exact moment that the ticket collector pulled open the gate and a despairing Olive was about to go through: then he was beside her, a platform ticket in his hand, having stepped out from behind a pillar and a baggage trolley where he had been waiting and watching for at least a quarter of an hour: even then, he made a detour around another trolley of luggage as he approached, using that as a screen when one of the slow-pacing constables returned. At least, he looked cleaner than when he had arrived at the flat, Olive noticed: he had washed and shaved and was even wearing the suit he had been carrying in the brown paper parcel: he looked altogether different as he lifted up the twins and moved swiftly through the gate: just a man seeing off his family at a mainline station rather than a hunted fugitive from the law – albeit British law.

Robert deigned to carry the twins any farther once they were through the barrier – 'In case I have to do a bolt,' he said. – but set them down despite their protests and, taking each by the hand, hurried them along as fast as their smaller legs would allow, while Olive followed behind with Michael, Joseph and his anti-gas helmet and respirator, the suitcase and the shopping bag all piled into the pram. Being the first in the queue to go through, they were well ahead of the rush and so had enough time to bundle the pram, with its Thurstone label securely tied, into the guard's van and still be first into the second-class carriage: she and the children were all settled in their seats either side of the window and the suitcase, the shopping bag, the gasmasks and Joseph's respirator were all up on the rack before any other passengers joined them.

'I suppose it's too much to expect you to see commonsense and go and give yourself up,' sniffed Olive while they were still alone, as Robert himself prepared to leave.

'I know what I'm doing,' he retorted, annoyed that she had raised the matter at such a moment. 'I'll be all right. Even if they catch up with those other lads, they've got nothing on me. And even if they do grab me, I don't know where they are so I wouldn't be much help to the police, would I? Anyway, I'd sooner go to gaol than be a stool pigeon for the English. It'd be more than my life's worth to inform on the likes of those lads. I'm no fool. I have to do it this way, Olive. I've no choice, I've told you that already.'

Olive resisted the temptation to tell him he was talking like a fool and settled for reminding him: 'You have got a choice. There's nothing to stop you from walking into the nearest police station and telling them you had nothing to do with it.'

Robert just dismissed the idea with a wave of his hand. 'Like bloody hell, I will,' he said fiercely.

'You can't run forever,' Olive snapped back. 'If you went to them rather than keeping on running or trying to they'd listen, I'm sure. The police aren't daft. A guilty man would never walk in and say he's innocent, would he?'

'They'd make bloody sure I *was* guilty! You know coppers,' Robert retorted sharply, as a soldier, with a kitbag on his shoulder, came along the corridor and stopped at the compartment door: his arrival cut short all further conversation on the matter: instead Robert became the sad-faced husband seeing off his wife and children.

'Well, I suppose I'll see you when I see you,' he said flatly, the way men sometimes do when parting from their wives, as if the whole thing were an embarrassment which they wished were over and done with. He took the key to the flat off Olive, but made no attempt to kiss her or the children goodbye and she did not follow him along the corridor to the carriage door as others might have done: instead, she sat down opposite the twins, alongside Michael and Joseph, who were both on the same seat, and busied herself with them.

Robert's face was a blank as he stepped out of the carriage door: and then, with a final raising of the hand to the twins at their window, he was gone, weaving his way back through the phalanx of soldiers, airmen, WAAFs, WAACs and civilians all hurrying down the platform to find a seat in the second and third class carriages. The train filled up rapidly after that, mostly with service personnel returning to their units: it left twenty minutes late so Olive was glad that the twins and Michael were too preoccupied with pressing their noses against the window and breathing on the glass to draw faces upon it to notice the manner in which their mother and father had parted.

NINETEEN

APART from two halts, one halfway through their journey when the slow, clanking train came to an inexplicable stop in open countryside with nothing but barren fields to look out upon for a half-hour, then another short delay at one of the towns en route, with nothing but a single passing boat on a brown, rubbish-strewn canal running alongside the track to distract them, the journey to the south Midlands town was uneventful – except for the time it took: two-and-a-half hours for what in peacetime normally took one-and-a-half-hours.

Fortunately, the rocking motion of the carriage soon sent Michael and the baby to sleep so for Olive it was a pleasant enough journey: the only discordant note came when she had to steer Thomas and John jointly along the crowded corridor to the lavatory, only to find there was not one in that carriage and she had to retrace her steps all the way to another carriage and across a rocking footplate: for the most part, the soldiers and airmen in the crowded corridor cheerily squeezed themselves into the doorways to let her and the twins by. A blonde WAAF in the compartment volunteered to watch the sleeping Michael and Joseph while she performed this task and, when she got back, she found the girl was cradling the baby in her arms and softly cooing to him, even though he was asleep. She could not have been more than nineteen or twenty and was pleasant enough to talk to: at least she seemed to understand Olive's stress, for she talked to the twins for much of the journey as they peered at the countryside passing slowly by, pointing out to them the horses, sheep and cows, other trains on the lines and the occasional vehicle on the roads crossing under the tracks or seemingly racing the train on near deserted roads.

The only irritation, more embarrassment really, came when Olive inadvertently let slip to her that she was on her way to Thurstone to see her three other sons. The WAAF was so surprised that she exclaimed loud enough for all in the compartment to hear: 'Seven boys! You have seven boys? My goodness! Seven! I don't think I could have seven children!' Then after a short contemplative pause, she added: 'Maybe two, a boy and a girl, say.'

Olive sensed there was a sudden surge of sympathy from the others jammed into the compartment, two young Scottish soldiers with their rifles and kitbags thrust up into the rack opposite and their glengarries tucked into their shoulder straps, a Royal Army Service Corps corporal with his kitbag between his knees and an airman reading a book by J B Priestley whose rank and job Olive was unable to determine. What annoyed Olive was that it was a mutual 'Catholic, poor cow!' sympathy which people express with their eyes when they glance quickly at each other to ensure that each is thinking alike, but which they never express in words

Notwithstanding, the young WAAF was still very helpful to Olive and kept the twins amused: she also told Olive all about what she used to do when she worked in a large store in Manchester before joining up so that the journey was not as tiring as she had expected it would be: even so, Olive was glad when the ticket collector announced after two hours and twenty minutes that they were approaching Thurstone.

As the train emerged from the long tunnel which lay before the town into a grey midday light, Olive saw again all that she had hoped she had left behind her: when she had left Thurstone ten months before, she had not expected to return so soon. To her, it felt almost like a failure, a defeat, as she stood in the crowded corridor looking out of the grimy window while the old train clanked and clanged over the Victorian viaduct, with the dull brown ribbon of the sluggish river flowing below, and came to a halt in the soot-dusted, redbrick station amid clouds of smoke and steam and the shouts of the guard and the porters and the banging open of carriage doors. As Olive was cradling Joseph by then, the blonde WAAF gently shook Michael awake and carried him to the carriage door, while the two Scottish soldiers between them took down the suitcase, the respirator, the gas masks and the shopping bag with the baby's things in it and deposited them on the platform: one even jumped out to help Olive lift the heavy, double-hooded pram from the guard's van. Perhaps he was a Scottish Catholic?

Thurstone did not seem to have changed one iota in the months Olive had been away: indeed she would have been surprised if it had: there was the same smoky smell of the factories everywhere and only a splash of green opposite the station where the shrubbery-shrouded castle mound stood. Lining Black Lion Hill were the same plain, grimy, terraced red-brick houses, while along the Mare Fair and Gold Street the same sad, peeling-paint shop fronts presented the same half-empty windows into which, in hope during her stay there, she had looked a thousand times, seeking something, anything, a dress, a scarf, a pair of shoes, that would distract her from the boredom of the place. Outside the bakery, the greengrocer's and the two butcher's shops, the self-same small queues, which she had once joined, were forming, people patiently waiting with the same pasty, blank, unenquiring faces: none recognised her: her sojourn in Thurstone had been too short. In the Horse Market and Broad Street, the shop windows seemed to have little to offer other than the same dull, unfashionable women's coats and the same dull, unfashionable women's dresses and the same dull, unfashionable women's shoes as they had always had. The windows of the men's shops were mostly bare: only one having a headless dummy dressed in a brown tweed jacket, grey flannel trousers and a green knitted woollen pullover to offer in exchange for someone's hard-earned cash – so long as they had the coupons, of course. Only a blue-painted UCP cafe on the corner of Grafton Street seemed to be doing much business: there at least people were going in and out, whereas, for a Friday midday, there seemed little other activity of note in that dull, dull town.

Olive's destination was one of the tree-lined avenues of bigger houses which branched off Barrack Road up near the boys' private grammar school and where, according to the letter Miss Grogan had given her, she would find lodgings for herself and the children already booked by telephone from London at number thirty-one St George's Avenue: and paid for, Olive hoped. Familiar as it all was to Olive during her stay in Thurstone, it still proved to be a tiring, uphill walk of a mile-and-a-half from the station, made all the more wearisome by the twins' persistent demands to be carried in the pram alongside Michael and Joseph, coupled with the weight of the suitcase, the respirator and anti-gas helmet and the shopping bag already piled in. At first, Olive tried to place the shopping bag atop the suitcase and Joseph's respirator and helmet on the pram's apron, but Michael, awake now, took exception to it blocking his view and kicked so vigorously that she ended up pushing the cumbersome pram with one hand while carrying the shopping bag with the other and keeping a watchful eye on the twins as she shepherded them along the pavement. Fortunately, there was hardly any traffic, a few cars powered by gas bags, a couple of coal lorries, some wagons and two or three buses going the wrong way for Olive to catch, so she was able to negotiate the wide cross-roads at the junction of Grafton and Broad Streets without any worries: when she turned into the avenue and found the house opposite the point where the grammar school stood behind a long frontage of trees and shrubs next to the recreation ground, it was a little after one.

The landlady at number thirty-one, a parsimonious-looking Scots woman named Munro, with a thin pinched face and greying hair, who looked nearer seventy than fifty, so Olive thought, let her in, read the letter from Miss Grogan, sniffed, eyed the children with more than a little disdain and open suspicion, gave another sniff and led Olive up to the second floor.

'Just bed and breakfast, is it?' she asked as they climbed the stairs, as if to ensure that what was requested was confirmed verbally and Olive would not be requesting anything for which she was unlikely to be reimbursed. 'For yourself and the four little ones? Three nights is it? Till Monday?'

Fortunately, the bedroom proved to be a large one, bay-windowed, linoleumed, with a double bed and a single bed, a bright, patterned red carpet, yellow wallpaper and a washstand, chest of drawers and dark wood wardrobe: it was a relief to Olive for it meant the children would have plenty of room to sleep and there would be room, too, for the twins and Michael to play on the floor if they wished. All the time she was surveying the room and acknowledging her satisfaction with it, Olive felt herself to be under the steady scrutiny of Mrs. Munro: it was as if the steely-eyed landlady could not make up her mind why a woman with four young children should be given such preferential treatment warranting a large front bedroom, the best bedroom, in fact, in her establishment: and all paid for, too, by the chief officer of the health department of a borough in London of which she had never heard. Most peculiar.

Olive did not feel at ease until she was able to strap Joseph and Michael back into the large double-hooded pram, which filled half the hallway, bump it back down the front steps into the street, chivvy the twins to keep up, and set off back down Barrack Road towards its junction with Grafton Street: there, she turned on to Grafton itself, which led across St Andrew's Road on to Spencer Bridge Road and, eventually the other side of the railway tracks, to Harlestone House, where Patrick was billeted. Fortunately, the hostel was no more than a steady threequarters-of-a-mile walk across town, so it was just after two o'clock when Olive finally walked up the shrubbery-lined drive.

It took a minute of ringing the bell before anyone appeared: there was a sound of young children's voices from around the back where the play area was, but there was no on else about: it was the deputy matron who answered, spick and span in her bright blue uniform and white cap.

'Is Mrs. McLaughlin in? I'm Olive Cullen. I've come about my son, Patrick. Patrick Cullen.'

The deputy matron looked flustered when Olive asked for the matron by name: Olive had briefly met her at the Christmas party given for the children while she had been living in Thurstone.

'Oh, oh dear,' said the deputy-matron, her face dropping. 'Mrs. McLaughlin is not here at the moment, I'm afraid. She's out. There's no one here except me.' The last words were spoken as though she hoped rather than expected they would suffice as an answer and the caller would go away.

'Can I see my son, Patrick, then?'

'Er – I'm sorry, no, Mrs. Cullen, you can't,' the deputy matron began, biting her lip. 'Your Patrick's not here anymore. He was moved this morning. They've taken him round to Upton Lodge. I am very sorry. We had no way of letting you know. I'm afraid he's been too much of a disruption here. We have had to move him. You know he ran away, don't you?'

'That's why I'm here.'

'He had to be moved, Mrs. Cullen, for his own good. You do understand, don't you?'

'No I bloody do not,' snapped Olive. 'I've come up from London to see him, I've walked all the way from St George's Avenue to here and now I'm told he's been moved to somewhere else! Who moved him? Who said he had to move?'

'Oh dear,' was all the deputy matron could say at first. 'Oh dear. You really ought to talk to Matron. I'm sorry to have to tell you this, but Patrick had to be taken to where – ' She paused while she searched for the right phrase. ' – to where he could be looked after better than we can here. Where the controls are tighter, so to speak. We're only a small hostel here. We don't have the staff or the time, you see. Matron took the decision. He was moved this morning. He hasn't run away just the once, you know – ' Another pause while she studied Olive's face. '– It's been several times.'

'Yes, I know all about that,' exclaimed an irritated Olive, waving the information away. 'What I want to know is where he is and why he was moved.'

'All I can tell you is that Patrick tried to run away again this very morning,' the deputy matron nervously informed Olive. 'That is when it was decided to move him to a more secure place. He was caught climbing out of an upstairs window at five o'clock fully dressed. We have no doubt where he was headed. I do not know what else we can do for him, Mrs. Cullen. Your Patrick is such a determined little boy, I fear we can do nothing with him here. That's why he has been taken round to Upton Lodge. They are more strict there.'

'What do you mean more strict?' Olive sensed there was more behind that simple phrase than the deputy matron was telling her.

'Boys who run away go to Upton Lodge,' the deputy matron said pointedly through thin lips. 'Upton Lodge is run by Mr. Grundwood. They are more strict there. Mr. Grundwood – he, er – ' Again she was searching for the right words. ' – he doesn't allow them to run away.'

It was an angry Olive who retreated down the shrubbery-lined driveway to the road and headed towards the Weedon road, following the instructions the deputy matron had given her to reach Upton Lodge: fortunately, Michael fell asleep in the pram halfway through the journey: and, as Joseph was already asleep, she had only the twins with which to contend and they found themselves sharply chastised if they lagged behind, Olive moving at such a pace that they had to cling to the side of the pram and run to keep up, all the while suffering to hear their mother's scolding voice.

Olive found the Lodge without too much trouble and walked up the shingled drive to a large, turreted, red-brick, mid-Victorian house, with wide bay windows and ivy-covered walls: the front door was recessed in a black-and-white tiled porch, the three steps to which were a clean, freshly stoned white: on either side of the porch stood two large ornamental plant urns, their greenery overflowing the sides and creeping across the entrance to the porch as if to deter any callers rather than to welcome them.

Olive parked the pram, with the sleeping Michael and Joseph in it at the bottom of the white-stoned steps and rang the large polished brass bell: when no one came, she rang again: it was only after she had rung a third time that a young girl of no more than fifteen or sixteen, with blonde hair and a bent nose, came to the door, drying her hands upon a tea-towel as though she were just completing the washing up.

'Everyone's out,' said the girl matter-of-factly, eyeing Olive suspiciously and at the same time imposing her body in the opening so that the twins did not rush past: for their part, they retreated behind their mother's coat hem and eyed the bent-nosed girl with open curiosity.

Olive felt her heart sink at the news. 'Where are they then? I've come up here all the way from London to see my son.'

'They're all down at the park, most like,' said the girl, a little too sniffily for Olive's liking. 'Doing their gymnastics. What's your son's name then?'

'Cullen,' said Olive forcefully. 'Patrick Cullen. He's eight years old.'

'Don't know any Patrick Cullen,' said the girl, wiping her nose on the tea-towel. 'Don't know that name.'

'I was told he was here,' repeated Olive, a little wearily, looking past the girl into the dark and gloomy hallway in the hope that she might see someone else who would know. Somehow she sensed rather than saw that there was some-one there listening, hovering out of sight in the shadows, but she could see no one: just a grandfather clock ticking away in the silence on one side of the hallway which was lit only by a narrow shaft of pale sunlight slanting through a window at the top of a wide stairs to form an elongated parallelogram on the polished checkerboard of black and white tiles.

'I've just come from Harlestone House,' said Olive curtly, 'and they told me my son was brought here this morning and now you tell me he's not here!'

Something must have dawned on the girl then, for suddenly her hand flew to her face. 'What did you say his name was?'

'Patrick Cullen?'

'Oh,' said the domestic and 'Oh' again. Her face seemed to have blanched and then to have reddened.

It was at that moment that a shadow in the hallway moved. 'All right, Aileen, I'll handle this,' a man's voice said from out of the gloom behind her: he had been standing far back in the shadows of the hallway, hidden by the grandfather clock, listening: Olive had been right.

TWENTY

THE DOOR was pulled half open to reveal a surly, heavy-set man of about fifty or so, with a florid face, uneven teeth, thick lips and pale-grey eyes magnified by the thick lenses of his heavy-framed spectacles: what remained of his hair had been greased and slicked behind his ears: the domestic, Aileen, immediately withdrew into the shadowed hallway behind him as if cowed by his presence.

'My name's Grundwood,' said the man, with an air of authority. 'I am the principal here. And you are – ?'

'Olive Cullen, Mrs. Olive Cullen. My son is Patrick Cullen. I'm told he is here and I've come to see him. The authorities have asked me to.' She answered with a firmness of her own, giving a satisfied sniff at the end of it as if she were trumping a card at whist.

Grundwood made a face and let out a low 'Hummph,' or something approximating that to Olive's hearing. 'You had better come in,' he said with a sniff of his own, opening the door wider to allow Olive and the twins to enter, at the same time directing the domestic to bring the cumbersome pram with the sleeping Michael and Joseph in it up the steps and to park it to one side of the polished hallway.

Grundwood, meanwhile, led Olive and the twins into a small office halfway down the hallway: it was simply furnished, with a well-worn patterned carpet over linoleum, a darkwood desk, two chairs, one for Grundwood and one for any visitor, and an old faded brown armchair set against one wall. Rows of sagging shelves occupied two-thirds of the wall space behind Grundwood's desk, all carelessly stacked, it seemed to Olive, with bulging, official-looking folders, piles of ribbon-tied papers and box file after box file, themselves bursting with papers: one careless tug of the wrong file would have brought the whole lot crashing down. High up on one wall were two framed certificates of some kind which Olive could not read clearly because the glass fronting them mirrored the daylight coming through a high window in the wall behind her: on the dark, polished desk were a black telephone, an ink blotter, an ink stand, two wooden pens, a paper knife and several brown folders: an unopened folder lay on the ink blotter. It was what was leaning against the wall which caught Olive's eye: a slim bamboo cane about three-feet long with a curved handle: she hoped it was just a walking stick, such as a man might carry, and was not used for any other purposes.

Grundwood motioned for Olive to sit on the chair before the desk and took the seat behind it himself. 'We were not informed you were coming, Mrs. Cullen,' he said, eyeing the twins with some misgiving as they jostled each other to sit on the solitary armchair against the back wall. 'There seems to have been a breakdown in communication somewhere. That is most unfortunate, most unfortunate.'

Olive produced the letter Miss Grogan had given her and slid it across the desk. 'This is what they gave me from the borough council health department in London,' she said, with enough defiance in her voice to let Grundwood know that he should not question her right to be there. 'It says for me to come up to Thurstone today, where I'm to stay and why. It's all there. Read it for yourself.'

Grundwood took his time reading the letter prepared by Miss Grogan, giving out the occasional throat-clearing cough as he did so: then he looked up.

'Your son, Patrick Cullen, is here,' he said at length. 'He was brought over from Harlestone House this morning.' There was a certain coldness about the way the man said it, Olive thought: it was like he was speaking of the delivery of a parcel rather than a child, a small being of flesh and blood, being taken from one place it knew to another it did not know and deposited there in surroundings totally strange to it. At least that is what it seemed to Olive and she took an even greater dislike to the man than she had at their first meeting in the doorway when he had hung back rather than come forward, almost as if he were hiding from her. 'It appears that they must have forgotten you were coming and so did not tell us. An administrative oversight,' he suggested, with the beginnings of a smile: Olive just maintained her usual blank face.

Grundwood paused, briefly steepled his fingers and then, with a deep sigh for no apparent reason, opened the folder in front of him and looked carefully at the writing on the top sheet of paper: having read it, he appeared to be slightly embarrassed.

'This is your son Patrick's file,' he said matter-of-factly. 'I see that he has been in four other hostels and has absconded nine times – ten with today's attempt. You understand what absconded means, Mrs. Cullen?'

Olive was not going to take that insult lightly: it was the snide way Grundwood asked that angered her, like he did not expect her to know anything. 'Of course, I know what absconded means! I went to school the same as the rest,' she said fiercely in a voice that so alarmed the twins still seated on the solitary chair against the wall so that John's bottom lip began to quiver. 'What's happened is all in the letter from the council lady. I *can* read you know!' Then, with a mother's intuition, she turned and gave the twins a reassuring look.

Grundwood seemed to realise that he had an adversary who was prepared to stand up to him. 'Quite, quite, Mrs. Cullen,' he apologised. 'It's just that nine times is a lot in so short a period – just a year. I see he has run away four times from Delapre Lodge, twice from Allott Gardens and three times from Harlestone House and all since he was evacuated here just over a year ago.'

'And he has been moved four times – three before this one!' protested Olive: it seemed to her that Grundwood was blaming her for Patrick's record of absconding. 'It's no wonder he keeps running away when they keep moving him about. When I left him in January, he was all right. He was with both of his brothers in Queen Eleanor Road. He would have been all right if they had stayed together, but no – ' Her tone was scornful now. ' – they had to go and move him to another hostel, didn't they? Delapre Lodge. Then they moved Jimmy to another one still. Gladstone Lodge. They said it was to do with the schools, but they could have gone to the same school, couldn't they? That wasn't too hard to arrange, was it? They didn't have to move him, but they did. They thought they knew best. Well, they've found out they don't. If I had still been up here, if I hadn't have had to go back to London, I would never have let them split them up like they have. They were happy together at Queen Eleanor Road. They had friends there. Jimmy had his friend there, the O'Connor boy. But they split them up and look what it's led to!'

'You were here, in Thurstone?' Grundwood queried, raising one eyebrow.

'Yes, I was here till January,' sniffed Olive, realising she had created a predicament for herself. 'I came up with them in the September when they all came up. I had lodgings in Southampton Road, but I had to go back to London. I was eight months pregnant with the baby. He was due and I had to go back in January to see my doctor, that's all.'

'Aah,' said Grundwood as though enlightenment had dawned. 'Aah. That would account for a lot, seeing that the first time Patrick absconded occurred immediately after your return to London. February the tenth.' He put one finger on the sheet of paper and traced it along. 'Then February the twenty-second. March the nineteenth. April the seventh, May the sixteenth – ' Grundwood broke off and looked up, a knowing smile on his face. 'It would seem that the trouble all began round about January, when you left and returned to London, Mrs. Cullen.'

'I had to go back,' Olive retorted: she was not going to have a man – and a stranger at that – tell her what she should and should not do. 'I had to go back to have the baby. I couldn't stay here. I had complications.' It was a lie, but Grundwood would not know that. 'I needed my own doctor, Doctor Kingston. My husband was working down in Plymouth. I needed to be in London where my doctor was, for the baby's sake.'

She was not going to say any more and felt that what she had said was sufficient: Grundwood must have realised that there was no point in continuing that line of discussion, for he slowly closed the folder and, looking straight at Olive, said through pursed lips: 'Then there is this morning. I understand there was another incident at Harlestone House. That is why your son has been brought here.' No longer 'Patrick,' Olive noted, but now 'your son.'

'You haven't let him run away again, have you?' she demanded.

'Oh no. No, no,' Grundwood quickly reassured her, steepling his fingers again and smiling a peculiar smile. 'It is something else.' He paused for a few seconds as if to ensure that Olive appreciated the import of what he was about to say, then continued coldly: 'I regret to tell you, Mrs. Cullen, that what Patrick did this morning, which led to him being brought here, was to bite the matron at Harlestone House – twice. It appears that he bit her on the hand and then, I am sorry to say, on the nose when he was found climbing out of an upstairs window in the early hours. We can only presume he intended to climb down the drainpipe and run off yet again in view of the fact that he had stolen some food to take with him. He was foiled in this foolish escapade by one of the staff and when the matron, who is a good woman, was called and tried to pull him back, he bit her hand. And when she took hold of him to remonstrate with him, he bit her on the nose.'

Olive was wise enough in the ways of children to know that they do not just bite people for no cause and she told Grundwood so quite forcefully. 'She must have been doing something to him to make him do that,' she protested in Patrick's defence. 'Boys just don't bite people for nothing! If she was hitting him – '

'I am not aware of what she may or may not have been doing or indeed whether she was doing anything at all,' Grundwood said, pushing the folder to one side. 'What is certain is that boys should not bite members of staff who only have their best interests at heart. That is why he is here – ' He paused. ' – What you must understand, Mrs. Cullen, is that the children who come here are sent here because they are disruptive in one way or another at their hostels or they are unhappy for some reason and cannot settle. Those who are unhappy, we try to help. Those who are disruptive, we – ' A deep breath here. ' – we deal with. We have a doctor, a specialist doctor to deal with such problems. Do you know what a psychiatrist is?'

'Yes, I know,' replied Olive, bristling up. 'What good can he do? Has he got children of his own? Does he know anything about boys? Patrick's an eight-year-old, for goodness sake! He's going to be just as disruptive here as anywhere else, despite what you say or do. He won't listen to anyone but me. I'm his mother, so I know. I'm the only one he takes any notice of. You'd better let me see him and have a talk with him. I can do more good in ten minutes than you and all your doctors and matrons put together could do in a month of Sundays.'

Grundwood ignored the outburst. 'Patrick is here, as I say,' he went on, quietly, 'but I am afraid he has been disruptive here, too. At this very moment he is in detention. We have had to lock him in – for his own good, you understand. Normally, we would not allow anyone to see him, but as you are his mother and you have come such a long way – ' He left the sentence unfinished and, as he rose to his feet, added with a wearied sigh: 'If you will be so good as to wait here – '

'I'll wait,' said Olive huffily. 'He's my son. Why shouldn't I wait?' And while Grundwood went out into the hallway jangling some keys he had taken from his trouser pocket, she sat calmly in the chair in the office, talking to the twins to reassure them, both of them having picked up their mother's resentment toward the surly, bespectacled man behind the desk.

Anyone observing Grundwood closely would have seen that he made sure the door to the office was firmly closed behind him before he crossed the hallway into a short corridor, really no more than an elongated recess, five or six feet in length, at the end of which was another door: this he opened by turning a key. Inside, all was dark: Grundwood carefully descended a flight of wooden steps holding on to the bannister rail: only at the bottom did he pause to flick a light switch. The harsh glare immediately exposed a cellar, some twelve-feet square, flagged by a dozen or so uneven sandstone slabs each about three feet in length by two feet wide, and all damp as if water had recently been sluiced across them: in the centre of the room above a drain and a tub stood an iron mangle: along one wall was a long flat tub lined with lead, while in an opposite corner stood a brick copper with a wooden lid and the ash of a recently lit fire spewing out from its grate: over it all there hung the sharp, nostril-pinching smell of soapsuds and ammonia.

Also against the wall opposite was the figure of a small, thin-legged boy with a pinched face: he was hunched up on the cold stone flags, shivering in the damp air: his grey bomber jacket was pulled tightly round him and his legs were drawn up to his chin: at the sudden brightness, he turned his head sharply away and screwed up his eyes. He looked to be grubby and unwashed and his trousers seat was covered in the grey-white soapy grime from the floor: when his eyes had adjusted to the harsh glare and he saw the bespectacled Grundwood, he did not move or flinch, but just stared defiantly back at him as if waiting to see what the adult was about to do next.

'Your mother's here, Cullen,' the principal said sternly. 'She's come to see you. She's in my office. You had better get up them steps and greet her. And you had better not tell her you were down here or what happened or it'll be all the worse for you when she's gone. Do you hear, boy?' A large hand reached out, took hold of the hair above the child's ear and twisted it, bringing him to his feet. 'You do understand me, don't you?' he queried, menacingly, before letting go and stepping back: a thin-lipped smile replaced the sneer.

'Now brush yourself off, Cullen! Get all that muck off yourself. You aren't going up there looking like that. Tidy yourself up, boy, and then get up those stairs. And look lively about it.'

Patrick Cullen did as he was bade, brushing at his trousers and jacket sleeves, before hobbling towards the steps: almost instinctively, as he passed the man at the foot of the steps, he read the signals in the principal's eyes, as small boys can, and ducked under the swinging hand and was scuffling painfully up the stairs, wincing as he went.'

Inside Grundwood's office, Patrick halted, still five or six feet from his mother, who had risen from her chair: he did not rush to her and bury his face against her and weep copious tears as some children would have done: but stood silently looking at her, as if first ensuring that it was his mother from nine months earlier standing there and also to gauge her mood: then he asked in a quiet, even, almost surly voice: 'Have you come to stay then?' It was almost as if he expected the answer, 'No.'

Olive did not answer his question: she had noticed something puzzling about Patrick's movements as he entered: he hobbled in, dragging one foot behind the other as though his legs were too stiff to walk properly: it puzzled her and, to a certain sense, it alarmed her. Patrick was generally a good runner: faster even than his older brother, Jimmy: so why would he limp, seemingly barely able to lift his feet? 'What's the matter with you?' she demanded. 'Why are you walking that way?'

Patrick did not answer, but stared back at his mother, frozen-faced, as if to say, 'I cannot give you an answer. You must work it out for yourself.' Then as a perspiring, grim-jawed Grundwood came up behind Patrick and placed a heavy hand upon his shoulder, realisation dawned upon Olive. 'What is the matter with him? Why is he walking that way?' she cried.

'He has been chastised,' Grundwood answered coldly, tightening his grip on Patrick's shoulder so that two of his talon-like fingers dug into the small area between his neck and collar bone: Patrick's blank face tightened against the threat of the pain such an action can bring.

'He's been what?' Olive exploded. 'You mean you've caned him.'

Quickly, adroitly, Olive seized hold of Patrick and pulled him from Grundwood's grasp: she stooped, spun him round, lifted up the back of his grey jacket, pulled out his shirt tail and peered down at his lower back: there were several red weals showing across his lower backbone and across his buttocks.

'You have, you've caned him!' she exclaimed: then as she counted the weals, 'Five, six, seven, eight!' her fury rose even more. 'A boy of eight! What for? What's he done to you that had to cane a boy of eight on his first day here? Who gave you the right to do that?'

'He was in a temper when he came, Mrs. Cullen,' Grundwood said, reddening. 'He tried to run out almost as soon as he came through the front door. Then he kicked the door and would not do as he was told. He was very difficult. He had to be chastised. There was no other way.'

'That's no reason to beat the boy!' shouted Olive: there was a fury in her voice now. Almost without realising what she was doing, she released Patrick and darted across the room to seize the thin walking stick leaning against the wall which she had noticed when she first entered: and before Grundwood could react, she was brandishing it in his face, even as the wide-eyed twins cowered away from her and an equally flabbergasted Patrick looked on.

'Who gave you permission to cane my son?' shrieked Olive, the tip of the thin walking stick less than an inch from Grundwood's nose. 'You are supposed to look after these children, not beat them! The Government sent them here to get away from the bombing, not for you to beat them when you think you will! So help me, I've a good mind to give you a taste of your own medicine! I've had bloody Germans bombing me for the last month trying to kill me so don't think I'd be bothered about you!'

Here Grundwood made an unfortunate mistake: he started to smile in disbelief: he did not expect her to carry out such a threat: after all, she was only a mere woman. Olive read the disbelief in his eyes, saw the smile at the corners of his mouth, saw his shoulders relax: and the next instant Henry Grundwood, the principal of Upton Lodge hostel for evacuees, felt the stinging lash of a bamboo cane across his left cheek, nose and ear. 'There! How do you like it?' shouted Olive Cullen. 'How do you like being hit for a change? You aren't such a big man that I can't hit you the way you've hit him. I'll teach you to cane my son!'

She did not strike a second blow: one was enough to satisfy her anger: instead she raised her leg and snapped the cane across her thigh then flung the two pieces sideways so that they rattled against the window pane above the startled twins' heads.

'Come on, you two,' she called as the twins leapt off their chair and scuttled to her. 'You, too, Patrick. We're getting out of here. I'm not leaving you here to get beaten by him or anyone.'

Grundwood was still standing in the doorway, clutching at the red weal across his cheek and eyebrow, his face screwed up in pain, but barring their way: undeterred, Olive pushed him aside so firmly that he staggered back against the doorpost: it was enough of a gap for Patrick to slip through, a mixture of concern and amusement showing on his face. His tears were forgotten, he was almost laughing with glee as he dragged open the heavy front door and scampered outside into the smoky afternoon sunlight.

There was no sign of Aileen as Olive wheeled round the parked pram, with the still sleeping Michael and Joseph in it, knocking one corner of the grandfather clock as she did so: then she out through the door.

Behind her there was a shout from Grundwood. 'You can't take him out of here!' he called out, as if expecting Olive would heed it.

'Can't I just! You just watch me!' she hurled defiantly over her shoulder as she bounced the heavy pram down the white-stoned steps on to the gravel drive. 'He's my son, I'm his mother. I can do what I want. I don't need to ask you or anybody what I do!'

TWENTY-ONE

OUTSIDE, Olive quickly lifted the twins on to the pram's apron so that they were back to back with their legs dangling over the side: it would speed their getaway: she needed to put as much distance between herself and Grundwood as quickly as she could. Matters were not helped by the fact that, in bumping down the steps, she had awakened Michael: he now began a vehement protest that his feet were being sat upon and, in his sleepy irritation, began kicking out at his two older brothers: this immediately brought howls of protest and retaliatory cuffs against him from them. Olive chose to ignore them all, hurrying down the path with Patrick shuffling alongside as fast as his bruises would allow, a sheepish smile on his face: but it was not without the occasional anxious glance behind in case Grundwood should be coming after them.

Olive had no thought as to what she would do next: she vaguely contemplated marching down to the council offices, but, it being late afternoon on a Friday, realised she might not get there before they closed their doors at five. Besides, why would she go there? It would only draw attention to herself and what she had done and might very well lead to Patrick being taken back to Upton Lodge, the very opposite of what she wished to happen from now on: no way was he going back there, she had decided.

But if she could not take him back there, where could she take him? It was late afternoon by this time: Olive's mind was in a whirl: she needed to be able to sit somewhere and to think about what she had done, so she headed for the Abbey Park, where she had sat many times with other mothers on grey, damp winter afternoons during her previous sojourn in Thurstone. Apart from what Grundwood might do, there was also the problem that Miss Grogan's letter had specified that she and the four youngest were to be given bed and breakfast: now, through her own temper and impetuosity, she had, a fifth child in tow, Patrick, and the early October darkness would soon be closing in..

Olive spent an hour just sitting on a bench in the park, watching Patrick playing with his new-found brothers, the twins and Michael, now out of the pram and happily toddling around everywhere. The questions she had to ask herself were: Would Grundwood tell of what she had done? He was bound to do so, duty bound to do so, she reasoned. So how soon would they come looking for Patrick? Did they know she was staying at Mrs. Munro's? If they did, they would be there that evening: they might even be there at that moment, waiting for her. But Patrick had to sleep somewhere: she could not leave him on a park bench for the night and, because of the younger children, she could not stay with him herself. So what to do? One possibility was somehow to smuggle Patrick into her room and let him sleep there for the night, on the floor with one of her pillows for his head, her overcoat and the carpet for a mattress and a blanket off her bed to cover him.

Dusk was descending when they finally left the park: it was too late in the day for Olive to call on her other two children, Jimmy and Jack, at their separate hostels: she would not be welcomed at either of them: it would be better if she visited them on the morrow, she decided, when they would be able to spend the whole day together. So she headed back into the town centre: the twins and Michael were complaining that they were hungry and she needed to give Joseph a warm drink: the rundown UCP cafe was the only place in which she knew she could get some hot water to make up his bottle, so she headed there. She had the money Robert had given her in her purse, so she was able to buy some buttered currant buns for the children and to placate the surly girl on the counter, especially when she asked for a cup of milky tea for them to share, which they did with their usual squabbling and boisterousness: fortunately, there were no other customers at that hour to be upset by them. For herself, Olive bought a cup of tea to refresh herself and a stale, dry scone several days old, the first meal she had had since breakfast.

When an hour later Olive pushed open the door of thirty-one St George's Avenue, with a limping and sheepish Patrick helping her to lift the pram across the threshold, she had decided honesty was the best policy: she would confront her suspicious, sour-faced landlady and appeal to her better nature, if she had one, and her maternal instinct, which Olive supposed all women should have somewhere deep down inside them: she did not hold out much hope of success: all she could do was to try.

Mrs. Munro was in the kitchen eating a supper of soup and bread. 'I've got my second eldest with me,' Olive blurted out, dragging the hovering figure of Patrick forwards from the hallway. 'I've had to bring him here. He keeps running away, you see, trying to get back home. He won't stay anywhere. That's why I've had to come up from London. I need to talk to him, to keep him with me for a while. Just a couple of days to try and talk to him. He's had a bad time of it lately, I was hoping he could sleep in my bedroom tonight, on the floor, if that's all right with you? He needs to be with me for a while. I can give him one of my blankets. I don't mind. He's been caned, you see, by the hostel manager – ten strokes they gave him. He's red raw down his back, he can hardly walk. I've taken him out of the hostel. I'm not letting him go back there. I'm not having them hitting him when they think they can.'

Olive knew full well she was asking a great deal of her landlady: that much was evident from the startled expression upon Mrs. Munro's face: but if the landlady minded at all, she was too taken aback at first to say so, which gave Olive the opportunity to add in desperation: 'I can pay for him if you want me to. I've got some money. I'm not short. My husband gave me some before I left.' The extra three shillings which she estimated would cover her request were already being held out in the palm of her hand.

Whether it was the pathetic look upon Patrick's face, the stiffness of his walk, or the knowledge of the ill treatment he had received, or just the desperation of his mother's plea, Olive never knew, but the look of sternness and disapproval vanished from the face of the white-haired Scot: the next instant, the suspicious, stern-faced, prim harridan who had first greeted her six hours earlier was transformed into a sympathetic, solicitous, grandmotherly friend.

'You poor woman, you poor woman,' she cried in a horrified tone, rising from the table, leaving her soup unfinished: concern was etched upon her face as she put her hand upon Patrick's shoulder and guided him to her own chair with the cooing words, 'You poor wee bairn, you poor wee bairn. Sit there, my boy, sit there.'

Picking up the coins Olive had placed upon the table, she returned them to Olive's hand. 'I'm not bothered about any extra payment, Mrs. Cullen,' she said. 'The room's already paid for so I won't charge you for him sleeping here for one night, not in view of what you've had to put up with.' Then when a red-faced Olive gushed out her thanks, she blithely waved them away. 'Oh, go on, girl, you've got enough to worry about with you four other bairns. What kind o' a woman would I be if I didna help one of my own?'

Bowls were produced from the dresser shelf, a saucepan already steaming on the side of the range was moved back across on to the glowing coke, a loaf was sliced and hallmarked silver spoons clattered on to the table: more chairs were fetched and, in next to no time, five bowls of hot homemade onion soup and a breadboard heaped with doorstep slices were being placed before four hungry-eyed children. They needed no urging: the dry bread was dipped into the bowls to stir the hot soup then lifted into hungry mouths with much smiling and blowing and licking of lips and chins. So taken up by her grandmotherly role was Mrs. Munro that when, to Olive's consternation, the twins blithely raised their bowls to their faces and eagerly licked off the last of the soup, she even smiled benignly, just like a real grandmother who had seen it all a hundred times before. And such was their sense of security in the presence of their new-found, kindly 'grandmother,' who was bustling about the kitchen setting down the butter and jam, that for once they were not even intimidated by the severe look which their mother gave them as she carefully tipped her own bowl away from herself and spooned up the soup in the proper fashion, while nibbling politely at her bread.

Later, when Olive returned to the kitchen after putting Patrick and the younger children to bed, she found herself being ushered into a spacious front parlour in which the scent of lavender and beeswax polish hung everywhere: dark red velvet curtains flowed to the floor in the bay window: a flower-patterned three-piece suite stood before a black marble fireplace upon which a gold-faced clock ticked below an ornate silver mirror: real oil paintings hung upon walls covered in blue-flowered wallpaper. No sooner had Olive slumped upon the flowered couch and eased off her shoes than Mrs. Munro had reappeared beside her, a concerned frown for the other woman's well-being, carrying a silver tray upon which were set a shiny silver teapot, a painted china cup and saucer, a small milk jug and a bowl of sugar lumps, not saccharins as Olive would have expected elsewhere, but actual sugar lumps.

As the two sat sipping their tea, Olive tentatively broached the possibility that she might even need to keep Patrick by her for a second night to settle him a bit more. 'What's one more little one?' Mrs. Munro declared with a wave of the hand. 'I don't expect he'll eat me out of hearth and home. The poor bairn looks like he needs a good feed. He's so thin, if you don't mind me saying so? He could do with fattening up a bit.'

Olive did not mind at all and Mrs. Munro went on: 'Don't you worry, Mrs. Cullen, there's plenty more in the larder where that came from. We Scots are no' all that you English make us out to be. Besides, your council in London is footing the bill. I'll bill them for a bit extra.' She gave a broad, knowing smile here. 'You keep your money, Mrs. Cullen. I'll not ask you to pay one penny o' it, not with five bairns to look after. You've given me all I needed, your ration books, so I don't need to take anything else off you, do I?' The smile grew even broader.

TWENTY-TWO

PATRICK spent a restless night on the floor of the bedroom: he slept in all his clothes with a cushion from an armchair as a pillow: Olive laid her own coat and one of the coarse wool blankets from her bed over him to give him some warmth as the knob on the central heating radiator was painted shut and it did not seem to be working too well. Several times in the night the chill in the air woke her and she lay in the darkness listening to the breathing and mutterings of her second eldest: he had always talked in his sleep and had sleep-walked at least twice while they were in the third-floor flat in Rupert Road: all the time she listened, Olive wondered whether it was just a bad dream he was having or was it something else at which he was occasionally crying out in pain and fear?

She had taken the single bed for herself: the double bed she pushed against the wall so that the four youngest children could sleep on it, or rather across it, the baby at the head and Michael next to him with their feet one way, the twins at the bottom half with their feet the other way: it had meant dividing the two blankets, but after their continual parade around Thurstone, the children had not seemed to care and were asleep almost as soon as their heads touched the pillows and well before she went back down to join Mrs. Munro in the parlour.

If Patrick felt the cold at all during the night, he did not complain, but awoke in the morning rubbing his eyes and smiling to himself at the realisation that he really was not waking up in Upton Lodge's cellar, or in Hartlestone House's dormitory, for that matter: he was in a bedroom in which his own mother was sleeping nearby: he even smiled to himself at her snoring and the fact that her false teeth were in a glass on the small bedside table. Several of Olive's teeth had loosened while she had been carrying Joseph and she had had them taken out by the dentist so that he could fit her with false ones: it was a drastic step, she knew, but one which she felt she had to undertake for the sake of comfort: and an expensive one, as it turned out, for someone so strapped for money: at the time, it had depleted her post office savings by more than half.

Mrs. Munro, despite her parsimonious air, provided a breakfast of porridge, milk and sugar, bread fried in dripping, with a fried tomato apiece, watery orange juice for the little ones and a pot of tea for Olive and Patrick: it was sufficient to bring a smile to the serious face of Patrick, who was, he told Mrs. Munro, eating 'the best breakfast I've had for ages,' a point which he underscored by wolfing down in the space of ten minutes his plate of porridge, three slices of fried bread and two fried tomatoes and drinking two cups of condensed-milk-made, saccharin-sweetened tea. That he was pleased to be away from Upton Lodge and the threat of Grundwood's chastisement was obvious.

After a while the landlady's curiosity got the better of her: she had read about the bombing of the capital in the newspapers and the fortitude of the Londoners, but to her it seemed the authorities were understandably reluctant to tell the whole story, or rather, the true story, not wishing to spread alarm and despondency among the population in other towns which might be bombed, as well as not wishing to assist the enemy in any way by informing him of his successes. Now here was a real Londoner, straight from the Blitz, sitting at her table, who had experienced it all: she had to know.

'How bad is it down there?' Mrs. Munro asked, quietly, sitting down opposite Olive in one of the chairs vacated by the twins, who, having been fed first,
had scurried off into the front parlour with Patrick, their new-found, unre-
membered older brother, to play with a half-broken wooden train found in a
cupboard the previous evening and put there by Mrs. Munro. 'We hear things,
but we don't know what it's like.'

'It's the bombing that gets you down the most,' Olive replied, pausing in her
feeding of Joseph to give the bottle a shake. 'There's no let-up. You are always
in and out of the shelter. You have to be there with the little ones by six or six-
thirty before the siren even sounds just to get a place or other people will take
them. They allocate them, of course, for the children, but even then you're not
always sure of getting one for each of them, not when you've got four of them
like me. I'm supposed to have one for myself, but you don't always get one.
Other people take them if they're empty when they get there and you can't
wake someone up if they're fast asleep, can you? They may not have slept for
three or four nights themselves! You just have to wait and hope they'll wake up
and give it up. Some will, some won't. I'm not the only one who's not getting
much sleep. And if you do get a bunk, it's hard sometimes to get a proper
night's sleep with all the noise going on outside and all the people around.
Some people have no consideration for others. You find that out soon enough,
especially with the men from the pub. No consideration for anyone, some of
them!'

She went on to recount two or three incidents which had occurred in the
shelter over the past month: but it was only when she recounted the devastation to the houses in Rupert Road which had been hit that Mrs. Munro showed
real anger. 'That bloody man, Hitler! Bombing people's property!' she said
with a true Scottish sharpness. Olive had related her experiences, not with any
intention of impressing Mrs. Munro with the awfulness of her plight, but simply because she considered that she was informing someone who did not know
and had requested to know what she and others like her had endured for so
long: and indeed would endure again that very night.

A curious change came over Mrs. Munro as she listened to Olive's ordeal –
'Twenty-eight consecutive nights in the air raid shelter, then I have had to
come up here to stop this one from running away back to it! Last night's was
the first proper night's sleep I've had since the bombing started.' – and her
sympathy and admiration for the younger woman grew: Olive, she found, with
her stoical, wearied but unbowed attitude, reminded her of her own mother
living in the poverty of the vast Gorbals tenements of Glasgow when she had
been a young girl before the turn of the century and the razor gangs had ruled
the streets at night.

'I wouldn't swap places with you for all the tea in China,' Mrs. Munro said,
aghast at what she had heard: then, almost reddening with the pleasure of saying it, she added: 'If you want to keep your older bairn with you a little longer,
that's all right with me. I won't charge you for him sleeping here a couple o'
more nights, not in view of what you've had to put up with and seeing as how
you've got troubles with him, too. Goodness me, no! And if you are going out
to see your other bairns, I dinna mind making some sandwiches and orangeade for the little ones and something for the baby.'

While Mrs. Munro busied herself about the kitchen preparing these, Olive
considered what she should do next: she was in a quandary and realised that
really she needed to go to the council offices and see the children's welfare officer: she needed to ensure that Patrick was not sent back to Upton Lodge: but

she could only do that on the Monday. The question was: if he were not sent back there, where would he be sent? There were only nine hostels in the town, three of them for girls only, and in little over a year Patrick had been in five of those for boys: that left only one to which he could go if he did not go back to Grundwood's Upton Lodge!

But first things first: her next port of call, she had long since decided, would be Queen Eleanor Road, the hostel where Jack was staying: he alone of the brothers had remained at the same place since his arrival, mostly because, being five at the time, and having had his sixth birthday in the July, for which Olive had sent a card, the authorities had decided to keep all the smaller children in the one place.

It was more than a mile-and-a-half to Jack's hostel: she found him in the garden at the rear, where about fifteen children in all were enjoying playing on the swing and slide and in the sandpit. Jack recognised his brother Patrick first, then his mother: nine months' separation had taken their toll on him, too, for he did not run up to his mother and hug her and expect or demand to be lifted up in her arms as some children might, but warily crossed the patch of worn grass which served as a lawn, halted four or five feet from her and stared up at her as though she were an apparition or a mirage emerging from the bright October sunlight. 'Is that you, Mum?' he asked, frowning as he gazed at her: and then the same questions Patrick had asked: 'Is Dad with you? Have you come to take us home?'

All Olive could do was nod to the first question and say a sad 'No' and 'No, not yet' to the second and third, all the while trying to smile though the tears poised at the corners of her eyes as she saw how reluctant Jack was to approach her.

'Have you just come to see us then?' The face crestfallen as the reply came: then a slight pleading and desperation in the voice. 'Why can't you take us home?'

'We're in a different place now.' A guilty sense of an invented answer from Olive. 'There isn't enough room for everyone. We've only got the one bedroom. And it's dangerous down there with the bombing. People get killed in bombing.'

'You mean killed dead? Dead for ever and ever?' Jack wanted to know, suspicious that his mother was really only making an excuse not to take him with her.

'Yes. A lot of people have been killed.' There was no sense in sparing the child the truth. 'And the Germans might come. You don't want to be down there when they come, do you? You're better off here. Safer.'

'Are they going to come and shoot us?'

'No,' an exasperated reply from Olive. 'Our soldiers will shoot them first. It's the bombs we have to worry about. They drop them from aeroplanes. Up here you don't get bombed.'

'We do. We've been bombed,' declared Jack, almost proudly, having shrugged off his earlier disappointment.

'When? When did they bomb here?' It was such a shock, Olive felt her blood momentarily run cold: she had read nothing and no one, not even Mrs. Munro, had mentioned the town had been bombed. Olive did not want to sound sceptical, almost scornful, but she was unsure whether she was being told the truth or whether Jack was not just exaggerating the way children are sometimes prone to exaggerate or embellish.

Patrick interrupted: 'A week ago. It was only the one night. They didn't do much damage. Two bombs landed in Abbey Park. Just made a couple big holes, that's all.'

When they had evacuated the children, it had been almost an unstated expectation, almost an unspoken claim, that they were being taken to a place which the Germans would never bomb because they had no reason to do so: Olive had believed it, Robert had believed it, all the other mothers had believed it: now here was her six-year-old Jack telling her he had been bombed in that safe haven.

'We all went and had a look at the holes,' Patrick added, referring to some of his friends. 'They've fenced them off with some barbed wire.'

After the past month in London, Olive had hoped she would be free of talk of bombs: it seemed to dominate almost every conversation in Rupert Road. 'Whatever would they want to bomb here for?' she asked herself: there were no factories other than the army boot manufacturers, two shoe factories, a button manufacturer, a biscuit factory, two tanneries, a brick works and an iron foundry which, when she was there before, was still making gratings for roadside drains: the town was far too small for any of the major wartime industries such as shell-making, aircraft assembly or tank production.

'If they're going to bomb us, we should go back to London,' suggested Jack hopefully.

'You can't,' Olive told him, a little too hastily. 'It's far too dangerous down there.'

'John, Thomas and Michael are down there,' said a sulking Jack, who, not knowing the baby Joseph, studiously omitted all reference to him. 'Why can't I be down there, too?'

'Because you can't!' snapped Olive. 'I have to have the others with me. They're too young to be left on their own. The twins are only three and Michael's not yet two. You're six now. You're much bigger than they are. You should be able to stay up here with the others.'

It was a mother's usual way of turning round an argument which she knew in her heart she could never rightly win, appealing to the pride and vanity of the older child by comparison with his younger siblings: but it always worked.

She quickly found the matron and explained who she was and why she had come: fortunately, the matron remembered her and, Jack, having retrieved his black mackintosh and cap from the peg in the hallway, was allowed to join the small group which left the gate and headed for the third hostel: it now was almost eleven o'clock on the Saturday morning.

As they walked along, Jack, by far the gentlest of the three eldest, seemed genuinely interested in the twins and Michael and the baby: he had, of course, not seen Thomas and John since the January and he barely recognised Michael as the same baby his mother had carried in her arms when she had travelled up with them on the train: the baby Joseph in the pram was entirely new to him so he was naturally curious.

'Is he my brother, too?' he asked as Olive trundled the pram back through the centre of the town, with Patrick shepherding along the twins. 'How old is he? What's his name?' To all of which Olive gave the wearied replies of a tired mother

It was as though, having lived for almost nine months without his family, he was pleased to be back amongst them: now he was no longer abandoned as he felt he had been back in mid-January when his mother had left him and gone back to London. Then the months had crawled by: the snows of winter had turned to slush on the paths and pavements and great puddles had formed in the infants' school playground: he had expected his mother to come back, but she had not. Spring had come and gone in alternate days of pale sunshine, icy blasts of face-chapping wind and cold, air-chilling showers of hail and rain: each morning he had awoken in the hostel dormitory with all the others around him, washed his face and knees in the communal sink, eaten his breakfast in silence at the long tables in the dining room and then joined the daily crocodile to school. Summer and the longer holidays had arrived, with long, hot days of blue skies and bright sunshine and endless hours spent playing with the other children in the hostel back garden: and still his mother had not returned. Summer had faded into autumn and he had returned to the infants' school, the daily crocodile and the line of quieted children forming up into an orderly queue at each playtime's whistle blast to go into their classrooms, out of the drizzle and out of the wind. Now, suddenly, on a sunlit morning when he had least expected it, his mother had suddenly appeared: or a woman who said she was his mother, who looked like his mother and who, because she was with Patrick, his brother, whom he did remember and whom he had seen only three times since the winter, must, therefore, be his mother.

TWENTY-THREE

FINALLY, they reached Cliftonville Lodge, the hostel in which Jimmy was living and which lay on the east side of the town, threequarters-of-a-mile from the centre. 'I've come to see James Cullen, my son,' Olive told the woman who answered the door: she seemed surprised and slightly disconcerted by Olive's arrival with her brood.

'If he's living here, he'll be out with the rest of them,' said the woman, not opening the door more than a few inches and peering suspiciously out as though she feared Olive had come to dump the children she had with her rather than to take one off their hands. 'I'm just the cook,' she added weakly as if by way of an apology.

'Out where?' Olive wanted to know: one thing upon which she had always prided herself was being able to discern when people were lying or not telling the whole story: it always showed in their face, in their speech and in their mannerisms: there was, she decided, more to Jimmy being 'out' than the speaker was telling her.

The woman heaved a sigh and then said nervously. 'They're all – they're all up at St Andrew's churchyard – at the funeral.' She paused and waited for the words to sink in before going on. 'One of the boys was knocked down by a bus last Saturday. He ran across the road and was killed by a double-decker. Went right under the wheels. Horrible it was. Very sad. They were all going to the morning pictures at the time.' There were tears forming in her eyes. 'Couldn't hold the funeral before because of the inquest on Wednesday. Accident, they decided. No one to blame. It's tragic. They're having to hold the funeral today without the parents. Poor little mite. No mother and father to see him off. Father's in the army abroad somewhere. Don't know where the mother is. Tried to find her in London, but couldn't. Gone away somewhere. No one knows where. The address we had's not there no more, so I heard. All that bombing, you know.'

'Yes, I know,' said Olive, surprised by her own inner calm: the awfulness of the child's death and the sadness that he was being buried in a strange town without his parents present made Olive's blood run cold: the thought came to her that it could so easily have been one of her own, Jimmy, Patrick or Jack.

'Having the funeral today, Saturday like, meant at least all the children could go, all his little friends,' the woman went on. 'I'd have gone, too, but someone has to stay here, don't they? Holding the funeral on a Saturday morning was for the best. That way they haven't had to take a day off school and miss their lessons. If your boy's here, he'll be up there at the churchyard, saying goodbye to the poor little chap with all the others.'

'Where is the churchyard?' Olive enquired, feeling somewhat disconcerted by some of the women's comments. 'I'll go and meet them.'

The cook's face seemed suddenly to brighten at the prospect of getting rid of the woman and her brood cluttering her doorstep: she had counted four that she could see grouped around the pram at the bottom of the steps and supposed that, it being a double-hooded pram, a fifth and a sixth must be in the pram itself. Quickly, she gave Olive her instructions: 'It's about a mile all told. Turn right out of the gate, then the third left and first right after the park. They should be coming back soon, so you might meet them on the way. They'll come across the park, most like, so if you want to sit in that, I should. There are some swings for the little ones and a slide. You can't miss them. About twenty boys and five adults, the matron, Mrs. Williams, her assistant, Mrs. Grindon, and the others.'

She was so enthusiastic about helping Olive – or getting rid of her and her brood: Olive was undecided – that she even walked down the drive to ensure that they turned the right way at the gate.

Olive followed the woman's instructions and found herself once again entering the Abbey Park, but through a different gateway than the previous evening: where she had sat previously, there had been a couple of mud-trodden football pitches and some rugby goalposts, but in this part of the park, the walk was lined with tall chestnuts, bare in the October sunshine: the children enjoyed kicking their way through the banks of fallen leaves which littered the way. Eventually they found the small area where the swings and slide were situated and the children played on them while Olive attended to the one thing she had been aware of during her walk to Cliftonville: that the two youngest both needed their nappies changing: the soiled nappy liners she deposited in a nearby waste bin. She also fed Joseph some carrots she had mashed and put into a small pot before she had left Mrs. Munro's kitchen, where she had also made up a bottle of sugar water for him: to Patrick, Jack, the twins and Michael she gave the sandwiches Mrs. Munro had wrapped for them: the kindly landlady had even included a piece of fruit pie for each.

Twenty minutes were to pass before she spied the crocodile of children and adults wending its way back along one of the paths from the far side of the park: quickly Olive gathered up her things, put the two youngest on the pram and set off after it, with Patrick and Jack, each delighted to be holding the hands of their younger brothers, trotting along behind: she timed her arrival at the hostel just after Jimmy and the others had filed in. The matron, a sandy-haired woman, wearing the same mid-blue uniform and white hat as the others, came down the path to meet her: she was smiling pleasantly, which put Olive at her ease: indeed, she seemed to recognise Olive, or at least to realise who she was. Perhaps she had seen Jimmy with Patrick and Jack before and seeing them with Olive gave her the clue: or she might have remembered Olive from an earlier meeting, back in December: either that or she had been forewarned.

'Mrs. Cullen?' she enquired. 'Have you come to see Jimmy?'

'Yes, I've come up to see all the boys,' Olive informed her. 'I got in yesterday afternoon. I've been to Hartlestone House and Queen Eleanor Road to get Patrick and Jack – ' She carefully made no mention of Upton Lodge in the hope the matron at Cliftonville would not know about that. ' – Now I've come here to see Jimmy.'

The matron, being a genial type, invited Olive and her brood into the hostel where they waited in a small seating area in the wide hallway: Jimmy was sent for and arrived looking in a sulky mood: his response to his first sighting of his mother for nine months was offhand to say the least: he acknowledged Patrick's and Jack's presence with a 'Hullo, Pat. Hullo, Jack' and, like them, asked straight away: 'Is Dad with you?'

'You know he can't get up here,' Olive exclaimed in exasperation, almost scoldingly, which immediately put Jimmy's back up: the very fact that she could not give the answer Jimmy required made her angry at herself.

From Jimmy there was just a return to his former surliness: 'Doesn't he want to see us then?'

'Yes, of course he does.'

'Then why hasn't he come up with you?'

'Because he's working right down in Plymouth and it's too far to come,' Olive repeated the answer she had already given to Jack less than an hour earlier. 'He has to work to earn money. How do you think I'd get along if your father didn't work to get money.'

'He spends most of what he does get on drink anyway,' said Jimmy harshly, but with a dismissive shrug, as though he did not expect his father to appear anyway.

It was dispiriting for Olive to hear her eldest son talking that way about his father, even if it were true. 'Well, he can't come,' she answered sharply, hoping to finish the conversation. 'I've come to see you. Isn't that enough?'

'And how many times have you been up to see us since you left?' sniffed Jimmy. 'None.'

'I've had things to do,' Olive pleaded.

'You wouldn't have come up at all if I hadn't done another bunk,' interrupted Patrick, moving closer to his brother as if in support: a bewildered six-year-old Jack looked on as the two eldest brothers argued with their mother: the twins and Michael, too, were looking distinctly ill at ease.

'Well, I'm here now,' snapped Olive, determined to end the conversation: it subsided more because the matron made a reappearance with a welcome cup of tea for Olive and a plate of small rock cakes for the children, all gleefully snatched at, notwithstanding the fact that they had just eaten all of Mrs. Munro's sandwiches and fruit pie. The twins, being the quickest, or the hungriest, snatched up two cakes apiece, each holding one to his chest while they ate the other, which caused Michael to pout because he was able to get only the one: Jimmy did not eat: but, in the presence of the matron, he at least became more subdued and sat watching the others.

Finally, as if to make amends for his earlier antagonism, he nodded towards the baby on his mother's lap and asked, still with his earlier surliness: 'What's he called then?' When Olive told him, 'Joseph, Joey for short,' he seemed to find the name amusing, smiling to himself as she said it, but making no attempt to cross either to his mother or to the child, almost as though, never having seen the baby before, it was of no consequence to him that he had a sixth brother: however, just before he went in for his dinner, he did turn and ask his mother apprehensively: 'You will come back, won't you?'

They called for him after lunch and then spent the afternoon wandering across the broad green acres of the Abbey Park before coming across a small pond where the boys fished for newts off a dead tree trunk lying half in the water: then they returned to where they had sat previously to play on the swings and slides. Jimmy and Patrick happily pushed the twins and Michael on the swings, even Joseph had a crawl around on the grass, but for some reason Jack did not join his brothers, but sat on the bench alongside his mother playing with a toy tin car.

Patrick, laughing as he pushed John ever higher on the swings in competition with Jimmy, who was pushing Thomas, not unnaturally was giving no thought whatsoever to what would happen in the days to follow: if he did not go back to Upton Lodge, but was moved on to yet another hostel, it would mean he would have to change schools again as well: he had already done so three times following his earlier moves. The matter was still occupying Olive's mind when, in the early evening as the dark was again closing in, she found herself near the station: an evening newspaper billboard outside the station kiosk halted her in her tracks. 'London latest: bomb shelter disaster,' it read: upwards of a hundred and fifty people, many of them children, had been killed when a basement shelter had collapsed upon them during a raid: Olive herself had not the courage to buy the paper: she preferred not to know about such things.

Because of Mrs. Munro's generosity in refusing payment for Patrick's overnight sleep, she still had two pounds and ten shillings in her purse and so she decided to spend a half-crown of it on the children in the small station buffet: it was only a cup of tea and a buttered scone for herself and some orangeade and currant buns for them, but it was good to see the whole family seated around the one table, all the boys together at last!

It was while she was sitting at the table, watching Jimmy and Patrick helping the twins to eat their buns and making sure they did not spill their orangeade, that the thought first came to her: she had enough money in her purse to purchase a ticket for Patrick to London. Then the thought came: why just Patrick? Why not Jack, too? And Jimmy? She could take all three back with her! Patrick was obviously unhappy and wanted to be with her or he would not have run away and headed for London nine times: Jimmy had been surly and unwelcoming when he first saw her and she had sensed his resentment still: clearly, he felt betrayed at being left behind in Thurstone. And Jack, the meekest among them, who used to climb on to her lap for attention sucking his thumb, now trailed five yards in her wake and would not even hold her hand: when they had met for that first time in nine months, he had stopped short of actually greeting her and now continued to view her from a distance as though he was unsure if she was real, considered her as an apparition perhaps and expected her to fade away before his very eyes if he got too close. When she had briefly left the table to go to the toilet, Jack had got up and followed her as far as the door: he would have followed her inside had she not told him to wait outside: even the twins had given no more than a quick glance when she left the table: but Jack could not even let her out of his sight: and two days from then, on the Monday morning, she was expected to get on a train to London and leave them all behind a second time.

'I'll just have to take the three of them back with me!' Olive thought to herself: and then she found herself saying aloud so that heads in the buffet turned to look: 'I'll just have to get a bigger flat, that's all. I'm not so hopeless that I can't do that!'

To Jimmy, Patrick and Jack, she announced: 'Tomorrow we're all going back to London. All of us! And sod the authorities. Sod the lot of them! You lot are coming back with me! The bombing can't last forever!'

The woman behind the buffet counter, who had looked on with some trepidation when Olive had wheeled in the pram, with Joseph asleep in it and Michael sitting up, to be followed immediately by five other children, allowed herself a smile, more of relief at the thought that at least the woman with the seven children would be leaving the town with her brood and they need not worry for the future of the salt and pepper shakers, which had slid ominously close to the edge of the table around which they all sat.

Jimmy was smiling wide-eyed, but there was still some disbelief showing: Patrick was chortling happily to himself at the realisation that it was his antics over the past nine months which had brought it about: while Jack was regarding his mother with the same suspicion which suggested he was waiting to be told it was not true and that it was really all a piece of fun done to amuse his older brothers: the twins, of course, just wondered why everyone was smiling, but joined in the grinning anyway.

That night when she had returned to her lodgings, Olive wrote out three letters, one each for the matrons at Jimmy's and Jack's hostels and a third, all encompassing one, for the children's welfare officer at the council offices to cover Patrick: two read quite simply:

'Dear Matron, I have decided to take James/Jack back to London with me as he obviously is not happy here in Thurstone. From now on, he will be with me. I am sorry I have had to do it like this so quickly without first telling you, but I see no other way. I've had to make a quick decision because I don't want anybody trying to stop me. I know what I am doing. Yours sincerely, Olive Cullen (Mrs.).'

No doubt, she thought that night, as she licked the envelopes and sealed each, she would be having a visit from Miss Grogan before the week was out. The decision made, Olive felt strangely relieved: it was as if a weight had been lifted from her shoulders: all the worries over the children she had left behind nine months previously were gone in that moment: now all she had to do was to get through the Sunday without anyone in Thurstone discovering her whereabouts and to carry out her plan.

TWENTY-FOUR

OLIVE was up very early on the Monday morning, before even the horse-drawn milk cart came trundling into the street: a surprised Mrs. Munro, herself an early riser, would have been even more surprised had she seen her guest peeking out of the bedroom window from behind a curtain to ensure that neither the police nor the children's welfare officer were waiting outside, which, fortunately, neither was. So immediately following breakfast at seven, Patrick, who had stayed a third night with his mother, was dispatched to the station with the suitcase: Olive had no intention of returning to Upton Lodge to collect whatever things he had left there: he would have to make do with the clothes he was wearing: there would be time enough, she hoped, to sort that out when they got back to London.

Instead, she hurried round to Jack's hostel, where she had arranged to meet Jimmy at eight o'clock: he was waiting nearby with a small newspaper parcel of his own things and was smiling broadly when his mother came hurrying up. They had not long to wait: soon a black-raincoated Jack came scampering down the driveway with a crowd of other youngsters, all heading for the nearby infants' school, seemingly having forgotten his mother's instruction of the previous evening to parcel up his socks and vests. Suddenly, he found himself seized by the hand by his eldest brother and hustled away along the pavement, watched by several curious friends: only then did it dawn on him that what had been promised by his mother in the railway station two days before was about to come true: that he actually was 'going home.'

Momentarily, his one thought was whether he should tell them that he did not have his toy tin car with him, because he was not allowed to take it to school, and that he wanted to go back for it: it had been a birthday present from the matron and staff and it was his pride and joy. But the prospect of returning to London with his mother and all his brothers, being with her and them again and perhaps even seeing his father, stilled the protest even as it formed on his lips and he allowed himself to be propelled along farther and farther away from the precious car which he kept hidden in a shoebox of things under his bed. He was never to know that the following day it was taken by one of the younger boys in the dormitory and three weeks later was stamped upon by one of the older boys in a pique of nastiness.

At the station, they found Patrick sitting nonchalantly on the suitcase just inside the entrance, paying attention to no one so that no one thought to pay any attention to him, taking him for what he was, a small boy guarding an adult's suitcase, probably waiting for his mother, which, in this case, he was. She arrived in a rush, wheeling the pram, with Michael and Joseph inside, the twins seated across the middle with their legs dangling over the sides and Jimmy and Jack hurrying along after her, determined to catch the first train back to London. She had just enough money to purchase two third-class single tickets for Jimmy and Patrick and, having her own return tickets already, seated the boys alongside her in second-class as the train rattled southwards. The ticket inspector gave them all no more than a cursory glance as he took the tickets from her, failing to notice – or, if he did, ignoring the fact –that two of them were in second class with third-class tickets: but then the train was full of soldiers, airmen, WAAFs and WAACs and he would not have wanted an argument with any of them over two small boys being in the wrong carriage: besides, with the train so packed again, there was nowhere for them to go any-way. So, giving a sigh, he clipped their tickets, and passed on: only when he had gone, pushing his way through the jam in the corridor, was Olive at last able to lean back in her seat and give a long sigh of relief: she had done it!

The train got in just after midday: from the station they went by Tube to the nearest stop to Rupert Road: as they came up the steps to the entrance, Olive again became aware of the familiar smell of smoke from the burned and, in some case, still smouldering buildings. It was only as they picked their way along the pavement towards Rupert Road that she noticed the increased dev-astation, the new buildings which had been destroyed and the extraordinary number of fire engines and ambulances parked on the High Road itself. Jimmy, Patrick and Jack, who had never viewed anything so apocalyptic be-fore, stared in amazement at the devastation: building after building along the High Road now gaped roofless and windowless. The High Road, which they vaguely remembered for its Saturday afternoon cinema, its two sweet shops, the public house outside of which they had occasionally waited for their father to emerge, the barber's where their hair had been cut, the Co-operative Society emporium where they had bought their grey trousers, grey socks, grey school shirts and grey bomber jackets, and the cobblers where their boots had been 'toed and heeled' with half-moon steel plates so that they could scuff sparks on the pavement – that street now was almost gone, vanished: for them, it would forever be a memory, littered with rubble and criss-crossed by hoses. Every-where there were firemen: some standing talking in small groups in front of what had been the Jewish tailor's: some sitting down with their backs against the devastated greengrocer's front, smoking: others queuing before a green WRVS van parked while two women in pinafores handed down mugs of tea through a hatchway: they all looked tired and sullen, and dirty-faced, like they had had a long night.

When Olive pushed the bumping pram, with Joseph and Michael both sit-ting up, past them and turned the corner into Rupert Road, she knew immedi-ately from the line of rooftops what had happened: where numbers forty, forty-two, forty-four and forty-six Rupert Road should have been, there was a wide gap and a great mound of rubble on which stood several tin-hatted men in dark overalls.

The road was taped off fifty yards down and the same policeman who had pushed back the crowd when number sixty-nine had been hit, was standing by a length of white tape. Whatever crowd he had been put there to hold back had long since melted away, so Olive was able to go straight to him: when she told him number forty-two was where her flat was, or had been, and that she had just got off the train from Thurstone, his mood softened. 'Yours took a direct hit on Friday night, missus,' he said sympathetically. 'Happened about two o'clock. The houses either side went with it. We've had two bad nights, real bad. Everywhere's taken a real pasting. We thought one night was bad enough, but they came again last night – got the factory and the warehouses and half the district as well. The worst is cleared up this end. Fires are out and that, but it still ain't safe to go forward, not for a while anyway. Some of what's left ain't too stable. Live there, did you? Well, I doubt there'll be much left of your things, missus. Not after a direct hit. You were lucky to be out of it, especially with your kids. They ought not to be here, anyway, not in the middle of this lot. They ought to be somewhere safe in the country. You were lucky to be away when you were, very lucky. Most of those from forty, forty-two, forty-four and forty-six were in the shelter at the time the bomb dropped, so they're all right.'

'Most of them?' Olive's heart sank.

'Aye, except for an old couple who lived right at the top of the one in the middle, number forty-two. They copped it, poor beggars,' said the policeman, slowly shaking his head. 'You must have known them. They say the old boy weren't too fit or something. Is that right? Had bad lungs. All right coming down the stairs, but had trouble getting up again. Seems he was ill so the old woman decided to risk it for a change and stay up there rather than go down to the shelter when the sirens went. Shouldn't have done it. Should have gone to the shelter like everyone else. But they didn't.' Another sad shake of the head and a shrug of the shoulders. 'There ain't nothing that can be done for them now. They're gone. Blown to bits, I'm sorry to say. Leastways, they ain't found anything of them. Not yet and I don't think they will either.' A pause and another grim sigh. 'It happens.'

Olive was almost too frightened to ask, but she had to know. 'Was there anyone else killed?'

'Not at number forty-two that I know of,' said the policeman to her great relief. 'Just them two. They were the only ones we know were up there. A neighbour said there was a man on the same landing earlier in the day, but she reckons he was just visiting. When the siren went, she tried to get the old couple to go down to the shelter, but the old woman wouldn't leave the old man. He was too ill. In bed coughing his heart up when she knocked, she said. The old woman wouldn't leave him. Refused point blank. So she had to leave them. She didn't see anybody else. At least, when they went, the old couple went together. That's something, I suppose. There were four other casualties next door. Mother and daughter and two old sisters at number forty. Silly fools all stayed down in the basement flat rather than go to the shelter. We dug them out yesterday morning. Girl was all right, injured like, but the mother and the old ladies are gone – ' That would be Mrs. Crow and her young daughter. Mary, and the two old Killane sisters, Olive thought to herself. 'I don't know of anyone else who was killed in forty, forty-two, forty-four or forty-six,' the policeman went on. 'Like I say, number forty-two took a direct hit so there wouldn't be much of anyone left after that, not if it's a direct hit. Anyone in particular you're looking for? Plenty of others killed in other roads. Sixty-six all told in the borough in one night. Worst we've had. Compton Road, Derby Street, Peel Street, Skipton Avenue and elsewhere. Kiddies among them, the bastards! Planning the funeral on Thursday, once they've got all the names together. It'll be a mass burial, I reckon. All in the same grave up at the cemetery. It's the only way. We took a fair pasting round here, I can tell you. Jerry had a right go at us. If you are looking for anyone special, the names of the dead and injured will all be down at the St Bartholomew's church hall. They should be able to tell you what hospitals they've taken them to – and what mortuaries. It'll be the Co-op in the next borough, I expect, since ours has gone. I should go down to the church hall, if I were you, and add your name to the survivors for a start in case there's anyone who didn't know you were away and is looking for you. And your kids, of course. You've got enough of them, missus. Someone will want to know you and they are all right, won't they? Authorities will want to know, for a start, so they can compile a list. At least they'll be able to cross you and the kiddies off one list, won't they? You were lucky to be away when you were, missus, very lucky. I wouldn't want to go through a night like that again, I can tell you.'

What Olive desperately wanted to do as she stood behind the tape, staring at the wreckage of her home fifty yards away, was to duck under it, leaving the children where they were, and run across to the mound of rubble which once had been number forty-two and scream at the top of her voice, 'Bob! Bob! Bob!' But she did not: she just stood there, trying to take in the enormity of what had happened while she had been in Thurstone. Where was Robert when the bomb was dropped? The man the neighbour had seen during the day on the top floor had to be him! It could not have been anyone else but him! So where was he? Had he been in the flat, sleeping, as he had said he would, when the siren sounded? Knowing Robert, she knew he would have been indifferent to the wailing of the siren and the droning of the bombers, almost contemptuous of them in his arrogance, as if, being Irish, he considered that it was not his war and, therefore, he would not get hurt in it. At that very moment, the thought went through Olive's mind, that he could be buried under the very rubble from which the small group of helmeted men in dungarees were still pulling wearily at blackened and smouldering timbers, twisting them out and pitching them down from the top towards the bottom, where others waited to load them on to a lorry parked by the pavement edge: but there was no urgency about any of it: it was just a job that had to be done at that moment in the lull between raids: they certainly were not looking for anyone alive trapped in the rubble: that much was obvious.

Olive wanted to join them, scrabbling at the ruins, searching for any sign of him, a hand sticking out from under a beam perhaps or a voice faintly calling out to her from deep down: but, curiously, too, she also found herself wanting to clamber over the rubble just to claim back what was hers, as if in defiance of the awfulness of the destruction: something that had been theirs together! A plate perhaps? A cup and saucer, a pan, the teapot, a cardigan, a blanket, the baby's christening spoon if she could find it, her own clothing if any remained of that, the children's toys even, but most her solitary wedding photograph, the photograph of herself and Robert and Muriel and Gerry, when she had half-hidden herself and her obvious pregnancy with two bouquets of flowers, and which had stood on the small chest of drawers in the bedroom.

Realising he was dealing with a woman in a state of shock, the policeman quietly repeated his advice: 'Best go round to St Bartholomew's hall in Haddon Road, missus. That's where they're taking in all the families that have been bombed out. You'll be needing accommodation of some kind during the next few days now you've lost your own. The WRVS are down there. They'll be able to fix you up with a cup of tea for yourself and a bite to eat for the kiddies. There's others down there all in the same boat so you'll all be together.'

Olive turned away, numb with shock, thinking only that she might have been there had she not gone up to Thurstone: even Jimmy and Patrick were subdued, shocked by the devastation which surrounded them: it was a silent, bewildered party which retraced their steps along the High Road towards the church hall.

TWENTY-FIVE

ST BARTHOLOMEW'S church hall, a large, red-brick, Victorian pile, was a jostling mass of people when Olive and the boys arrived at its high arched entrance: from inside came a babble of voices, pierced by the shrill shouts of children and the echoing clump of hobnailed boots across its bare, wooden floor. Where normally three-hundred would have gathered under the high, vaulted ceiling for harvest festivals, children's Christmas parties, amateur plays and the like, six-hundred now were congregated in a fractious, bewildered melee of the homeless.

For the purpose, the hall had been divided lengthways into three sections, separated by two narrow aisles: down the centre, a rudimentary attempt had been made at organisation by using benches and chairs to create elongated compartments to divide family from family, while down the right-hand wall a number of 'curtained' cubicles had been improvised by the simple expedient of tying ropes at six-foot intervals from the central strut running the length of the hall and pegging blankets and sheets to each sagging line. For every family space, the borough council had provided either a solitary double mattress or two thin single mattresses, plus two blankets: families now slept body beside body, mothers, fathers, children and grandparents all together.

Inevitably, the first-comers had taken the 'curtained' cubicles down the right-hand side and the second-comers had taken the narrow central compartments: the left-hand side had been left for the latecomers: Olive discovered why when the woman from the council, seated at the entrance to compile a list of the homeless as they arrived, directed her and her brood down that side.

'You're lucky, we've just got one place left,' said the woman from the council, before adding brusquely: 'You're only allowed to stay for one week, you know. That's the council's rule. After that, you'll have to find somewhere else. We've got people coming in from all over. Hundreds are being made homeless every night. We've even got people from three other boroughs sleeping here at the moment as well as our own. No one can stay more than a week. We don't want people camping here permanently.'

'Who would want to?' Olive thought to herself as she steered the pram round a group of prone figures on the floor: although it was early afternoon, some doughty souls were attempting to sleep despite the noise all around them, worried perhaps that they might not get any sleep that night if a third raid came. From time to time, a shrouded figure would stir itself, shout something at one of the noisy children nearby and then irritably turn over and pull the coarse grey blanket closer under their chins.

On one bench two yawning, red-eyed mothers sat cradling their squalling babies, trying not to doze while giving them their feed, too weary even to chatter to each other: on another a mother was angrily scolding two runny-nosed toddlers, who had sought to extend their boundaries by crawling away from her under the rows of benches: their chastisement over, they gleefully proceeded to make another attempt. As Jimmy and Patrick passed one space, a surly youth in an open-neck shirt with a grimy face stared hard at them, as if regarding them as a threat, while behind him two sullen-faced girls, one in patterned dress, the other in a navy gymslip, wept quietly with their heads bowed as if overwhelmed by the very hopelessness of their situation; there was no sign of their mother or father.

Some of those slumped upon benches down the centre of the hall Olive knew by name from when Jimmy and Patrick had attended the local school: others she recognised from the long crocodile queues which had formed daily outside the greengrocer's, the butcher's, the fishmonger's, the fish and chip shop, or she had met when she had taken the twins to the swings in the park. Those with whom she had conversed in the various queues simply nodded their acknowledgement of her arrival: but others, bigoted and cynical and knowing her to have married a Catholic, turned away: they saw Olive's arrival with her Catholic brood as an encroachment upon their rightful Protestant spaces, uncaring that, simply by being there, she was now in the same boat as were they: homeless.

The reason the spaces down the left-hand side had been left for the late-comers, especially for strangers from other boroughs, was simply because the windows on that side had all been shattered by a bomb blast during one of the raids: an attempt had been made to cardboard over some of gaps, but it had not been completed, or it had been abandoned. Nor were there any blankets to divide one space from the next, just chalk marks scratched on the floor and by then all but eliminated by innumerable scuffing feet: the mattresses, too, were older and more grimed and the blankets more frayed.

The space to which Olive was directed lay right at the end of the line, directly beneath a large, arched window, broken like the others and open to the elements: thus, anyone lying beneath it would get rained upon and would have to sit and sleep in a permanent draught: it was also nearest to the women's and girls' toilets and suffered an unending stream of people coming and going that way.

'Good God! Olive! You too?' said a voice as Olive negotiated the marrow, crowded aisle: it was her sister-in-law, Muriel: she was sitting on a mattress in the penultimate space down the left-hand side: her two girls, Anne and Jean, were stretched out on one of the two single mattresses, reading comics, while the baby, Peter, slept behind his mother on a cushion against the wall. Hearing Muriel's voice at least brought Olive out of the trance-like state into which she had slipped while walking to the church hall: she had arrived there more by instinct than actual thought as to where she was going. At the door, she had answered the woman's questions in a zombie-like fashion, especially when the woman had innocently asked: 'Anyone else in the family?' 'No, no one else,' Olive had replied, biting her lip.

'Yes, me too,' she said wearily in reply to Muriel's exclamation. 'The whole house has gone, the flat with it. I can't even get down the road. They've blocked it off. Everything I'd left there has gone. You?'

'The same,' said Muriel with a tearful catch in her voice, from which she quickly recovered. 'Ours happened on Friday night. It wasn't a direct hit. The bomb fell over the back of us, but ours got damaged in the blast. All the windows were blown out at the back and the roof and the ceilings caved in. They said it was too dangerous for us to go back in with the wall all cracked. That's why we're here. We managed to get some stuff out, clothes and food and that, and our ration books. I asked one of the ARP men if he'd do it. He was very obliging, not like some of them – ' A slight waspishness in her tone here before she brightened again. ' – Thank the Lord we were in the shelter at the time, that's all I can say. We wouldn't be here now talking to you if we hadn't have been. We've been here since Saturday afternoon. The council say they'll try to find us somewhere else, but I don't know where they think they are going to put us, especially with all the houses that have been bombed. Other people need places, too. In their eyes, we're Catholics, anyway. We're married to Irishmen so I can't see them putting us ahead of that lot – ' A meaningful nod here towards the noisy mass in the church hall. ' – I think they just say those things to keep people from worrying. I've made up my mind, though. We're moving out first thing tomorrow. I'm going back home, back to Hertfordshire. I'm taking the girls out into the country, well away from all this. I don't think I could stand much more of this place. There's some real bigots in here, Olive, so watch yourself.' The last words louder and with undisguised contempt for anyone who might hear her.

'Is Martha all right?' Olive had wanted to ask the question as soon as she saw her sister-in-law, but had not dared in case she received a reply for which she was not prepared.

'She's all right,' answered Muriel, a little sourly. 'Her flat was damaged the same night as ours, probably in the same raid, but not as bad. Bad enough, though, for them to have to move out. She fell on her feet. She got in at Father O'Canning's church hall, at Our Lady's up by the playground. The place was crowded out by the time we got there, so they sent us over here. She says she's fed up with the bombing and she's going back up to Glasgow – taking the girls and just going.'

By this time, Olive had parked the pram and lifted off the twins, who had immediately scuttled over to where Anne and Jean smiled their greeting: Jimmy, Patrick and Jack hovered awkwardly behind their mother, awaiting word from her as to what they should do next and, from the reddening of their faces, acutely aware of the coy interest being shown in them by their female cousins.

Olive looked with some distaste at the two soiled single mattresses and the rumpled pile of blankets left in the space by the previous inhabitants, a family of four who that very morning had entrained at Paddington for the West Country: no wonder no one had moved in to occupy it!

'Are you all right yourself?' asked Muriel, rising to her feet and joining Olive, who was lifting Joseph out of the pram: Muriel lifted out the bemused Michael and set him down on one of the mattresses. 'He needs changing. He feels a bit soggy,' she said matter-of-factly: and, without waiting, she proceeded to do just that, pulling a dry towelling nappy from Olive's shopping bag, kneeling upon the mattress in the empty space and tipping the surprised Michael on to his back.

Beside her, Olive was doing the same to Joseph. 'I'm all right,' she replied. 'I've been up to Thurstone. Went up on Friday to fetch these back. Problems with Patrick – I'll tell you about it later. Only got back this morning. That's when I found out about the house. Took a direct hit, the policeman there said. It's just a pile of rubble now. I've lost everything, clothes, food, furniture, crockery – everything' The tears were beginning to fall as her resolve not to cry gave way with the unburdening.

'It's not me I'm worried about, it's him,' she just managed to whisper through a choking sob: 'He came home on the Thursday night full of himself. Sneaked into the flat while we were all in the shelter. Lying there asleep, he was, large as life, when I got back. You wouldn't have thought the police were looking for him. He was there all day, sleeping, like he didn't have a care in the world. He saw us off at the station on the Friday when we went up to

Thurstone. Didn't seem to care if the police were looking for him. Said he had nothing to hide. Said he was going back to the flat and then he was going to see a friend about getting work in London. Said he knew people who didn't ask too many questions, who he was and where he was from. Said he was going to change his name, too, if he had to. Get a new ration book and identity card from someone who could provide such things. Black marketeers no doubt! Big ideas like that. Crazy ideas. Said plenty are doing it. The thing is, I don't know whether he did go back to the flat after he saw us off. I don't know if he was sleeping there when the house was hit. I just don't know. I just don't know. I hope to Gawd he wasn't! I hope to Gawd he had enough sense to go down to a shelter somewhere! The last thing I want is to lose my husband. Not now. Not now I've got the boys back. I just don't know whether he was there or not, Muriel. I just don't know.' The tears were streaming down her cheeks: only the fact that her head was bent away from them and her back was turned to them prevented the children from seeing her cry: as it was the two girls, who were cuddling the twins like two possessive mothers, had noticed something was wrong and were looking at her out of the corners of their eyes.

'Old Ma and Pa Parrett – the old girl and her husband who lived on the same landing as me – they both got killed,' Olive went on, wiping her eyes, embarrassed to be weeping in front of her sister-in-law. 'They stayed in the flat when the siren went. Didn't go down to the shelter like they usually did. The old man couldn't get up the stairs very well. I hope they didn't stay up there because I wasn't there. I just don't know whether he – ' Meaning Robert. ' – was in the flat when it got hit or not. I can't get near enough to go and look. I'd know if he was, I'm sure. All I can do is hope and pray he wasn't there. If he wasn't, surely he could have come down here and left a message with someone, just to say he was all right. He'd know I would have to come here when I got back. There isn't anywhere else. They wouldn't have known who he was or anything, would they? He could have left a message, couldn't he?'

The tearfulness of her dilemma brought a touch of sympathy on her arm from her sister-in-law's free hand. 'Steady, girl, steady,' counselled Muriel, pausing in her ministrations with Michael. 'You could hardly expect him to come here and announce to everyone who he was, especially with you-know-who looking for him. Your Robert's a lot smarter than that. Don't worry, girl, I'm sure he'll turn up. He always does. You don't know whether he was in the flat. After he left you at the station, he could have gone somewhere else, looking for a job, maybe. Even if he did go back to the flat, it doesn't mean he stayed there. If the truth be known, if he was dodging the coppers, he might even have been in a pub somewhere where he wasn't known. Up West even. He could have gone farther afield, to a shelter where he wasn't known, where there'd be nobody looking for him, couldn't he, girl? The problem is he hasn't got anywhere he can leave a message – not now, not now all three of us have been bombed out. There's nowhere for him to go. Ordinarily, he could have gone to mine, or Martha's, but we're not there any more. We're heading out to Hertfordshire and Martha's heading for Scotland. I've managed to get a telegram off to Gerry and Martha has sent one to Brendan telling them we're all right but bombed out. I just hope the army gives it to them. Chances are Robert will make contact with them sometime, Olive. He's bound to, sooner or later – his own brothers! Then you'll know for sure where he is. You're like me, girl. You can't do anything but wait. That's all the both of us can do for now. Wait and hope, girl, wait and hope.'

For the rest of that afternoon, while Michael slept and the twins toddled off led by Muriel's daughters, while Jimmy, Patrick and Jack read comics lent by their cousins, lying on the single mattress they had been allocated, Olive and Muriel talked: all the time Olive kept one eye fixed upon the bustling aisle, in the vague hope that Robert would perhaps suddenly appear. Muriel's presence at least calmed her worst anxieties: but, in truth, she recognised she was in a state of shock and just sat upon the mattress, oblivious to the draught streaming down upon her through the broken window above, gently rocking the baby, drinking the cups of tea and munching on biscuits provided by a woman wheeling an urn on a trolley.

TWENTY-SIX

AT LEAST, camping out in the church hall was a novelty for the children: the afternoon passed into early evening: and, when just after five the tea urn returned, corned beef sandwiches were handed out to eager hands, along with small cakes. Later, the air raid wardens came in and the families began packing for their traipse to the shelter: Olive and Muriel joined them, both eager to get a bed for their children. Olive managed to park the pram beside one set of bunks so that Michael, Joseph and Muriel's baby could sleep on the lower one: the twins would occupy the middle bunk with Jack, and Jimmy and Patrick would sleep together on the top: Muriel's girls, Anne and Jean, had found one for themselves. It was the first time Olive's three eldest had been in a shelter under such conditions and they considered it as much an adventure as travelling on a train.

Fortunately, when the bombers came as usual, they went elsewhere in the capital and Olive was able to get some sleep, though Joseph woke midway through one raid and only a bottle of powdered milk and a half-hour of rocking quietened him.

When they returned to the church hall the following morning, the WRVS provided a breakfast of porridge and fried bread: for dinner, there was a steaming plate of mash, sausages, peas and gravy, then bread, butter and strawberry jam and a cake apiece for tea, each meal accompanied by mugs of near-scalding tea. In between, a succession of council form-fillers descended on Olive and the other newcomers and there were innumerable forms to be filled in and for Olive to sign, from what schools Jimmy, Patrick and Jack would attend now that they were back to obtaining free orange juice and powdered milk for the babies, as the slow wheels of bureaucracy creaked into motion. Olive did not hold out much hope that any of what she had lost would ever be replaced: certainly not what she held most dear: you cannot replace trinkets which had memories attached, or the sole wedding day photograph she possessed, or the one photograph, taken by Gerry with a box brownie, of her and Robert sitting on the sunlit grass in the local park when Jimmy and Patrick were their only children and the marriage had been happier.

The saddest part was when Muriel and the girls departed just after midday, as they had said they would: the two women tried not to let the tears fall so that they would not upset the little ones and for the most part they succeeded: but they could not prevent the misty eyes as Muriel and the girls walked off towards the Underground carrying what few worldly possessions they had managed to save in two suitcases and some shopping bags.

'Don't worry, we'll keep in touch,' Muriel assured Olive as they parted: both girls turned to wave to their cousins as they walked away and smiled shyly back at them, but the boys, unused to such displays of emotion, just stood there looking embarrassed and did not return their farewell.

Miss Grogan was most displeased when she learned that Olive's trip up to Thurstone, which her department had financed, had been used to bring back three evacuees which she had seen off there a year previously.

'It really is very foolish of you, Mrs. Cullen, to bring the boys back from

where they were safe,' she declared, unexpectedly materialising out of the
throng in front of Olive on the second day.

Olive, however, was in no mood for her carping. 'I'm not taking them back.
They're staying with me, whether you like it or not,' she snapped. 'If you don't
like it, you know what you can do!' Not unnaturally, it did not go down well
with Miss Grogan and she went off in a huff.

They remained three days at the church hall: most of the time, Jimmy, Patrick and Jack joined the other children playing outside on the asphalt yard or
went roaming by themselves among the newly bombed buildings, eager to see
what they could find. It was no use Olive trying to stop them: they had been
free of her influence too long to listen to her: besides, bombed buildings were
magnets for inquisitive, devil-may-care boys: and natural playgrounds: there
was danger in them, adventure and excitement: there was no way Olive could
have prevented them from going! Fortunately, further attempts were made by
one of the church workers to cardboard up the windows which had been shattered so that at least in the afternoons the two youngest were able to get their
sleep on the thin mattresses before their inevitable traipse after tea to the shelter.

It was not until the afternoon of the third day that Olive was at last able to
walk up Rupert Road and stand in front of the mound of rubble which had
once been her home and beneath which she fervently prayed her husband
Robert did not lie. Jimmy and Patrick were piggy-backing the twins some
twenty yards behind so there was no one to hear the gasp which escaped her
lips or to see her wipe at the tears which glistened in the corners of her eyes as
she stood there: had she been on her own, they might have rolled unstoppable
down her cheeks: but the children were there and she did not want to embar-
rass herself in front of them again: so she sniffed back the tears and set her
mouth in a determined line.

Of forty-two Rupert Road, only the four steps up to the front door and a
small section of wall each side the two bay window sills were recognisable as
having once been a part of the four-storey building in which she had lived:
apart from that, it was just a great pile of rubble and dust twenty feet high
where the house had imploded into the basement flat of old Solly Weiseman
and his short-sighted, pebble-bespectacled son, Sidney. Debris lay scattered
everywhere over the boot-compacted surface over which the rescuers had
toiled in vain: single bricks, small sections of joined wall, some internally
painted, some externally dark and soot-blackened, broken joist beams with
white splintered ends, nail-studded floorboards, pieces of multi-patterned linoleum, shattered window frames, slivers of glass glistening in the grey murk
of the drizzling day, fractured half-buried roof slates and, worst of all, the forlorn, rain-soaked possessions of the departed occupants, the ash-streaked
pieces of broken furniture, split tables, crushed chests of drawers, twisted and
splintered dark wood wardrobes, legless kitchen chairs, strips of tattered
clothing, torn pillowcases spilling feathers on to the dirt, mantel ornaments in
pieces, a wall clock with bent hands stopped at four o'clock, the time of the
raid, fragments of plain and patterned plates, cups, jugs, vases and an old
bucket, a wireless with its front trodden in by a boot and the valves hanging
out the back, lengths, too, of sodden, water-stained wallpaper and rent and
burnt linoleum. There was nothing that was actually recognisable to Olive as
her own, or anybody else she knew, not the legs of a table stickling up from the
dust, not the bent black iron framework of two tangled bedsteads, an upside

down armchair nearby, a ripped mattress, or the seat-less brown wooden chair standing squarely on top of the rubble upon which some weary rescuer had perched his aching frame during a pause in the digging, perhaps to drink a cup of tea from the WRVS van or munch on a ham sandwich: not even the wallpaper still attached to one large section of brickwork which lay exposed to the rain was recognisable to Olive as being from this or that flat: it could have come from any of the ten flats in the building.

Just looking at the devastation, she knew in her heart that nothing could have survived the blast. Nothing and no-one!

Even the boys remained silent as their mother contemplated the awfulness of the scene: she had not the courage to tell them that their father was buried under that mound: but then she had not the courage even to think it and, when the thought came into her mind, she vigorously shook her head as if to dislodge it from her brain: it was as if by thinking it, she might somehow make it come true.

It was several moments before an awed Jimmy broke the silence. 'Is that where you were living, Mum?' he asked, almost disbelievingly, picking up a half brick lying on the cracked pavement and pitching it back on to the mound.

Patrick began to snigger. 'Not much left of anything, is there?' he giggled, one hand over his mouth as he spoke, carefully shifting away out of range of his mother's reach in case her hand should fly in his direction.

The thought that he was actually standing in front of his father's 'grave' and laughing was too much for her. 'Shut up!' Olive scolded. 'People died in there. And next door. Have some respect do!'

'If that's where we were going to live, what are we going to do now?' Jimmy asked, sensibly. 'If we can't stay in the church hall, we'll have to find somewhere else, won't we?'

It was then that Olive made her second momentous decision of that week: before she realised it, almost as if it were a message from her own subconscious, she found herself thinking:. 'I'll go back to the country. That's what I'll do – I'll go home. I'll leave London.'

And leave behind, too, the bombing and the shelters and the smell of smoke and the perpetual taste of dust in her mouth. Leave also the fear and the danger and the lack of sleep: taking the children out into the countryside, where they could run free, in the clean fresh air. Going home, that is what she was doing: going home. Home to Gledlang, home to the village, home to where she grew up, home to the people she knew!

She stopped short of the last thought: 'Home to the family!' But even as she made the decision, the doubt arose within her. 'There's nothing else I can do,' she told herself as, with a heavy heart, she wheeled the pram round and set off back towards the church hall, ordering the others to follow.

She would have to tell Miss Grogan, of course: she would need her help to get another railway warrant as she had very little of her own money left: just what was left in her post office savings. She was at least comforted by the thought that Miss Grogan would be so glad to see her go that there would be no hindrance from her.

TWENTY-SEVEN

'THERE'S trouble up ahead. The buggers are bombing Melchborough now!' the railway guard announced in the gruff rural speech of his county as he came crunching along the cinders beside the track, the tone of his voice more one of resignation than anxiety. 'Bloody Germans! Whatever next? First London, now us. Must be after Hockmann's. I reckon we'll have to stay here a while, folks, till we get the all-clear. Don't know when that'll be, though.'

It was an unnecessary remark: what was happening ahead was clear for everyone to see: some three miles from the halted train, a red glow lit up the horizon and the stiff beam of a single searchlight roamed the sky: far off, beyond silhouetted trees and hedgerows of that undulating region, there were bright gun flashes, followed by loud explosions high up among the scattered clouds. Olive, like the rest of the passengers, was leaning out of the window on one side of her compartment, gazing along the length of the train towards the burning town and listening to the distinctive crump of exploding bombs: on the other side of the compartment, Jimmy, Patrick and Jack were doing the same, having pushed open their door so that all three of them could hang out to view the sight: in their eyes was not shock and trepidation but awe and wonderment.

Two hours earlier, long after the October darkness had closed in, Olive and her brood had finally taken the train from Liverpool Street to Wivencaster via Melchborough and Hamwyte: the previous day she had sat all morning outside Miss Grogan's office awaiting her return from whatever busybody duties she had been upon so that she could request a travel warrant for herself and the children. Only after much questioning and repeated assurances, that on no account would she return to London, had the spinster children's officer deigned to issue a letter to the Great Eastern railway company requesting that they furnish the necessary tickets which would allow 'one mother and seven children, herewith named, two classed as babes-in-arms, to travel on the morrow to the small town of Hamwyte,' forty miles up the line. Having made up her mind to go, Olive wanted to go quickly, if nothing more than to leave behind the draughts and the overcrowding and the smells in the church hall as to escape the bombing itself. Though many were leaving, more and more people were coming in daily as each raid destroyed more homes: and, though other halls and an empty school had been opened up in the same district for the ever-growing number of homeless, the spaces in St Bartholomew's church hall were being squeezed by officious supervisors.

Unfortunately, on the day Olive chose to go, only half the trains were running: those leaving from Broad Street and going via Old Street were running on time, but trains leaving from the Great Eastern platforms through Bishopsgate and Shoreditch past the goods station via Bethnal Green junction were seriously delayed. In fact, when Olive and the boys arrived at the mainline station in mid-morning, they found the station a seething mass of humanity: the queue for tickets alone at the Great Eastern window stretched almost out of the entrance.

Having finally obtained her tickets from an overly suspicious and almost disbelieving clerk, Olive found that on the concourse itself, such was the squash of people, the police had tied tapes across the gateways and were determinedly holding everyone back. Midway along one of the half-dozen long platforms on the Great Eastern side, which, as bad luck would have it, served those heading for Melchborough, Hamwyte and Wivencaster and the wide open rural spaces beyond, a gang of men was loading rubble and twisted girders on to two parked lorries with the help of a small mobile crane. During the first of four raids that night, a bomb had plunged through the station roof, exploding between platforms thirteen and fourteen, bringing down a pillar and a several ornate cast iron girders from the roof, as well as buckling the rails and creating a hole: consequently, there was chaos and confusion everywhere. Nothing could get into or out of those two platforms, or others alongside, and, consequently, no trains at all were running through Bethnal Green junction, those in front told them, adding rather pessimistically that none would be leaving 'before mid-afternoon at the earliest': all the people could do was to join what would have been the normal queue for Melchborough, Wivencaster and beyond and hope.

There were trains standing at almost every other platform: everyone was being held up and, such was the crush of people hoping to get on the first of those trains when eventually they did leave, that it was clear a wholesale flight was under way: some people manifestly did not seem to care where the trains for which they were waiting were going so long as it was 'away,' away from London, away from the bombing. Like Olive, they were simply people who had had enough of sleepless nights, weariness and, above all, the terror of the bombing: mothers with children, whole families in some cases, grandfathers and grandmothers included, the majority of them homeless already: some sleeping as they waited, others sitting silently on suitcases, or just standing talking, waiting. Most waited patiently, but there was some bickering and grumbling and arguing and even some pushing and shouting and flares of temper: for some, it seemed, losing their places in the actual queues was more of a concern than the actual bombing which had driven them there: all they could do was wait until the time when the policemen would remove the tapes and they would be beckoned forward and allowed to shuffle through whatever gate they were at: and nobody knew when that would be.

Olive was still waiting in the queue, seated uncomfortably on a folded coat on the bare concrete of the concourse, when just after four o'clock the sirens sounded again: the Germans were mounting another of their sneak afternoon raids. Twenty-five bombers, escorted by forty fighters, had followed the southern railway line into the heart of London intent upon dropping high explosives and incendiaries on the Hackney Road gas works, a cable factory in West Ham and some petrol storage tanks beside the railway in Canning Town. When the dreaded wail began, the steel helmeted and overalled workers had just finished loading the rubble and girders on to two parked lorries: a helpful passing porter had announced that the railway gang had filled in the bomb hole, which had not been too deep, and had just about finished replacing the last of the buckled tracks and splintered sleepers, so there was a good chance the trains would be leaving soon. 'Certainly within the next hour,' he had said.

As the sirens started up a great groan went up on the concourse and from the various orderly lines came the sounds of much cursing and swearing as the sleeping were shaken awake, the seated struggled painfully to their feet and the children looked about them in bewildered alarm. Some panicked, but most did not: the crying and the wailing came mostly from the suddenly lost children, the scolding shouts from irate mothers seeking to locate them in the great disorderly surge of luggage-laden people heading back towards the Underground: the cursing and profanity emanated mostly from the more elderly males, who, having sat or lain for hours on end on bare concrete, were too stiff almost to move. Given the choice, they would have remained where they were and said 'Bugger the Germans!' but the police blew their whistles and herded them all back towards the long white-tiled transit tunnels of the Tube, where they waited while the raid went on overhead: it lasted no more than twenty minutes and no sooner had the all-clear sounded than there was a great rush back towards the concourse.

Jimmy and Patrick carried the twins, running ahead with the general stampede back while Jack helped his mother with the pram, but, in spite of this, Olive found herself almost at the tail of the self-same queue she had been in before: then, before the siren sounded, having arrived two hours before the train was scheduled to depart, she had been at least halfway along the line. At one point, after an hour of waiting, the whole queue was unexpectedly directed on to the tail of another queue waiting at another gate four platforms away: they all shifted over grumpily in the hope that a train would leave from there, but a half-hour later were all sent back to their original queue, only to find that forty others had taken their places in front of the Melchborough and Wivencaster gate and they were not going to move aside for anyone!

The crowd on the concourse had diminished considerably by six o'clock as various crowded trains left for other places: finally, Olive and the children were ushered through the gate by a haggard-looking ticket inspector, who had been on duty since four that morning, and could barely stifle a yawn let alone raise a smile as he waved them past. Being now near the front of the queue of those who were left, they managed to commandeer a whole eight-seat compartment at the back of the train to themselves by the simple expedient of manoeuvring in the bulky pram and using it to block the platform-side doorway, while inside everyone who could occupied one or other of the seats to fill them and then Jimmy and Patrick glared out of the carriage door window as other desperate passenger seeking a seat went rushing past towards the front and ignored the decrepit third-class rolling stock at the rear.

It was a good half-hour before the train finally left: and when it did it clanked along at a crawl as if it were gingerly testing the newly laid rails: the true reason for the whole day's delay became evident when the train passed through one of the long, cavernous, soot-blackened tunnels which lie a mile or more outside the station: beside the track, giving the thumbs up sign to the puzzled passengers staring out of the windows, stood four muddied and grinning soldiers from a bomb disposal squad: a second, delayed-action bomb had crashed through into the 'tunnels' and buried itself six feet down beside the line: consequently, no trains could pass anywhere near in case their rumbling set off the timer. The soldiers had been working for almost thirteen hours, since first light, and had successfully defused and removed the bomb, which was a long, slow and extremely dangerous business: but all their thumbs-up signs and grins drew from the tired and fed-up passengers staring out at them were bemused looks and hostile glares as if they rather than the Germans were to blame for the excessive delay: by then, Olive had hoped to have been stepping off the bus in Gledlang.

The train took an hour to reach Shenbrook and a further hour to reach Stonegate: they were well out into the countryside when the sirens began to wail again and the train came to a hissing, jerking halt just before nine o'clock with the lights extinguished. Unfortunately, being a compartmentalised, non-corridor train, made up of old, dilapidated carriages, it had no toilets: not having had a drink since breakfast and having eaten only an apple, Olive herself felt she could wait: but the boys could not. There was nowhere to change either Michael or Joseph than upon the seats upon which they sat, much to the grimacing disgust of Jimmy, Patrick, Jack and the twins: when the smell assailed them, they gagged noisily and jostled with each other to stick their heads out of the door and breathe in the fresher smelling night air: the linen liners which Olive used in the nappies went out the other window on to the up line along with their contents. When it came to the twins, once Shenbrook was behind them and they were making the longer run to Melchborough, Olive was able to sit them in turn upon the chipped enamel bowl under the lee of the pram: though the rocking of the train did cause some spillage on to the floor, most went out the same window as the soiled nappy linings.

Jimmy, Patrick and Jack did not seem to want to go till the train came to its juddering halt outside Melchborough: then it was a case of, if one wanted to go, they all wanted to go! The carriage door was flung open and all three happily peed out into the darkness: Jimmy and Patrick were just finishing when the guard came crunching along the cinders beside the track.

'Hey, you! What the bloody hell do you think you are doing?' he barked. 'Close that bloody door and get back inside!'

Then, seeing Olive herself appear in the doorway as she pulled the two eldest back by their bomber jackets, the man altered his tone. 'Sorry, missus,' he said, slamming the door shut, 'but you'd best keep the boys inside. They could fall out if the train jerks sudden like. We could also get shrapnel falling from that lot up the line. There's guns going off everywhere. It ain't safe for you and your boys to be sticking their heads out, not with all that stuff coming down. You don't want to take a chance on one of them getting hit or falling out just for having a wee, do you, missus?'

'They needed the toilet,' Olive tried to explain, glad that the darkness hid her reddening cheeks. 'People have to go to the toilet and there's no toilets on this train.' Then after a hesitation: 'How long are we going to be here? Does anyone know?'

The guard paused and looked up so that the distant flashes among the clouds and the red glow on the horizon reflected on the glass of his spectacles. 'I only hope they're hitting a few with all that stuff they're putting up,' he said half to himself, before turning back to Olive and adding: 'I can't say, missus, I can't say. Soon I hope. I'm sorry there ain't no toilets. It should have been an all-corridor train, but this was the best we could do after last night. We lost a lot of rolling stock in last night's raid on the yards. We had the bomb in the station and then there was that unexploded bomb at the side o' the lines delaying everything. We didn't think it would take this long to get here. Can't tell exactly when we'll get going again either. One thing's for sure, though, we won't be moving till that lot have gone. So long as they're up ahead of us bombing, we'll be staying put. This track runs right past Hockmann's so we can't go ahead anyway. We have to stay here till we get the all-clear. We'll be all right so long as we don't show a light. My job now is to phone back down the line and make sure all the other trains are stopped on both the up and down lines. Last thing we want is for a trainload of people to get mixed up in that lot. Pity the poor buggers in Hockmann's, though. They'll be having a rougher time than we are. I hope they're in their shelters, poor sods. Bloody

Jerries, the trouble they cause! Bombing people! Interrupting the trains!' And with that he went crunching away into the darkness towards a small hut by the side of the track, from which, Olive presumed, he would make his telephone call.

What the delay meant, of course, was that they would not arrive at Hamwyte, nine miles beyond Melchborough, until well after ten and there would be no prospect of catching the 'Crab and Winkle' train to Maydun: it made its last seven-mile run between the mainline station and the little two-platform station at the foot of Maydun hill at nine-thirty. To miss the connection to Maydun was a blow to Olive: when she had made her plans to leave London, she had hoped to be in Hamwyte by three o'clock, take the four-fifteen 'Crab and Winkle' to Maydun, buy some chips for the children, perhaps in the little cafe by the bus station, if it were still there, then, if it still ran, catch the six o'clock Bourne Brothers' bus to Gledlang, some five miles from Maydun along a winding B road which followed the long, bleak Langwater estuary eastwards. Now she faced the prospect of a seven-mile walk by dark and high-hedged, narrow back lanes between Hamwyte and Gledlang, bypassing Maydun altogether and cutting across country, with just the pram to carry the two youngest and possibly the twins: the suitcase and shopping bags and all the other paraphernalia would have to be carried by the three eldest.

TWENTY-EIGHT

JUST as the guard had speculated, it was well over two hours before the train jolted into motion and crawled forward towards the smoking ruin of Hockmann's. The ball-bearing factory did indeed stand alongside the track at Melchborough: the actual workshops were no more than fifty or sixty yards from it as one passed along a high embankment at the same level as the rooftops of its single-storey buildings before crossing a viaduct over the town's main street: so the passengers were all able to gawp unobstructed from their windows at the inferno of fire and smoke which greeted their eyes. In the yard around the shattered, roofless buildings, from which roaring pillars of orange flame shot skywards, there must have been twenty or so fire engines: every tender in the immediate district, it seemed, had answered the call: and so fierce was the conflagration that, as the train rumbled by, Jimmy and Patrick, both now hanging out of the door window on that side and fending off Jack, who also wanted to look, shouted that they could actually feel the blasts of hot air from the leaping flames.

The bombers had arrived over Melchborough precisely at nine o'clock, which meant Hockmann's Saturday night shift would have just about gone on as the first bombs started to fall. Like many factories, Hockmann's had just begun working seven-day-a-week, round-the-clock shifts: being an essential war industry, it was a prime target for the German bombers, even though it was located in a small country town. Olive, like all those leaning out of carriage windows to stare, hoped the shift workers would all have been in the air raid shelters when the bombs began to rain down: they were, but thirteen still died that night when one of the shelters took a direct hit.

A grim-faced policeman in a steel helmet and gas cape was standing at the side of the track to wave them through: behind him, in the factory yard below the embankment, scores of firemen, other helmeted policemen and soldiers and air raid wardens, workers and ambulancemen were milling around in an area fifty yards by fifty yards: dozens of hoses sprouted from the sides of parked fire tenders and snaked away across the cinder ground and through huge puddles of water which reflected the lurid light of the flames. Atop four towering turntable ladders, pairs of firemen were spraying, futilely it seemed, feeble jets of water over the burning sheds, which, even as they did so, seemed to burn even more fiercely as if in defiance of their puny efforts. Suddenly, the roof of one collapsed inwards with a deafening roar and smoke and sparks billowed up into the reddened night sky: it so startled Jimmy and Patrick that, instinctively, they ducked back inside the compartment before giving each other a nervous grin and resuming their positions at the open window: clearly, they had never seen anything so marvellous before.

At one point, an over excited Patrick leaned so far out of the window to get a better view and to 'feel the heat' that Olive feared he might topple out or be tipped out by his jostling brothers and seized the band of his jacket to pull him back. 'Aw, Mum!' was all he said in utter disappointment and within seconds had thrust his head and torso out just as far again. Jack, like his mother, contented himself with pressing his face to the glass to ensure there was at least some protection between himself and the heat of the fires.

On any other night, faced with a two-hour halt in the utter darkness of the countryside, the boys would all probably have fallen asleep with the sheer boredom of it all: but not that night: there was too much to see. Mercifully for Olive and the other adult passengers still awake, the train's halt at Melchborough station a half-mile farther on was brief, no more than a couple of minutes or so, made amid urgent shouts and banging doors as those leaving the train were hurriedly shepherded down the steps, through the booking hall and out into the High Street: then, with a single blast on a whistle, more scurrying footsteps and more frantic shouts, the train rolled forwards again. As the fires fell behind them, Jimmy and Patrick grudgingly hauled up their window and flopped back down upon their seats, muttering to themselves, as if they were being deprived of something, like sulky children forced to leave a fireworks display before its end.

When the train eventually steamed slowly into Hamwyte, the station clock showed well past eleven: it was a tired and weary Olive who shook the sleeping twins awake and, with Jimmy's help, lifted them protesting and whining out on to the platform and the cold night air: then, as she and Jimmy returned to lift out the pram and the babies in their turn, Patrick and Jack lugged out the suitcase, their gas masks and the four shopping bags. Others detrained, too: some soldiers and some girls, who went off together, and various others, but none offered to help Olive. The yawning ticket collector was in the process of closing the gate when from the far end of the train, through the clouds of steam, came the figure of a woman pushing a pram, followed by five children, two of them mere toddlers looking to be asleep on their feet almost and being dragged along by their bigger brothers.

'Late out with them young'uns, aren't you, missus?' he said bluntly, giving the children a quizzical stare as he took the tickets. 'I hope you ain't got far to go? They ought to be in bed.'

It was really just a comment, but it was a disapproving remark and it angered Olive: it was not her fault that they had arrived so late. 'We would have been if your trains ran on time!' she retorted sarcastically, pushing past. 'We haven't got that far to go. Far enough, but we'll get there one way or another. So I don't need you or anybody else telling me what I should or shouldn't be doing!'

Hamwyte station has steep steps up to the road some thirty feet above the platform: her show of annoyance precluded any help from the flustered ticket collector and it was her three reluctant older sons whom she pressed into service on the two trips up and down, first to help her to carry the heavy, double-hooded pram to the exit without disturbing the sleeping babies and then to fetch the suitcase, the gas masks and the shopping bags. The sleepy-eyed and tottering twins flopped down on the bottom step in the hope that their mother and their bigger brothers would return a third time to carry them up: but all four were too exhausted by their efforts to go back down again, let alone carry them up thirty steps, and it took a harsh shout down from their mother at the top that she would leave without them if they did not hurry to bring them scrambling up to the top, blubbing and protesting and pleading for her to wait.

With the prospect of a seven-mile walk ahead, Olive quickly realised that, if they were to complete the journey at all, the twins would need to be carried in the pram for part of the way at least: they certainly could not walk all the seven miles and neither could she expect her two eldest to carry them the whole distance. There was nothing for it but to move the sleeping Michael's and Joseph's legs to one side, shift the baby's anti-gas helmet and respirator and to sit the weary, yawning John and Thomas in the middle of the heavy pram, with their legs dangling over the sides, just as they had done in Thurstone: Olive would have to push all four of them all the way. The suitcase, since it was the heaviest and Jimmy was the eldest, she handed to him to carry along with three of the gas masks: the four shopping bags and other four gas masks she divided between Patrick and Jack, giving the two heaviest bags to Patrick.

With the three eldest leading, a half-mile down the blacked-out High Street, with not a soul in sight anywhere, they took a side road, which, though tarred and dashed with a layer of tiny stones, was as unlike the smooth pavements of London as it could be. After a mile or so even the tar and pebbles petered out and it became what was little more than a crude shingled cart track, with puddles and potholes and grass growing down the centre. Fortunately, the night, though cold, was dry, with breaks between the clouds and a half moon to light their way, for in the narrow confines of dark, high hedged lanes one side road looked much like another: and every half-mile or so, it seemed, another side road would branch off their way into a hidden and seldom-travelled labyrinth of shadows and silence. Such were the number of high-hedged lanes criss-crossing their way that an unwary walker could, on arriving at another un-signposted junction, unwittingly take the wrong fork and head away from the very route he was attempting to follow.

The juddering and jolting of the pram over the rough surface was so severe at times that it awakened Michael and twice Olive had to stop and coax him back to sleep again so that he would not wake Joseph squeezed to one side at the head of the pram: the twins, meanwhile, had settled themselves into their positions back to back and were asleep within five minutes, heads lolling on their chests, oblivious to the bumping and bouncing of their journey. Indeed, so tired were they, they would both have toppled sideways on to one or other of the babies had Olive not called Jack back, hooked one of his shopping bags over the pram handle and commanded him to trot alongside the pram and push the twins upright whenever one or the other was about to fall.

Jack, it seemed, was particularly glad to do so: his two older brothers, sensing his nervousness, had begun to tease him about ghosts in the darkness all around them and monsters waiting to spring out from behind the tall hedgerows and carry him off.

'Shut up, the pair of you!' scolded Olive when she came level with them as they stood laughing by the laneside. 'Can't you see, you're scaring him with all that nonsense.' An attempt to cuff a laughing Patrick, the nearest, failed to connect as he dodged nimbly away.

After that, the two eldest quickened their pace and ensured that they led the way some thirty or forty yards ahead, pausing only at the junction of one winding lane with another to wait for their mother to catch up and point which way they should go: but no sooner had she directed them than they raced ahead again: tired as they were, they were revelling still in the adventure upon which they had embarked. Even the week-long stopover in London had been something different from the hard and aggravating discipline of the hostels. They had, for instance, twice ridden on a proper train again, once from Thurstone and once from London, and that was something to be excited about: in London, they had slept in a refuge for the homeless, albeit a church hall, and from there they had rushed laughing and eager to the shelter when the sirens had sounded and had slept all night in that. On the train again from London, they had watched the guns firing and seen the searchlight beams aimed at the German bombers: then they had passed a whole factory ablaze and seen some twenty fire engines struggling to deal with it: now they were walking all through the night down dark and scary lanes to who knew where. To them, it was great fun: some people could live a lifetime and never have such fun!

It was Jack who was Olive's main concern: by the time they had reached Hamwyte station, they had been more than five hours on the train: unlike the four youngest, he had not slept at all, but had been inveigled by his brothers into joining them in looking out of the window to see what they could see. In the end, Olive took the second of the shopping bags from him and hooked that over the pram's handles along with the other, leaving him just the two gas masks to carry: it added to her exertions, but it meant at least that Jack should be able to keep up. However, after a mile or so trotting alongside his mother and performing the duty she had set him, he quietly let go of the handle and began to drop back: his walking was sluggish and he was meandering with weariness: in no time at all, he was twenty-five yards back: then fifty, then a hundred. Reluctantly, Olive called on his two brothers forty or so yards ahead of them all to slow their pace: if Jack fell too far behind on that twisting, meandering route, he might not see them take a particular turn and, if out of sight, he could easily go the wrong way down one of the many dark side roads. It slowed their progress greatly and was particularly galling for Jimmy and Patrick, striding on ahead, oblivious to the dangers of the dark and anxious to get to their destination and chatting away to each other like two old tramps on the road in the night.

Eventually, after three miles, as they came out of the shadows of some roadside trees, Olive called a half-hour's halt, as much to rest herself as to allow Jack, by then almost a hundred-and-fifty yards behind, to catch up: it also gave her the opportunity to feed a fractious and awakened Joseph the remainder of his bottle, cold and unwelcome as it was, before rocking him to sleep again: the sleeping Michael she left in the pram. It was an opportunity, too, for the others to go to the toilet: Olive shook the dozing and immediately protesting twins awake and held them by the backs of their coats to prevent them falling as they peed into the roadside ditch: Jimmy and Patrick, as was to be expected of them, gleefully treated it as a game, competing to see who could pee the highest over a farm gate. A tired Jack, however, had to be cajoled even into 'trying' when he finally trooped up five minutes later: he simply flopped down alongside the pram and fell asleep with his head upon his knees. Olive knew she had to wake him and did so with a guilty scolding, knowing full well that he was completely exhausted: but they still had four miles to go and she could not let him sleep. Had there been room, she would have put him in the pram, but there was none: he would have to walk, the whole seven miles, six years of age or not!

For herself, Olive, not wanting to go with her children all around her, slipped away behind the hedge to perform that function while the boys waited on the damp verge guarding the pram in which both the babies slept soundly again and in which the twins had resumed their back-to-back doze.

When they set off once more, Jack again trailed some twenty or thirty yards behind, this time with the pitiful refrain, 'I'm tired, Mum. My legs hurt. I want to go to sleep.' All Olive could do was to exhort him to keep up and to stop his whining: she was still doing it when at last they crossed the ridge road where the silent windows of the Compasses public house look out on to a triangle of green: before them, lay the last stage of their journey across the two miles of the Greater Tottle plains, a low-lying expanse of marshy ground and the loneliest stretch of all, for in the damp October dark flat, ploughed fields stretched seemingly endlessly away on either side, while over it all a grey tide of mist was rising from the ploughed furrows and the ditches which drained it. Only one farm lay along this hedgeless route, its long, low buildings lining both sides of the road so that one passes between them, into and out of their shadow as though through the actual muddy farmyard itself. At the end, where the route made a blind, right-angle turn, an ancient black barn leaned out over the road, its open, darkened doorway looking for all the world like the gaping mouth of some huge-headed, sleeping monster: it was noticeable that even Jimmy's and Patrick's enthusiastic chattering fell silent at this point as they hurried past, while a laggard Jack suddenly found the strength to run up to join his mother and was holding on grimly to the pram handle when they turned the corner.

On the far side of the plains, the road rises up again and runs along another ridge between the scattered village of Lesser Tottle and the more compact village of Gledlang: dawn was breaking grey and pink in the lower reaches of the eastern sky when, across the fields, Olive at last saw the dulled silver line of the distant Langwater estuary. Gledlang lies on the north bank of the bleak and desolate river estuary which runs in off the North Sea for some eleven miles up to the hilltop market town of Maydun.

Ahead, amid the gloom, she could just make out the red-roofed houses grouped around the village's square and the grey flintstone tower of the Norman church rising out of the cluster of tall elm and horse-chestnut trees which surrounded it: in that moment, the weariness which had dogged Olive for the whole of the journey fell away: for in that moment she knew then that she was home: home again after fourteen years!

TWENTY-NINE

GLEDLANG is built upon a barely discernible knoll which rises up no more
than a few feet above the level of the sea midway between the mouth of the
Langwater and the narrowing of the estuary at Maydun: seen upon a map, the
four roads which make up the village, the Maydun road, Tithe Street, Shoe
Street and Hedge Street, form an upright printed figure '4.' The sloping side of
the right-angled triangle is the Maydun road, winding southwest off the bottom of the figure for five miles to the hilltop town, all the way paralleling the
course of the estuary over flat, hedged fields, most of which themselves lie below the level of the sea. From the top of the triangle Tithe Street plunges due
south down into the village Square, which is really no more than a widened
junction where three roads meet, Tithe Street coming down from the north,
Hedge Street crossing horizontally from the Maydun road along the bottom of
the figure, and Shoe Street, the leg rising gently up from the river.

The Square is the hub of the village: the whole of its east side is taken up by
the cream-walled Chessman public house, with the square-towered, grey,
flintstone Norman church alongside: next to that, a short way up Tithe Street,
is an old tithe barn and a two-roomed, redbrick school standing side by side
opposite the Stanson sisters' farm. The cream-walled farmhouse and the long
wall of a cowshed front on to the road opposite the school and beyond that two
linked cottages and two groups of terraced, red-brick cottages, white-stepped
and white-windowed, with doors opening directly on to the street, curve away
towards the Bowler's Rest public house halfway up. The blacksmith's forge
under its spreading walnut tree lies directly across the road from that and,
right at the apex of the figure, in its own grounds, surrounded by gardens and
trees and thistly meadows lies the multi-chimneyed, twenty-roomed, eight-
eenth-century Gledlang House, the oldest of three parsonages in the village.

On the north side of the Square is the post-office-cum-grocery store: next to
that is a house and the entrance to Male's builder's yard with its two petrol
pumps set in the garden wall, while the south side is mostly taken up by a
chest-high brick wall masking the Chessman's allotment patch, in front of
which stands an old iron-wheeled pump alongside a broken circular granite
ciderstone embedded in the earth, a red telephone kiosk and a wooden bus
shelter. Hedge Street itself enters the Square from the west between the bus
shelter and Male's walled front garden: fifty yards along Hedge Street, set back
behind a low wall and a patch of grass and dwarfed by a horse chestnut tree, is
the mullion-windowed parish hall, while just thirty yards down Shoe Street
from the Square, just where a line of plaster-fronted terraced cottages curve
away following the line of the road, is Fred Thorn's bakehouse.

From the top of Tithe Street, two other roads divert left and right: the right-
hand one is a continuation of the Maydun road, which there becomes the
Salter road, running northeast over undulating ground to the next village of
that name, some three miles distant, while the second, narrower route, really
no more than a tarred and gritted lane, disappears between ten-foot-high
hedgerows as it begins its twists and turns towards Lesser Tottle.

It was along this second meandering route that, as the first light of dawn
spread over the ploughed and dew-soaked fields, a weary Olive and her yawn-

ing, red-eyed brood approached the village. They debouched from the shadowed gloom of the narrow Tottle road on to the wider, metalled Maydun road soon after six, at a point where two cottages stand in a depression as if built down in the bed of a dried-up pond: but instead of continuing on towards the straight run of Tithe Street and the centre of the village, Olive turned right along the Maydun road towards where Hedge Street has its junction with the backroad: the house she sought lay on the right side of that road, one of a line of eighteen, just before the junction.

To Olive, seeing the village again after so long a time away, it all seemed exactly the same: in fourteen years, nothing had changed: the two red-brick cottages on the sunken triangle were as dilapidated as when she had last seen them: the pond where the village boys searched for newts and tadpoles in the summer and where in the winter they slid on the often dangerously thin ice, was covered by the usual scum of algae: the paint was still peeling on the picket fence in front of the plain, lopsided cottage a quarter-mile down: and on the opposite side of the road, the signs outside Sam Gale's backroad shop, set up in the front two rooms of his bungalow, were as rusted and rain-streaked as ever. Beyond that, nothing had been done to improve the way where one corner of Johnny Coxwaite's house projected into the road, forcing any pedestrian walking on that side to hug the wall and to look behind them as they passed or risk being bowled over by whatever traffic came by, though there was not much to worry about then, except the occasional farmer's lorry and those bicycling farmworkers who went that way to and from work.

It was only after passing this point that Olive was at last able to get a view along the row of eighteen houses lining the right-side curve of the Maydun road almost to its junction with Hedge Street: the very last of these brown, semi-detached, pebble-dashed dwellings, solemn and silent behind their privet hedges and front garden apple trees, was the house which Olive had left fourteen years before. Seeing them again, so grim-looking and so unchanged, her heart sank momentarily: whether through apprehension, nerves or resignation, she did not know: but she took a deep breath, steeled herself, and pressed on.

The very sight of them had brought the memories flooding back: of herself at the age of three trotting with her younger sister Theresa, then two, alongside their mother as she wheeled the pram containing their baby sister Alice to the church to be christened: of the sunny April morning of her fifth birthday when she and her mother had walked to the two-roomed church-run school in Tithe Street for the first time while her two laughing older brothers, Percy and Hubert, had walked on ahead: and the tears she had shed on being left that first time. It was a journey she was to make as a schoolgirl six times a week for the next eight years, five times during the week and once each Sunday to Sunday school, till she was thirteen and left: then each day for five years after that when she had returned to it as the young, poorly paid but happy assistant to Old Mother Jepson, the old infants' teacher. Really she had been no more than a helper, taking the little ones 'across the yard,' helping them button their coats, put on their mittens, tie their shoe laces and wash their hands after playtime: sometimes helping them with their lettering, counting and reading.

There was a memory, too, of the countless times she and her best friend, Ethel Garner, had rushed in their early teen years from the house, fastening their coats with one hand as they ran while trying to hang on to their straw hats with the other, shouting 'Wait! Wait!' as the Bourne Brothers' new two-o'clock Saturday bus turned the corner of Hedge Street and headed off towards Maydun. But the saddest of the memories was that of herself, aged nineteen, walking slowly arm-in-arm with Theresa and Alice behind their stooping, solemn-faced father and their unemotional, seemingly unaffected brothers, as they followed the polished, flower-laden hearse bearing their mother's coffin to the churchyard.

It was Jimmy who broke her reverie. 'Is this it?' he asked. 'It's the middle of nowhere, this place!' It was the first time he or any of the boys had seen their mother's home village and clearly he was not impressed: neither was Patrick. 'Bit of a dump, isn't it, Mum?' he scoffed, in support of his brother, before adding a grumpy 'We aren't going to live here, are we?'

The sullenness of the boys' faces as they looked about them in the early morning gloom told of their disappointment and their contempt: to them, the houses bordering the road along which they were trudging seemed haphazardly scattered and isolated in relation to each other, with a hundred yards of hedge between some: the more compact roofs of the village proper lay a good threequarters-of-a-mile away directly across barren ploughed fields, seemingly huddled and remote around the square church tower. At that hour, the rising sun behind the tower was still obscured by cloud and there were no street lamps lining the Maydun road and no pavement upon which to walk, just black, skeletal telegraph poles spaced at fifty yard intervals and overgrown grass verges: long fingers of rainwater lay in the furrows of the fields on either side and there was already a coldness and a dampness to the coming day: and such was the silence all around them, it seemed physically to hang in the air and rustle in their ears.

To Olive, it was a blow: when she had told her two eldest that they were leaving London and heading for the country, they had grinned excitedly, welcoming it: anything was better than their brief stay in the church hall crowded with other bombed-out Londoners and no way did they want to go back to Thurstone. Even the grindingly long wait at the railway station had not dampened their enthusiasm: and the train ride, slow as it was, had been an adventure: after all, it was not every day that they had a grandstand view of firemen fighting such a huge blaze, especially one at a factory which they had actually seen being bombed! They had even undertaken the long walk cheerfully: now they were complaining of the village's isolation: it exasperated Olive: what else did they expect of a village in the countryside but that it would be isolated!

'Where else would we live?' she snapped. 'We haven't got any other place to go except here.' Then a contemptuous sniff. 'You'll get used to it. You'll just have to learn, that's all. We'll all be living here for the next couple of years, at least till the war's over, so you might as well get used to it now.' The boys, suitably chastised, said nothing more, but followed their mother reluctantly to the very last of the houses in the row of eighteen and then waited at the gate while she walked up the path.

It was only after several minutes of knocking that Olive heard the tread of feet on the uncarpeted stairs, accompanied by a gruff voice announcing, 'I'm coming, I'm coming Hold your horses!.' A bolt was slid back and the door was tugged open a few inches: a scowling face peered out: it was her father. Clearly, he had just got out of his bed, for he was in his stockinged feet and was holding up a pair of brown corduroy trousers which he had hastily drawn up over what was most probably his usual night attire, his long-johns. Olive tried not to react, to control her emotions, but could not: she let out a silent gasp as an inner shock jolted through her: in the fourteen years she had been away, her father had aged more than she had imagined. When she had left, he had been in his middle-fifties, upright and muscular still and with most of his hair: now, nearer to seventy, he was stooped and shambling: a three-day growth of beard covered his chin and he was completely bald except for two grey tufts above his ears. His preference for wearing a flat cap at all times was marked by the fact that his bald pate was almost milk white, while the brow itself and the lower part of his face was the beetroot red of a countryman who had spent long years out in all weathers.

It was not solely the sight of her father which made Olive step back off the doorstep: it was the smell emanating from the house which, even after so long a time, she recalled had certainly not been there when her mother was alive. Then there had been a different smell, one of polish and warm cooking and scented lavender in a vase on the living room table: even in her last days, before she was taken up to her bed, her mother had been in the habit of going into the garden to pick the early flowers of the season, bluebells, daffodils, tulips, grape hyacinths. Now the smells were unmistakably male smells: the sudden waft of stale cabbaged air which drifted out of the small hallway, the smell of sweat and long-worn, unwashed clothes: and, permeating it all, the nauseating stench or urine from the pot her father was carrying and which he had not had the gumption to put down when he answered the door.

'Good Gawd! What the hell are you doing back here, girl?' was all the exclamation her astonished father could muster as he peered out into the morning gloom and recognised his eldest daughter standing on his front doorstep. No greeting by name, no greeting at all, in fact: no smile, no gladness, no moistening of the eye: just disbelief, then annoyance.

'We've been bombed out,' Olive told him flatly. 'We've been living in a church hall in London for the past week. We haven't got anywhere else to go.'

Arthur Chapman looked past his eldest daughter towards the gate to where Jimmy, Patrick and Jack were standing beside the pram upon which the twins were still sagged in semi-sleep. 'You ain't brought your whole bloody brood down here with you, have you?' he asked, incredulous. 'How many have you got now anyway?'

'Seven,' Olive replied, her sharpness of tone matching his.

'Seven!' her father coughed in surprise. 'The last I heard from your sister you only had three.'

'That was four years ago,' Olive retorted, recalling the last time she had written to Theresa: then Jimmy had been just five, Patrick four and Jack still two: she had not written since. 'I've had the twins, John and Thomas, since then,' she announced as if challenging him to disapprove. 'They're three now. I had Michael eighteen months ago and the baby, Joey, at the end of February.'

'Gawd, girl!' her father repeated: and, opening the door fractionally wider, he peered out the better to see his grandchildren, but made no signal to acknowledge them, or to smile at them, and nor did he step aside to allow them and their mother entry. 'Well, why have you come here?' he asked after a pause as if genuinely puzzled. 'What do you want with us?'

'We've just walked from Hamwyte,' Olive told him bluntly, 'the whole seven miles, on foot. It's taken us all night. The boys are tired out. They need somewhere to sleep and so do I.'

'More fool you for walking all that way,' said her father gruffly. 'Why didn't you wait till today and come on the bus from Maydun? You wouldn't have had to walk then.'

'We came yesterday because we had train tickets for yesterday. It wasn't our fault the trains were delayed because of the bombing.' Despite herself, Olive's manner was still sharp. 'We should have caught the midday train, but every-thing was held up. They'd bombed the station and the line and it took us five hours to get from Liverpool Street to Hamwyte because of hold-ups of one kind and another. We didn't get in till well after eleven and we had to walk. We had no choice.'

Her father cleared his throat and sniffed again. 'Well, I don't know what you expect me to do about it all,' he said with a shrug, rubbing a hand across his bristly chin. 'We ain't got no room for you or them here. You know that. We've only got the three bedrooms and one of them's small. I've got my bedroom, Percy and Hubert have got theirs and Alice has got the other, the small one that you girls slept in. There just ain't no room for anyone else. Certainly not for eight of you, anyway. Whatever were you thinking of, coming here? You must be daft to think we could put you up. Goo back to London, girl. We can't put you up. Not eight of you, for Gawd's sake!'

Olive had not expected to be welcomed with open arms: but she had hoped that somehow he might grudgingly let them all in: give them a chair each, somewhere to sit and to rest: maybe with a pot of tea and piece of toast or fried bread: but nothing: her father just stood there with his growly face, blocking the doorway.

'We just need a place to sit down for a while and something to eat?' cried Olive, angered by the bluntness of his refusal. 'That's not asking too much, is it? They're your grandchildren. Can't you at least let us in?'

'If we let you in, girl, we mightn't git you out again,' a voice called out from the darkness behind her father: it was Percy, the elder brother: the raised voices on the doorstep had brought him down from his bed. Olive groaned in-wardly: if one thing were guaranteed it was that Percy would oppose anything which she suggested or requested, just out of sheer bloody-mindedness: had her father been on his own, she might have been able to persuade him to re-lent and let them in, even if just for an hour or two while they rested: the ap-pearance of Percy dashed that small hope.

'She's been bombed out, she says,' Arthur Chapman told his son, again with an indifferent shrug.

'Well, it ain't no good her coming here, is it?' Percy declared, sourly, in the peculiarly deep gruff voice with which he spoke. 'We ain't got no room. Any-way, we don't want her here, or any of them kids – if they are all hers.'

As he came more into the light, Olive saw that he, too, had changed: he had always been lean, with a square head and cropped hair: now he was fatter around the middle, with the beginnings of the belly men get from too much beer-drinking: his face, too, was fatter, more jowly, and he looked more surly than he ever had before: even though he was still only in his late thirties, his hair was receding fast: and, like his father, he, too, was dressed in just a vest and corduroy trousers.

'Git yourself back to London, and your old man, girl!' snorted Percy, placing his somewhat ample bulk in the centre of the doorway alongside the father, the better to ensure her entry was barred. 'If we weren't good enough for you when you lived here, we won't be good enough for you now! You chose to leave here and goo up to London. It was your choice, just as it was your choice to marry that Irish fellah you call your husband. Where is he, anyway? You ought to be with him, not back here bothering us. Goo back to London, girl. It ain't our problem if you've been bombed out. There ain't nothing we can do for you here.'

Before Olive could reply, matching his scorn with scorn of her own, there was further movement behind the two and Hubert, the second brother, came forward out of the darkness to peer over the shoulders of his father and brother at the boys by the gate.

'Whatever were you thinking, bringing all them kids here and expecting us to put you up?' he demanded in a voice equally as gruff and as booming as his brother's. 'Whatever was in your head, girl? It weren't common sense, that's for sure, bringing half-a-dozen kids all this way for no purpose. If you want somewhere to stay, goo round to your sister's in Shoe Street. You and she always were as thick as thieves. Maybe you'll find some room there, though I doubt it. Her place ain't big enough to swing a kitten in, let alone a cat! There certainly ain't no room for you and that lot here, You ought to have known that. Goo round to your sister's.'

With that, the door was banged shut.

Seeing their mother was not even being allowed to cross the threshold, Jimmy had again picked up the suitcase and Patrick and Jack had taken up the shopping bags: they had already wheeled the pram back across the verge and on to the road, ready to leave.

Olive's tears as she walked back down the path were induced as much by the anger she felt at that moment as the humiliation she had suffered: she had hoped for help of some kind at least, if only the provision of some bread and butter for the boys, a cup of hot tea for herself and a room in which they and she could sleep for a few hours: she had received nothing.

'Don't they want us?' Jack asked, his brow furrowed in a frown.

Olive did not answer: she just wiped away the tears which kept welling up in her eyes.

'Come on, Mum,' a stony-faced Jimmy said sympathetically, saddened by his mother's tears, at the same time nodding in the direction they had been walking, but waiting for his mother to take the lead.

Alongside him, Patrick was looking downcast for the first time since they had left Hamwyte. 'Where to now, Mum?' he asked cautiously, the way children do when they think their mother might fly at them if they ask an obvious question in the wrong manner.

'Into the village,' Olive replied, seizing the handles of the pram and setting off for the centre of the village.

As they walked away into the gloom of the morning, Olive turned for one last look at the house in which she had passed her childhood and her adolescence: at an upstairs window, framed by the pane, she saw a white face looking out. The features were blurred by the condensation on the glass, but Olive knew who it was by the shape of the face and the darkness of the hair surrounding: it was her sister Alice, her crippled sister Alice, three years younger than Olive and, to her father and her two brothers, no more than a drudge who cooked and cleaned and washed for them and led the very life from which Olive had fled fourteen years before.

THIRTY

THE FACE which came to the window of the little house in Shoe Street in answer to Olive's knocking was thin and haggard beyond belief: it made Olive gasp and shudder to see it. Briefly, the face disappeared from the window and there was a second drawing back of bolts: then Theresa, her other sister, a year younger than Olive, was standing in the doorway in her nightdress, sleepy eyed, with her hair dishevelled, but managing a weak smile of greeting. Even as Olive regarded her sister in the half light of morning, she felt a sensation akin to a cold shadow pass over her: Theresa was much thinner than Olive remembered her: her cheeks were sunken and her eyes were ringed through lack of sleep: there was a frailty about her: indeed, her whole frame seemed to have shrunk so that the flannel nightdress she was wearing appeared to be overly large for her body. Olive had seen the same thinness, the same paleness, the same emaciation in her mother a year before she had died of breast cancer. It had always been one of Olive's greatest fears, that she would contract the same terrible affliction as had affected her mother in the last year of her life: almost daily she and her sisters had watched their mother's strength and cheerfulness drain away almost as if life itself were leaking from her body.

Theresa spoke first. 'Good God! Olive! You of all people' she gasped in surprise and delight at finding her eldest sister standing on her doorstep for the first time in fourteen years. '! I never expected to see you here. And the boys! All of them! And the babies, too! I'm glad to see you all. How many have you got now?' And when Olive told her, rather self-consciously: 'Gracious, Olive! And there's me with just my Dorothy! I always said I should have had another. I would have liked another, but – ' A wistful smile and a shrug before a final disbelieving: 'When did you come, girl? There aren't any buses at this time of the morning. You should have let us know you were coming. Come in, come in, all of you. Gawd, girl, you must be all in, the lot of you.'

She ushered a weary Jimmy, Patrick and Jack past her into a small parlour where a fire burned low in a black-leaded grate, emitting more smoke than actual flame or heat: without further ado, the boys each took one of the three padded chairs set around the polished central table and, with their heads resting upon their arms, immediately closed their eyes and attempted sleep: the long weariness of their journey had finally caught up with them, too.

Olive, meanwhile, had lifted the half-dozing twins from the pram and led them, yawning, stretching and complaining in after their brothers: slumped upon a high-backed, black-covered horsehair settee under the window, they leaned against each other like two groggy old men.

The introductions were made, for this was the first time any of the boys had met their aunt: but to Olive's chagrin, only weary nods and mumbled replies were given in return by her three eldest dozing at the table, while the twins closed their eyes, jerked themselves awake and closed their eyes again, hovering between wakefulness and sleep yet still oblivious to their new surroundings. Theresa, however, did not seem to notice and, instead picked up a poker to stir the coals into life. 'You boys must be starving hungry as well as tired out?' she said, stating the blatantly obvious before adding, as the fire blazed up: 'Don't worry, we'll soon get you something to eat. How about a nice piece of fried bread and some scrambled egg?'

The settee upon which the twins now sat had obviously been Theresa's bed for the night, for a pillow and some rumpled blankets were still upon it: as she helped Olive to manoeuvre the pram past a bicycle in the narrow passageway leading to a tiny kitchen at the rear, Theresa felt a sudden need to explain herself. 'I have trouble sleeping sometimes,' she confessed, rather guiltily, glancing at her sister as if trying to discern whether she had guessed her secret. 'I sleep down here so I don't disturb Alf and Dorothy.'

Olive looked at her sister for a few seconds and was about to ask why, but decided to stay the question, fearing to hear the answer even though the evidence, in the emaciated form of her sister, was staring her in the face: talk of that would keep until another time: the moment of their first meeting after so long a time was not the occasion: her priorities were to feed Joseph and Michael and to change them, to feed the sullen twins and get them ready for the day, if she could wake them, and the provide something for the three eldest and herself: then, mercifully, to sleep: all other conversations could wait.

In the kitchen, while Theresa busied herself relighting the range to boil the kettle for tea and placing some bread and dripping in the frying pan and whisking up some milk and dried egg powder in a pan, Olive knelt on the floor to change Joseph and Michael in turn: that done and the two returned to the pram, looking anxiously at their mother for the hoped-for food and drink, she poured some orangeade into what glasses she could find and took them into the parlour. It was the first drink any of the boys had had since the halt halfway to Tottle almost five hours before and no sooner had the three eldest awakened themselves and gulped it down than they all resumed their former slumped postures at the table. The twins she could not wake at all: they had stretched themselves out upon the crumpled blankets on the settee and, undeterred by their strange new surroundings, were making up for the jolting discomfort and the all too frequent awakenings to which they had been subjected on their journey. When, five minutes later, Olive carried in the fried bread and scrambled egg, she had to shake the three eldest awake a second time to eat it: but within a minute of finishing, all three were fast asleep again: exhaustion had taken its toll: the twins' bread and drink she left on the floor beside the settee and returned to the kitchen.

It was later, as the sisters sat drinking tea, Olive with Joseph in her arms, Theresa with Michael on her knee as she watched over his eating, that Olive told of her father's and her brothers' cold welcome and how they had sent her round to her sister's house: it at least drew a murmur of sympathy from Theresa.

'It doesn't surprise me,' she said, carefully spooning some bread she had mashed into warm milk into Michael's mouth. 'He ain't really got the room, not for eight of you, not with four of them as young as they are. He ain't got the patience either. His nerves and his health ain't good. And it would be putting a lot on Alice the way she is. She does as much as she can, but she's limited. That lump Percy don't do anything except eat and drink and Hubert ain't no better.'

She explained how after their mother had died, their father had become a much harder man, more morose, more insular, angrier with everyone, more suited to the grousing company of the drinkers, smokers and swearers in the Chessman vault or the Bowler's Rest snug, where in the months which followed he had spent many of his nights. 'You wouldn't know, you were up in

London away from it all,' said Theresa. 'That's why I got out. That's why I married Alf. I wasn't stopping there after you left.'

The question which Olive had been partly dreading was asked by Theresa at this point: 'Where were planning on staying tonight?'

'I don't know,' Olive sighed wearily, holding a bottle of warmed milk for the cradled Joseph to suck. 'I didn't think of that before I came. I just came. I had hoped they would let me stay round the road, but – '

The pained expression on Theresa's face forewarned Olive. 'We haven't really got the room for all of you here either,' her sister said sympathetically. 'We've only got the two bedrooms or else you could stay here tonight. We're just a two-up and two-down with the lavatory out the back. You can get a bit of sleep once Alf's gone out. He'll be off to his allotment this morning, I expect. He will be when he sees this lot!' She gave a little laugh which produced a wry smile from Olive. 'The three oldest can go up in our bed then and you can go in Dorothy's when she comes down. At least you'll get some sleep. Dorothy and I'll look after the babies while you do.'

Olive was not put out by her sister's refusal: it was no more than she expected with her sister living in such a small cottage and she genuinely sympathised with her dilemma, accepting the obvious: that eight was too great a number for any one household in a village of small cottages to take in: she was just grateful for the opportunity to put her head down for a few hours and catch up on her own lost sleep: besides an idea was already forming in her head.

'I'll find somewhere for tonight,' she reassured her sister with an enforced optimism which belied her own doubts. 'Tomorrow I'll have a good scout round. Do you know of any houses that are vacant?'

'None that I know of in the village,' replied Theresa. 'There might be outside of Gledlang, over Tottle way, perhaps, but I don't know of any in the village itself. We've got the army here now because of the invasion alert. They've taken over the whole of Gledlang House and the Park for their soldiers. They've got a searchlight battery up on the Park and an ack-ack gun. The old thatched cottage opposite the Park was empty, but they've taken that over for one of their officers and his wife. They're even using the old coach houses and stables belonging to the Big House to park their vehicles in. There's only forty or so of them so things aren't too bad. It's worse at Salter. They've got half a Scottish battalion there camping out in the fields, even on the cricket pitch behind the Red Lion. About five hundred of them. Got machine-guns and mortars, so Alf says. At least our lot are English, except for a couple of Welshmen among them. They've livened up the village a bit, I'll say that for them. Especially the Chessman on a Saturday night, not that I go in my condition. It's just what Alf tells me. You can't get in the place some nights for soldiers, he says. They've had a couple of dances, too, in the parish hall. Things are certainly livelier round here since they came. But as for an empty house, well, I can't think of any. What there was have all been taken by strangers, people I don't know. We've had several come into the village since the bombing started in London. To be honest, girl, you'll be lucky to find anywhere, anywhere at all.'

THIRTY-ONE

THEIR conversation at this point was interrupted by the sound of a footfall on the stairs: it was Theresa's husband, Alf: the two sisters exchanged nervous smiles. It being a Sunday, Theresa had expected him to sleep on till well after nine o'clock: only on weekdays and Saturdays did he rise early to begin work at seven at Blythes, along the Tottle road, one of the three large fruit farms which surrounded the village to the north, east and south: it was a little after seven: the sound of two women's voices talking in the kitchen had made him curious.

Alf Braybrook was a bony, round-shouldered, thin-faced, man, with tobacco-stained teeth, somewhat of a squint and the deep, ruddy complexion and calloused hands of a farmworker: though only in his late thirties, his hair was already receding and his first action each morning was always to put on his cap, even before he put on his trousers. He must have looked through the door into the parlour when he reached the bottom of the stairs, for there was a snort of disbelief followed by a loud exclamation. 'Bloody hell! Where did you lot come from?' His five nephews were still sprawled in various stages of sleep, three at the table and the twins lying asleep on the settee.

'What are we now, a home for waifs and strays?' demanded Alf loudly of his wife as he came clumping into the kitchen with the untied laces of his boots trailing.

Seeing Olive sitting at the table, with the baby Joseph balanced on her knee, patting the infant's back to burp him, his mouth twisting into a sneer of recognition. 'Huh, I might have known it would be you,' he declared: and then realising his wife was holding another infant, Michael, he cried: 'Gawd! How many more are there?'

He made no attempt to greet Olive by name – nor did she expect him to do so – but sank with a scowl on to the chair his wife had vacated for him, with the words: 'I hope you lot are not stopping.'

Theresa quickly explained Olive's plight and her reason for being there: and how she had suggested that Olive and the three oldest boys take up their two beds during the day. 'I said they could get some sleep in our beds as soon as you've gone out,' she told him.

Alf Braybrook answered it with one of his typical grunts which sometimes passed for his comment upon a subject. 'So long as you ain't expecting to stop any longer?' was his way of acquiescing to his wife's suggestion.

'I'm not intending to,' Olive replied with an exaggerated sniff, but managing to control her anger: she did not want to antagonise her sister's husband at their first meeting for fourteen years. She had known the squint-eyed Alf Braybrook when he was just one of the youths who nightly congregated on the broken ciderstone in the Square, where all the village's boys gathered to while away the tedious hours of evening with banter and talk: she had not cared for him then and had been surprised when Theresa had written within a month of her leaving to say that she was marrying him. Of all people, she would have hoped Theresa would choose someone better than Alf Braybrook. It seemed to Olive that Theresa was acting out of desperation, for one reason or another: especially as, with her blue eyes, white skin and wavy fair hair, she was, in

Olive's opinion, the prettiest of the three Chapman sisters and could have had her pick not only of the village boys but of several others from other villages who had remarked upon her good looks: the truth came out when Dorothy was born within seven months of Olive leaving.

Olive did not expect anything but suspicion and hostility from Alf Braybrook: though older than Olive, he had been at the village school at the same time as her and, whereas Olive had been considered one of the brightest pupils, Alf had been seen as a true dullard: it had been no surprise when, like most of the boys who left the village school, he had gone straight into farmwork. Olive knew that he resented the fact that Olive had returned to the school only two weeks after leaving to become the teacher's helper in the infants' room, the Little Room, as it was called, until her mother's illness and subsequent death had driven her off to London.

'What brought you back here then? London getting too dangerous, is it?' Alf sneered as, behind him, his wife, still holding Michael, dropped two pieces of bread into the frying pan: clearly, he now found it somehow pleasing that his old adversary was back in the village from which she had disappeared, back with seven scruffy children in tow and looking for somewhere to stay. He knew his own wife looked up to her older sister and he resented that, just as he resented the fact that Theresa had wanted to send Olive the fare to come to their wedding in the village church, but Alf had vehemently objected to such 'waste,' declaring that they needed the money themselves. As it turned out, Olive would not have been able to go anyway because her employers, the Wilcoxes, had a dinner party arranged for that evening and would not give their new assistant cook the time off: she was needed to help the older cook.

'I had the children to think of,' declared Olive. 'London's no place for children. It's not safe! They're safer here, out in the country, away from the bombs.'

'Well, if you're looking for a place to stop, you won't find one round here,' sniffed Alf, reiterating what Theresa had already told Olive, but with unmistakable scorn attached. 'What there was went weeks ago, right after Dunkirk. People know if the Germans come, London'll be the first place they make for. Stands to reason. There's bloody newcomers everywhere! We've got half the army in the village as it is.'

'I'll find somewhere,' replied Olive, injecting a note of defiance to counter his sneer. 'I've got a few places in mind.'

'Where?' demanded Alf, scornfully. 'You'll be lucky to get anything this side of Wivencaster, I'm telling you. There ain't nowhere to be had, not for love or money, not even a bloody pigsty or a cowshed!'

From behind his back, his wife gave Olive another of those knowing, telepathic sisterly glances and barely discernible shakes of the head which say, 'Don't rile him. He's always like this! Wait till he's gone, then we can talk properly.' And to distract him, she slipped the first of his fried bread on to the plate in front of him

But having always been, stubborn, proud and defiant, Olive pointedly refused to let any man belittle her, particularly one as simple-minded as Alf Braybrook, even if he were her sister's husband. 'I don't give up that easily,' she snapped back. 'If there's a place to be had, I'll find it. So don't you go worrying yourself about me. I'll find somewhere. I'll keep looking as long as I've got breath in my body.' And, taking her sister's hint, she rose to her feet and went out into the hallway to lay a gurgling Joseph back in his pram, but more to the point to turn her back on her gleeful brother-in-law and hide her reddening cheeks.

Alf stuffed a piece of dripping-fried bread into his mouth and chewed noisily. 'I ain't the one who's worried,' he sniffed as Olive returned to the table, her cheeks flushed with anger. 'It's you who should be worried, not me.'

When the usual questions followed, such as, 'Where's your other half then? Gone back to Ireland, has he?' Olive simply gave all the same answers she had given everyone else who had asked: that he was down in Plymouth, working in the docks with his two brothers and that he had urged her for the children's sake to seek the safety of the country. Alf, knowing nothing different, had to accept her explanation, which he did with a sour look, accompanied by a low grunt.

Defeated there, Alf chewed on his fried bread as if searching in his brain for another subject: then, the way some men will to belittle women when they believe they have some kind of ascendancy over them, he gestured with his greasy fork towards his pale, red-eyed wife and asked with an unexpected bluntness: 'I don't suppose she has bloody told you about herself yet, has she?' He must have thought he was reading the answer in Olive's eyes when, in fact, they were blank, for he plunged on without waiting. 'No, I didn't think so! Daft bloody, woman! I don't suppose she's told you about that?'

'Told me what?' demanded Olive, trying to inject a note of surprise into her voice, as though she could never have guessed what was quite obvious about her sister's health to everyone who saw her: that she was dying.

'Didn't tell you she waited too long, did she?' continued Alf. 'Didn't tell you she waited till it was too late – too late to do anything about it? Didn't tell you she should have gone to the doctor months earlier when they might have been able to do something. Didn't tell you that – that she waited till it had got a hold, till it was too late for them to operate? No, I thought not. Didn't tell you she was too frightened to go to the doctor in case he told her what was bloody obvious from the start?'

Behind him, Theresa, who had just poured her husband's tea, was replacing the teapot on the range near the coals to keep it hot: tears welled up in her eyes at the harshness of her husband's remarks: her hands began to shake and Olive, fearful lest her sister scold Michael, whom she was still holding, jumped to her feet and took him from her. Again, the glance between the two sisters was enough for Olive to realise that Theresa had only been waiting for the right moment to confide in her about her illness: her husband's footfall on the stairs had come too soon.

Theresa's lips quivered. 'I'm under the doctor,' she answered, almost in a croak, at the same time wiping a tear from the corner of one eye. 'They reckon I might have the same as Mum had. I get weak sometimes and I have to take morphine now and then. I've been taking more just lately. That's why I sleep downstairs. Some nights I don't sleep at all. I just sit here and think. I was up when you knocked. That's why I answered the door so quick. You and I saw Mum, how she was before she died, so I know what to expect. We both know I ain't going to get any better. It's just a matter of how long.'

'Should have gone to the doctor sooner,' repeated Alf, a clear resentment in his tone, a churlish petulance almost of one who was about to be denied something, in this case the final thirty or forty years of his wife's life!.

There was a wistful smile at the corners of Theresa's mouth. 'This time next year, I could be pushing up daisies,' she said, giving a weak smile. 'I've told Alf where to put me – just in front of Mum so we're together. I've already put my money down on the plot so no one else'll be buried there ahead of me. If it's going to come, you have to face it. You can't run away from it, can you?'

To Olive, it was as if the room had suddenly gone cold despite the blaze in the range grate and the steam from the kettle: a shiver ran down her spine: it was like sitting in bright sunlight one moment and then finding herself in a cold shadow as a cloud passes in front of the sun. She wanted to put her arm around her sister, but knew that, were she to do so, the stoicism, almost indifference to her fate which Theresa was showing at that moment would crumble and she would weep for the life from which she was soon to depart, as well as for the life she knew she would never experience: not seeing her fourteen-year-old daughter, Dorothy, still asleep upstairs, growing into womanhood: and, of course, never knowing her grandchildren when Dorothy married. Almost by instinct, Olive knew that it was that which troubled Theresa the most: it was not death itself: it was not dying and leaving her husband, as much as she might or might not love him: it was dying too soon and leaving her daughter too soon: that is what hurt Theresa the most.

'Does Dorothy know?' Olive asked gently.

'No, she doesn't know, not everything,' replied Theresa, still a little tearful, but managing to smile shyly now, almost as if it were an embarrassment being the subject of so much concern. 'She knows I'm ill and that it's going to take a long time for me to get better. But she doesn't know what with. Dorothy's left school now, but she won't go looking for a job till I'm better, she says. Says she'd rather stay home and help me. I have to say, I'm glad of her help. I couldn't manage otherwise. She thinks I'm going to get better, though.'

In the second little bedroom above them there was a sound of feet padding across the linoleum-covered floor.

'Shhh, here she comes,' cautioned Theresa. 'Don't let on you know whatever you do.'

'Perhaps you will get better?' Olive tried hopefully, but unconvincingly. 'People do, don't they? So they say.'

'So they say,' repeated Theresa, managing another weak smile. 'You can but hope.'

Her husband, swallowing more tea before forking up the last of the fried bread, gave no sign that he detected the tearful catch in her voice, but just chewed noisily on.

THIRTY-TWO

OLIVE'S first meeting with her niece, whom she had never seen, was a surprise: Dorothy proved to be a blonde, wavy-haired, blue-eyed, beauty, slim and graceful, with smooth white skin and a shy, almost demure way of smiling: she was, Olive saw, the very image of her mother when she had been the same age.

Dorothy acknowledged her aunt's unexpected arrival with a shy and flustered 'Auntie Olive!': thankfully, the presence of Michael on his mother's knee gave her the distraction she sought, for no sooner had she sat down than she was playing peek-a-boo behind her hands with the giggling child. Later, Michael was to be found lying upon the floor by his new found cousin's feet while every now and again she would break off from eating her own breakfast of porridge and fried bread to 'dive-bomb' with her fingers the ticklish points of a near hysterical child. Not unexpectedly, his screams of laughter soon awakened the twins in the parlour and they came creeping cautiously into the kitchen to find their mother and also to discover what all the noise was about: soon they, too, were competing with Michael to be tickled by their 'new' cousin. Olive saw Theresa looking at her daughter as she played with the children and guessed what she was thinking: that she herself would never see Dorothy playing with her own children in that way, those who someday in the future would be her own grand-children.

Three children lying around his daughter's chair all waiting to be tickled till they screamed was all too much for Alf: his breakfast done, he muttered to himself that he had 'things to do' and left their company: it really was too early to go to his allotment, but he went anyway, just to get away from a house full of squealing children and tearful women. He could while away the morning there, for he knew others would arrive eventually to work their allotments: inevitably, from noon onwards they would all drift into the Chessman vault to join the other Sunday lunch drinkers: and none would be back home till the pub closed at two. Except that this time Alf did not return for his Sunday dinner, but went back to his allotment for the afternoon as well: so Olive and Theresa were able to talk more freely once the three eldest had been cajoled from their slumped positions in the parlour and coaxed up the stairs into the bigger bedroom to finish their slumbers: their mother would follow them later to the smaller bedroom. But first she had to talk: she had much to talk about: for it was only then that Olive felt she was able to tell the truth about Rupert Road. Olive knew that she would have to say it sometime: and there and then seemed to be the most opportune time.

'I think I've lost Robert,' she began, swallowing hard and wiping away a tear, as the two women stood at the wash tub, rinsing the babies' and the twins' clothes in warm water before putting them through the mangle. 'The house where we had our flat got bombed a week ago. It happened while I was up in Thurstone bringing back the boys. Robert was sleeping there at the time. He'd come up from Plymouth where he'd been working with his brothers. I think he's gone. I think I've lost him.'

She went on to explain to her silent, astonished sister the circumstances of Robert's arrival from Plymouth: the unexpected police visit, though without mentioning the guns they had carried: how Robert had sneaked back into the flat, how he had daringly seen them off at the station before going back to Rupert Road and how the house had been bombed while she was away. Only when she told of how they had all arrived back to find the road taped off, guarded by a policeman, and nothing but a great mound of rubble where the house and the adjoining properties had been did she momentarily let her emotion show and let the tears fall again. And, worst of all, she told Theresa, was that she could not inform the authorities of his loss because the police were after him and he should not have been there: and neither could she leave word where she had gone because there was no longer anyone she could tell.

'There wasn't anything left of the house except a mound of rubble,' Olive added after a pause. 'The policeman said no one could have survived the blast. An old couple on my floor got killed. We know that. They stayed in that night because he was too ill to go down to the shelter. They were there when the bomb hit and they didn't find either of them. Nothing at all.'

She broke off, unwilling to recall the thought. 'We lost everything, everything we had in the flat. I've only got what we had with us when we went up to Thurstone.'

When Theresa asked why she had not gone to her two sisters-in-law, Olive had to give the simple answer: 'They got bombed out, too. All three of us on the same weekend. Muriel, Gerry's wife, lost most of her stuff so she couldn't give me anything. She's got girls, anyway. Same with Martha, my other sister-in-law, Brendan's wife. Muriel and I were together in the church hall till she left, but the place was noisy and you had no privacy. Kids, people everywhere. I only had a week there anyway. They don't let you stay too long. That's why I've come down here – to get away from all that. There's nothing up in London for me now to go back to, neither home nor husband. Things weren't that good between us. Hadn't been for a long time, not since I first went up to Thurstone when it all started. Though if I'm honest, it started before that. I sometimes wish I hadn't gone up to Thurstone this time. But I had to go to see Patrick.' She explained why and also why she had brought the boys back with her. 'I wanted to keep the family together. Perhaps, if I'd been there that night, we might all have been in the shelter together.'

'Oh God, Olive!' was all her shocked sister could say.

'All I've got left are the things I had with me when I went up to Thurstone,' went on Olive, 'those and what we could get from the handouts they gave us at the church hall. That was only a few woollens for Joey and some cardigans for Michael and changes of clothes for the twins. The others have got the things they brought back with them, but not much else. Just a shirt and vest apiece, socks and jumpers. I haven't got a lot of money either, just a few shillings and some post office savings. Luckily, I took my post office book to Thurstone with me, so at least I've got that. It's not much, but it's something.'

'Oh, Olive,' repeated Theresa in commiseration. 'Oh, Olive.' For the first time since the two had met, the sympathy was flowing the other way.

'I'll help you with what I can,' Theresa promised, 'but I haven't got much. Things are getting tight what with the Government rationing everything. They seem to be adding something else every week. Perhaps Alice might be able to help, if you can get to speak to her without him or them being there.' She meant their father and their brothers.

One thing Olive had intended to do as soon as she and Theresa were alone was to find out how the youngest sister was faring. 'How is Alice?' she asked, grateful for an excuse to change a painful subject. 'I thought I caught a glimpse of her up at the window when I called there this morning first thing.'

'She's all right, I expect,' was Theresa's casual and surprising reply.

'Don't you know?' an astonished Olive asked.

'I don't see much of her these days,' an embarrassed Theresa admitted, her cheeks reddening. 'She don't come round here and I don't go round there for obvious reasons. I don't think I've seen her to talk to for seven or eight months, not since I stopped her in the Square as she came out of the post office one day and told her about myself. Even then she was hurrying off back to the house. I think it shocked her too much hearing about me, frightened her, especially after seeing Mum go the way she did. It's either that or they won't let her come round. She does all her shopping on the back road at Sam Gale's now so she don't have any reason to come round to the Square unless it's to the post office or the butcher's and she gets her bread delivered by the baker's boy. The only time she sets foot outside the house is when she goes up to Sam Gale's for shopping. Otherwise she don't go nowhere. Too busy washing, cooking and cleaning for that lot!'

'Told not to come, most likely,' said Olive bitterly: like Theresa, she, too, was prepared to hazard a guess as to why the youngest sister did not visit Theresa, even though they lived less than a mile apart. There was scorn in her voice, too, now. 'A thirty-year-old woman letting herself skivvy for them. No life of her own.' The anger rose within Olive and a fierce determination welled up in her to see her youngest sister again, not just a white face at a window: but first she had other concerns, the main one being where to find some accommodation for the night: in that respect, the idea had already formed.

When the two sisters parted, dusk was creeping in and a fine rain was falling, growing steadily heavier as the darkness deepened. Jimmy, Patrick and Jack were already waiting with the twins by the gate simply because there was no longer any room in the pram for John and Thomas to ride. Out of sight of her husband, who was skulking in the kitchen, having finally returned dripping wet and in a bad mood from his allotment, Theresa had secretly pushed into the well of the pram a shopping bag of her own containing a half loaf of bread, a small pat of margarine, a half-finished pot of homemade greengage jam, some pre-boiled sugar-sweetened milk for the two youngest in a capped lemonade bottle, a second capped bottle of diluted orangeade for the twins and the older boys, as well as some cheese, a half packet of tea, and a cold apple pie, plus a quarter packet of porridge oats, a small lidless saucepan, a larger one in which to cook the porridge oats, a half-box of matches and a candle, three old plates, some unwanted spoons and knives, and two patched brown blankets, folded to cover everything from her husband's prying eyes: all of which Olive gratefully acknowledged by pausing to lay her hand gently upon that of her frail sister as she and Dorothy manoeuvred the overladen pram, with Michael and Joseph perched on top, across the threshold and out into the damp evening air.

It was left to Dorothy to show concern. 'Wherever will you go, Auntie?' she asked, her forehead creased in a frown as she contemplated the twins waiting forlornly at the gate with their older brothers.

'Never you mind, girl, never you mind,' smiled her mother darkly: and then she compounded the secrecy with a laughing, 'Rather you than me, Olive! Rather you than me!'

'Don't you worry, Dorothy,' Olive reassured her niece, 'I've got a place in mind. We'll find somewhere.'

THIRTY-THREE

INSTEAD of turning up the hill towards the Square, Olive turned left and led them down the gradual slope of Shoe Street towards the river. It was only then she became aware that there was an eerie silence about the village: normally, at that time on a Sunday, the church bells should have been ringing, calling the faithful to evensong: but because of the threat of invasion the bells of all the country's churches had been ordered to remain silent: they were to be rung only as a signal that an invasion had begun.

'Where are we going, Mum?' Jimmy asked, puzzled as to why he and his brothers could not have stayed longer in the warmth and dry of the house with their frail, thin auntie and their friendly blonde cousin.

'Down here,' was Olive's unhelpful reply as, at the bottom of Shoe Street, just before a white-painted, five-barred farm gate, she turned abruptly left on to a sandy path which tunnelled for two hundred yards or more beneath high overhanging hedgerows of blackthorn, crab apple, holly and wild oak. To the left of the path, behind the hedgerow, was an orchard of mature apple trees, one of three old orchards which ran all the way up the east side of the village and protected it from the bitter winds which howled off the sea and up the estuary in winter and which, some said, came all the way from Siberia, across the Russian steppes, the Hungarian and German plains, the lowlands of Holland and Belgium and the grey heaving emptiness of the North Sea. To the right was a rough, uneven meadow, still bearing the look of land reclaimed from the estuary, fenced off by barbed wire and dotted with the silent forms of a half-dozen cows huddled motionless in the weeping rain.

The tunnelled path led to Gledlang Shoe, an inlet which formed the vague shape of a giant shoe stubbed into the flat fields which lie all along the estuary's shoreline, the whole surrounded by an earthen seawall some twenty-feet high which runs for mile after endless mile, twisting and turning to enclose creeks and inlets, from Maydun five miles to the west to the estuary mouth by Strood island six miles to the east: and beyond that for a hundred miles or so, right up to the Stour Gap in the next county. Along the southern shore, the same seawall meanders, twists and turns around similar long and wide inlets all the way back to the estuary mouth before plunging southward towards the eventual wharves and hards of London itself. It is a wild, bleak and desolate place, a place of emptiness and of loneliness when the sea retreats beyond the broad mouth to leave vast expanses of brown, salt-sheened mud, inky black beneath the surface and vile of smell when that surface is broken by treading feet. Great trenched banks of marran-grassed saltings choke its smaller inlets, while along its entire length it is bisected by a wide main channel from which shallow creeks meander across the glistening mudflats to either shore. Out there, where the gulls soar and dive and the waders tread, and the sounds of the land are too distant to be heard, one can sink to one's thighs in the black slime underneath and no one would ever know one was there, no one would ever hear your cries.

The high seawall is wide enough and flat enough on top to take a pram, even one as large and as cumbersome as Olive's double-hooded contraption. When they reached the end of the path, Olive simply shouted, 'We're going along here!' and, without pausing, ran the pram up the steep slope in one frantic push to be met at the top by a saturating curtain of fine rain sweeping in over the mudflats. From both Jimmy and Patrick, following behind with the twins, there came undisguised howls of dismay as the full force of the rain hit them, while the twins themselves darted behind their mother's coat-tails and regarded the bleak, windswept scene with fear and alarm: Jack, for his part, just burrowed deeper into his raincoat and clung on more tightly to the handle of the pram.

Only after a mile of walking in the sweeping drizzle did their destination finally appear out of the rain and deepening gloom: a large, cream-painted bathing hut, one end of which rested atop the seawall itself while the remainder projected out over the seaweed-covered foreshore, supported on thick, slime-covered wooden piles driven deep into the shingle. The hut stood at a point where the winding seawall turned at a right angle and a shingle bank ran out from the land to form a headland beach: the Shingle Bar, as the locals called it. This was where most of the villagers swam, where Olive herself had swum as a young girl with her sisters and paddled with her mother, even her father once, but never with Percy or Hubert that she could remember. At the juncture of the shingle bar and the seawall, the villagers had cleared away all the rocks, which the County Catchment Board had carefully laid to protect the seawall from erosion, in order to make a small cove for themselves which provided a sheltered and accessible bathing place.

The hut, however, had always been considered out of bounds to the villagers: Olive herself had never been inside it: and only once had she ever sneaked along the plank walkway which surrounded it, though there had always been some bolder village boys prepared to defy their elders and betters to jackknife, swallowtail and bellyflop, or just jump, off the two stout diving boards which stretched at different heights out over a rock-free patch of sand.

Access to the walkway was barred by a spring-controlled gate: a sign warning that all trespassers would be prosecuted and fined was nailed to the planking on the side of the hut: this time even Olive ignored it and pushed the pram through, holding carefully on to the wooden railing as she did so in order not to topple on to the sand twenty feet below. The realisation that their mother was going into the hut brought Jimmy, Patrick, Jack and the twins scurrying up the slope of the seawall: for the past threequarters-of-a-mile, they had been trudging gloomily along the bottom in a futile attempt to keep out of the sweeping rain, all the time complaining miserably of how wet they were and wondering why on earth their mother was taking them along such a God-forgotten place.

Fortunately, the door on that side of the hut was fastened only by a small padlock which Jimmy soon prised off with his jack-knife: clearly, the owners considered it unnecessary to padlock it more securely in the clear expectancy and knowledge that no one from the village would dare to use it: to do so would have brought the wrath of the owners down upon their heads: and the farmworking families of the village could not afford that. For the bathing hut belonged to the Godwins, one of the biggest and the most disliked of the farming clans in the region: they allowed no one but members of their extensive family to use the hut and woe betide anyone they found inside it, or even just sunbathing on the plank decking or diving from the two boards. Anyone so much as treading the walkway or damaging a single plank would be, and had been, prosecuted severely: Old Man Josh Godwin, the septuagenarian patriarch of the clan, was himself a magistrate and had friends among their kind who would ensure that his property was not defiled by the likes of any village types. Over the years three village youths had found to their cost that trespassing on Old Man Godwin's property was frowned upon by his cronies at Wivencaster's magistrate's court and they had paid literally for their audacity with fines which, as poorly paid landworkers, they could ill afford: so the locals generally gave the hut a wide berth, and ensured their children did so, too: not so much out of fear of the family but out of common sense. Why antagonise people who had the law firmly on their side?

The Godwins had always been the biggest landowning family in the area: Old Josh still bossed his own farm and lived in a large Georgian house right on the estuary shore about a mile from the hut as the seawall winds: the eldest of his four sons, Doug, actually worked it for him, while his other sons, David, Dick and Don, possessed farms of varying acreage of their own surrounding their father's, so that from Gledlang to Salter, a distance between the two villages of some three miles, the Godwins owned more or less every square inch of land, right down to the water's edge and for several miles inland as well. Indeed, locals said there was not much that they did not own and such was the power the family exercised in that small pocket of the county that they had provided two of the village's vicar and an archdeacon for Wivencaster in the past hundred years: they had also built separate homes for each of them in Gledlang, funded the building of the village's two-roomed, redbrick church school seventy years before and also paid for the erection of the mullion-windowed parish hall in Hedge Street. No, one did not upset a Godwin lightly, not in Gledlang, not if one lived and worked upon any of the farms around the area, where a quiet word from a Godwin could blight a man's employment prospects even on another farm.

But Olive neither worked upon any of the farms nor cared: she needed a place for herself and the children to stay the night, out of the rain and out of the cold, and this was the only place of which she could think: the Godwins' bathing hut.

Even as she had left her tearful sister's, Olive had asked only one question: 'Is their hut still there?'

When her sister had chortled with glee at her audacity and nodded 'Yes,' Olive had whispered: 'You'll find me there then – at least for tonight. We'll worry about tomorrow when it comes. If I can't find a place by tomorrow, we'll just have to sleep there till we do.' Her sister's intake of breadth and warning that 'The Godwins won't like that!' Olive blithely ignored.

The hut actually comprised two roomy compartments, each twelve feet by twelve and each with its own entrance, one in which the women and younger children of the separate Godwin farming families changed and one in which the men and boys changed: and among the Godwin clan there were many of those: Olive and the boys had broken into the men's part. With the matches Theresa had given her, she lit the candle, placed it carefully in one corner in case of draughts and looked about her: the place appeared to be clean and free of dust, as if recently swept, and the candle flickered brightly enough to show there were no worrying draughts. 'It'll do,' Olive said aloud, 'it'll do.'

The boys were less convinced: but it was there that the family ate their frugal fare and spent the night, the younger ones covered by the two blankets, lying on the floor of a creaking bathing hut perched atop a high seawall along a remote stretch of a bleak tidal estuary, while outside the rain lashed against the board walls and the cold and dark of the October night closed over them.

THIRTY-FOUR

'YOU in there! Don't you know this is private property? Come on out, the lot of you!' The words were shouted outside: then the door was tugged open and a tall, thin man in his late twenties, with fair receding hair, burst into the hut waving a thick, knobbed hornbeam stick menacingly before him.

'You ain't got no right to be in here,' he bellowed, halting just inside the door and glaring down at the children stirring from their long night's sleep. 'This is private property and you're trespassing. What's the matter, can't you lot read? There's a notice outside, "Private property: trespassers will be prosecuted".' Apart from shouting loudly and holding up the stick, he made no other move to accost them.

'Yes, we can read,' Olive retorted, turning to face the newcomer and defiantly standing her ground: fortunately, she had awakened a good half-hour previously, just as the morning sun was cresting a line of pink clouds beyond the estuary mouth, and was already collecting up their things when the man burst in.

'There's no need to come in here shouting the odds,' she told him. 'We aren't doing any harm to your precious hut! We came in here to shelter from the rain. That's all. What did you expect us to do, sleep outside in the wet all night?' She was not going to let herself be intimidated by any man's shouting and, at the same time, she was incensed that his shouting had upset her children, especially the four youngest

When the man burst in, the twins had been curled up on the floor beside the pram: their terror at finding him towering over them, a raised stick in his hand, had sent them scuttling behind their mother's skirts: Michael, whom Olive had been about to place in the pram, had burst into tears which could not be stifled and baby Joseph, taking his cue from his older brother, had also begun to howl: the whole place was filled by the noise of their wailing. Neither Patrick nor Jack was immune to the threat: Patrick, who had been lying just inside the door, had immediately propelled himself backwards on his buttocks into one corner to put as much distance between himself and the newcomer as he could: while Jack had wriggled away into another corner as though trying to shrink himself into the darkness: only Jimmy had the presence of mind to jump to his feet and place himself squarely alongside his mother, jaw set, fists clenched, ready to defend her and his brothers.

The man eyed them all coldly, a peculiar sneer upon his face. 'Come down from London, have you?' he asked disdainfully. 'Come to get away from the bombs? Come to the country to be safe? You people ain't got no right to be here. You ought to stay where you are up in London where you belong. We don't want your sort round here causing trouble.'

'What if we have, Don Godwin, it's none of your business,' Olive snorted in reply, visibly bristling with indignation. 'We aren't beholden to you or your family. We don't have to ask you or them what we do. Not like some poor souls who live here. I don't bow or curtsy to no man, especially you and your kind. What if we have come down from London to get away from the bombs, what business is it of yours?'

Olive's use of his name brought a look of surprise to the man's face and he peered more intently at her, frowning as he did so, seeking to discover her identity.

'It is when you prise the lock off and break into a place. That's breaking and entering,' said the man coldly: he must have realised that Olive and the children presented no threat, for his tone lost much of its belligerence and he lowered his stick: he still continued to stare hard at Olive, finally asking somewhat tersely and with a puzzled frown: 'Do I know you?'

'No you don't, but I know you,' Olive answered with a smirk of satisfaction and then blatantly turned her back on him and bent over the pram to console the fearful Joseph, at the same time fastening the whimpering Michael into the pram as well. Only when she had done that and had taken a firm grip on the handle did she address the man again. 'We had to prise the door open to get in out of the rain. We weren't going to sleep out there in the rain. What if we did "break and enter," as you call it? There's no harm done. You haven't lost any money over it. We didn't damage your precious lock. It won't take you five minutes to put a couple of screws back. None of it gives you the right to come barging in here waving a stick about and frightening my children!'

The man almost choked at the brazenness of her reply: but before he could comment himself, Olive was pushing past. 'Come on, let's go,' she called out, thrusting the pram ahead of her so violently that he had to step quickly aside or receive one corner of it in his groin. Jimmy and Patrick, meanwhile, had scooped up the suitcase and the shopping bags and, holding the twins by the hand as they negotiated the rickety railed walkway, quickly followed in her wake, each of them giving the man their own defiant smirk as they ducked by him: last out was Jack, darting from his dark corner with a panic-stricken cry of 'Wait for me! Wait for me!"

Once they had all passed through the spring-loaded gate and were on the neutral ground of the seawall path itself, Olive half-turned and defiantly flung back at the man: 'Olive Cullen's my name, if you want to know. I was born in Gledlang, so don't you tell me I've got no right to be here. I've got as much right as you, Don Godwin! As much right as you and any of your kind! So there!'

There was such a defiance in her tone, such a challenge, that Jimmy and Patrick looked at each other in surprise: ahead of them, her head held contemptuously aloft, pushing the bouncing and juddering pram, their mother strode purposefully on: behind them, a bemused and red-faced farmer was still trying to puzzle out who this woman was with a pram and seven children, who had slept overnight in his family's private bathing hut, who knew him by name and who seemed not to fear him: her name he knew, but it meant nothing to him.

'Where to now, Mum?' Patrick asked as she led them away.

'I don't know,' said Olive with a sigh. 'I haven't a clue where we're going next.'

THIRTY-FIVE

WHERE Olive did go, it being a Monday and still early, was back to her sister's house in Shoe Street, being careful to arrive after husband Alf had left for work: there, she and the boys were all given a breakfast of porridge and dripping-fried bread, with mugs of hot tea for herself and the three eldest to restore their spirits and orangeade for the twins and Michael. Then, all having finished breakfast, Olive set off at ten o'clock with the three eldest and the babies in the pram to scour the village and its surrounds, leaving the twins happily playing on the floor with Cousin Dorothy and their aunt.

'If it weren't for him – Alf – I'd willingly let you stay here,' said a sorrowful Theresa as they left, 'but I don't want to upset him, not the way things are.'

'I know, I know,' Olive reassured her. 'Don't worry. I'll sleep in the bus shelter or the church porch if I have to! One night won't do any harm.'

Olive spent the whole of the morning walking round the village and then out along the Maydun and Tottle roads, carefully inspecting every house for signs of occupation: or, more correctly, for signs of non-occupation: uncurtained windows, overgrown gardens, unpainted doors and windows. She knew it was futile even as she set off: but she had to do it in the hope that there might just be an empty house or cottage somewhere about which her sister and brother-in-law had not heard or which the army or the host of newcomers fleeing London had not commandeered. Of course, she found none and, indeed, met hostility from those whom she asked: some who remembered her, who had grown up with her, were sympathetic and just shook their heads, though as surprised as her own relatives that she should have returned to the village for such a purpose. What did quickly become apparent was that her brother-in-law and her sister had been right: there was not a house or a cottage to be had of any kind, neither in the village nor out of it.

'You'll be lucky!' one woman said brusquely, almost as if in protest at the question being asked: then, eyeing the three eldest with barely concealed distaste, she exclaimed: 'A woman with so many children ought to have got a place sorted out before she come, not just come in hope, especially now!' With that, she remounted her bicycle and pedalled away: Olive cursed her under her breath: she remembered the woman as a pious, simpering type, who, in her opinion, would have 'crawled to church on her hands and knees even if she were dying just to ingratiate herself with the vicar.'

When Olive called in at Sam Gale's back road shop halfway through her search, hoping that, since it was a place where women met and gossiped, the shopowner's fat, bespectacled wife, Winnie, might know of somewhere, she found her equally as unsympathetic. 'Go to the council at Wivencaster, girl. They're the only ones who can help you!' was her unhelpful advice when she found that Olive was not there to purchase anything but only to seek help.

'I'd sooner sleep in a tent than go to those busybodies!' declared Olive angrily, storming out. 'I don't need council help!' What she could not say was that she dared not ask for the council's help: the less they knew about her till she had found a place the better. True, she knew that she would have to contact them eventually, to renew her ration books, for the boys' schooling and to get the allotted powdered milk ration and orange juice for the babies: but till then she preferred things the way they were: the authorities at Wivencaster did not know she had arrived in Gledlang and she was not going to tell them till she was ready! A single letter from them to Miss Grogan about her difficulties, perhaps just enquiring who she was and why she had come – and with seven children in tow – might lead to a further letter being sent to the authorities in Thurstone and that was the last thing Olive wanted: the Thurstone authorities, particularly Grundwood, would probably very much like to know where she and the three eldest were. One letter back from them, she feared, could very well lead to Jimmy, Patrick and Jack, maybe all seven of the boys, being taken into a hostel again, perhaps even an orphanage, especially if she and they remained homeless. No, she would continue asking and continue looking on her own account: sooner or later she must find something, she reasoned.

'If I knew of a place, I'd be after it myself for my sister!' declared another woman, who was a customer in Ma Rowthey's post office-cum-grocery shop in the Square when, after a futile morning, Olive called in just after midday to ask the same question. Then, as Olive left, she overheard the woman say to the postmistress: 'Whatever does she want to come back here for asking about houses? Good Lord! There ain't enough for people in the village as it is, what with the newcomers taking over everything. We don't want any more outsiders taking our houses. Them that's moved away should stay away!'

'You've got some hope, Olive Chapman,' a fourth woman snorted, remembering Olive and using her maiden name as she tugged open the shop door to leave. 'There ain't nothing to be had. My own daughter and her three children are having to live with me and mine while her husband's away in the army. The six of us are in a cottage where there's not room to swing a cat let alone live and sleep. As it is, they're in one bedroom all together and we're in ours. What are you doing back here, anyway? You ought to have more sense than to come back here at this time with the army all over the place.'

The signs of the army were indeed everywhere: two trucks and an armoured car were parked on the triangle of green where the Salter road begins and immediately drew the interest of her three eldest: more lined the sandy drive up to Gledlang House under the rhododendron bushes and horse chestnut trees: a 'War Department Property' notice was fixed to the hurdle fencing fronting on to the road. As they walked up Tithe Street at the start of their search, a small group of soldiers had come strolling casually down towards the Square, presumably to go to the village shops there: Olive did not let it upset her that the young soldiers, seeing an older woman in her thirties pushing a pram with two young children visible in it and three others following along behind, stepped aside to allow her to pass and not one so much as turned to look back so disinterested in a mother-of-five were they.

It was a weary and dispirited Olive who, just after one o'clock, having made a complete circular tour of the village and out along the Maydun and Tottle roads, sat herself down upon the broken ciderstone embedded in the earth beside the iron-wheeled public pump to unwrap the sandwiches she had made for herself and the boys. They, as usual, ate theirs greedily, but, rather than drink from a lemonade bottle of water which Theresa had provided, they preferred to drink from the pump, cupping their hands at the spout to drink in turn from that. Discovering how the pump worked made the three eldest forget their troubles: the pump machinery stood to one side in an upright metal casing and was worked by a large iron-wheel: the water poured from two spouts, one high up, one low, which projected from a boxed-in, vertical pipe, some ten feet high. All went well until Jimmy found that, by giving a deft twist and lift of the lower 'tap,' he could close that spout and then, by vigorously working the iron wheel faster and faster, could make the water spurt solely from the top spout with the force of a hosepipe, enough to drench anyone standing underneath: and poor Jack was the one who was standing underneath! It took an angry threat from their mother to curb Jimmy's and Patrick's hilarity at their dripping younger brother's misfortune.

The boys were playing 'fivestones' with pebbles nearby and Olive was still sitting there when the village's vicar, Reverend Handle, came pedalling slowly down Tithe Street leading a gaggle of a dozen or so girls between the ages of seven and eleven from the village school which was no more than a hundred yards farther up the street: the vicar, a bony, white-haired man well into his seventies, carefully dismounted at the gate, took off his bicycle clips and, rubbing his aching knees, ushered the girls through the gate before wheeling his bicycle after them. Olive guessed that the children were probably going for a choir practice: she had done the self-same thing herself twenty-three years before when she had been at the village school: and Theresa had told her in general conversation that very day that there was going to be a funeral two days hence, that of the ninety-five-year-old matriarch of another of the area's farming clans, the Peakmans, who had given money to the church to repair the organ and who was to be sent on her way to heaven to the sound of its playing and the singing of a choir of village girls.

It was then that the thought came to Olive: why not ask the vicar if she could use the parish hall in which to sleep? It was run by the churchwardens for the good of the village and the vicar was the voice of the churchwardens, was he not? It stood no more than fifty yards away in Hedge Street and, though there might not be any beds in it and only a few chairs and fold-up, baize-covered card tables as furniture, it would be roomy and dry and had an outside bucket lavatory and a coke stove.

'Come on,' Olive cried and, in no time at all, she was marching across the Square with the boys trotting at her heels.

They caught up with the crocodile of girls just as they were entering the church porch: the white-haired vicar, hook-nosed and with a high domed forehead and prominent cheekbones, came forward out of the dark interior when he spotted Olive, a thin smile of greeting upon his lips, peering closely at her as if seeking recognition.

'May I help you, madam?' he asked, but in the manner people adopt when they consider the prospect of actually having to help someone would be an imposition on their time and their charitableness.

'I was hoping you might help us find some accommodation,' said Olive, perhaps a little too brusquely. 'I need somewhere to stay for me and my family. We've looked everywhere, but there's nothing to be had anywhere.'

'Accommodation!?' Clearly, the vicar was taken aback by the unexpectedness of the request. 'How can I help you there, madam?' The emphasis was on the 'I' and the words were spoken coldly, unsympathetically.

Olive did not know the Reverend Handle: he had come to the village after she had left: from looking at him, she assumed he could only have been given the living as a sinecure by some kindly bishop to ease him towards the end of his days: with only a hundred or so houses, Gledlang was really too poor a place to attract higher, ambitious clergy: it was a place of retreat and at his age, Olive thought, Handle must be thankful for a living of any kind.

'Do I know you, madam?' he asked, frowning, still squinting hard at Olive and the boys through pale, narrowed eyes as if he considered them trespassers on his territory. 'Are you local or are you a stranger? Have I seen you and your boys in my church before?'

'The boys go to a different church,' Olive declared huffily.

The expression on the vicar's face changed abruptly 'Oh, I see,' was all he said through pursed lips as if something had suddenly dawned upon him.

Olive realised immediately that what she had done was to inform a long-standing Church of England bigot of the old school that the boys were Catholics – of a religion he despised: it was no good telling him that she herself was still Church of England and had at one time sung in his very church and, indeed, had been baptised there: that her very own mother and grandparents were buried in the churchyard! The damage had been done: she was unlikely to get help from him now, she realised, but she would try anyway!

'I'm just looking for somewhere to stay for myself and the boys,' she rushed on. 'I know you and the churchwardens are responsible for the running of the parish hall. I was hoping you would let us stay there for a while, just for a few days until we can find somewhere properly. We've only just arrived in Gledlang. We could sleep on the floor. We've got blankets and things. We don't need anything fancy.'

The vicar began to bluster: 'The parish hall! I, er – We – er – ' Then he found his excuse: 'I'm terribly sorry, madam, but I don't see how we could let you stay there. It's not suitable, not suitable at all. It has no running water, no cooking facilities. Besides, the new Local Defence Volunteers have asked if they can use it for their headquarters. They've formed a platoon in the village – the invasion scare, you know. They are due to move in this very week, I believe. They obviously take priority. I mean, I don't know you, do I? You are a stranger to me. You are not from round here.'

'Just one night till we've found somewhere?' Olive pleaded one last time.

'Not even for one night, madam' the vicar said icily. 'I just could not take the responsibility.' He ended it with, to Olive, an insincere, 'I'm terrible sorry, madam, but I'm afraid I just can't help you,' and began pushing the girls inside the church as if impatient to get on with his choir practice.

Or won't help, thought Olive, not a family of Catholics in the midst of a Protestant community!

'If that's your attitude, you can keep your damned parish hall! See if I care! I'll find somewhere else!' she cried, her irritation exploding into anger as she wheeled the cumbersome pram round and headed off back down the path. 'Huh, and I thought vicars were supposed to be Christians!'

Among the older girls, the nine-year-olds and ten-year-olds who watched the strange angry woman heading back down the path, pushing her double-hooded pram and leading three scruffy boys with her, there were giggles and whispers behind raised hands. The arrival of three unknown boys in the village meant new boys attending the village school and, for them, the prospect of a different attraction from the ones they already knew: new blood, so to speak, which Nature decrees the female of the species will always seek out.

Two of those boys, however, were too busy studying a plane high in the sky which had crossed a gap in the canopy of trees which overhung the path.

'It's a Halifax,' Patrick was claiming.

'No, it's a Stirling,' his older brother was insisting.

'A Halifax,' insisted Patrick, 'you can see by the nose.'

'A Stirling,' replied Jimmy.

The two were still arguing as they followed their mother out on to the road, now over the number of guns in each, which flew the fastest, the size of their bombload and, of course, in which they would rather fly to bomb Germany!

THIRTY-SIX

HAD the boys not been arguing about aeroplanes, Olive might never have thought of Beckenden aerodrome, the old First War site which lay a mile-and-a-half outside the village: and, more specifically, she might not have thought of the 'aerodrome cottage.' Had she not done so, the boys would not have found themselves an hour later trailing their mother through the gloom of late afternoon drizzle along a lonely road well out of the village, each step taking them farther and farther from their hoped-for sanctuary.

On leaving the churchyard, Olive had returned briefly to her sister's cottage to collect the twins from a disappointed Dorothy and to load all their things, suitcase, shopping bags and gas masks, into the pram: as far as Theresa and her daughter were concerned, she was returning to the bathing hut for a second night: she had not told them anything about Don Godwin and their hasty eviction.

However, once her sister's door was closed, instead of continuing down Shoe Street and back towards the river, she had turned the pram around and quickly led the boys up the street, across the Square and up Tithe Street: past the church, the tithe barn and the empty school, past the Stanson sisters' farm and the two rows of terraced cottages, past the Bowler's Rest and the old smithy with its cluttered yard, and out along the Salter road past the Park where the army searchlight and the ack-ack guns pointed skyward and two black huts formed the soldiers' barracks.

It had begun to rain before they had even covered a quarter of the distance: one glance towards the western horizon and the darker clouds scudding up over Maydun hill five miles distant told Olive that the rain would soon be falling much more heavily. As she had told no one where she was going, there was no one to deter her: if they failed to find a place that night, she and the boys would just have to seek shelter in a ditch if needs be, she told herself. Several times she was tempted to turn back: in her wilder thoughts, she vaguely contemplated camping in the church porch overnight, just to cock a snook at the vicar, or even breaking a window of the parish hall, lifting the lighter Patrick through to undo the door for the rest of them: in the end, she did neither of those things, but pressed on towards Beckenden, driven by desperation as much as anything.

Olive's one concern was to keep Michael and Joseph dry: they happily were asleep in the pram, with the hoods up and the suitcase and the other things heaped between them in the place where the twins normally sat when riding upon it: consequently, John and Thomas were having to trot alongside Jack and their mother and both were whining constantly. Dawdling some thirty yards back, bent and huddled against the fine rain sweeping over the fields and muttering to each other, were Jimmy and Patrick: both were soaking wet and feeling thoroughly fed up with all the to-ing and fro-ing to which their mother had subjected them: there was between them the first simmerings of a rebellion, which only the sharpness of Olive's tongue was for the moment able to quell. To them, what had started as an adventure – the flight from Thurstone, the time spent in a crowded church hall with other bombed-out families, nights sleeping in a shelter while the bombs rained down, then a train journey past a factory going up flames, followed by a night-long walk down scary country lanes – that had all been fun, of a kind: now it had all soured. First had come a rain-soaked traipse along the shore of a bleak estuary, followed by an uncomfortable night in a bathing hut of all places: then that had been followed by their ignominious ejection by an angry farmer, another futile traipse around the village seeking an empty cottage that was nowhere to be had: now, in pouring rain, their mother was making them tramp along yet another road through the same bleak countryside as they had encountered upon their arrival. In their disillusion, they saw only flat fields of bare brown earth stretching endlessly away upon either side to a distant, misted horizon which merged into the rainy sky: there was not a house or a cottage to be seen anywhere and nothing to distinguish the landscape but occasional leafless trees spaced at intervals among high, dark hedgerows.

The road to Beckenden was no more than an old chase, gravelled to facilitate the passage of carts: it diverts off the wider, metalled Salter road a mile out from Gledlang, then climbs a long slope towards a flat-topped ridge upon which the tall red-brick tower of Beckenden church rises high and solitary above the surrounding fields. The old church, by then, was scarcely used: Gledlang's vicar conducted occasional services there to keep it holy, communion being offered monthly, evensong quarterly, but they were sparsely attended: sometimes, it was said, Reverend Handle and the organist were the only ones there, for Beckenden was no longer a village as such, just a place name on the map. There was no population to speak of save for the inhabitants of two farms remote and distant from each other and one ageing bachelor farmer, who lived in a moated glebe farm, the so-called Beckenden Hall, alongside the ancient church: the aerodrome had been built on what had once been his land. Even he was seldom to be seen, being too aged and infirm by then and preferring to remain behind a high crenellated wall which surrounded his place like the battlements of an ancient castle, as if to keep out all intruders: his land he rented to the other farmers, his nearest neighbours, as it just so happened two of the Godwin clan and they had divided the land between themselves.

With none caring for the church or using it, the gravestones and crosses in its grounds year by year were disappearing beneath tall hummock grasses, rampant briars, waving ferns and ever-spreading thistlebeds: the forgotten dead were vanishing into a second oblivion. It was towards this lonely and forbidding place that Olive led her brood through the enclosing gloom and sweeping rain.

In reality, Beckenden aerodrome was never even a proper aerodrome: just two fields on either side of a narrow, high-hedged lane which diverted for a hundred yards off the Beckenden route threequarters-of-a-mile from the church: one field was a flat cindered meadow two-hundred and more yards long from which the aircraft took off and upon which they landed: the other 'field' was little more than a square enclosure, a one-time horse paddock across the lane, fifty yards by fifty yards, also overlaid with a cinder hard, or stand, upon which the aeroplanes had been parked and where they had undergone repair.

The aerodrome itself functioned only from the middle of Nineteen Seventeen to the summer of Eighteen: it came into being almost overnight when the threat from the German Zeppelins and the lumbering Gotha bombers was such that it became necessary to base a squadron of RE8 biplane fighters there to protect the capital. They chose Beckenden ridge because it was flat and because the winds which blew there would aid the planes at take-off: and also because much of the rest of the land around and along the estuary's shores was below the level of the sea, reclaimed marshland, and thus prone to water-logging in winter: and a waterlogged aerodrome would have been of no use at all.

The aeroplanes began their taxi-ing on the smaller cinder hard on one side of the track, then gathered speed as they crossed the way itself and took off from the long meadow's cindered runway: two thirty-yard gaps had been cut opposite each other in the two hedgerows either side to allow this and a red flag was hoisted on a pole as a warning that aircraft were crossing, though except for an occasional farm wagon, a herd of cows wandering past alone late in the afternoon on their way to be milked or an occasional bicycling farmworker, nothing ever passed that way or had need to do so. The track to the aerodrome was a dead-end: the only motor vehicle ever to stir the dust there had been the bi-monthly supply lorry!

Olive remembered how, as a girl of nine on a blackberrying outing in the autumn of Seventeen, she and her mother and sisters had unexpectedly come across the aerodrome after forcing their way through a hedgerow: she had heard rumours that there were 'aeroplanes at Beckenden to shoot down the Zeppelins,' but had never expected to see them close up. When, she, her mother and her sisters had burst suddenly into the lane, they had found themselves halted on the track by an overalled airman, while flimsy, canvas-covered biplanes trundled across right in front of them causing the dust to fly into their eyes: it was the only time Olive had ever been near the place: it was from that time she remembered the 'cottage.'

As she and the boys neared their goal, the memory also came to her of the many times she had lain in bed with her sisters listening to the aeroplanes from Beckenden flying low over the village rooftops as they flew out to sea on night patrols: night was the favourite time for the Zeppelin raids and she had often wondered what happened to the young airmen who rose up to meet them. One of them she did know about: a young lieutenant named Watkins had taken off one September night in Seventeen to shoot down the first Zeppelin ever brought down over England: it had crossed the North Sea under cover of dark to bomb the factories at Melchborough, among them Hockmann's, the very works which the German bombers had half-destroyed two nights previously: clearly, they had not forgotten its existence. The Zeppelin had crashed on farmland to the north of Strood island, close by the estuary mouth, killing two of its crew: a police constable, who had seen it go down, rushed to the spot on his bicycle and by the light of his headlamp came across a dozen or so of the German crew marching in step behind their officers along one of the back lanes looking for someone to whom they could surrender. All the astonished constable could do was to point with his truncheon and lead them by the light of his bicycle lamp to the nearest army camp at Wivencaster eight miles away: it had been one of the wonders of the time.

It was not all humour, though: the bodies of two other of Beckenden's young fliers, a lieutenant and second-lieutenant observer, are buried in Gledlang churchyard: they were burned to death when their two-seater biplane crashed one afternoon in a ploughed field behind Old Man Stanson's farm opposite the village school: several of the village men ran to help, but could not get them out: Olive remembered standing in the school yard and seeing the column of smoke from the burning plane rising skywards behind the farmhouse. The whole village turned out for the funeral, the children from the little red-brick school lining the path as the coffins were carried up to the church door: she also remembered how frightened she had been when the six soldiers from the Wivencaster garrison forming the honour guard had fired their rifles in two salutes.

The so-called 'aerodrome cottage' was really nothing more than a single-storey, plain, cast-concrete, utilitarian building, some thirty feet long and painted a creamy white, which had served as a barracks and a mess for the dozen young Royal Flying Corps pilots briefly stationed there: it was given the name of 'cottage' by an itinerant family of farm labourers, who had moved down from the next county just after the First War to work on the nearby glebe farm and had taken up residence there, till the bleakness and loneliness of the place and the agricultural slump of the Twenties drove them back whence they had come.

THIRTY-SEVEN

WHEN eventually they turned into the enclosure where the so-called 'cottage' stood, Olive's heart sank: before her lay a moonscape, a place of utter dereliction: mound upon mound of grey smothering ash lay everywhere, while interspersed among it were other heaps, of clinker, of clay, of yellowed chalk and tar-blackened aggregate, of cement and rock, concrete and masonry, all the unusable, unwanted industrial detritus of three nearby towns, in fact! Beckenden aerodrome had become a dumping ground, a great rubbish tip!

For eleven years, unbeknown to Olive and of little concern to the villagers of Gledlang since it was so far from them, the separate councils of Wivencaster, Hamwyte and Maydun had combined to dump the whole of their refuse there. The cindered smaller 'field' was ideal for the purpose: it was in open country, there was no village of any size nearby and it had lain abandoned ever since the great push of August, Nineteen-Eighteen, when the victorious Allies had driven the Germans back from Amiens to the very slagheaps of Mons, where they had first clashed with Britain's 'Contemptible Little Army' four years before: two months later the war had ended. The larger cindered meadow, from which the planes had actually taken off, had been reclaimed for agricultural purposes by the glebe farmer soon after the Peace: its gap had been rewired, the cinders from it raked up and dumped on to the smaller stand and then it had been reploughed. But, with the market slumping in the early-Twenties, the old glebe farmer had deemed it not worth the trouble and effort to reclaim the smaller enclosure and it had remained unwanted and unfarmed, as had so many fields in that region.

Besides, the Government still owned it and they, it seemed, had forgotten its existence, which was not surprising since, on an Ordnance Survey map, so small an enclosure would have appeared as no more than a tiny oblong, with only a single building upon it and a narrow, winding lane leading to it, barely worth the effort of reclamation: the hand-painted notice declaring it to be War Department property, which had stood at the entrance, had long since fallen and now lay rotting in the lank grasses, along with the pole upon which the red warning flag had once been raised.

The three councils had reasoned that it was never likely to be used as an aerodrome again now that the war to end all wars had been fought and won: and, as they needed a place which was remote and unwanted, yet accessible, in which to dispose of the refuse from their growing towns, the enclosure at the forgotten Beckenden aerodrome was ideal for that purpose: besides, it was already being used by the farmer as a dump for the cinders he was raking off his other field: so what better place to use! It even had a cinder stand upon which their carts and lorries could turn. So to it, beginning in Twenty-Seven, the year after Olive had left the village, they had trundled cartload after cartload and lorry load after lorry load of clinker and ash from the three gas works of Wivencaster, Hamwyte and Maydun, plus all the waste from their various factories, from the iron works, the cabinet-making factory and the agricultural machinery makers at Maydun, the window makers, the fan makers, the boiler makers and the iron foundry at Hamwyte, the iron works, the steel foundry, the furniture factory and the implement makers at Wivencaster. Added to these were the weekly lorry loads of ash from the rows upon rows of terraced houses of all three, unwanted rubble from demolished buildings, dried red clay from sewer excavations, road-building and other pipe laying schemes, stones and black tar from road workings, the very sweepings of the streets even: all had been tipped there week after week, month after month, year after year, till mound after mound of it filled almost the whole of the smaller field.

But it was not this which so disheartened Olive: it was the utterly ruined state of the so-called cottage: it was roofless and windowless: and, worse, the greater part of it, two-thirds, in fact, lay buried under another great mound, a mound of household refuse some twenty to thirty feet high which threatened to engulf it entirely. For as well as the industrial waste, the good burghers of Wivencaster, Hamwyte and Maydun had over the intervening years trundled there on their carts and lorries everything that the town-dwellers no longer required: old armchairs, broken dining chairs, halves of tables, broken bed-steads, ripped mattresses, door-less wardrobes, drawer-less bureaux, rusting mangles, rusting tin baths, rusting frames of old bicycles, rusting metal pots and pans by the thousands, tin cans by the tens of thousands, bottomless buckets, lengths of splintered, nail-spiked timber, utensils with handles, uten-sils without handles, wheel-less prams, pram-less wheels, pane-less window frames, unwanted fenders, fire grates, rotting wooden doors, sawn floor-boards, cracked roof slates, lumps of rock and concrete, shattered crockery, shattered mirrors, shattered everything and anything: and ten score other things as well: everything which the three councils needed to dump well away from their own environs.

Lorries reversing on the hard had at first dumped their loads up against the walls of the cottage: then, when the walls themselves tumbled inwards, they had tipped their loads into it: only the need to preserve a turning space on the stand itself had prevented the whole building from being buried. The weight of refuse piled up against it and over it had eventually caved-in the roof, first at one end and then in its entirety: now, of the four external walls, only the gable end nearest to the road remained upright: of the rest, all that stood was a twelve-foot length of the front wall, encompassing a porch entrance and a soli-tary square window from which the frame and glass had long since disap-peared, plus an even smaller windowless section of the back wall which served to keep the other two standing. Only when the great mound could be seen from a mile away rising higher and higher above the intervening hedgerows had the two councils reluctantly ended their dumping and moved to another site in a disused sand and gravel quarry some five miles away. Over the years, wild grasses, thistles, nettles, clumps of ragwort and docks and spreading brambles had colonised the Beckenden mounds to mask the worst of their ap-pearance: but what was still visible told any passer-by that the place was and remained and would forever be a dump, a rubbish dump! It was to this place that Olive had brought her family through the now-teeming rain.

She had not expected to find a palace: she had just hoped that the cottage would be in a reasonable condition, one which she could clear out and clean so that it would at least be habitable and offer them some shelter in the winter months ahead. To her, as she looked at the ruined building, it seemed that she had made the journey through the rain for nothing: and had the twins and Mi-chael not been looking at her to gauge her reaction, she might well have bro-ken down in despair.

The doorway to the cottage itself was blocked by rubble and refuse so they could not even gain entry and, though the darkness by then was fast closing in,

Olive could see enough through the small solitary window to realise that the interior was as clogged with rubbish as was the outside: even the half-dozen triangular timber struts over which the laths and the roof slates had been nailed had fallen inside and now, rotted and shattered, poked up at all angles. All Olive could do was to push the pram under the lee of the gable end to shelter from the rain and curse herself for having made what had proved to be such a futile journey to so outlandish and forbidding a place: and to curse, too, those who had so wantonly destroyed the building which had been her last hope.

Beside her, the twins, trying to gain extra shelter up against the pram, were looking up at their mother, waiting for her to decide what to do next: alongside them, Jack shivered, his teeth chattering: in the pram the sweeping rain was spattering upon an awakened and upset Michael. Olive herself felt numbed and chilled: the horizon was a darkening curtain of gloom: nothing, not so much as the glow from a single paraffin light in a solitary farmhouse window, could be seen: they were cut off from the world, it seemed.

It was Jimmy and Patrick who noticed the chimney pointing up into the sky from the slope of the great mound no more than a few yards from where they stood: the two boys looked at each other, frowned and then, ignoring the rain, splashed through the puddles towards it, determined to find out why a chimney should be sticking up from there of all places. Beneath it, there was a sacking flap hanging from an iron bar: Olive, being more concerned with the twins and trying to keep herself and Michael dry under the lee of the wall, did not notice her two eldest lift the sack and disappear into what seemed to be an entrance to the mound itself: in less than twenty seconds they had reappeared, shouting excitedly.

'Mum, Mum, we've found somewhere! Come and see!' That from Jimmy as he and his brother splashed back towards the group huddled against the wall.

'It's got a stove in it with a chimney!' That from Patrick, eager to have his say.

'And a room with two mattresses,' from Jimmy again, pointing towards the entrance and setting off back across the puddles, in his excitement oblivious to the rain.

'And a roof to keep the rain out.' from Patrick, beckoning his mother to follow.

'And a door.'

'And a place to light a fire.'

'Where?' demanded Olive, taken aback by their unexpected exuberance: even though she could see the chimney and the entrance for herself, she could not bring herself to believe them: surely they were exaggerating?

'Over here, Mum,' cried Jimmy, pausing to ensure she knew where to follow him, 'over here where the chimney is.'

Olive allowed herself to be pulled by Patrick across the intervening space, wheeling the pram: Jack and the twins followed reluctantly, unhappy at having to leave the shelter of the wall: ahead of them, Jimmy had already disappeared behind the sacking.

'We just took a look to see what was there,' Patrick shouted. 'We saw this doorway and we found this place.'

'Come in, Mum, come in and take a look,' Jimmy was shouting from inside. 'In here.'

Patrick gave his mother a broad grin and disappeared behind the sacking to join his brother: Olive knew that she had no choice but to follow: rivulets of water were running down her own face and that of the exposed Michael, while Jack, John and Thomas cowered beside her, hoping her height would shelter them. It was almost with a sigh at her own foolishness that she lifted the sacking curtain.

Behind it, was a warped, blue-painted door still fixed by its hinges to one side of a half-broken lintel: the lintel itself had been crudely repaired with sections of another and rusted nails driven into it: Jack and the twins scurried inside: Olive followed, pulling the pram after her.

THIRTY-EIGHT

TO HER surprise, Olive found herself in a crudely-built chamber, some eight or nine feet square, and just high enough for her to stand upright: the walls were all fashioned from doors – pale blue doors, green doors, yellow and brown doors, white doors, some already beginning to rot – all placed upright and held in position by lengths of wood nailed across them at knee and eye height. Down the centre of the 'room' was a long central beam, an old floor joist, from which other 'beams' of various thicknesses, laths, lengths of skirting, parts of door lintels and window frames extended to the sides where they rested on the tops of the various doors: these lesser 'beams' supported the ceiling, which had been constructed from what looked like the splintered doors of some old wardrobes, plus some sections of rusting corrugated iron sheeting. To support the central beam, a cast iron post had been driven into the ground, wedged with bricks at the bottom and tacked in position at the top with nails: the floor itself was made of other old bricks laid dry on the earth.

What immediately caught Olive's eye was a black, cast-iron range filling one whole wall, complete with an oven, a grate and a fender: on top of it, stood two battered, blue-handled aluminium saucepans and an old iron kettle, all of which bore the signs of having been recovered from the dump outside: blackened food had congealed at the bottom of the two saucepans, though what it was, or had been, even Olive as a cook was unable to say. At the back of the range, a screen of loose bricks had been built to contain any heat and prevent anything outside catching fire, while a chimney, made from a length of cast iron downpipe such as is found on the outside of houses to carry away effluent from toilets, had been fitted to the range using a section of a flanged tin can tightly bound with wire to seal the join: there was a second such seal where the chimney exited the chamber. The fire grate itself still contained ash, showing that a fire had once been lit there: if others could light a fire safely, Olive reasoned, then so could she: a fire meant warmth, cooked food eventually and dry clothing for her and the children.

In front of the range lay an old sacking rug, upon either side of which were two rickety kitchen chairs, their legs sawn down to half their height, either to level them or to cut off splintered or rotted wood. It was, an amazed Olive realised, a tramps' den, built patiently and skilfully of materials recovered from the rubbish heap itself. Whoever had built it had first burrowed into the heap to clear a space large enough for their purpose: then they had collected the various doors, nailed them into place to form the walls so that the den was sturdy and secure: after that, they had put up their central pillar, laid the various beams across, placed the corrugated iron sheeting and other doors on top, then weatherproofed it by the simple expedient of piling all the rubbish they could find back on top. Somehow they had managed to drag in the discarded range, connect the downpipe chimney and then drive that up through the rubbish piled on top. With scrunched newspaper and kindling wood, some of which still lay in the carefully bricked hearth, as well as some logs and pieces of coke in a handleless pail alongside, they had lit a fire in the grate to warm the place and to do their cooking: it was almost as if whoever had built it had left everything so that it would be on hand when they returned.

Momentarily, Olive had a frightening thought that whoever had built the den might at that very moment be walking back towards it through the rain and dark outside, but then she dismissed the thought: clearly, the place had not been used for sometime: the dust on the floor, the cold ash in the grate and the mouldy, congealed food in the two saucepans told her that. Besides she had Jimmy and Patrick with her and the aggressive Jimmy could more than hold his own, even at the age of nine: all that mattered was that she was there with the children, in the dry, out of the rain and cold and, once she had got the fire lit, in the warm.

'Look in here, Mum.'

Jimmy had swung open one of the doors which formed the wall to the left of the range to reveal a second smaller chamber, again fashioned from doors the same as the first, with the same central pillar supporting a cross-beam holding up the ceiling, it, too, built from the lighter materials and corrugated iron sheeting. The floor again comprised the same loose bricks and on it were laid two single mattresses: both were covered in dust and dirt and Olive shuddered at the thought that the 'dirt' was most probably rats' droppings. She knew that, even if the dump had lain disused for a number of years, such a place would inevitably have attracted rats: it was ideal for nesting and, even if all food dumped there had long since rotted away, they would still forage among the fields and ditches and hedgerows all around: they would be there no matter what and Olive gave an involuntary shudder at the thought of a rat scuttling under her feet or, worse, sitting on the sleeping forms of a blanket-wrapped John, Thomas or Michael: but with the rain teeming down outside, she had to discount the rats and her fear of them and remain.

Along one wall in the first chamber was a crude shelf upon which stood a bottle with a candle jammed into its neck: it was covered in dust and cobwebs: a box of matches lay beside the candle: the box was slightly damp, but inside were several unstruck matches among the many blackened ones which Olive was able to add to her meagre supply. The only way to test the range and find out whether the chimney operated properly was to light a fire: the exit was immediately behind her so there was no real danger if the place became too smoky: all she had to do was push the pram out into the rain and make sure that the others followed. As a precaution, she turned the pram to face the door and had Jimmy take hold of it ready to rush it outside if the worst happened: as a further precaution, she made Patrick, Jack, the twins and Michael all stand behind her nearest to the door while she raked out the ashes as best she could with a length of wood, laid the fire with the scrunched-up newspaper and kindling, placed one of the small logs upon it and, crossing her fingers, lit it with a match, which fortunately flared at the first strike.

It took a quarter-hour to get the fire going properly: much to Olive's amazement and relief, the chimney drew well: and once the fire had caught, she was able to place a second log upon the blaze to keep it going, then a third and some of the coke from the pail: eventually, the heat was such that the boys were able to gather round it to warm themselves, Jimmy and Patrick bagging the two chairs, while the others seated themselves upon the sacking rug. Consequently, their tea-cum-supper consisted of slices of toasted bread spread with margarine and jam, but at least it was something and the boys ate it with satisfied smiles before a warming fire: the adventure, Jimmy and Patrick now acknowledged, had resumed!

They could not go straight to sleep, of course: before any of the boys could settle down for the night in the inner chamber: the two mattresses had to be cleaned, which Olive did as best she could by giving them a good shaking in the open doorway, with the rain pouring down outside, then scraping off the dust and grime with a flat piece of wood. Fortunately, there was no evidence of any rats' droppings as she had feared so, in the absence of anything better, she replaced the mattresses on the floor, spread the two blankets and settled Michael, the twins and a very tired Jack upon one of them. Michael fell asleep within minutes of lying down, contentedly sucking his thumb, followed a short while after by the twins and Jack. Jimmy and Patrick occupied the other mattress and, as boys will, remained awake for a good hour or so, talking about all manner of things, but mostly about aeroplanes, before they, too, fell silent: all slept in their clothes, with their jackets pulled over them for warmth.

There was no sleep for Olive, however, till she had fed, burped and changed Joseph: he was not happy to be awakened and required much coaxing before he took the milk: Theresa had made up a bottle before Olive left the house, but the best she could do to warm it was to hold it in front of the fire.

The range fire was beginning to die when Olive finally bowed her head upon her knees, sitting with her back against the door wall in the outer chamber and her coat drawn up around her: the last thing she remembered before she, too, succumbed to tiredness was the noise of the rain drumming on the refuse outside.

THIRTY-NINE

WHEN Olive awoke, she found herself curled up on the bare brick floor, with her cheek and forehead pressed against it and aching terribly: painfully she climbed to her feet, massaging the unexpected stiffness in her joints. A thin sliver of light was showing through the gap between the door and the lintel: outside, when she lifted the sack curtain, she found that the rain had stopped, though there was a cool breeze blowing and somewhere behind the grey wash of the sky skulked a pale watery sun.

Olive's first thought was that she needed to wash her face, as much to shock herself into full wakefulness as to cleanse herself of the brick dust: too many nights in the air raid shelter at the end of Rupert Road and Robert's long absence had of late induced in her a less fussy approach to her hygiene: too often, on arriving back at the flat, she had simply splashed cold water on her face and reapplied her cheek powder. In the past week, since returning from Thurstone, she realised, she had hardly used her lipstick and face powder at all.

Not that she was not clean, she told herself: at Theresa's, after she had slept that first day, she had had her first proper wash in over a week, albeit at the kitchen sink while still wearing her slip: but at least she had been able to spray on some eau de cologne. Her sister and niece had bathed Joseph in a bowl while she slept and had then given Michael and the twins a wash, standing them in the sink: even Jack, too, after his sleep, had allowed his smiling cousin to sit him on the kitchen table while she washed his legs and upper body as well as his face and neck, though he refused to take off his trousers. It was the two eldest who concerned Olive: Jimmy and Patrick had resisted anything other than a cursory wipeover of face, hands and knees with a damp flannel, insisting, as was to be expected, that they did not need a wash then, but promising that they would agree to having one later, on the following Friday night, say! At the time, Olive herself had been too tired to argue: now she intended to see that all the children, the two eldest included, were properly washed.

When they had first arrived at the aerodrome, out of the corner of her eye, she had noticed a pump standing behind the cottage, at the far end and almost buried by the same debris which smothered that end of the building. Though the ground behind the cottage was still sodden from the rain, she was able to pick her way to it through the puddles and smaller scattered mounds: it was a matter of moments before she had pulled aside some old pram wheels and some twisted sheets of galvanized iron which leaned against it. A quick test of the pump handle determined that it was not too rusted and, though it was stiff and squeaked alarmingly, a few vigorous leverings up and down worked it loose: after a few moments, water began gushing from its spout. At first, the water was stained a reddish brown, but that did not deter Olive: such a thing was to be expected when a pump had not been worked for sometime, especially in an area where the water was drawn up through heavy red clay. It took only a minute or so of steady pumping before it became clear: cautiously, Olive cupped her hands to drink and was surprised and pleased to find that the water was, after all, quite palatable, though icy cold.

After washing her face, neck and arms and drying them on the hem of her pinafore, she returned to where the children were still sleeping, took out the two saucepans Theresa had given her and carried them back to the pump to fill: when she returned to the hideaway, she found Jimmy and Patrick both stirring, rubbing at their eyes and stretching and yawning, awakened by their mother's movement. It was an effort to get them outside, but, reluctantly, they went to the pump to wash their faces and knees, though whether they washed anywhere else Olive considered it unlikely: they dried themselves on their pullovers.

By the time Jack and the twins had awakened, Olive had the fire blazing up and water boiling in the saucepans so she was able to dip a shirt-tail flannel into one of them and wash their faces, ears, necks and knees and dry them on her pinafore without too much protest.

That done, food became the priority, especially for the two youngest and the twins: Olive was thankful that no scum had formed on the water as it boiled in the two saucepans, so when it had cooled a little she was able to make up a bottle for Joseph with the last of her powdered milk: as she cradled the hungry baby in her arms, she was glad to see he sucked eagerly and seemingly contentedly at it.

For the others, it was a matter of sharing: there was only the last of the bread which Theresa, had given her and the porridge oats. The old bone-handled knife, which Theresa had included with the other cutlery, was not at all sharp, almost blunt, in fact, and Olive had struggled to saw the bread as thin as she would have liked: consequently, she had used up most of it in making the toast the previous night: now there was only enough bread left for four slices. Jimmy and Patrick seized the first two for themselves even as they fell away from the loaf, pushing their younger brothers aside to snatch them up: then, mindless of the others, they spread them with the last of the margarine and rather too liberally with what remained of the jam so that there was little left for the others. Olive's anger towards them fell on deaf ears and they giggled as they sat together on their mattress wolfing down the bread. The third piece she buttered herself, spread it with what little jam she could scrape out and cut it in half for the twins to share: it meant poor Jack and Michael had to make do with the harder crust, half each, and the scrapings of margarine, but no jam. Jack did not seem to mind, for he made no complaint: Michael, however, set up an immediate wailing when he found he could not tear his half of the tough crust properly with his tiny teeth and, in exasperation, Olive took the bread from him and dunked it in one of the saucepans to soften it. By that time, the porridge had boiled up in Theresa's bigger saucepan and they ate that in turn off the three plates: Jimmy, Patrick and Jack first, then the twins and Michael: however, with no sugar to sweeten it and no milk to cool it, there was much grimacing and screwing up of faces as each blew upon his before putting it into their mouths: but at least they ate it and Olive had the satisfaction of seeing all her offspring eat.

After that, their breakfast finished, such as it was, the boys went outside to explore their new-found home: only then was Olive able to make tea for herself in the smaller saucepan from the leaves Theresa had given her, though she had to use what was almost the last of the baby's powdered milk to thicken it and, again having no sugar or saccharin to put in it, grimaced with every mouthful: but at least it was hot and, after the weariness of the night, restored her spirits as she sat beside the range, listening to the shouts and laughter of her offspring outside as they climbed one mound after another and shouted defiance at each other the way boys do, before jumping down into the deep valleys between.

The irony of the situation – that she and her family were sheltering in an abandoned tramps' den built into the side of a mound of rubbish on a deserted dump – did not escape Olive: those in London who knew her would have been astonished by how far she had fallen: but she consoled herself with the thought that someone somewhere was probably worse off. It suddenly struck her as amusing and she found herself smiling at the thought, that the previous afternoon, as the fine rain began sweeping across the open fields, she had angrily whirled on her tardy, sour-faced brood and, in order to keep them moving and to stifle a rebellion of the two eldest, had sarcastically promised: 'Don't worry, we'll find somewhere even if we have to sleep in a haystack!'

She had said it laughingly, but as the rain grew heavier and more sustained, the worry had grown in her that they might have to do just that and burrow into a convenient farm straw stack: that was why she pressed on to the aerodrome cottage, in the hope that she would not have to do so. At the time they were passing just such a straw stack: it stirred memories of how she and her two sisters, as young girls, had themselves once burrowed six or seven feet into the side of just such a stack to create a den: there in the warm and dry, they had hidden themselves away from their brothers and the other troubles of the world, lost in their own secret place. They never considered there was any danger in what they did, no country child did, so long as one was not foolish enough to light a match or a candle or build a fire in the den, and also so long as one remembered to prop up the tunnel entrance in case of collapse. Olive and her sisters had used a thick branch broken off an old elm in a gale: there, in their secret place, they had sat for the whole of one summer afternoon away from their brothers and the rest of the world, until hunger and the approach of teatime had forced them home.

However, that had been in a past which now seemed almost idyllic and pleasant by comparison with the grim and uncertain present. A little while later, as Olive sat on a dry lump of concrete outside the abandoned den, cradling Joseph, with Michael alongside cheerfully banging on two different-sized tin cans with a piece of wood, watching the others scrambling over the various mounds, she was acutely conscious of another fact: that if they did not find somewhere else to stay, they might have to spend the next few nights in the hideaway: perhaps even the next week or fortnight! Or the next month! Not that Olive minded so much: it had been warm and dry when the fire was lit, the chimney at least drew out the smoke and none had filtered back into the two chambers, which, given a good sweep, could be made reasonably habitable: it was just the stigma of being forced to live in a hole in the side of a rubbish tip of all places which grieved her.

FORTY

SHE let the boys play all morning: most of the time, Jimmy, Patrick, Jack and the twins seemed content to roam across the tops of the various mounds, particularly the mound half-covering the cottage with household rubbish as though they expected whatever they were seeking would be found there: what that was Olive had no inkling. Every now and again the boys would stop and wrench at things half buried by other refuse: a shout at some discovery would go up, they would spend the next few minutes or so tugging it out, carelessly throwing aside other refuse to get at it, then all would gather in a huddle as if inspecting it and discussing its merits or otherwise. Some things the boys hauled out were greeted with whoops of delight: others were tossed aside with glum faces: to Olive, it was just something which boys did to occupy themselves.

The purpose of all their activity soon became evident when a number of tyreless bicycle wheels, the rusting frames of three bicycles, a selection of pram wheels and pieces of wood of various lengths and practicality, were all dumped in a pile on the bare cinders outside the entrance to the den. Some of their finds, like the splintered fruit boxes, it was clear, would be good only for kindling: but the remainder, pieces of broken laths, quarter-lengths of planking and short, sawn floorboards, sections of warped cupboard doors and the like, despite their degree of decay, Jimmy and Patrick stated quite categorically would be turned eventually into at least two carts, while the various bicycles would be rebuilt into untreaded, chainless boneshakers, one each for Jimmy, Patrick and Jack.

It was near to noon, after Joseph's second sleep and bottle, that Olive finally placed him and Michael in the pram, hoisted the twins back into their usual back-to-back positions and called for a reluctant trio of searchers to join her.

'I have to go back into the village. We need some more food,' she informed them and was rather glad when the three said they preferred to remain at the dump to continue their building work: it meant Olive could walk there and back more quickly without having to turn constantly to hurry the three eldest. Even as she had sat outside that morning, watching the boys leaping across the various mounds, she had calmly conceded to herself that they would have to spend another night there: and perhaps another night after that: and still more nights after that.

When she reached the village, Olive called first at Theresa's cottage to reassure her sister and her niece that they were all safe and well: Dorothy had had as sleepless a night as her poor mother worrying about the babies and the twins: Olive's news cheered them both. 'I've got somewhere at Beckenden. I found it last night. It's a bit out in the wilds, but it'll do,' Olive told them, giving no more detail than that. Not unnaturally, her sister and her niece were just pleased that she had 'found somewhere,' never suspecting that the 'somewhere' was an abandoned den on a rubbish dump' on the old aerodrome site down a track which diverted off the Beckenden road itself. As the way to Beckenden was no more than a cart track itself, it was unlikely that anyone would realise her family were there unless they actually saw them on the tip itself: and, since it was so far out of the village and in so obscure a place, Olive considered that was highly unlikely. During the whole of the time she had sat there that morning, not a single vehicle of any description, not even a bicycle or a horse and cart, had climbed the ridge along the Beckenden road: and, as the grass growing down the centre of the track which ran off it to the old aerodrome was such, Olive was convinced that no one had been past the entrance for a good few months, perhaps not for a year or more. Her secret was safe for the moment, so long as the children did not blurt it out: the babies could not yet talk and the twins would not say anything, she knew, because they accepted their circumstances no matter what and knew no different. However, she would need to have a word with the three eldest, especially Jack, and coach them into what they were to answer when asked where they lived. 'We live in Beckenden,' was all they needed to say: no more than that.

She did just that when she called in at the butcher's shed in Hedge Street to register with Old Man Moulton and to buy a half-dozen sausages and some scragend meat, giving her address as no more than 'Beckenden road' as she handed over her coupons and most of her remaining change: Old Man Moulton accepted it without so much as a raised eyebrow, for it was well known there was no shop of any kind anywhere near Beckenden and the three isolated farming families living there always came into Gledlang to shop. Olive did the same at Fred Thorn's bakery at the top of Shoe Street, where, with the very last of the money from her purse, she bought two loaves. Her third call was by necessity at the post office-cum-grocery store in the Square because she needed to cash the last of the stamps from her post office savings book to make her purchases: in doing so, she also used up the last of her food coupons but was able to buy a full packet of Quaker porridge oats, a tin of condensed milk, two allowed tins of powdered milk for the baby, a green waxed packet of American dried egg powder, some saccharins, a half-pound of margarine, one jar of homemade loganberry jam, thickened with carrot, six pounds of potatoes, two sticks of rhubarb, two onions, a parsnip, a pound of rice, a tin each of processed peas and haricot beans, a half-pound of American prunes and four rashers of bacon as well as some cooking fat. It was a joy to do such a big shop without having to wait for an hour in a queue: Olive did not mind even having to field the usual questions from the nosy postmistress, Ma Rowthey, as she filled in the obligatory 'newcomer's' registration form before handing over the necessary food coupons.

'Address?'

'Beckenden road.'

'Since when?'

'Since yesterday.'

'Didn't know there were any places up there vacant?'

'We found one.' Contemptuously from Olive: then sarcastically: 'Some people don't look hard enough, do they? They give up too easy. This place was empty and we're living in it – for now anyway. It's small, but we'll manage. At least we'll be in the warm and dry this winter.'

There was no query other than that because, although Beckenden was a hamlet in its own right, it was considered part of the parish of Gledlang simply because Gledlang's vicar preached in both churches and thus the parishes were linked: people in Gledlang were used to seeing what few people from Beckenden there were in their midst and almost regarded them as Gledlangites. Besides, Ma Rowthey was too busy writing to notice Olive's cheeks reddening with the shame of the deception and instead greeted the news with a sniff. 'How many children have I got to put down?' she demanded.

'Seven,' answered Olive quietly.

'Seven!' acknowledged Ma Rowthey unfazed: she was used to registering families of seven, eight, nine and ten children: such were the times. 'What ages are they?' And so on.

The food would be enough at least to last the family for the rest of the week and beyond. After that, Olive's priorities were quite simple: to continue her search for a cottage and to find work and earn some money from somewhere, any work. However, to meet either of her priorities, she first needed to disencumber herself and to get Jimmy, Patrick and Jack into the village school: that way she would be free to continue her search both for a cottage and work, even if she had to push the pram halfway to Wivencaster to do it! The need to find work became even more urgent as she stood at the small post office grille and watched the fat postmistress cash the stamps in her post office savings book: she had money for the moment, but where would she find work?

By the time she returned to the aerodrome field, Jimmy and Patrick had built the first of their boneshaker bicycles and were taking it in turns to race around the remaining part of the clear apron amid much whooping and shouting. They were not at all pleased when their mother told them, that on the morrow, they would be going to school: only Jack seemed pleased.

'You know you can't stay off school for ever,' Olive told them bluntly. 'You have to go to school sometime so you may as well start now!'

They would need clean clothes, or at least clothes cleaner than those which they were wearing: they had not changed those since they had left London. As none of the boys wore underpants – Olive had always considered them an unnecessary luxury she could not afford on what little money Robert used to give her for housekeeping – she decided she would have to wash and dry their trousers, jackets, shirts and pullovers and dry them overnight: and she knew full well what protests that would bring from all three. She could almost imagine the chorus of bleating which would arise when she ordered them to strip: but nighttime really was the only time when she could do it: the boys would just have sleep in their vests while their clothes dried in front of the range.

FORTY-ONE

OLIVE duly carried out her threat the next morning, marching Jimmy, Patrick and Jack back down the muddy and potholed Beckenden track and along the smoother surfaced Salter road to the two-room village school in Tithe Street: her two eldest were in a sullen mood, dawdling as much as they dared some forty yards behind their mother all the way: several times Olive had to turn and angrily call for them to catch up, which they did with ever greater reluctance the nearer they got to the school.

Jack, however, walked beside his mother: ever since she had brought him back from Thurstone, he had remained close by her at every opportunity: when they walked with the pram, while Patrick and Jimmy were piggybacking the twins or walking on ahead, or even lagging behind as they did that day, Jack would always be alongside his mother, hanging on to the pram handle: saying nothing, just keeping pace with her: he would even sit beside her, when they stopped. Sometimes she would look down and find him gazing up at her, expressionless, as if trying to read her thoughts: it was as if he were afraid that she might disappear again and not reappear for a further nine months, like before, or perhaps never, and he was determined not to allow it to happen by having her always in his sight. As they pushed open the wooden gates and entered the school's potholed playground, his face was a solemn mask that did not reveal anything about what he might be thinking on having to start at another school: he more than the other two, worried Olive.

Though she had been able to wash and dry the clothes of her two eldest overnight, she had had no means of ironing them: consequently they were all crumpled: nor had she been able to darn the trouser seats of either, much as they needed attention, or the elbows of their bomber jackets. It did not help matters that both preferred to wear their socks down around their ankles rather than tie them with elastic under their knees: and, despite Olive's best efforts to get them to rub a rag over their boots, the footwear of both was still mud-splattered. Only Jack looked neat and tidy, but then Olive had washed his face, hands and knees herself, combed his hair into a parting and rubbed his boots till the toecaps shone.

It was a quarter past ten, the time of the morning break, when Olive pushed open the wooden gates and wheeled the large pram towards the porch, with the twins trotting alongside and the three eldest following. Curious children paused at their games to stare: several of the girls, recognising Olive as the woman in the churchyard, began to giggle: others, seeing the dishevelled state of Jimmy and Patrick smirked at them: a group of boys kicking a rag ball at a 'goal' drawn in chalk on a high brickwall stopped their game and warily eyed the newcomers to see if they presented any threat: mostly their eyes were on the taller Jimmy.

A sharp-nosed woman in her fifties was supervising the children and came forward as Olive neared the porch: she introduced herself in, what was to Olive, a near-unintelligible Scottish accent with the words, 'I'm Mrs. Mackay, the infants' teacher.' Then fixing Jimmy, Patrick and Jack with a stern gaze, like the beady eye of an eagle settling upon its prey, she demanded: 'Are you bringing these three to school here? You're a little late. They should have been here at nine.'

Olive, who had timed her arrival to coincide with the morning playtime so that she would be able to see the headmistress and not disrupt classes, replied equally as curtly. 'I realise that! I've just come to register them. I wouldn't expect them to start before tomorrow. I haven't seen the headmistress yet!' The older woman reddened at the slight: at the same time, Olive thought of her own years in the 'Little Room,' helping the younger ones to take off their coats, escorting them 'across the yard' when they needed to go, reading to them from a book of fairy tales, helping them with their letters. How many cowed and trembling five-year-olds, she wondered, looking at the hawk-nosed woman – how many trembling five-year-olds had wet themselves rather than raise their hands and incur Mrs. Mackay's wrath by asking if they could 'go to the lav' across the yard?

Mrs. Mackay huffily allowed Olive to leave the pram with Michael and Joseph still seated in it at the porch entrance so that they could watch the other children at play, then curtly directed her to the main arched door, unaware that the younger woman had passed through it thousands of times during the years she had spent at the school, first as a pupil, then as a teachers' assistant, helping the ageing Mother Jepson look after the infants in the self-same room in which Mrs. Mackay now taught: until her mother had fallen ill and she had left to look after her.

Stepping into the high-ceilinged porch again after so many years brought back all the old memories for Olive: for a brief moment, it was almost as if she had never left. The tiny corner sink at which the children queued to wash their hands at the end of their morning and midday playtimes was still there, as was the grubby roller-towel alongside. As she lifted the latch on the brown-painted main door and stepped again into the 'Big Room,' where the seven- to eleven-year-olds were taught (in her day, the seven- to thirteen-year-olds), she felt a sudden pang of nostalgia: the same wooden desks stood in the same four lines of five. They were the self-same desks which had been installed when the school had opened seven decades before, with cast-iron legs, hard wooden seats, double inkwells covered by sliding brass caps and scratched and gouged tops which lifted to reveal a narrow shelf underneath upon which exercise books, pens, pencils and rulers were kept, though, in Olive's time, all that had been kept there had been a framed slate for each child, some broken pieces of chalk and a cleaning rag.

The high, vaulted room was still painted in the same two tones of green as it had been when she had sat in it, dark on the lower half and a lighter tone on the top half, with a narrow darker brown line, almost black, dividing the two: it was as if time had stood still. Indeed, it was obvious to Olive that the walls had not been painted since she had left: in several places, thin catkins of flaking paint hung down from the lower edges of bare, discoloured patches, while around the room, in an attempt to hide these, various children's pictures had been pinned, of the kind Olive herself had drawn as a nine- and ten-year-old: washing lines on windy days, sailing boats on the estuary, cows and horses indistinguishable from dogs grazing in vivid green meadows with bright yellow suns spinning overhead in scratchy blue skies.

In the middle of the facing wall was a second arched door, which led to the 'Little Room,' where Olive had spent her happy years helping Old Mother Jepson: immediately to the left of this door stood a black cast-iron stove, caged by a three-sided fireguard, inside of which stood the ubiquitous blue coke scuttle and poker: next to that was an open cupboard, its lower shelves piled with various books and boxes, mostly of chalk, and its top shelf lined with a row of gluepots and small coloured tins and jars. The headmistress's desk, at which in Olive's day, had sat the prim, stiff, grey-haired spinster, Old Ma Lewis, was in the farthest corner, facing the rows of desks occupied by the oldest of the boys and girls: the four seats at very front of the row, those nearest to the headmistress's desk, were always occupied by the four brightest of the older scholars: the rest sat in serried ranks behind in diminishing order of competence and comprehension: from those who one day would take their place on the front rank to the hopeless dullards right at the back. Olive had sat on the front rank for her last three years there as a pupil, constantly praised by Old Ma Lewis: conversely, her best friend, Ethel Garner, had sat at the back, constantly chastised. In her last year as a pupil, Olive had been awarded a prize for gaining a hundred marks out of a hundred in an arithmetic test: multiplication, long division and fractions, plus having to solve difficult sums about trains travelling at different speeds to pass each other and questions about how many differently priced apples could a certain amount of money buy: she had also scored a further eighty-nine marks in her spelling test: strange that the one word which had stumped her that day, she recalled, should have come back to haunt her: it was 'accommodation': she had spelled it with only one 'm.'

Olive also had the best attendance record and, as the star pupil at thirteen, had been presented by the vicar at that time, Reverend Jolly, with a painted wooden pencil case at the end-of-year prize-giving: it angered her still how she had hurried home to show it to her mother, only for a jealous brother Percy to gleefully stamp on at the first opportunity a month later.

It was because of Olive's brightness and her willingness that Old Ma Lewis had recommended her as a helper to the ageing Mother Jepson, then in her sixty-sixth year and all too prone to doze in her chair beside the stove on cold winter afternoons, leaving her charges to do whatever they wished: till Olive, just fourteen, was sent in to bring some organisation. She would dearly have loved to have become a proper teacher, but knew that could never be: the times conspired against her and her kind then. At least, helping Old Mother Jepson gave her the chance to dream as she taught the younger children: it also raised her status in the village, too, which some resented and others commended. 'Fancy, little Olive Chapman being given such a post! A teacher's assistant! The very idea!' from the disagreeable. And 'Good luck to her! One in the eye for those two doltish brothers of hers!' from the agreeable.

How those who envied and despised her then would laugh now if they knew from where she had walked that morning: from a tramps' hideaway on an abandoned rubbish dump! It would all filter out sometime, Olive knew: but till then she would endeavour to keep it secret.

Olive pushed the whole matter from her mind as she ushered the twins through the door and, with a withering look, commanded the two eldest and Jack to follow.

Old Ma Lewis had long since gone: at the headmistress's desk now sat a woman Olive did not know and about whom she had only heard from Theresa: 'She's a widow. Come here from Dudley in the Midlands. Husband had cancer. Committed suicide, they say. Cut his wrists with a razor in his bath, then hit himself over the head with a hammer!'

Mrs. Popplewell, or Old Ma Pop, as the children had quickly nicknamed her, turned out to be a bespectacled, grey-haired woman in her early fifties, with a wide smile: she was dressed in a sober pleated, brown tweed skirt, cream blouse with a lace front and a beige cardigan: she was seated at her desk at the far end of the Big Room, holding a cup of tea in one hand and nibbling on a biscuit. On the desk in front of her were two piles of green exercise books: one pile lay open and she was ploughing through it with frequent despairing sighs before transferring each book to the closed pile with much headshaking.

On hearing the rattle of the latch, the headmistress looked up and removed her spectacles, then quickly stood up in surprise when she saw Olive advancing towards her leading two wide-eyed toddlers by their hands while three others, two of whom looked distinctly surly, waited just inside the door, unwilling to enter too far into the lion's den.

'May I help you?' Mrs. Popplewell began, coming forward a little way: it was a much kinder, more welcoming tone than the vicar had used two days before, Olive noted.

'I've come to see if I can get the boys in school,' said Olive. 'We've just come down from London three days ago. My name's Olive Cullen. I was a girl here till I left and went up to London to work. We've been bombed out so I've brought the boys down here. Jimmy is nine, Patrick is eight and Jack is six. He's started school, but only in the infants. I'd like to get the three of them in here as soon as possible. They need to be back in school.'

Unused to mothers arriving mid-morning with children in tow, demanding places at her school, the flustered teacher had to return to her desk to consult what Olive recognised was the long, narrow, black-covered registration book: as there had never been more than sixty children at the school in her day, thirty-eight in the Big Room and twenty-two in the Little Room, Olive knew that there were always one or two desks vacant in both rooms.

After several seconds of lip-pursing, Ma Popplewell raised one eyebrow enquiringly, as if seeking Olive's permission, and announced with a bemused smile: 'They can start tomorrow if you wish.'

'The sooner the better as far as I'm concerned,' declared a thankful Olive. 'They're only mooching about where they are. Patrick's good at sums, Jimmy's more practical – good with his hands. Jack? He's just started, but I'm hopeful he'll do well.'

As the teacher carefully wrote down the names and dates of birth of each with a dark blue fountain pen, the inevitable question came.

'And what is the address?'

'Beckenden Road.' Olive replied in the same casual manner as she had in the post-office-cum-grocery store. 'I've got a place this side for now, but I'm hopeful I might get something here in the village eventually rather than being stuck out there. There aren't the places about at the moment, but I'm still looking.'

The explanation, vague as it was, seemed to satisfy the headmistress. 'I must say I don't know Beckenden at all,' she confided as she wrote. 'I have only been here two years myself so I don't know the area at all well.' Her disclosure pleased Olive: it meant no exact explanation of where in Beckenden they lived needed to be given.

The registration accomplished and the day for their start settled, Olive also disclosed the relevant facts that her two eldest had had to change schools a number of times in the past year while they had been in Thurstone as a result of being moved from one hostel to another: it brought a murmur of surprise from the teacher, but she made no comment other than that. Instead, she asked about each boy's health, whether they had ever had ringworm or impetigo, mumps or measles, when they had last been checked for head lice, etcetera, writing down Olive's replies on a sheet of paper before informing her that the district nurse would be making her quarterly visit to the school in the next month and she would ensure they were each given a thorough check-up.

Patrick and Jimmy were not at all enamoured of the school. 'It's a bit small,' was Patrick's verdict as soon as they were outside.

'I don't think much of this place,' was Jimmy's comment as they crossed the playground towards the road and he returned the stares of the other boys. 'It's a bit of a dump? Do we have to go there, Mum?'

'Of course, you do!' hissed an irritated Olive. 'Why else would I go through the bother of registering you? You start tomorrow and like it, all three of you!' Her thoughts were dwelling on something else: there was something she needed to ask her sister Theresa.

From Jack, holding on to the pram handle beside her, there was just silence: his face had not changed since entering or leaving: Olive did not know whether he was pleased or apprehensive.

FORTY-TWO

THE NEXT morning they set off for the village just before eight, after a break-fast of toast, porridge and tea: though, with just saccharins to sweeten it and condensed milk to colour it, the tea drew grimaces from the twins. For lunch, Olive cut Jimmy, Patrick and Jack a sandwich apiece and spread butter and jam upon it: Jimmy would carry them and distribute them to the others at dinnertime. Ma Popplewell had promised she would apply to the school board for free meals for the three of them when the daily dinners were delivered to the school in the little green van from Maydun, but that might not be for a week or two, she had said, and Olive was being cautious. She did not want the boys to go all day without something to eat, even though they had twice done that recently, waiting patiently, confident that their mother would eventually provide something, no matter what: she always did, whether it be plain bread and butter or soup or stew from a tin.

When they arrived at the school, there were a few pupils already there and others were arriving, most walking, including the little ones whom Jack would join: on Jimmy's face as he slouched in was the hard expression of one ready to take on all-comers if necessary: on Patrick's face was a look of wry amuse-ment: Jack meekly followed his brothers, not wanting to be separated from them.

Olive quickly pushed off with the pram, this time making the twins walk either side of her as she headed down towards the Square and Theresa's house in Shoe Street: there, having made the arrangement previously, she left the four to be cared for by her sick sister and Dorothy, the latter delighted at the chance to play mother again to three toddlers and a baby, especially Joseph: the three toddlers were ushered into the cramped parlour to play before they had even taken off their coats.

That day Olive had a mission in mind: two days before, as she left the post office-cum-grocery store with her shopping, she had spotted a notice, hand-written on a plain postcard, stuck near the bottom of the window: it was sun-curled and, from the amount of condensation which stained it, had obviously had been there some time. It read: 'Husband-and-wife labourer's help and cook and cleaner required. Monday to Friday. Immediate vacancy. Good wages paid. Apply Richard Wakenham, Follenfaunts House, Gledlang.'

The name 'Wakenham' was new to Olive: she had not known anyone of that name when she had lived in the village: that is what she had spoken about to Theresa the previous day after registering the three eldest at the school.

'Don't know much about him,' Theresa had informed her. 'He's a queer cove by all accounts. Come here seven years ago. Nephew of Old Silkins, who farmed Follenfaunts when you were here. Inherited Follenfaunts from him. Lived there with his widowed mother when he first come. She was elderly. First winter saw her off like the next one's going to see me off.' A sigh and an ironic laugh here. 'One of the village boys, young Colin Bow, worked there, but he's gone into the army now. Volunteered just to get away, they say. Should have been deferred. Follenfaunts ain't a big farm, not like some round here. About a hundred and fifty acres, I suppose. Nowhere near as big as any of the Godwins' farms. Bloody land grabbers, they are! Taking over everything left, right and centre, anything they can get their hands on! You can't move around here for Godwins' land, especially out on the Salter and Beckenden road. They would have had Wakenham's, too, if it were bigger. Too small for them. Two people can work it easy. Trouble is he don't pay much. Bit of a skinflint, the old man, so I've heard. Seems to think people live on sunshine. That's why the Bow boy left. Better off in the army, he reckoned. Wakenham himself don't know the first thing about farming. Leaves it all to Old Jim Borne. You remember him? Lived two doors away from us. The one who was a bit simple. Not right in the head. He was there under Old Silkins before you left. He still works there. Does ninety per cent of the work himself, I shouldn't wonder. He could probably do with some help. Wakenham's no help to no one. He's got lazyitis, that man! Too fat and too lazy to do a thing for himself. Got things wrong with him, they say. Don't know what, though, except laziness. He ain't never married. Perhaps that's why. Ain't likely to neither. You'll see why when you meet him! Gave me the creeps just to see him, though, fortunately, he don't come into the village much. Ugh!' She shivered dramatically: even Dorothy giggled a little at her mother's remarks.

A few minutes later Olive was hurrying up Tithe Street towards the white entrance gates to Follenfaunts: the farm itself lay up a sanded drive which began just at the point where the Tottle road debouched on to the Maydun road: Olive had passed right by it on her entry into the village two days before. The drive ran straight for half a mile between two orchards, one of apples and pears, the other a mixture of cherries and plums: at the end of it stood a large, ten-bedroomed, cream-washed Georgian mansion, common to that region. The house was surrounded by a wide expanse of lawn and stood on ground marginally higher than the village: as such, it commanded a good view of Gledlang itself and the dulled silver ribbon of the Langwater half visible through the intervening elms and horse chestnuts which dotted the hedgerows and clustered around the church tower. Alongside the house stood a dilapidated, black-creosoted barn and an open-fronted, red-brick wagon shed, while to the side and behind it were the eleven arable fields it possessed and its sole meadow, in which stood two huts for turkeys centred in wire enclosures. A half-dozen chickens, which were pecking about on the lawn, scattered as Olive pushed open the second gate and crunched up the gravel path to the front door.

Lifting the brass knocker, she rapped it hard against the unpolished button: the sound of it echoed in the silence inside: after a few moments, there was a sound of footsteps shuffling slowly towards the door: two heavy bolts were drawn back and a laboured breathing became apparent as though the effort of even coming to the door was almost too much for whoever was pulling it slowly open: then Dick Wakenham appeared.

He was everything that Olive had expected from Theresa's description: grotesquely fat, short in stature, with a heavy belly swelling over the waistband of his trousers and folding down towards his groin: where his chest should have been, he had flabby breast-like mounds: he was, in fact, one of those kinds of men who made Olive shudder just to look at him. His face was heavily jowled, his lips thin and colourless, his nose like a tiny beak: his hair, tightly waved, almost crinkly, brown and heavily greased, was parted in the centre and plastered down on each side of his head. By his looks alone, he appeared as flabby in mind as he clearly was in body, as though there was not an ounce of strength or energy in him and no willingness to make an effort to overcome that deficiency: a man who moved only short distances at a time, stages measured in yards rather than half-miles or miles, breathing in heavy gasping bursts at the end of each as though movement of any kind were too much of an effort for his larded bulk and his lungs were unable to pump enough oxygen around his overweight frame to get him going again. Any man regarding him would have grimaced at the thought that there probably was not an ounce of testosterone in his body. 'More female than male,' some undoubtedly would have said. 'A repulsive toad,' women, more cruel, might have added, shuddering in disgust. When Wakenham spoke, his voice was little more than a squeak, like that of a child still and, like a child, he seemed to have a perpetual dribble at the corners of his mouth: it was no surprise, therefore, that he was, as Theresa had remarked with a sniff, a bachelor. Unhappily for him, he was also a diabetic and a chronic asthmatic for whom movement of any kind seemed too much of an effort: sadly, too, he was burdened by other ailments: an under active thyroid, profuse sweating and halitosis, which Theresa had not remarked upon, but which Olive now discovered to her discomfort: carefully, she took a step backwards.

Nor was Wakenham a farmer by birth or breeding or inclination as were most who worked the land in that region, men who were born to it, the sons and daughters of generations of farming folk, brought up to all the rigours and hardships of its life, but loving the land, knowing it as children, the shape and lie of every field, every headland and hedgerow, every tree and track, every ditch and dip, the very nesting places of the different birds: blackbirds in the whitethorn and hazel hedgerows, rooks in the elms, plovers along headlands, partridges in the fields. They knew, too, the signs of the seasons changing: the first budding of the hawthorn in spring, the green shoots pushing up in the fields, the mammoth cloud-filled skies bringing the rain from the west: in summer, the distant blue shimmer of heat-hazed hedgerows, a blistering sun beating down over parched fields from an azure sky, dust devils whirling like mad dervishes along the headlands: then, in autumn, a subtle change in the brightness of the sun, a cooling of the air, a chill in the morning, the grass heavy with dew, cobwebs stringing between the fence posts: followed all too quickly by the first signs of winter, a cold wind streaming in from the northeast, blustering around the barn and the cowshed, plucking the leaves off the elms and the horse chestnuts and penetrating even the narrowest of gaps in the timbers of the barn, and, after that, the grey, smothering fogs, the carpeting frosts freezing the ground bone-hard as driving lines of sleet and snow sweep in off the estuary.

All of that meant nothing to Dick Wakenham: he was London-born and London-bred: he had grown up indulged and lonely, in poor health, for long periods confined to his bed by his diabetes and asthmatic attacks: he had spent a life being shuttled between his own bedroom, sanatoria of one kind or another and foreign health spas. It was a life freakish enough in itself, but one which had been compounded by his parents' mollycoddling, as well as by luxury and ease: he had been a boy who had never walked in the rain when he could ride in a carriage or a motor car, who had spent his childhood playing alone in a nursery in which a roaring fire always burned, lonely and friendless: who in his formative years had a nanny to bathe and to dress him and later a housemaid to lay out his clothes and to fetch and carry for him. His father, a wealthy banker, had also suffered from diabetes and chronic asthma and had died suddenly from an attack when the son was just eight, leaving the indifferent young widow and his son a large house in a prosperous part of London and sufficient funds to hire a private tutor to educate the bed-ridden boy and, in between the stays in bed visits to sanatoria, to take holidays abroad, inevitably at spas in Italy, France and Switzerland, with the tutor always on hand as the family's sole friend. The years had just seemed to drift by for Dick Wakenham: his life was very much a monotony of nothing, each day the same as the one before it and the next likely to be the same, an existence rather than an actual life, with no reason or rhyme to it: when Wakenham had inherited Follen-faunts from his uncle at the age of fifty-six, seven years before, he had not done a single day's work in the whole of his life.

His move to Gledlang was one of the few decisions he ever made himself: and that done in the vague hope that the salty fresh air of an estuary village might help to ease his chronic condition: it did, in the summer, but in the winter the fogs and frosts which plague that part and the howling gales which blow up the estuary threatened his health just as much: aches and chills and bronchitis, pleurisy and pneumonia became his new dreads: so much so that for days on end, weeks on end sometimes, when the winter weather was particularly bad, he would not set foot outside the house. He bemoaned the loss of his mother within six months of his arrival in Gledlang: bronchitis did for her and he blamed himself for her death, even though she was over eighty when she died and from the time she arrived till the day she died she had never once ventured out into the village. 'It took a hearse to get the old girl even to go to church!' the locals joked, cruelly. But then they had no sympathy for Dick Wakenham and he had no interest in them: thereafter, he lived by himself, a lonely, disconsolate, figure, never fitting in with the locals, never mixing with them, speaking only to the two who worked for him, the young Colin Bow, now gone, and Jim Borne, the simple-minded landworker he inherited from his uncle. All else, groceries, coal, milk, post, bread were delivered to his house and bills settled monthly or quarterly by cheque: the man had become a virtual recluse.

FORTY-THREE

'I SAW your card in the post office and was wondering if the two jobs you advertised were still open,' Olive blurted out, almost before Wakenham had swung the heavy door fully open.

Wakenham eyed her carefully as might any employer finding someone standing on his doorstep answering their advertisement. 'Yes, they're still open,' he said. 'Are you and your husband applying?' He looked past Olive, expecting to see a man standing behind her.

Olive took a deep breath. 'No, just me,' she declared as levelly as she could. 'I'm applying for both jobs, as a labourer and as a cook and cleaner. I was hoping you'd let me do both, part-time in the fields for so many days and then part-time in the house for the rest of the week. I could manage it, I know.'

For a few seconds Wakenham was so taken aback by her proposal that he did not answer: then he recovered to splutter: 'B-b-but I was looking for two people, one to work on the farm and one to do the house cleaning and a little cooking for me, a husband and wife together, not just one person. Two people. And not to live in either. I wouldn't want that.'

'I haven't got a husband, not any more,' said Olive flatly. 'He died. I've come down here from London to get away from the bombing. I used to live in the village once .That's why I've come back. I've got a family to keep. I need to find work of some kind so I can look after them. I've got seven, all boys. I've got my own place so I wouldn't want to live in anyway.' She smiled, hoping that her honesty would impress him: Wakenham just made a noise and looked surprised. 'And I know you wouldn't want seven boys cluttering up your place, would you?'

A dumbfounded Wakenham shook his head.

'I've done plenty of cooking and cleaning in my time so I know what to do,' went on Olive. 'Before I was married, I was an assistant cook and housemaid for a family named Wilcox in Highgate. I did do some farmwork when I was a girl living in the village so it won't come as a shock to me.' The latter was a fib more than a clear lie: Olive had worked briefly on the land as a fourteen, fifteen and sixteen-year-old, pea-picking and bean-picking sometimes with her mother and sisters for an hour or two in the very early morning before taking up her post at the school: she went off to the school at eight o'clock and they stayed in the field. Her only other work on a farm had been a month's fruit-picking one August, again with her mother and sisters when the school had closed for the summer and had remained closed for an extra two weeks because of a diphtheria scare: she did it solely to earn some money: the church-wardens refused to pay her the pittance they generally paid while the school was closed and she was not working.

'I'm not afraid of hard work,' Olive added quickly when Wakenham appeared about to waver and to close the door on her. 'I've done plenty in my time. You wouldn't regret it if you hired me, I promise you.'

Wakenham rubbed the end of his nose, then stroked his flabby chin: almost with a sigh of resignation, he added: 'Well, you are the first to reply. The post-card has been up for over a month. I was beginning to think no one would come. It seems people don't want farmwork now. They all seem to want to go into the munitions factory at Wivencaster. I had almost given up hope of hiring anyone to replace young Colin and Jim does need help.' Then reluctantly, almost grumpily, he added: 'Well, since you are the only one who has bothered to enquire, I suppose you had better come in.'

He turned and, in the same laboured manner as before, shuffled back down the wide hallway in his tartan carpet slippers, breathing hoarsely again as if the exertion even of walking to the door and back again were too much for him. The floor, Olive noted, was covered by a long roll of faded threadbare carpet: doors leading to the rooms off were painted white, but seemed to be shiny with grease: cobwebs covered the bottom few panes of a tall arched, blue-glass window high above on a wide central stairway at the far end of the hallway: a grandfather clock stood against one wall, its pendulum swinging noisily in its glass-fronted case: there was a smell of mustiness and dustiness about the whole place: Olive recognised the unmistakable signs and smells of bachelorhood.

Wakenham led her to a small room off the hallway which served as his office: it contained a roll top desk, a swivel chair, a mahogany cabinet and was almost obliterated by mounds of papers of every kind, from newspapers to letters, envelopes, magazines, bills and forms: a silver teapot stood on a silver tray perched on top of all this along with a gold-rimmed cup, a silver sugar bowl and a white milk jug.

'I don't see myself how a woman can do both farm labouring and cleaning and cooking,' Wakenham began as, with an effort, he lowered his bulk into the chair and turned to face her, his paunch settling over his groin like a deflating balloon. 'Cooking, yes, cleaning, yes, but not farm work, too, surely? Proper farm work is a man's business, it's not properly for a woman, in my view. I have one farm labourer, Jim Borne, and I did have a lad from the village to help him, but the silly boy has gone off into the army to get himself shot no doubt when he could have stayed here. Farming ought to be a reserved occupation, in my opinion. Now I have no one to help Old Jim and I cannot help him. My health is not good. I have chronic asthma and other things so I cannot do much.'

'Can't do anything,' Olive would have substituted, looking at him, grotesquely fat and breathless from even the smallest exertion: but, of course, she did not: she kept her face blank.

Wakenham regarded her again, still pondering upon the idea of a woman doing the two jobs. 'I really was wanting a married couple, a husband-and-wife team,' he sighed, 'another man to help Old Jim.'

Olive had her answer ready. 'There aren't the men about at the moment,' she interrupted. 'Not young men. They're all in the forces where they should be. You could wait forever for a man and his wife to come along, but I'm here now and offering to do the work. I could work in the house cleaning and cooking two days a week, Tuesdays and Fridays, say, and the rest of the week I could help out with farmwork, hoeing and the like. It wouldn't be too hard and I'm not asking for a great deal for it, just what you would normally pay a woman, one wage for two jobs, so to speak.'

It was a bold offer: Wakenham wrinkled his beak-like nose, contemplating. 'There are more things to be done on a farm than hoeing and picking,' he said. 'A man would be expected to be able to do all the jobs on a farm that needed doing and much more. Much, much more. You are a mere woman. Do you really think you can do proper farmwork – like ploughing, harrowing, drilling and harvesting and all the other things Old Jim does? They say they're going to form a Land Army of women workers to take over from the men in the army. I should like to see it! Whether they ever will, I don't know. My need is now, not sometime in the future.'

'Then take me on,' Olive pleaded. 'I'm here now asking to do the work. All I need is the chance. I can't give you any references because I don't have any. I had to leave off working when I got married and had my family. That's one of the problems. I've got kids to see to before I start. That's why I can't go into a factory. It means I couldn't get here before eighty-thirty, not till I've seen the three eldest into school and dropped off the twins and my two youngest at my sister's in Shoe Street. I couldn't bring them with me.'

With a great effort, Wakenham heaved himself to his feet: then, with a sigh of resignation, he said: 'Well, I suppose I shall have to give it to you since no one else has applied. I've no choice, really, have I? It'll be just a tryout, mind, for a couple of months to see how things go. You'll work with Jim Borne and do as he says. He'll be in charge. He runs the farm for me and could do with some help. You start on Monday.' Then remembering what she had said about her children. 'Eight-thirty prompt.'

They settled on Olive's suggestion of Tuesdays and Fridays in the house and the other days helping Old Jim: the wage which was offered, and reluctantly accepted by Olive, was a measly thirty-five shillings a week, poor by any standard, even then, but it was money and Olive did not want to argue over it and have Wakenham change his mind.

When she walked back down the long chase between the orchards, all her misgivings about leaving London and bringing the children to her home village were gone: she had work, or at least the promise of work, a tryout though it was: and work meant money and money meant food: and warmth. As a pale, seemingly heatless sun struggled to burn off the damp morning mist, for the first time in a long time Olive was smiling to herself.

FORTY-FOUR

'I'M GLAD you're here,' said Alice, opening the door. 'I saw you from the window before. I wanted to come down, but I daren't. Not with them the way they were. I just had to hope you would come back. I knew you would, though. Don't worry, there's nobody here. They're all out at work. Him, too.' The latter remark referred to their father: she was smiling as she said it, like a child doing something which it should not.

After she left Follenfaunts, Olive had walked back through the village to collect the twins and the babies from Theresa and Dorothy: then she had walked round to her father's house on the Maydun road. It was just after eleven and she knew that she had an hour or so before her brothers arrived home for their dinner, as they usually did whenever they were in the vicinity of the house.

Whether her father would also be at the house, Olive was unsure, but decided to take the risk: she did not particularly want to meet him again, not so soon after he had turned her and the boys away. She recognised that at times her temper was such that she might say, or perhaps do, something which would further widen the rift between them, especially if any mention were made again that she should return to London, as she knew he was quite likely to suggest: she was in Gledlang to stay and they might as well accept it.

When her mother had died, she knew her father had looked to her and considered that, by going to London as she had, his eldest daughter had let him down, deserted him and the family when they needed her most: betrayed them, in his eyes. That was why he had turned her away: because of that and his own pride: he had managed without her for fourteen years and would go on managing without her. Any encounter with him, she knew, too, would most likely be reflected back upon Alice after she had departed and she did not want that: Alice suffered enough as it was.

Fortunately, her father, though approaching his seventieth year, still insisted upon working whenever he could to supplement his old age pension, hedging and ditching for any farmer who could not get anyone else to do it, even though his health was poor. October was generally the last month during which he could work properly, for he suffered from a continual chest cough and had to give up once the November fogs, December rains and January snows closed in: when they did, he went weekly to the snug at the Bowler's Rest to fill a small medicine bottle with whisky: it eased his cough, he said.

For two sisters who had last seen each other fourteen years before, it was an unemotional greeting between Olive and Alice: there was no handshake or hug or kiss such as more emotional townies might give: just a 'Hullo, Alice' and a 'Hullo, Olive,' a smile and a nod of the head from both of them, one to acknowledge the arrival of the other, the other to welcome her sister home, the way people did in that region: with no fuss or histrionics.

'I see you're still here then,' Olive said, following her sister into the parlour: it was not meant as sarcasm, but was just a further part of the greeting.

'Yes, I'm still here,' Alice replied with a weak smile: the fourteen-year separation might as well have been the previous day or the previous week.

It was no surprise to Olive that Alice, then in her thirtieth year, remained unmarried: one night as a ten-year-old, descending the stairs in a hurry, she had fallen heavily and awkwardly and had broken her thigh bone near the hip: the doctor, an ageing, disillusioned man, had been under the influence of drink when he arrived to reset the bone, a not uncommon trait with him, as all the villagers and those in the surrounding district to whom he ministered well knew. It was only after he had splinted the leg and the bone began to knit that it was realised how poor a job he had made of it: Alice's leg had become twisted and the foot was splayed out almost at right angles to what it should have been. Olive, her mother and Theresa had all begged their father to take Alice to a hospital to have the leg rebroken, as gruesome a course as that might be, so that it could be reset straight: but he had refused, saying that he could not afford the money it undoubtedly would cost unless they could get her into a funded hospital, of which there was not a great deal of hope.

Olive had always regarded Alice as prettier than herself, almost as pretty as Theresa, as had their mother: even the old schoolteacher, Ma Jepson, had once described Alice as 'a pretty little thing': but, as a result of the accident, Alice thereafter walked with a pronounced limp: and, from being a cheerful, laughing girl who loved to skip and to dance, she had become withdrawn and shy: she had remained a spinster simply because no man in the village had bothered to court a girl who, to them, had always been a cripple.

As she sat opposite her sipping her tea, Olive's first thought was how pale and thin Alice looked and how dowdily dressed she was and seemingly unbothered by her appearance: still with a pretty face, but so thin. Olive guessed that Alice's thinness was down mostly to poor eating habits just as she guessed that her drab manner of dressing, darned red cardigan pulled over a shapeless flowered dress, her hair straight and slightly greasy looking was down to her own disinterest in life beyond the house.

Throughout her marriage, Olive had always taken pride in her own appearance: she had always tried to wave her hair as best she could and had powdered her face, pencilled in her eyebrows and always put on lipstick even when Robert was not there. Before the war, when they were living in their first flat in Rupert Road, before she had fallen pregnant with Joseph, she had even sprayed on eau de cologne on occasions whenever she had gone to the pub with Robert and his brothers and Martha and Muriel, leaving the children in charge of a young sixteen-year-old girl from one of the lower flats. Her one great disappointment was the loss of six teeth as a result of her gums softening during the seven pregnancies. 'One for every child,' the women at the clinic had said: in Olive's case, it had almost come true, but, as they were all on her upper back teeth, she could still smile without worrying too much: at least she still had hers: her sister-in-law, Muriel, had had all hers taken out as a birthday present from her husband, Gerry, and false ones fitted: and she only had the three!

After Joseph's birth, during the long hot summer, she had also managed to retain her dress size, which saved her the trouble of letting them out, though it was down more to eating less due to a lack of money and the beginnings of food rationing than a desire to achieve a chorus girl shape: it would, she had hoped, also help to eliminate the stretch marks on her stomach and the veins on her breasts and thighs.

Alice put the kettle on to boil and laid out the cups and saccharins and placed a plate of homemade scones on the table for the twins to eat: while she did that, Olive went through the ritual of pointing out which twin was which and of informing her sister how old was Michael and how old was Joseph. Alice, for her part, smiled and cooed at the baby in the pram, while Michael, who sat upon his mother's lap, eating a scone, looked on frowning as if to ask: 'Who is this strange thin lady?' The twins, however, emboldened by their mother's relaxed and calm demeanour, were starting to wander about the room and eventually climbed on to the settee under the window to look out: exclamations from the window told Olive that they had seen a bird land on the grass border around the flower beds: it was a distraction for them and an excitement, seeing a bird up so close.

Now, sitting at the table, the two sisters were able to talk properly.

'How are you these days?' from Olive as she sipped at her tea.

A phlegmatic 'I'm all right. And you?' from Alice.

'I'm all right. Nothing to worry about. Sleeping's been my problem, getting enough of it, what with the bombs and that.'

'Was it bad up there? We only heard about it. We could see the flames from here some nights. Sometimes the whole sky was lit up.'

'What from here?'

'Oh yes,' replied Alice, nodding and coughing as she half-choked on a scone. 'We could see the clouds turned bright red sometimes over London so we knew there was a raid on. Some of them looked very bad. They say there's lots of people been killed?'

'The raid a week ago was the worst,' said Olive calmly. 'A lot of people were killed in that one. We lost the flat in that one. That's why I've come down here with the children.'

'Where did you go when you left here?'

'I went to see Theresa. You ought to go round. Never mind what they think.'

'I thought you might,' replied Alice, reddening a little. 'How is she these days?'

A shrug from Olive. 'As well as can be expected considering what she's facing. She's putting a brave face on it, but it can only be a matter of time. She knows that. It's Dorothy she's worried about, leaving her.'

'Perhaps I ought to go round?' suggested Alice, a little guiltily.

'I think you should. She is your sister!'

'I know, it's just that it reminds me too much of Mum. I just don't like to see it, that's all.' There was an awkward pause before she changed the subject: 'Did you sleep there that first night?'

A laugh from Olive. 'No, we slept in the Godwins' bathing hut.' No mention of the fact that Don Godwin had appeared and they had been evicted, or that she had traipsed round the village for half the day and later as far out as Beckenden in the pouring rain to find somewhere, or that she had had a row with the vicar over his refusal to allow them into the parish hall. Just a matter-of-fact: 'We've got a place in Beckenden at the moment. It'll do for now. It was empty. When you're desperate, you'll take anything. It's a relief to get away from the bombs and the guns so I suppose I can't grumble.' The words 'a place' she knew would suggest that it was a cottage or a house: she did not really like to deceive either of her sisters, but her pride was at stake: time would reveal the truth, but not that day.

FORTY-FIVE

'WE'VE got a couple of guns round here, too,' Alice said suddenly, changing the subject, thinking she was telling Olive something which she did not already know. 'We've got a searchlight battery in the village now. On the Park. About thirty or forty soldiers under a captain?'

'I know, Theresa told me,' said Olive: then, in jest with a laugh, she added: 'You want to make an effort, girl. You never know your luck there.'

'They're all too young for me,' replied Alice with a shy smile: but Olive had detected the blush which had come to her cheeks and read the signs as only a sister could: Alice, realising she had been caught out, added with a smile: 'Except for the cook. John. He's a couple of years older than me. I've spoken to him a couple of times.'

'Spoken to him?' a disbelieving Olive asked.

'Well, you know,' shrugged Alice, blushing even more.

Olive understood perfectly. 'Is he married?' The obvious first question from one mature woman to another.

'Says he isn't.'

'How old is he?'

'Thirty-four, so he says.'

'Where's he from?'

'Up North somewhere. Place in Yorkshire, he said. He was wounded during the fighting at Dunkirk. Got hit in the leg by a bit of shrapnel.' She smiled to herself as if picturing something. 'He's got a bit of a limp, too. We make a fine pair, the two of us limping along together.'

'Ah, so he is courting you then?' Olive asked, now more than interested: here indeed was a piece of glad news: her youngest sister courting! Alice, with a limp, whom all the local youths had been more inclined to tease and jeer at: Alice the cripple courting!

Alice blushed again. 'Sort of,' she proffered shyly. 'They've had a few dances in the parish hall. I went. I sneaked out. I never told them or him – ' meaning her brothers and her father ' – I just went. I met him there. They were just village dos. It was the first time I had been out for months, years. First time, I had a couple of dances with him, not that I can dance that well with my leg, though he wasn't much of a dancer either with his leg, but we managed a couple of waltzes together and the hokey-cokey.' The latter mentioned with a smile. 'Mostly we sat and talked and he walked me home.'

'Did you stop off anywhere?' Another obvious question from Olive which caused Alice to blush even more.

'Not the first time,' said Alice, reddening again. 'Third time we did go for a walk down the seawall.' In Gledlang, going 'down the seawall' for a walk along the estuary was a euphemism much used by courting couples for finding a lonely place where they could do what they wanted to do out of sight of others.

'Well, I might as well take the chance while I've got it,' Alice added with a shrug and a smile of her own. 'I haven't had any other offers. Take it when you can get it, I say.'

'Are you all right?' A frown and genuine sisterly concern from Olive.

'Yes, we used as French letter,' said Alice with an amused smile, nodding.

A sigh of thankfulness from Olive: and the next obvious question: 'Have you seen him since?'

'A couple of times. On the sly, though. Just for a walk. You know. Don't want them finding out, do I? His leg is more or less healed now, though he still limps. He's away at the moment – Sussex somewhere – the army moved him. I shall just have to wait till he comes back – ' She paused, almost as if not wanting to finish the sentence, for the next phrase had two meanings. ' – if he comes back. He's written to me and I've written back a couple of times. He sends his letter to next door so Dad and them two won't find out. I told him it would be safer and asked Mrs. Coxwaite – ' their neighbour ' – if she minded. She hands them over the fence when they're out. She doesn't mind. She thinks it's a great laugh, them not knowing.'

Olive just smiled her understanding: if their father and their brothers learned of Alice's liaison with a soldier, even her interest in one, she knew that they would certainly attempt to end it somehow: they would not want to lose their unpaid skivvy to a soldier.

'Well, at least he's showing an interest,' said Olive in encouragement.

Alice heaved a sigh. 'Yes, I suppose he is, though I'm not counting on anything,' she said gloomily. 'If he comes back, well and good. I want him to, but I'm not taking anything for granted. I shall still wind up an old maid, I expect.'

'Don't give up yet, girl,' Olive counselled, still smiling. 'You're only thirty. You haven't lost the chance yet.'

'I'm not so sure I want it,' replied Alice with a shrug.

'You should have got out when you had the chance.' For Olive, it was a tart remark, but she felt it had to be made.

'It's easy for you to say,' declared Alice, again with a shrug. 'Where would I have gone with my leg?'

'You could have come up to London with me,' answered Olive. 'You could have gone somewhere, anywhere, so long as you got away from them and him.'

There was an awkward silence after that: Olive had spoken sharply simply because of her own disappointment at her sister's lack of verve: for a few moments the old sisterly antagonism returned, but then just as quickly vanished: now was not the time to have an argument. Instead, they agreed to differ by ending the matter there and taking the twins and Michael on a tour of the garden to show them the gooseberry bush, the apple tree, still with its windfalls littering the ground under the branches, a row of raspberry bushes, the half dug row of potatoes and the new digging just begun, as well as the pullets in their hutch at the top of the garden, which stretched back for almost fifty yards. It was a pleasurable sight for Olive to see Alice so taken by her young nephews, for, despite her limp, she took the twins' hands and led them round much the same way and with the same eagerness and enthusiasm as the soon-to-be-motherless Dorothy had done on first seeing them. They returned to the parlour after a half-hour or so and were still talking and drinking a second cup of tea when the latch on the back door was lifted and Percy and Hubert came stamping in together: being close to the village, they had decided to call home slightly earlier for their dinner: Olive had mistimed her leaving.

Just as it infuriated Olive that Alice had never had the nerve to leave home and make a better life for herself, so it rankled with her, too, that her two brothers had never made any effort to better themselves, working in a factory, say, or even as farm labourers: but they were content to be roadsweepers and roadmenders and would remain so till they retired and drew their pensions and died. In the summer they swept the network of lanes and B roads around

the village, cut back the miles of overhanging hedgerows and scythed mile after lonely mile of wildflower-and-weed-covered verge: in the autumn, they
swept up the leaves and the other detritus of summer: in the winter, they
sanded the icy patches where the snowfalls had compacted and deepened the
roadside ditches to run off the floodwater: and in spring, with another year
gone by, they unblocked the drains and pruned off the lower branches of any
trees which overhung the road and patched with tar and gravel any cracks and
holes the winter weather had caused.

Olive had always hoped – forlornly, she realised – that they might have
been more amiable men if they had had better jobs and took more pride in
themselves: but they did not and their reaction at finding their eldest sister
sitting in their parlour, with four of her children littering up the place, sipping
tea and eating scones which were meant for their tea, was exactly as Olive expected it would be.

From the stouter, surlier-looking, gruffer Percy, a predictable and inevitable, 'What the hell are you doing here, woman? I thought we'd got rid of you
and your brats.' Followed by a sneering, 'Come for a handout from your sister,
have you?'

From Hubert came an equally uncharitable, 'Well, you won't get one here.
We ain't got no money to spare, none of us. We need what we've got to buy
food for ourselves and pay our own rent.'

A smile from either of them for the children was too much to be expected:
instead they received a hard glare, which was enough for both John and Thomas to scramble off the couch under the window and scurry back to their
mother's protective arm, while an apprehensive Michael climbed upon her
knee: only Joseph, back in his pram in the hallway, was oblivious to the little
scene.

'I haven't come to see you or to ask for money,' Olive snapped, deliberately
exaggerating the contempt in her voice. 'I don't need charity from you or anyone. I came round here to see my sister. Since when did I need your permission to do that?'

'Since you left and didn't bother to come back,' growled Percy, somewhat
taken aback by the defiance in Olive's tone. 'You don't live here no more, Olive.
We told you that before. You left. We stayed. We live here now, so we have a
right to say who sits in this house and who don't.'

'It's not your name on the rent book,' an angry Olive declared. 'There's only
one person who's got the right to throw me out and he's not here!'

A snarl from Hubert. 'I can soon go and fetch him. After the other day, I
think you know he'd tell you to git as well.'

Olive could have answered him, but deemed it more prudent just to give
him a scornful look: she had noticed how concerned, fearful even, Alice had
become listening to her sister brazening it out. When the brothers had entered, she had limped quickly into the kitchen to fill the kettle from the pail of
water which stood just inside the door, then limped back into the parlour to
place it on the range: now she was hovering in the doorway between the parlour and the kitchen, her eyes, silently pleading with Olive not to go too far in
antagonising her brothers, not like she used to do fifteen years before when
they were both girls and Olive was still living in the house.

Suspicion now from Hubert and a question gruffly addressed to Alice, spoken as though Olive were not even there: 'What were you talking to her about
anyway?' The clear implication was that she should not even be talking to her
sister at all.

A sharp 'It's none of your business!' from Olive spared Alice: then a sardonic: 'I was telling her how to get out of here and away from you two, if you want to know!'

'It was women's talk, nothing for you to worry about,' a meek but timely interruption from Alice, still hovering by the door. 'We were just talking, that's all.'

'Don't you go getting any daft ideas like her?' a glowering Percy warned his crippled sister. 'You've got enough to do here, girl. She ain't exactly covered herself with glory, has she? Seven kids, no husband and no home.'

'And no money either,' a cynical Hubert added.

Olive was already on her feet, gathering up her things and putting on her coat: it was time she went, before she said something which she might regret and which might deflect their ire from her on to Alice after she had gone: and she did not want that. She had had her talk with Alice: the fourteen-year gap had been bridged: she was eased in her mind and, what was more, she was content for the moment.

'I'm going,' she announced, gathering up Michael and motioning for the two pale-faced twins to leave ahead of her.

'Good riddance,' said Percy.

'And don't come back,' said Hubert.

'I'll see you about. I'll let you know about things,' Alice whispered in the hallway as she helped the twins into their coats: then another whisper: 'Here, take this.' A ten shilling note was pressed into Olive's hand: tears of gratitude welled up in Olive's eyes. She wanted to ask if her sister could spare the money, but knew that any prolonged discussion might well alert the brothers to what was happening: Alice, she knew, could only have taken the money from the housekeeping as she had none of her own: somehow she would have to cover up that fact. Certainly there was never any to spend upon herself the way other women did: that was obvious enough from her dowdy clothes and lack of make-up: perhaps John the cook's return might change her. Perhaps.

Alice helped lift the pram down the two steps on to the path and gave a smile and a wave as Olive and the children departed: then, her face resumed its dreary, disinterested expression for life and she went back inside to get the brothers their dinner.

FORTY-SIX

THE too soon return of her brothers had soured Olive's reunion with Alice: she felt they had not had long enough to talk as freely as she would have liked. That evening, huddled in the den in front of the range, with the children asleep in the inner room, Olive spent a long time staring into the fire and mulling over the incidents of that day.

Just as Percy and Hubert feared, she had wanted to tell Alice to stand up for herself, to oppose them, even to leave the house, not to remain there and allow herself to be treated any longer as a 'doormat' by them, a skivvy, a nothing. More than anything, she wanted to tell Alice that she deserved a life of her own: she had mentioned the army cook, John, from the searchlight and ack-ack battery, and it was obvious that there was an interest there. What a good thing it would be for Alice, she thought, if the army cook really did court her, even if nothing came of it in the long run: what a blow it would be to her brothers and her father: the thought of it was too good to contemplate.

'It would be one in the eye for all of them!' she suddenly heard herself saying aloud: she had grown up fighting back at her brothers and defending her two younger sisters when they had been picked upon: the taunts and teasing of Percy and Hubert had been a daily source of unhappiness for them all from their earliest days. If there was a doubt in Olive's mind, it was because she knew Alice: she knew that because of her disability she would not do anything to forward the liaison, or romance, or whatever it was, even though her soldier, John, was similarly disabled or at least had a limp of sorts.

Just sitting in the house, drinking tea and walking in the garden had brought back old memories for Olive, memories long suppressed because, in effect, they were old wounds, too. Just hearing Alice's greeting had reminded her of the afternoon when she was returning from helping at the school and found the younger Alice hurrying as fast as her crippled leg would allow along Hedge Street to meet her: because of that leg, Alice remained at home after she left school at thirteen, ostensibly to help her mother about the house, but more because their mother had been in poor health for sometime, complaining of sickness, not wanting to eat and feeling tired all the time. Percy had even made her a walking stick out of a blackthorn branch he had cut from the hedge at the top of the garden and she now shuffled about the house on it.

A weeping Alice told Olive of how that morning she had gone upstairs to her parents' bedroom to mop the linoleum and, on moving the bed, had found several blood-stained rags lying under it, obviously pushed there by their mother to hide them. Later that afternoon, Alice said, their mother had been standing by the window in parlour, looking out, when she had suddenly slumped to the floor: Alice had managed to get her on to the couch, but had been unable to bring her round and, in a panic, had hurried out of the house to meet Olive, knowing that she would be on her way home from the school at that time. Olive had rushed home well ahead of the limping Alice and, on entering the house, had found their mother sitting up, looking flushed and bleary-eyed, but otherwise seeming none the worse from her 'collapse.'

'I'm all right. My walking stick slipped on the rug,' she just replied when Olive questioned her. 'I just had a dizzy spell. It was just one of my headaches.'

When Olive broached the subject of the blood-stained rags which Alice had found under the bed, their mother had impatiently, almost irritably, dismissed her concern, saying it was something that happened sometimes to married women and they had better expect it to happen to them as well when they got a husband, without explaining anything further, leaving the girls to form their own conclusions. Then, seeing their concerned looks, she had added with a laugh: 'You aren't going to get rid of me that easy. No one is going to carry me out of here in a box till I've seen all three of you married off!'

But there was a falseness about the way she laughed, a mock bravado, which both Olive and Alice were easily able to detect: when she rose to her feet and moved off, there was pain etched upon her face. Olive and Alice had looked at each other, knowing that something was wrong, but not knowing what.

Matters came to a head one Sunday dinnertime some months later: Olive, by then eighteen, a sixteen-year-old Theresa and Alice, fifteen, were sitting round the dinner table with their enfeebled mother and Percy and Hubert: their father, as was usual for him on a Sunday dinnertime, was drinking in the Chessman with the other men of the village and was not expected to return until after two o'clock when the pub closed: his dinner was in the oven, being kept warm.

Earlier in the meal, Olive had expressed her disgust at the way her two brothers were eating, making loud masticating noises and windmilling the food into their mouths with the next spoonful going in almost before the previous one had been swallowed.

'Do you have to eat like pigs?' she had demanded.

'What's wrong with the way we eat?' an injured Hubert had protested.

'If you don't know, I can't tell you,' Olive had scoffed with disdain.

The two brothers, Percy, then twenty, and Hubert, nineteen, had looked at each other, puzzled, and resumed as before: later, while their mother was washing the plates in the scullery sink, the two had set about their suet pudding 'afters' in the same way: suet pudding just happened to be their brothers' favourite dessert, which they badgered their mother into cooking almost every Sunday and which they always ate covered with masses of treacle.

None of the girls would eat the fattening pudding and so when it was tipped hot and steaming out of the basin on to the plate and the cloth unwrapped, it was simply divided into three, between Percy, Hubert and their absent father: it exasperated Olive no end. 'Can't we have something other than suet puddings every Sunday?' she had cried, loud enough for her mother in the scullery to hear above the clatter of plates and pans.

'We like it,' a bloated Percy had countered.

'It's nothing but fat!' Olive had declared in disgust. 'It's just fat, that's all. Suet! There's no goodness in it.'

'It don't do us no harm,' Hubert had added in support of his brother.

'Huh! That's a matter of opinion,' Olive had scoffed. 'You should go and look in a mirror. You look like suet puddings, the pair of you!'

There was silence for a few seconds: then, with a roar of anger, both Percy and Hubert sprang to their feet, flung back their chairs and attempted to seize their sister. Olive, however, was too quick for them: she made a dash for the back door and, laughing and sniggering as she went, raced up the garden path, pursued by a roaring Percy and Hubert: it ended with Olive being cornered near the pullets' run and Percy and Hubert throwing her on to the ground and slapping her about the head and cheeks with no little force.

What upset Olive was that their desperately weakened mother had hobbled up the garden after them in order to intervene: halfway up the path, her walking stick missed the edge of the path and went into a hole and she pitched headlong among the rows of potato plants. Olive remembered it particularly because of the terrible cry her mother gave as she hit the ground, a shriek of pain which stopped her brothers in mid-slap. A bright red stain had appeared on their mother's light-coloured dress as she stood up: the wound on her breast, which she had attempted to conceal from everyone, had opened and started to bleed. Olive and Theresa helped her inside and removed her blouse and slip so as to wash and bandage her: it was only then that she saw the extent of the wound: it was a cancerous growth.

Olive had frequently seen her mother massaging her breast, almost self-consciously, as if to ease some ache or tenderness in it, but she had not dared even to think of the dreaded illness, as if merely to mention the name of it would cause it to appear. She telephoned from the kiosk in the Square for the doctor to come and dress the wound: this time he was sober when he arrived, but all he did after the examination was to shake his head and to arrange for the district nurse to attend. She visited twice a week after that to change the dressings and it was she who, rather bluntly, told Olive the truth: that her mother had a 'massive cancer' and that it was 'terminal,' a phrase Olive had not heard before. When Olive had looked blankly at her, she had said somewhat harshly: 'Your mother is dying, Olive. It's only a matter of time. Months! Five months, six months – who knows? She's riddled with cancer. She can't survive it.'

Theresa and Alice, standing beside their elder sister, had burst into tears and Olive herself had felt the tears coming at the prospect of losing her mother so early, before she had even seen her grandchildren.

'Your mother knows,' the district nurse said sharply, as if imparting that knowledge should be enough to stifle Theresa and Alice's tears. 'She's no fool, you know. She's been keeping it from you on purpose. When things get too bad, the doctor will give her something to help with the pain. That's the best we can do. It is only a matter of time now.'

From that point onwards Olive's mother seemed to give up and she entered into a long, slow, painful decline, masked as much as was possible by the medicine the doctor prescribed: it made her so drowsy and weak that she took to her bed for weeks at a time. It meant the girls would have to care for her. It was too big a job for Alice alone by then: Theresa had just started as a housemaid at the big parsonage where the Tottle and Salter roads diverge from the Maydun road and did not want to give it up: as a result, the burden of care fell squarely upon Olive's shoulders: that was the reason she had to give up her post as the infant teacher's helper at the village school – to care for her mother.

Their mother's fight lasted for ten months, into the following spring: late one evening, Olive and Theresa looked in upon her and found she had died quietly in her sleep, wasted away: it was a grim-faced Olive rather than a weeping Olive who stood in the churchyard that pale March morning beside her two sisters and watched their mother's coffin being lowered into the grave. After the ceremony, when her father and brothers had slipped away into the Chessman, next door to the churchyard, for a drink along with Alf Braybrook, who was then just Theresa's boyfriend, she had walked home with her two sisters, emptied the little silver tin of the money she had saved, packed her suitcase and hidden it under the bed to wait for the next morning.

Olive's father, perhaps not unnaturally, expected that his eldest daughter would continue with the running of the house, undertaking the same cooking, washing, cleaning, ironing and darning duties which his wife had done, and that this would continue indefinitely, or at least until she got married – 'if anyone'll have her,' the men had laughed among themselves. For Olive was considered to have too quick a temper and to be too willing to answer back, even to return blows against her with blows of her own as Percy learned when he was aged sixteen and his sister was fourteen.

That happened one Sunday: during a dispute with Olive, Percy had laughingly pulled a pair of her patched drawers off the washing line and run around the garden flaunting them on a stick like a flag for all the neighbours to see: Olive, screeching with fury, had chased after him and, after several circuits of the apple tree, had felled him with kick across his heels and had him pinioned to the ground: she was belabouring him with her fists as best a girl can when a youth is lying there laughing his head off and feeling no pain when their father wheeled his bicycle through the gate. Not knowing what had provoked the fight, he saw only his oldest daughter kneeling upon a poor breathless Percy, who was laughing so much that he could not defend himself: and, not wanting his children to be fighting, he had dragged Olive off. To do so, he had to cuff her twice as she would not stop striking at her brother, even kicking at him as she was pulled clear. Much to his shock, an hysterical, wild-tempered Olive had flown at her father, screaming defiance at him, believing he was taking Percy's side: to subdue her, he ripped off his leather belt, with a brass buckle the size of a beer mat and gave her three swipes with it around the head and shoulders which left clear red weals.

Olive never forgot the humiliation of those blows, witnessed by neighbours who had come to their doors to see what all the screaming was about: after that, things between Olive and her father became estranged, icily estranged: so much so that, as her mother's death neared, it became self-evident that she would not remain in the house to act as cook and cleaner for her father and brothers. The morning after the funeral, when she came downstairs with her suitcase in her hand in good time to catch the morning bus into Maydun, she found her father and two brothers waiting, determined to prevent her leaving.

'And where the hell do you think you're going?' her father had demanded, positioning himself in the hall so as to block that doorway: Percy and Hubert were already blocking the exit through the scullery.

'London,' Olive had answered defiantly. 'I'm not staying here to be a skivvy for you lot even if you think I am.'

'You ain't going nowhere, girl, least of all up to London,' her father had shouted, bristling up.

'I bloody am,' Olive had shouted and swung the packed suitcase against her father's knees so that he reeled backwards against the door lintel, allowing her to force her way past. 'Bugger you all! I'm going and you're not going to stop me!'

'You come back here or I'll land you one!' her father roared somewhat helplessly as he regained his balance: but, by then, Olive was halfway down the path and heading for the gate.

'You'll be back within a fortnight,' was the last she heard a contemptuous Percy sneer as she hurried down the road to the corner.

It was followed almost immediately by a jeering shout from Hubert: 'You'll be lucky if you don't wind up walking the streets like the other tarts in Piccadilly!'

The last cry she heard from her father was 'If you go, don't you come back here if things don't work out. Don't you come back here!'

Olive paid him no heed: she caught the Bourne Brothers' brand new eight-thirty bus into Maydun, took the puffing 'Crab and Winkle' train to Hamwyte to get the mainline train up to London and hardly gave life in Gledlang a thought until the Blitz and Ma Parrett put the idea of returning into her head.

It all came back to Olive as she sat there in the hideaway as the wet wood crackled and hissed in the grate: in the end, to escape the sadder memories, she had to turn her mind to the events of that afternoon.

Her reason for collecting the children from Theresa and Dorothy had been twofold: she had wanted to show them to Alice and also to take them to the clinic which, she had learned from the parish notice board, was to be held in the parish hall that very afternoon. Two district nurses and a WRVS helper toured the villages north of the estuary every three months to check the health of the children under school age: fortuitously, on this day; they were to be accompanied by a council worker who was doing her usual round of doling out new ration books to villagers. As Olive had retained her identity card and her previous ration books, the new ones were issued without fuss: it meant she did not have to go to the council offices in Wivencaster to get them and that spared her greatly, for it was a day's bus journey there and back.

But mostly Olive wanted the youngest of her brood to be seen by the nurses before she began work as she did not know when she would be able to take them again: she also wanted to obtain her full share of the extra free powdered milk for Joseph and Michael, which the Government allowed all young children, and also to obtain some free bottles of orange juice for the twins. At the same time, the nurse was able to give all four a thorough examination: Joseph and Michael were weighed in the wicker basket and found to be slightly below whatever weight they should have been, according to the district nurse: but as Dorothy and Theresa had given them all a good scrubbing in the tin bath that very morning and Olive had washed their clothes and socks along with those of the three eldest the previous evening, no comment was made about their cleanliness: nor did the nurse make any remark when Olive gave her address as 'the old Aerodrome Cottage, Beckenden Road.' Obviously, she did not know it.

'They're healthy enough, though a bit underweight. They need a bit of feeding up,' the district nurse, a small, dark-haired Welsh woman in her mid-forties, said in her sing-song accent as she lifted a wide-eyed Joseph out of the wicker basket and handed him back to his mother.

'If only you knew the half of it, madam,' Olive thought to herself, as she laid Joseph in the pram. 'It's not surprising they're a bit underweight, when they have hardly eaten properly for nigh on two weeks.'

The nurse's comment irritated her: she felt it was unwarranted criticism after all she had done since the family had been made homeless: none of the children was what anyone could have called malnourished: a bit thin, perhaps, but a long way from starving: neither did they have any coughs or runny noses: there were no impetigo scabs around their mouths or bald ringworm patches on their heads and nor were there any nits in their hair.

Indeed the twins and Michael and Joseph, just like Jimmy, Patrick and Jack, seemed to be thriving on the open air life, though for the twins thus far it had consisted of long, long walks under cold grey skies and in either drizzling or pouring rain while clinging on to their mother's pram.

FORTY-SEVEN

OLIVE'S work on the land began precisely at eight-thirty on the following Monday morning. After shepherding the still reluctant Jimmy and the less reluctant Patrick and Jack to school, she took the twins and the babies to her sister's house in Shoe Street. Olive had agreed to pay her niece a small amount, one shilling and sixpence a day, to care for the four youngest: it would eat into her wage and she could ill afford it, she realised, but without Dorothy looking after them, she would not have been able to work anyway: Dorothy was happy because it meant she was, in fact, earning while staying at home to care for her mother.

Only Alf balked at the arrangement, not wanting 'bloody kids running about the house all day!' But the women took no notice of him whatsoever. 'You're out at work all day, Dad, so they won't be bothering you, will they?' declared an unexpectedly bold Dorothy. 'I'm happy to do it and Auntie Olive is paying me!'

This was followed by an equally blunt exclamation from his wife: 'Don't be daft, Alf, you can't have babies out in the fields in winter. Dorothy wants to do it, so let her. She's going to be here anyway, looking after me, so she might as well do both. I'll be glad to have them. It'll give me something to do as well.'

'Well, on your head be it,' her husband sniffed back. 'Just make sure they're gone afore I git home. Having four kids running around the way you are, you could find it's too much.'

'So what!' declared Theresa. 'They're my sister's children, my nephews. Get off to work if you don't like it.'

A suitably chastised Alf did not mention the subject again and in time would even come to play with the twins, albeit in a gruff and grumpy way. Having the little ones there, both Olive and Alice hoped, would help Theresa, giving her something else upon which to concentrate other than the slow, painful progress of her illness: on her bad days, if she needed quiet, Dorothy would put the babies in the pram and walk them round the village streets, suitably wrapped up, of course.

When Olive reached Follenfaunts, Wakenham's sole employee, the stooping, gaunt, shy-smiling Jim Borne, was waiting for her in the yard, having been informed of her coming. Olive had known 'Old Jim,' as everyone called to him out of his earshot, since she was a girl: he lived a contented bachelor's life in the same row of houses on the Maydun road as had she herself before she left the village and early in the morning she had often seen him pedalling off to work on his high-handlebar woman's bicycle. Though not yet in his sixties, because of his emaciated form and his eccentric way of dressing, he always looked ten years older than he actually was and, among villagers, was regarded as simple minded. He had a habit of always wearing three or four tattered blue boilerman's jackets at the same time, the one over the other: when one became frayed, he simply bought a new one and put that on over the others to form one bulky garment: he did the same with the blue boilerman's trousers he also wore. Some in the village, noting peculiar bulges about his person, were convinced that that was where the old bachelor sewed all his money, so that he could carry it about with him: more than one claimed to have heard the jingling of coins when he cycled past.

In reality, he was just one of those dour countrymen who lived alone and cared little for the outside world: his life revolved around work, sleep, rest, growing vegetables in the large garden at the back of the houses or, in the evenings and at weekends, working on one of the allotments he rented in a field just across the road. He had worked at Follenfaunts since boyhood, seeing no need to change, seeing no need to go elsewhere to seek a bigger wage or better conditions, not that either were to be had over the previous two decades when the agricultural industry in that part of the country was in sad decline. He was simply content with his way of life and wished for no other: in all his fifty-nine years, he had never been away from the village for as much as a single night and the only coach trip he had ever taken away from it was to London four years previously to see the Coronation decorations of George VI, which when he talked of London was the only subject he ever mentioned!

He recognised Olive and greeted her with the same shy smile and nod as he had when last he had seen her fourteen years before, the morning she forced her way past her father and ran out of the house with her suitcase, heading for London: such was Old Jim's lonely, withdrawn way of living that it would not have surprised Olive if he did not even know she had gone up to London, stayed for fourteen years and only recently come back.

Jim just continued to give his shy smile, mumbled something about the barn and set off towards it at a slow amble: Olive followed. They spent the day winnowing corn, that is removing all the stones, dirt, thistles and the like from the grain sacked during that year's harvest but which was not clean enough for milling. After threshing, it had been stored in sacks in the barn: Olive's task was to climb up into the loft where she had to pull the two-hundredweight sacks down from the stack, drag them across the floor to the mouth of the hopper, cut the string binding them and lift and tip the grain into the chute. Below, as the grain cascaded down on to a rocker, Old Jim turned a handle to spin a big drum at one end of which was a fan: everything rocked and shook, the corn dropped on to sieves and the wind created by the fan blew off all the rubbish and light corn, leaving clean corn. This was re-sacked and weighed and, with a strength and agility which belied his apparent frailty, Old Jim humped it up a ladder to another loft the other side of the barn where it awaited the arrival of the lorry from the flour mill at Tidwoldton.

When midway through the morning, Olive needed the toilet, she was directed by a blushing Jim to an open-fronted privy with an earth closet behind the wagon shed: it was little more than a hole in the ground covered by a wooden seat with a large hole cut in it and squares of newspaper hanging on a nail for toilet paper.

Old Jim hardly spoke ten sentences all day, except to pull out a big brass pocket watch at twelve o'clock and say, with a sheepish look, 'Dinner,' and then at forty-thirty to look at his watch again and mumble another sheepish, 'Packing-up time.' Fortunately, at Theresa's, Olive had been able to make herself two sandwiches of cheese and piccalilli: but, having no tea bottle, such was her thirst at the end of that first morning that she went out into the yard and drank from the water tank from which the horses also drank, consoling herself that the water was clear and, therefore, must be clean and that was all that mattered. At the end of the day, her face was covered in a fine dust, her hands were black, her hair matted on her brow and her finger nails broken and split from continually tugging, dragging, gripping, lifting and tipping the hessian sacks.

'Good God, you look a sight!' Theresa cried when at last Olive knocked on the door of the house in Shoe Street and the twins came scrambling along the passageway to greet her, full of delight and smiles. Olive had washed her face and hands under the yard tap on leaving, but, having no mirror, had not realised her neck and clothing were all still coated in a fine layer of dust from the day's work.

'I've had a hard day,' was all she could think to reply as she slumped on to a chair in the parlour. 'I wouldn't want too many of those, I can tell you.' Her sister just smiled in commiseration.

While Olive washed herself as best she could at the kitchen sink, Dorothy brewed some tea and gave what Olive considered an overly enthusiastic report on the children's behaviour. 'As good as gold, as good as gold,' she enthused: the smirking faces of the twins peeping round the door at their mother rinsing her face and neck told a different story, but Olive did not pursue the matter and, after drinking her tea, set off for 'home,' pushing the pram, with the twins walking alongside, as the raw winter dark was closing in.

At the den, she found Jimmy, Patrick and Jack were waiting when she pushed open the warped blue door, having made their own way home from school: their first comment to their mother was, not unexpectedly, 'What's for tea, Mum?'

Fortunately, thanks to the money Alice had given her, Olive had been able to call at the post office-cum-grocery in the Square on her way to her sister's cottage and add to her recent purchases, which surprised Ma Rowthey, though she said nothing of it to Olive. In consequence, the meal that evening was somewhat more sumptuous in comparison to the frugal fare of the recent past: two tins of sausages in brine heated in the smaller saucepan, some potatoes boiled in the larger one and carrots and parsnips cooked together in one of the tramps' discarded saucepans which Olive had cleaned under the pump: though lacking enough plates, she spooned the twins' helpings into the two tins which she had rinsed out, while she herself ate from a saucepan and Jimmy, Patrick and Jack ate from their three plates.

It was a slightly more reassured Olive who finally leaned back against the door wall on her side of the den as the rain teemed down outside and the heat from the range held back the biting damp: she and the children were in the dry, they were warm, they had been fed and they were secure for the moment. Joseph was sleeping with his dummy dislodged from his mouth and hanging across his face as he usually did, Michael was sucking his thumb as he always did, John was sleeping up on his knees with his face pressed against the mattress and his bottom in the air and Thomas was sprawled akimbo: Patrick and Jimmy had wrapped their bomber jackets over their chests, Jack was curled up on the edge of their mattress, with his jumper for a pillow. In fact, it was so warm in the den that Olive herself had drifted off herself, lying on her overcoat on the hard brick floor with one of the children's pram pillows as her own pillow.

She awoke just as the rat poked its nose through the gap between the door, which was slightly ajar, and the lintel: then it began to creep forward, sniffing the air as it came, perhaps drawn by the smell of the food there or even the warmth from the range. For a second Olive froze: ice was in her veins. Then, with a fury which surprised even herself, she reacted: before the rat could even turn about, she had pulled off her shoe and flung it hard and accurately at the vermin, which spun and darted back the way it had come. The shivers remained with Olive for a long time after that: she kept her eyes glued on the spot from which it had emerged and listened hard for sounds of others, scrapings or patterings above the ceiling and behind the walls of doors: but, though she imagined many, she saw none: and soon she was yawning again.

The next thing she knew was that it was morning and Jimmy was stepping over her to go outside.

It was the shock of seeing the rat which determined Olive's next move, though it took the appearance of several more rats and a month to come about.

FORTY-EIGHT

'I WANT to see this place properly,' said Olive, standing in front of the half-buried cottage four weeks later, a determined look on her face: she had seen the rat twice more, the third time on the previous evening, and that had made up her mind.

'I want to see if we can clear it out and live in it,' she announced to Jimmy and Patrick, standing beside her. 'If the walls are safe, I don't see why we can't put a roof of some kind on it to keep the rain off, put a door on and mend the window. You two could do that. You're good with your hands. Then we could move all the things from there – ' meaning from the den ' – into here.' – meaning the cottage.

An incredulous Jimmy and Patrick exchanged glances and gave her a strange look, as if to say, 'You don't really mean that, do you, Mum?'

But Olive did mean it and was already pulling at the rubbish surrounding the doorway: then, slipping and sliding, she climbed a low mound of ash which had been tipped against the side and which filled the doorway to within three feet of the lintel cross beam: squeezing underneath, she was inside for the first time since they had taken up residence at the old aerodrome more than four weeks previously.

Olive had looked inside a couple of times, but the rubbish filling the place had deterred her from even considering what she was considering at that moment: that and work and tiredness. Now she was desperate: four weeks in the cramped den were beginning to take their toll on her nerves: apart from the return of the rat, both Michael and Joseph had coughs: the twins, too, were running around with snotty noses: Jack was starting to shiver at night as the draughts became more evident and she herself had woken a couple of times in the night with her teeth chattering. Christmas was approaching, the weather was daily growing colder, much colder, and who knew what the depths of winter would bring?

They needed to find somewhere else and the so-called cottage was the only option available to them. Only the two eldest did not seem at all bothered at having to live in a den built into the side of a rubbish mound: to them it was an experience to be savoured: it made them feel like the trench soldiers of the First War about which they had read. And on Saturdays and Sundays, away from the tribulations of school, the moonscape of mounds surrounding them echoed to the sounds of new battles being fought against the old German foe, albeit with wooden guns and half bricks for grenades.

If Olive had been honest with herself she would have admitted that her real fear was that someone from the village would discover how they existed: someone would see her and the children there, or find out somehow, and spread tittle-tattle. Were that to happen, she would never be able to hold up her head in the village again: the mere thought of it dogged her waking hours and troubled her in her sleeping hours: her pride was at stake. She had even considered camping in a barn somewhere if the weather got too bad, but dismissed the idea almost as soon as it came into her head: no farmer would tolerate having a homeless family on his property. As it was, they gave short enough shift to any roving 'didikyes' they found straying on their land with a caravan: so how would they react to a whole family sheltering in a barn half full of grain and used to stable the farm's cart horse? 'Set the dogs on us, most likely,' Olive thought. No, sadly, the cottage, half-buried as it was, was her only option.

Just as she had feared, the rubbish in the cottage was piled six or seven feet high against the two fully remaining walls: a layer of earth, ash, clinker and lime three or four feet deep in places filled the whole of the floor area and on top of that was the three and four-foot layer of the same rusting, rotting, discarded junk as had been dumped on the main mound outside.

And such was her dismay that Olive almost turned back: one glance was enough to tell her that it would take the boys a week or longer to clear the place: it was past mid-November then and the days grew dark too soon after tea for them to work for more than a couple of hours after arriving home from school. Olive herself would not be able to help: most days, darkness would have already begun to close in by the time she returned home: and she had their tea to get and then other things to do after that: Jimmy and Patrick would have to do most of it on their own.

The two came scrambling through the gap after their mother: they had already been inside the cottage to see what they could find so the height of the rubbish came as no surprise to them: almost idly, Jimmy pulled at a piece of rotting timber and, as it snapped, other rubbish rolled down upon them, so that they all three had to jump hastily back. Ignoring Olive's reprimand, Jimmy laughed and pulled at more of the rubbish and, before she could stop them, he and Patrick were picking up all manner of things, cans, bottle, lengths of this and that, and aiming them through the solitary window, laughing as they did so: they had found a new game!

'Be careful!' an angry Olive admonished, but neither paid her any heed and enthusiastically tugged at whatever came to hand before hurling it out: in doing so, they created so much dust that Olive had to retreat outside, away from the billowing clouds and out of range of the objects which continued to fly out of the window till they littered the ground all around. In high dudgeon, Olive returned to the den, where a patient Jack was sitting shivering in front of the range, trying to warm himself, at the same time keeping a watch on the twins and the two youngest safely asleep under their coats and blanket in the inner chamber.

Later, crouched over the dying range fire and sipping saccharin-sweetened tea, Olive pondered on whether she was doing the right thing in attempting to clear out the old cottage at all: her main fear was that, having done all the work, they would find the walls too cracked and unsafe for them to live in it. If they were, she sighed to herself, they would all just have to remain where they were: perhaps even into the spring and summer: there would be nothing else they could do.

The boys had been set a challenge and, as boys will, they made their preparations on how best to carry it out with all the thoroughness of a military campaign. Returning from work the next evening, after picking up the twins and the two youngest from Theresa's, Olive found Jimmy and Patrick outside the den hard at work finishing off a sturdy cart-cum-barrow which they had constructed from a wooden box: the wheels they had taken from an old pram and the chassis was just two pieces of planking fastened together into a T-shape with copper wire via a hole burned through the wood with a length of metal heated in the range fire.

Olive's first action, not unnaturally, was to demand why they were wasting their time building a plaything when thcy should have been starting on clearing out all the rubbish: Jimmy's grumpy, 'It's not a plaything. It's a cart. You'll find out,' was revealed on the next night.

When Olive returned from Follenfaunts the next day, she found Jimmy and Patrick had disappeared into the evening murk with their newly made cart, without waiting for their tea, leaving a scared and lonely Jack sitting in the den, lit only by the light of a stuttering candle flame. When Jimmy and Patrick returned more than three hours later, dripping wet from the evening mist and rain, they were wheeling a folded tarpaulin on their cart.

'We found it,' was all either of them would say: though Olive knew full well that what they had done was to climb on to some farmer's straw stack and drag it off, fold it on to the cart and wheel it home. That was why they had gone out in the dark: so no one would see them: and that was why they had built so sturdy a cart: they had been planning just such a thing all along.

'I just hope you went far enough so that no one will suspect us,' an angry Olive declared.

'We did, we aren't fools,' said Patrick, looking peeved because his mother was angered by their initiative rather than praising them for it. 'We went a good three miles at least, didn't we, Jim? No-one'll know where we got it from or where it's got to.'

'I hope you're right,' said Olive as Jimmy nodded agreement with his brother. 'I hope you're right.'

Olive was just fearful that the farmer might have followed them back to the old aerodrome to find out where they were taking it and then come rampaging in amongst them to seize it back: she knew enough of the ways of some farmers in that region to fear their wrath. Some, she well knew, would not hesitate to cuff the ears of any boy they found trespassing on their land: or, if they were stealing, chase them off with dogs: and some were not averse to loosing off with their shotguns at departing trespassers, especially at nighttime when they could give all manner of excuses as to why they fired. Some farmers seemed to believe it was their God-given right as landowners to do what they pleased in defence of their property and livelihood and to hell with everybody else!

With luck, however, Olive reasoned to calm herself, the particular farmer from whom they had stolen the tarpaulin would think that only someone with a lorry could have taken such a heavy thing: he would never guess it had been spirited away by two boys with a homemade barrow and trundled three miles: so he was unlikely to come looking for it in their area, was he? Besides, there was no name stencilled on it and, unless the farmer knew every mark and tear, it was unlikely he would be able to prove it was his even if he did come upon them. So when, after two days, no one came, Olive decided not to make them take it back: and they had a roof ready to be put on.

They began emptying the cottage after school the next day: in fact, so keen were the two eldest that they started as soon as they got back from school, still wearing their bomber jackets, best trousers, shirts and pullovers: by the time Olive and the others returned at six, black dust was billowing everywhere and both Jimmy and Patrick and their clothing were in need of a good rinse under the hand-cranked pump. 'Take them off, you clowns!' she cried. 'They're your school clothes. Gracious! I'm not made of money! I can't afford to buy you new ones. Take them off, the pair of you! Have sense, do!' Even then, it was only the threat of a box around the ears that persuaded the laughing pair to stop and put on their more ragged and only other clothes which they had brought from Thurstone, though Olive conceded that, such was their state, there was not much difference between the first and the second.

Having washed their school clothes only a week before, she now would have to rinse them all over again and then hang them over the range fire to dry overnight: it made her angry: it was another unnecessary job which she would have to do after a hard day's work at Follenfaunts. But do it she did, cursing the pair of them for their lack of thought and foolishness: she did not want people to say she sent her children to school looking like tramps: though, had she let them, the two eldest would have gone to school the next day in their dust-covered jackets, trousers and shirts without so much as a care: they were boys, after all.

After their earlier dubiousness, Olive had not expected them to approach the task with such enthusiasm: but not only was it a game to them, it was also a challenge and they willingly accepted it. The topmost rubbish, the lighter items, were simply flung over the walls or out through the window in a steady stream: then, when they covered the cinders outside, they pitched them up on to the mound which half-covered the cottage already, vying to see who could throw each object the farthest, hoping they would stay where they were when flung and not roll back. The heavier debris, however, lumps of fractured concrete from what once had been a dividing inner wall, as well as a heavy iron-work spar, half-rusted, which had once run the length of the building, they carried off on the cart.

By dint of effort, at the end of their first session, Jimmy and Patrick had cleared an area several feet square: and by the third evening they had emptied the top layer of rubbish down to the level of the mound of earth, ash and clinker.

That was a different proposition, however: to clear that, they would need a shovel and they did not have one: so Jimmy fashioned one from a length of timber and a flat sheet of metal which he nailed together using a brick as a hammer: the shovel had sharp, jagged edges and had to be wielded carefully in such a confined space, but it served its purpose. Each evening over the rest of the week, the soil and ash, clinker and lime, which had been tipped in or which had blown in over the past thirteen years, was scooped out square foot by square foot, tossed into the cart and hauled away to the far side of the dump by two black-faced, black-armed, black-kneed, black-trousered, black-shirted boys.

After a week of labour, working all Saturday to complete the task, they were all able to stand that evening in the centre of a flat area, twenty-five or so feet by twelve feet, with two full walls and one part wall rising up around them, the beginnings of a house, in fact!

Having cleared the cottage, they now had to make it habitable: the doors making up the den wall they dismantled one by one, starting on the Sunday, working from after breakfast till the evening dark: then, after two cold and uncomfortable nights under a tarpaulin 'tent,' completing it on the third evening, thanks mainly to Olive's foresight in asking Theresa if she could borrow Alf's claw hammer. Much levering, cursing, frustration and sweat were needed before the long nails holding the doors in place came out and they were able to twist, kick and rock them free. Jimmy extracted what nails he could from the original lengths of wood, but some had been hammered in so far all he could do was to hammer them in completely. It took the both of them to carry each door into the cottage and to erect them to form the walls of one larger single room enclosing the space they had created, joining them in much the same fashion as they had been joined together in the den. Olive was happy to let two eldest do it their way, with some help from Jack: and, though the work was crudely done, with not every door nailed squarely or properly upright, it would do, it would do.

They even recovered one of the cast iron roof struts and secured that in place with some wire to form a 'tented roof' of sorts so as to run off the rain: it was rudimentary, done the way boys would do it, crude but safe: and once the tarpaulin had been dragged fully across from wall to wall, tented and tied down with the attached ropes and salvaged electric flex and the cottage rain-proofed, Olive and Jack proceeded to sweep it out and then sluice down the concrete floor with water from the pump.

The hardest task was having to drag the heavy cast iron range across to give them heat and warmth: Jimmy's more practical skills found a way. 'Turn it over on its back so it's upside down and slide it along pieces of wood like rails,' he suggested airily after they had disconnected the downpipe chimney: apparently, he had seen a similar thing done once by some workmen: but they were much older and stronger: men, not mere boys and a woman!

Whatever lengths of wood they could find were laid to create the 'rails': then, standing at either end of the range, well out of the way of the weight of it, and, with much heaving and grunting, they began to tip it slowly away from themselves on to a pile of rubbish laid specifically on the floor of the den to cushion its fall.

'Crikey! It must weigh half a ton,' gasped Jimmy as he, Patrick and his mother struggled to lift it even a few inches off the ground: a worried Olive made sure the twins, the two youngest and Jack were out of the den and well away before the manoeuvre began. The three of them finally had to tip it inch by inch, wedging rubble under the front legs till they reached the critical point: after that, all they could do was to let it fall: it hit the floor with a loud clang, crushing the rubbish and shattering a score or more of the floor bricks, but, fortunately, without cracking any part of it. The weight now being all in the lower section, it was an easier matter to get it over on its back and unbroken.

The wooden 'rails,' of course, offered less resistance as they sought to manoeuvre it: with more panting, pulling, pushing, twisting and cursing and a little help from Jack this time, they wiggled the upside down cast-iron range inch by inch out of the den and along the rails towards the porch door. Their only setback came when a length of rotten lath broke and the range top grated on the rough cinders of the old hard: they had a struggle even to manoeuvre it back on to the rails.

The hardest part, though, was dragging it up the small incline to the porch door: Patrick solved the problem by untying a piece of rope from the tarpaulin roof, winding it around the front legs of the range, then he and his eldest brother threw the loose ends over their shoulders and hauled it up the slope like two horses towing a barge while their mother pushed from behind and Jack kept a brick wedged up against it so it would not slide back.

Eventually, after a half-hour of near superhuman effort and with many pauses to regain their breath, and having re-laid the 'rails' inside the cottage to the corner where they wanted it to stand, Jimmy and Patrick faced the final headache, tipping the range back on to its feet. They were both so exhausted by their efforts in getting it there that they had not the energy to lift it: even when Olive and Jack joined in, the four of them could raise it only a few inches. It was enough, however, for the quick-thinking Patrick to ram a brick under either end to hold it in place: then, with Olive, Jack and the twins bringing more bricks, Jimmy and Patrick together were able by degrees to lever it up with a length of iron from an old bedstead until, after much shouting and with clouds of ash billowing up, they finally managed to tip it upright on to its legs with another loud clang, in the right place, or as near as they would ever get it. Ten minutes later, Jimmy was fixing the chimney back in place and poking it up through a tear in the tarpaulin and sealing the hole with one of the tins.

Draughts, and there were plenty of those, they blocked with cardboard: the old den door was nailed up to replace the rotted cottage door: the shattered window was covered by the sacking flap from the den, and an old length of paint-splashed linoleum was rolled out over the concrete: finally, somewhat ingeniously, Patrick suggested building two 'brick beds' on which to put the mattresses to lift them off the floor till they could retrieve an old bestead they had spotted buried in one of the mounds. So with the range fire lit and the chimney thankfully drawing as well as ever – 'Better,' Jimmy said – some potatoes, carrots and peas bubbling together in a saucepan on the flames and mince and onions in the other pan waiting to go on, by the third evening of the second week of their labours they were happily settled in their new home, warm and dry, with a meal cooking and their blankets and mattresses awaiting them. They had done it! They had a new home. The boys felt that their achievement was as good as a Christmas present to their mother.

FORTY-NINE

A COLD January wind was streaming across the snow-carpeted fields as Jimmy and Patrick crept towards the potato clamp: all around the dark, skeletal hedgerows and gaunt, leafless trees stood out stark against the white: the blizzard which had blown in so suddenly off the estuary had abated: only eddies of loose snow now drifted across in the bright moonlight.

'Hold the sack open,' Jimmy ordered his brother as he took a flat piece of wood from inside his bomber jacket and, half-crouching, began gouging into the layer of earth and straw which covered the long, low mound: in no time at all some thirty large potatoes had tumbled into the sack.

'That'll do,' Jimmy commanded, rising from his crouch and pushing the length of wood back inside his grey jumper: Patrick rose alongside him, teeth chattering with the sudden re-exposure to the wind. Carefully, Jimmy resealed the hole, smoothing the muddy earth and pressing the straw back over it: he even scooped up handfuls of snow and patted that down on to the straw as well. Then, with a quick look towards the farmhouse sixty yards away, the two scurried back to the gap in the hedgerow, ducked between the strands of barbed wire and, with heads down against the wind, hurried back up the lane.

At any moment, they expected to hear the farmer's loud bellow behind them and were poised ready to run: but no shout came: all was silent except for the crunch of their feet over the frozen snow. With luck, they said to themselves, grinning through chattering teeth, a fresh fall of snow would cover their tracks within hours: with luck, too, the farmer would never even know he had been robbed, so carefully had Jimmy concealed the hole: and that meant they could go back for more. Better still, the clamp was over two miles from the cottage so no-one would suspect them: they would not even know about them: and it was a ready supply of needed potatoes!

The two had slipped away from the cottage after tea. 'Just going outside, Mum,' Patrick had called as he disappeared through the doorway with his brother: Olive was standing by the blazing range, adjusting some washing she had hung on a string line tied from one wall to the other and paid them little heed: by then she had become used to her two eldest roaming across the dump at all hours, even at night when there were two to three inches of snow lying on the ground, ice on the puddles and the beginnings of a blizzard streaming across the flat fields. At times, they seemed to spend most of their free hours outside, leaping from one mound to the next or digging down into the ash and earth and rubbish in search of something: invariably when she called them in for bed, they were hauling out something from somewhere or other to inspect it for possible use somehow.

Jack, of course, knew where they were going and, not wanting to be left out, wanted to join them, but had been told quite sharply by his two older brothers that what they were about to do was far too dangerous for him: if the farmer saw them, they would have to make a run for it: and, while they could outrun any fat farmer, 'You'd get caught and spoil it because you can't run as fast as us,' they told him. Nor was Jack allowed to tell his mother why they were going to be away for so long: nothing was to be said till they returned with their spoils: what they were doing, they were doing for her: but she was not to be told until after it had been done because then it would be too late for her to do anything about it: so a sulky Jack was made to cross his heart under the threat of a punch from Jimmy.

When two hours later the grinning, snow-caked pair came stamping back into the cottage, brushing the snow from their hair and clothes, and tipped a pile of potatoes on to the floor at their mother's feet, a weary Olive was dozing beside the range, seated on the small white-painted chair with the sawn-off legs with her stockinged feet resting on an upturned box.

'Where'd you get them?' she demanded, sitting up as the potatoes tumbled on to the floor.

'We found them,' laughed Jimmy, surprised that his mother should even ask what to him was obvious. 'We found a whole pile of them so we took some. No one saw us. No one'll miss them. Anyway, you said we needed more food. So who cares?'

'I care,' snapped Olive. 'I didn't mean stolen food. I meant food I pay for. I like to pay for what I get with what I earn. That way I can look people in the face each day. I don't hold with stealing and never have. You don't know you weren't seen. Someone could have seen you and followed you here. I don't want any trouble. I've had enough of that already. And I don't want you two put in gaol for thieving either.'

As if to make her point, she went to the door and looked out: but there was nothing except the rush of the wind around the cottage and spumes of snow blowing off the mounds. The boys knew their mother's action was just a pretense and shrugged, as if to say they did not care either way if someone was or was not out there: they had brought the potatoes home because their stock of food was running low and needed replenishing and their mother was forever complaining that she did not have enough to give them and worrying herself over it: it was as simple as that. They did not expect to be thanked and they knew their mother would be angry: as far as they were concerned, they needed food and all they had done was to go out and get some, even if it was only potatoes.

'You think you're so clever!' scolded Olive, responding further to Jimmy's and Patrick's shrugs as she lifted the makeshift front door back into place. 'You two, be careful. You don't go around stealing things! Not round here! People don't go in for that kind of thing. This is not London or Thurstone. If anyone catches you round here, they might decide to do more than just clip you round the ears. Round here farmers have guns. And some of them aren't above taking the law into their own hands.'

But Jimmy and Patrick were only half-listening: by this time, the two exhausted boys had flopped down upon their shared mattress and were busy tugging off their wet boots and socks and shaking the snow off their bomber jackets: the boots they stuffed with newspaper and placed before the range fire, the socks and the jackets they draped over the broken end of a sheep hurdle which served as a clothes horse and stood propped against one wall more or less permanently to one side of the range. They were unsure what their mother was trying to say to them? Was she forbidding them to steal the potatoes? Or was she just telling them to be careful in the future and not to get caught?

Olive was surprised at her own lack of anger: in her heart, she knew that Jimmy was right: they did need the potatoes: they needed any food they could get. Food had been getting steadily scarce since Christmas: daily she had watched her supply, kept in an old bushel fruit box in one corner, dwindling till there was nothing in it except for the usual half-loaf of uncut bread, a packet of margarine, a half-used jar of jam, some flour in a tin, a half empty box of porridge oats, the remains of the cheese, some sliced spam wrapped in greaseproof paper, two tins of sausages in brine, a half-pound of rice in a blue bag, plus the last of a few seeding potatoes, two carrots, an onion and some cabbage leaves. It was not enough to feed five hungry boys and two infants, plus herself, over the next few days let alone the next seven before she received her next measly wage from Wakenham and would be able to buy more.

It was for that reason she just sighed and pushed the quarter-sack of potatoes into the corner: after all, she could hardly ask them to take them back, could she?

She even blamed herself for unwittingly setting them upon that path: the week before Christmas, she had called at Moulton's for her weekly ration of sausage meat and mince: it just so happened all the boys were with her: in the butcher's shed, a few scrawny chickens were hung up along with a gutted rabbit. When Patrick had laughingly asked, 'Which is our Christmas dinner, Mum, the rabbit?' Olive had rounded on him with a terse, 'None of them. I can't afford any of them. You'll get what you're given.'

The guilt that she could not provide them with a proper Christmas dinner stayed with her all the way back to the aerodrome, especially as she was already worrying whether the three eldest were getting enough food. All three had been growing thinner of late: or taller: Olive was not sure which, but their clothes seemed to hang upon them more: and, while buttoning Jack's shirt cuffs, she had noticed with alarm that the grey woollen shirt, which he had filled when she had first brought him down from Thurstone, was loose upon him and his ribs stuck out.

She could only surmise that Jimmy and Patrick must have smarted under her rebuke, for on the Friday before Christmas they came hurrying up the lane holding a dead rabbit by its ears: if their mother could not afford to buy them one for their Christmas dinner, then they would go out and catch one: except they had not caught this one, they had stolen it from someone else's snare! The rabbit was duly gutted, skinned and boiled and Christmas dinner was grey rabbit meat, boiled potatoes, greens, parsnips and gravy: 'afters' was 'spotted dick,' made with carrot and turnip pieces, boiled in a cloth in a cracked china basin.

Just as Olive had felt guilt at being unable to provide the boys with a proper Christmas dinner, so it rankled with her, too, that she had no money to spare for presents: everything went on food, household necessities such as soap and the small round tins of toothpaste. The three eldest did not even ask what she was buying them: they took it for granted that they would not be receiving anything, shrugged their shoulders and made their own presents for each other: matchbox cars with drawn cardboard wheels stuck on with flour and water paste for the twins and Michael, a balsa wood destroyer for Jimmy and a balsa wood aeroplane apiece for Patrick and Jack, made from pieces of shot-down aeroplanes they had found washed up on the Langwater's foreshore. Happily, those were not the only presents they received: for the three eldest, their aunts Theresa and Alice and cousin Dorothy had knitted each a balaclava from recycled pullover wool and for the four little ones there were a pair of mittens apiece.

Reluctantly, Olive had come to the realisation that, on her money, she could not even afford the price, little as it was, of the school dinners which arrived daily from Maydun in a little green van: so each morning she cut two doorstep

slices of bread for the three eldest, sometimes spread with just butter, sometimes with jam, but mostly with the dripping which Theresa gave her from her
own cooking: cutting the bread and wrapping the slices in newspaper for
Jimmy to carry to school was her first task each morning.

Invariably, it meant the boys came home hungry: not that they complained
overmuch: just muttered to themselves as they inspected the 'larder' box,
more in hope than anything. At dinner, they accepted and ate whatever their
mother put in front of them, generally a stew of gristly meat, carrots, swede
and onions, with flour and suet dumplings and gravy, all cooked together in
the large handleless saucepan so that the lid rattled from the escaping steam.
The 'meat' was often little more than scragends which she obtained from
Moulton's at a lesser price than other leaner meat but at the same number of
coupons. Olive tried to dole out the portions as fairly as possible, with the biggest going to Jimmy and Patrick because of their greater need and a slightly
lesser portions to herself and Jack, less still to the twins and Michael because,
while the three eldest were losing weight, the four youngest were all gaining it
at her sister's.

Even then, there were occasional flare-ups between the two eldest when one
thought the other was getting more meat, or more carrots, or more potato on
his plate: the only thing they did not seem to squabble about was when one
was given more cabbage: lately, even that had disappeared from the 'larder'
box.

The weekly money which Wakenham paid her just did not go far enough: he
made no concession to the number of children she had by adding any extra if
she worked a little later than normal or did any extra cleaning on the two days
she went into the house: he knew the number of children she had because she
had told him, but it did not seem to influence him in any way: he had agreed
the wage with her at the outset and that was that.

On her 'house' days, as she called them, each Tuesday she would spend
cleaning, polishing and dusting in each of the ten rooms, laying his fires, carrying up his coke from the cellar, scrubbing out his bath, toilet and pantry,
even washing down the windows: on the Fridays when she went back, she
would spend the morning cooking for him: apple and plum pies from the fruit
gathered from his orchard, rice puddings, made and stored cold: lemon curd
tarts, baked and cooled in the pantry: that kind of thing. In the afternoons,
came the part which often made her shudder, for then she washed and ironed
Wakenham's things, his shirts, his vests, his trousers, pullovers, socks, waist-
coats, handkerchiefs and the part which made her shudder the most his long
underpants, silk pyjamas and his bedsheets and pillow cases. Wakenham's
bulk and inability to move, she soon saw, led to some obnoxious stains on his
pyjamas and bedsheets: sometimes, she thought, he probably did not bother to
get out of bed in the middle of the night, but just did what he had to do there
and hoped it would be dry in the morning: at least that is what Olive suspected
as she cast yet another load of soiled sheets on to the washing pile.

To add to her worries, she was having to give half of the twins' and the babies' food coupons to Theresa: for, just as Dorothy had bowed to the carping
and grousing of her father and had reluctantly accepted some money from
Olive for looking after the four youngest, so now Theresa had been hectored
into asking Olive if she could 'spare some of her food coupons to help out.'

Husband Alf had done all the complaining, of course, though not when
Olive was there. 'If we're going to feed her kids and look after 'em every day,
it's only right she not only pays Dorothy to do it but forks out some of her cou-

pons for the food we provide. It's only fair, ain't it? By rights, she ought to be feedin' them herself. Things is hard enough for everybody without adding to our troubles. Food is getting scarce and we're feeding four extra mouths off our own backs. That ain't right, is it?'

Olive had to concede that Alf had a point or sorts: Michael, now two years of age, was having a growth surge and eating far more than he had ever done: the twins, too, were eating everything put in front of them: and Joseph, for whom everything was now being mashed, happily ate anything that was not bland in taste or off-putting in colour.

Making the payment to Dorothy had at least eased Olive's conscience: she knew what effort it involved looking after four young children every day: she knew, too, what a grump her brother-in-law could be – and would be when he and Theresa were alone together – and she did not want to add to her sister's suffering. It pained her each morning to see her sister's frailty, just as it relieved her each morning when Dorothy smiled her bright-eyed welcome to the twins and Michael at the door and lifted Joseph out of the pram to give him a kiss and to make him laugh.

Left to themselves, Dorothy would have quite happily looked after the twins and the babies for nothing and Theresa would never have dreamed of asking for half of the twins' and Michael's coupons, but food was getting scarce for everyone, even country folk unless they had an allotment or a large garden. The war was dragging on into another year, with no one knowing when it would end – or how: every square acre of land was being ploughed, every square foot dug up and planted and regulations were flying out of the Ministry of Food almost daily. Worse, little men with clipboards were spreading out over the land determined to regulate everything in the name of the national interest, to collect up everything and to channel everything, so it seemed to the countryfolk, towards the populaces of the cities.

One Whitehall-type in a spotless suit, a pristine mackintosh, an immaculate striped shirt and old school tie, and wearing unsoiled wellingtons, had even driven up to Follenfaunts and toured everywhere with his clipboard in his hand, much to the headscratching bemusement and bewilderment of Old Jim. Why a man from London should come all the way to Follenfaunts to tell him what he should grow and how he should be growing it, Old Jim did not know: they did not have farms in London, did they? So what would this man know? In the end, he just nodded his head in agreement at whatever the man said and forgot about it as soon as he had gone.

FIFTY

JIMMY and Patrick were unsure exactly what their mother had been trying to say to them in her harangue. Was she forbidding them to steal? Or was she just telling them to be careful in the future and not to get caught? The mildness of her rebuke, bearing in mind others they had received in the past, accompanied by cuffs, slaps and screeching sermons, left them confused: and, in their bewilderment, they took it to mean she was not unduly concerned if their nocturnal activities continued: which they duly did.

Over the next few months, the intrepid pair – for that is how they saw themselves: as the saviours of the family – made several more raids on the self-same farmer's potato clamp, careful each time still to take just enough, no more than a hundredweight over ten weeks, so that they would not be missed: and each time they carefully resealed the mound. On other nights, as the weather grew warmer and the evenings lighter, they went foraging farther afield, sometimes two to three miles off, often not returning till late when their younger brothers had long since been asleep and even their mother was dozing in her usual place on the cutdown chair before the range fire. Over time, quarter-sacks of sprouts, spring cabbages, spring onions, early beans and peas, all picked by themselves in the centre of a field in the dark, were added to their store of vegetables: and they did not just raid the straw-covered clamps or pull up from the fields, but crept into barns to obtain turnips and swede from the piles there and, on one occasion, even climbed down into straw-covered pit for mangels, robbing the cattle of their very feed.

It was always with risk: several times barking dogs alerted the farmers and Jimmy and Patrick had to flee across the fields in the dark, stumbling across ploughed, waterlogged furrows, crashing through hedgerows and diving under barbed wire: though to them, it only added to the fun.

On one occasion, a farmer shouting behind them threatened to fire off his shotgun if they did not stop: they did not and Patrick swore he heard a hornets' flight of pellets zinging through the air above his head as he and Jimmy dived headfirst into a ditch. One spring night, as they were picking onions in a field, a farm labourer, who had been working exceptionally late, came peddling along the dark headland with a clanking milk can hanging from his bicycle handlebars: the two froze as the torchlight splayed right across them. Fortunately, they were lying full length in a puddled furrow and the man did not see them: his thoughts and eyes must have been elsewhere, for he passed within fifteen feet of them and they were able to scuttle away along the headland, chortling with relief at their own audacity.

As the weeks passed into May and the days grew warmer and the evenings lighter, it was almost with relish that Jimmy and Patrick contemplated the approach of summer: for they knew that in a few weeks there would be field upon field of red and black currants, gooseberries and strawberries, peas and beans to raid: and such was their planning these were always across in one of the surrounding parishes so as to be well away from the cottage. In the high summer and early autumn, too, the number of plum, apple and pear orchards which surrounded the village to the east, south and north promised an equally fruitful harvest: they were almost rubbing their hands with glee sometimes as they went out on their Commando-style scouting trips, crawling along ditches, wriggling through hedgerows, sliding under barbed wire fences, balaclavas pulled up to mask their faces, all talk conducted in a hushed whisper and hand signals used wherever possible: boys at war!

The only time that Olive protested at their nocturnal activities was the one time they took Jack along to act as a lookout. 'You just shout if you see anyone,' were his instructions as he could not yet whistle properly: nothing happened: no one saw them, chased them or caught them, but Olive was more furious over that than the actual thieving.

'I don't want him going with you two,' she shouted as the two eldest came through the door with their latest haul, followed by a sheepish Jack. 'He's too young. You do it if you like. I don't want him doing it!'

It was not such an unthinking thing to say as it might seem: as a girl, after she had left the village school and before she took up the post as the assistant to the infants' teacher, Olive had spent a couple of weeks working alongside the other women as a piece-rate picker in the fields around the village, just to earn some money: at the end of the day, all the women, her mother included, had helped themselves to 'a few peas in the shopping bag' or 'a handful of beans' or a 'half punnet of gooseberries or currants or plums.' Startled as she had been by their audacity, it was the sight of her mother doing the same which had shocked Olive: her willingness to take the risk, knowing that the farmers would have barred any of them if they had been caught. It never deterred the women: they seemed to think it their right to take a few of this and a dozen of that: just a few, not too many. Only one group never took anything: those who worked for the cantankerous, bullying Rex Book on his apple farm beside the church: he was not above waiting at the gate to peer into the shopping bags of his pickers as they left: anyone caught with so much as a worm-infested windfall was barred on the spot!

When they were not foraging far afield, the three eldest could often be found riding their bicycles, or the latest variations of those they had built with the finds they had made when they had first scoured the dump and since crashed and buckled and rebuilt several times over! New finds now were hauled from the depths of the dump with the same expressions of thankfulness and delight as a gold miner might make when prising a glittering nugget from the earth. The wheels were inevitably tyreless, the once-black, once-shiny frames reddened by rust: handlebars were added and saddles or sorts fashioned by winding a piece of sacking round the saddle horn and tying it with string. In time, too, missing pedals were replaced and broken chains added to give them proper propulsion, the more mechanically-minded Patrick deftly repairing broken links with wire: often, the whole assembly was held together by means of twisted wire and nuts taken off other finds. Thus, on lighter evenings as the warmer May weather arrived, three of the machines rattled and squeaked over the cinders of the apron, careered up and down the mounds of ash, earth and lime, and sped along the track and out on to the stone-dashed surface of the Beckenden road: had there been a regular flow of vehicles along that way, one or other of them might well have been injured or worse, for they rode recklessly, as boys will, and of brakes there were none. The inevitable crashes and tumbles at least gave the twins something to laugh at and some excitement before they were chased off to bed.

The routine in the cottage, too, had settled down: a tin bath had been found with its bottom unholed and, cleaned and scrubbed out, it now provided weekly baths for them all: the twins and the babies on the Friday night and

Olive on a Saturday afternoon behind a crude curtain made from two sacks she had smuggled out of Follenfaunts in her shopping bag and sewn together with binder string: bathtime for Jimmy, Patrick and Jack was always on Sunday night so that at least they went to school on the Monday morning clean. Subsequent washes from a bowl during the week were expected to be performed without being asked, but did not always happen: and when they did there was often pushing and shoving, even fisticuffs, between the two eldest as to which of them should be first to use the clean hot water and which would get the dirtier tepid water. Usually Jimmy won that argument, bundling the slighter Patrick aside and raising his fists should he attempt to challenge him: often Olive had to step in to stop the two from pummelling each other.

Life was hard, they were poor, but they were surviving.

FIFTY-ONE

THEN one morning, crossing the Square, Olive found Dorothy waiting: she was crying. 'Mum's gone!' she blurted out, tears streaming down her face. 'She died in the night. Dad found her when he went in this morning.'

Olive felt as if a crushing weight had suddenly descended upon her shoulders: had she not been gripping the handles of the pram, her knees would have buckled: tears welled up in her own eyes. She had always known the day would come, must come, right from the very first meeting with her sister on her return to the village: instead of a smiling, slightly plump, blonde-curled Theresa, she had found a sad, thin, wisp of a woman, with hollowed eyes, sunken cheeks and all life seemingly draining slowly from her, But for her to die on a such a bright, sunlit May morning, with the sky a clear blue above, the air shimmering with light, the first flush of green already showing on the hedgerows and the first swifts and swallows darting among the houses in search of nesting places – to die on such a morning of promise only made Theresa's death more tragic, more poignant, more unbelievable.

Olive had sensed that there was something wrong as soon as she saw Dorothy standing forlornly by the ciderstone: she had brought the house pail to fill at the pump, but had not returned with it and instead had waited for her aunt.

'Don't worry, dear,' Olive said softly, brushing away her own tears and placing a hand on her niece's arm. 'I'll come back with you and see everything is done right by her. At least, she's at peace now.' She was aware of the hollowness of her remarks: and that they would bring little comfort or understanding to a girl who had passed her fifteenth birthday only three weeks before: to her, they were meaningless platitudes, spoken at such moments to comfort the bereaved: but in the shock of the moment, Olive could not think of anything else to say.

At the house, while Dorothy took the pail of water into the kitchen to brew tea ready for whoever might come, guiding the twins, Michael and the toddling Joseph ahead of her, Olive went into the sitting room where she knew her sister would be lying. Theresa was on the couch, her body covered by a sheet, except for her face which remained exposed: beside her on chairs, as if on some ritual sentry-duty to keep the corpse company, sat two of the more elderly village women whom Olive knew, one at the head, one by Theresa's feet. When Olive entered, they were sipping tea and talking in whispers almost as though Theresa was only sleeping in the gloom cast by the drawn curtains and they did not want to wake her. The women exchanged weak smiles of sympathy when they saw Olive and stood up so that she might get a better view of her sister's corpse: as is usual in death, the face had lost much of its pained thinness and her cheeks had regained their smoothness: only the blue tinge on her lips and the blood-drained pallor of the skin confirmed her death. What made Olive catch her breath as she looked down was how much Theresa looked like their mother had looked upon her deathbed: to Olive, for a moment it was almost as if her mother had returned in death and she was almost overcome: she felt the warm tears trickling down her cheeks again.

In Gledlang, Old Ma Chapple, a wrinkle-faced spinster with a rounded back and arthritic hands, who lived across the road, and her companion, Mother

Paine, a red-faced widow, who lived up near the Square, were the two most commonly sent for when a corpse needed to be laid out for the callers to see before the undertaker arrived to box it.

'We've washed and dressed her and combed her hair and put a bit of lipstick and powder on her so she'll look all right,' said Ma Chapple quietly. 'We've made her look as good as we can under the circumstances. She looks fine, I reckon, like she's sleeping.'

Her companion nodded and gave the corpse almost a glance of admiration: the gruesome details of their work could not be ignored. 'She cleaned up all right. There wasn't a lot, just the usual,' Mother Paine explained.

'Alf found her on the floor when he come down this morning,' interjected Ma Chapple. 'I reckon she must have tumbled off the couch as she was getting up. Alf heard her fall. Dorothy says her body was still warm when they lifted her back. They thought she had just fainted. They only realised she was dead when she didn't come round.'

'We've sent word to Alice and your father. I expect they'll be here eventually,' said Mother Paine, eager to get some word in. 'We've asked Charlie Male to come and he says he'll be here sometime this morning to do what's necessary. We'll stay with her till then, keep her company, like, her and Dorothy, if you have to get off to work somewhere. It's no bother.'

Olive was not sure whether that was a criticism of her working at Follenfaunts or not: but decided to ignore it: the two women read the question in her eyes in the pause.

'Alf? Oh, he's in the backyard, poor man. In shock, I shouldn't wonder,' Mother Paine went on, giving a sad shake of the head. 'It's Dorothy I feel sorry for, losing her mother at her age, and her so young!' She tut-tutted and sat again on her chair, blocking Olive's view.

Olive found the chain-smoking Alf in the back garden, pacing up and down in a semi-daze: though he also had known her death must come, lately, since Olive's return, he had gone down to breakfast on so many mornings to find his wife sitting up, talking and smiling, that he had started to forget how serious was her illness: it was almost as if he had pushed all thoughts of it out of his mind. He did not stop his pacing, but acknowledged Olive's arrival with a sideways glance.

'Are you all right?' Olive asked, tentatively.

'Yes, I'll be all right, eventually,' replied Alf, the irritability of his reply suggesting otherwise. 'You see to Dorothy. She needs more help than I do. You don't have to worry yourself about me, I'll be fine. You see to Dorothy.'

In the cramped kitchen, a sad-faced Dorothy, still visibly shocked, but managing to control her tears in front of the children, was holding Joseph in one arm and standing by the range waiting for the kettle to boil so that she could make tea: she had already reheated some leftover porridge for the twins and Michael seated around the table: unusually for them, they ate in silence: somehow they sensed the sombre mood of the adults and were nervously looking from face to face to ensure no transgression on their part had caused it.

Dorothy answered her aunt's query without being asked. 'I can still look after them, Auntie,' she said quietly. 'It will give me something to do and Mum would want me to do it. I'll be all right. Don't worry about Dad. I've already told him I'm going to continue so you don't have anything to worry about. It's my decision, not his.' She paused as a thought came to her. 'I knew it was going to happen someday, it's just that I wasn't ready for it. I just wasn't ready, that's all.'

With that, she burst into tears and a worried Joseph looked beseechingly towards his mother as his cousin sobbed into his knitted blue jacket: in the end, Olive had to take the child from her and wash the children's plates and make the pot of tea herself while Dorothy sat upon a chair and quietly cried, all the time apologising for her 'foolishness' and vainly trying to smile so as not to upset the twins and Michael, who regarded her with bewilderment.

Alice arrived just after nine, as tearful as Dorothy. 'I came as soon as I could,' she apologised as Olive ushered her into the parlour and the two women again rose so that the newcomer could view the body. 'Percy and Hubert had already gone to work when I got the news, so I don't suppose they'll be here till dinnertime. He – ' meaning their father ' – says he'll come later.'

Back in the passageway so that they could talk, Olive gave a quick glance towards the parlour where the two women had resumed their positions. 'Can you stay with Dorothy and see she's all right?' she asked, almost in a whisper. 'I have to go to work and I don't want to be here when any of them come. I'll come back later and we'll sit with her for a while this evening. I can't stay too long, I've got the children to think of .'

It was well after ten when Olive finally arrived at the farm: fortunately Wakenham, as was often his habit, was still abed: so she was able slip into the barn to gather up her hoe and return to the field where she had been hoeing for the past few days without being seen, except by Old Jim, of course, working in another field alongside and, like her, hoeing: but all he did was give a shy smile and resume his work.

Such was Olive's turmoil that she would not have cared if Wakenham had seen her, not that day: she had been working at the farm for six months, labouring for three days in the fields and cleaning and cooking in the house for two days each week and Wakenham seemed to be satisfied with her work: leastways, he had not said anything to the contrary. She had helped Old Jim with trimming hedgerows by hand with a billhook in the depths of January and February: and alone she had dug out ditches and water courses with a spade and plastered the mud on the banks to ensure the smooth flow off of the winter rainwater. On other frosty winter days, she had cut kale, pulled mangels and topped and tailed turnips which caused deep sore cracks on her hands, into which she had to rub the baby's Vaseline to ease the soreness: she had helped to build the two mangel and turnip clamps, beds of straw on which the mangels and turnips were tipped, covered in a layer of straw and earth so that they would last through the winter into the spring – and when they were needed as food for the horses, she had opened up the clamps on freezing mornings, forked out the roots into a wheelbarrow and wheeled them to the barn to be diced like chips and mixed with bran and oats.

Only when she was alone in the middle of the field with just her thoughts and her memories to keep her company did the full realisation properly strike her, that she had lost her sister forever, a sister with whom she had grown up, with whom she had played, fought with at times, laughed with on other occasions and sometimes cried with: and it devastated her.

Old Jim waited till midday before he walked over to stutter his usual 'G-g-good day' as she sat under the hedgerow eating her dripping sandwich, but he did not stay long: when she told him the sad news, the old farmworker looked embarrassed as if he had intruded upon her grief, mumbled something in a mournful fashion, which Olive took to be his attempt at a condolence, and wandered off towards the barn to sit in the company of his horses and eat his piccalilli sandwiches there.

FIFTY-TWO

THERESA was buried in the little churchyard on a typical late spring day of hard, bright sunlight, with great rain-filled clouds drifting across the blue, while off the river an east wind chilled the mourners to the marrow: there were a good number of villagers there, mostly the women, for the men were at work.

At the graveside, Dorothy stood with her two aunts, Olive and Alice, weeping quietly: Alf, ashen-faced and red-eyed, stood alone, a stunned look upon his face, as though he was unable still to believe or to accept that his wife was gone. Percy and Hubert were there, dressed in the only suits they possessed, navy blue pinstripe, with the turn-ups too short, but at least wearing dark ties and clean white collars for the first time that Olive could remember. It was the appearance of her father which shocked Olive the most: she had not seen him since she had called at the house on her first day back in the village seven months before: except for the time she had visited Alice and argued with her brothers, she had avoided going anywhere near the house in the weeks since. In that time, her father seemed to have aged beyond his years: he looked frail and hollow-eyed and stood before the gaping grave, open-mouthed and staring-eyed, hunched up inside his overcoat against the streaming wind, a mere husk of the man he once had been, as though he himself had slipped suddenly towards his own end.

Throughout the short graveside ceremony, he leaned upon the arms of his two sons and allowed himself to be guided everywhere by them, a tottering, stumbling old man seemingly bewildered by the goings on, as if he did not comprehend for what purpose he was there: to bury his second daughter! All three stood a few yards apart from everyone else, including the other villagers, as if they were unsure of what to do at a funeral and were confused by its rituals: nor did they come forward to throw a handful of earth upon the coffin lid in the symbolic acceptance of death and burial.

Olive made no attempt to speak to either brother, merely acknowledging their presence through thin pursed lips and then looking away: they, in turn, made no effort to speak to her, just grunted at her presence, returned her stare and stood steely-eyed, talking to each other, their arms linked through their father's. Several times her father looked across at her, but there was not a flicker of recognition in his eyes: they were blank and unseeing and the cold thought struck her, even as she followed Alf, Dorothy and Alice in throwing her handful of red-brown clay on to the coffin lid, that she would be back there soon looking down upon her father's coffin.

For a few moments a droning aircraft towing a long canvas target overhead, while a second aeroplane swooped down behind it, distracted her: then, as she looked down upon the polished brass nameplate, the memories returned: of the times she and Theresa had been together as children: how, when their mother had died, they had walked arm-in-arm up the same sandy church path behind her coffin, the three together, Olive in the centre, the strongest of them, Theresa to her right, Alice to the left: ahead of them their similarly stunned father and beside him again their gloomy brothers. The three girls had remained clinging together by the graveside just to get through it all, walking away together still arm-in-arm back to the house and sensing how empty it was without their mother's presence, even her invalid presence, there.

Still earlier memories came tumbling back, too, as Olive stood brushing at her own tears: memories of herself aged seven, Theresa aged six and Alice just four then, seated in the dirt of the back garden on a sunny day, holding a tea party with the rag dolls their mother had made for them from old woollen stockings: she was hanging out the washing on the line which ran parallel to the path: in memory, everything was white and flapping in a gentle breeze against a blue sky. Then Percy and Hubert, hoeing the lines of beetroot nearby with their father and ever willing to spoil their sisters' games, had surreptitiously begun to flick dirt at the group: an infuriated Theresa had jumped to her feet to scold the bullying brothers and had fled tearfully into the house when they stood laughing at her – until their father clipped their ears and told them to get on with their hoeing.

After that had come the long years at school, Olive and Theresa sitting side by side in the little infants' room and then again, when Olive was promoted to the Big Room itself, walking home together, leading the younger Alice by the hand.

To describe what existed between Olive and Theresa as love would have been embarrassing had it been expressed: love to Olive was something she had felt on first seeing Robert and which had grown and remained with each passing year, despite the trials and tribulations they had suffered when he had been out of work for weeks on end, months sometimes, and there had been no money. Olive, too, would have been the first to acknowledge that there had been times when she and Theresa had decidedly not loved each other: when, in fact, they had screamed their hate at each other, particularly in their adolescence, when they had argued fiercely and even fought each other, scratching at each other's faces and pulling at each other's hair. Once Theresa had even thrown a pair of scissors at Olive which had stuck in the door panel at eye-level just to the side of her head: yet through all that, the affection, though tested by life and their poverty, had survived to be strengthened by their years apart. Like in most families, it was an affection which went unacknowledged: it was just there and nobody remarked upon it or questioned it or fussed themselves over it: as far as all of them were concerned, they were just sisters, part of a family, the same as each other, with the same mother, the same father and, unhappily, the same two older brothers.

For some reason, as Olive stood there, the memory of the time the ten-year-old Alice had fallen down the stairs and broken her thigh came into her mind's eye: Theresa had been the first to reach Alice and to comfort her, before even her mother: and it had been Theresa who had held one of Alice's hands as she lay whimpering with pain upon the kitchen table, held down by her two brothers while the drunken doctor did his inexpert work. It had been Theresa, too, more than any of them, who had pleaded again and again with their father to take Alice to a hospital and have the leg rebroken so that it could be set straight: when her brothers, siding with their father in his refusal, had chided her, she had flown at them, raking her nails down Percy's laughing face and had tearing out a hank of his hair.

That was the Theresa whom Olive recalled in that brief moment when the coffin was lying in the hollow of the grave and the earth was being tossed down upon its lid: then she was walking away with the limping Alice and the tearful, sad-eyed Dorothy.

A month later, in the June, she was back, looking down at her father's coffin just as she had feared.

FIFTY-THREE

THE BLACK, rain-spattered Humber had been parked in the narrow lane between the grey, stained wall of the bank on one side and the windowless, red-brick sidewall of the Co-op emporium on the other for almost an hour: ten yards ahead of it, a steady stream of shoppers was crossing the gap where the lane joined the High Street of the small West Midlands town. Few, if any, gave the parked car so much as a glance: their heads were bent and their umbrellas were raised to shield themselves from the spring shower: in any case, their minds were on other things.

In May, 1942, nothing about the war was going right: it had been a succession of disasters: a full-scale retreat was underway in Burma, a full-scale retreat was going on in North Africa and the advance of the Germans in Russia and the Mediterranean and the Japanese in the Far East seemed to be unstoppable: small wonder then that the men, mostly older men, those under eighteen and those deferred from active service for one reason or another, slouched past with hunched shoulders, depressed. The women, too, looked glum and, if they spoke at all to a companion, it was to moan about their inability to buy decent clothes of any kind, at having to make-do and mend and the incessant queuing they undertook just to obtain their family's miserly food ration. Only two adolescent girls chattered wonderingly about a convoy of American airmen which a friend claimed she had seen the previous day driving along one of the county's roads towards a Royal Air Force aerodrome. 'Truck after truck of them, whistling at her and shouting things out, so she said,' commented one.

In the black Humber, three men sat nervously watching as a fourth man in a soiled fawn raincoat and brown trilby pulled down over his forehead came hurrying back through the rain, clutching at his hat lest it be blown away in the gusting wind. The lane really was no more than a short alleyway off the High Street, with just enough room for the lean, dark-haired man in the soiled raincoat to tug open the front passenger door of the black Humber and squeeze in alongside the driver.

'They've just opened up,' said the man in the fawn raincoat, turning to face two others in the back seat. 'They're all inside now. There's only the four of them, no one else. It looks easy enough. Is everybody ready? Liam?' He spoke in a broad Irish accent.

'Ready, Sean,' a thin-faced, hook-nosed youth, with flaming red-hair, answered from the back seat, taking a heavy revolver from inside his coat and breaking it open to check the chamber before snapping it shut again. His accent was also Irish, but with a broader County Mayo brogue.

The flat-faced man beside him, with a pudgy nose and a mop of wavy brown hair, had reached inside his own jacket to produce a similar revolver to that of his companion, National Army issue, Nineteen Twenty-Two: he, too, spoke with an Irish accent, but more northern, Derry or Donegal. 'Aye, I'm ready, Sean,' he replied. 'Let's get it done.'

The dark-haired man in the trilby had produced a heavy pistol of his own from his raincoat pocket and he, too, was checking the magazine. 'Make sure your safety catches are on,' he ordered his two companions in the back seat, ramming the magazine back. 'We don't want any bloody guns going off by mistake! We don't want another bloody fiasco like that time in Plymouth. So keep your catches on and your guns hidden till we're inside. Then get them out. Business as usual.' The two men in the backseat smiled.

The man in the fawn raincoat and the trilby turned to the driver, a thin-lipped, bespectacled man in his early twenties, and gave him a hard look. 'You know the drill, Charlie,' he said, grim-faced. 'Follow us as soon as we turn the corner. Park the car outside and wait – and be bloody sure you keep the engine running! Don't worry about the bloody petrol. Rationing's for others. We can allus get some more on the black market. If anybody looks queer at you because you're wasting precious petrol, just smile and say the engine's queer. What I don't want is to come rushing out of there with all hell let loose behind us and find you can't start the bloody car! All right?'

Charlie, the driver, nodded a nervous understanding and gripped the steering wheel even more tightly: beads of perspiration glistened on his forehead: after all, this was his first time.

'Right then, boys, let's get on with it,' said Sean, pushing open his door and swinging out his legs: he did not stand up straight away, but turned to eye the two in the back seat. 'For the Cause,' he said softly, raising one querying eyebrow.

'For the Cause,' said the red-haired youth with the hooked nose, nodding and opening his door.

'For the Cause,' repeated the flat-faced man with the pudgy nose, a grim look upon his face as he slipped the revolver inside his coat pocket and slid out after his red-haired companion.

The inside of the bank was small, with just enough room for four or five people to form a queue before a long open counter which crossed from wall to wall and divided the room: a line of three desks lay behind the counter and beyond was a solitary door with the word 'MANAGER' inscribed upon it: the walls were painted a light green. At the open counter, a young, grey-suited, dark-haired clerk of no more than sixteen or seventeen was writing in a ledger with a scratchy pen, carefully blotting each entry as he made it: so engrossed was he in his work that he did not look up as the three men entered. Immediately behind him, half-hidden by the height of the counter, another, older clerk, bald-headed, in his late fifties with a drooping grey moustache and steel-rimmed spectacles, sat at the first of the dark mahogany desks: he was sipping a cup of tea and sheafing through a pile of papers: he did look up, but saw the three only from the lower chest up. In one corner, a third clerk, young like the counter clerk, also dressed in a plain grey suit, was flicking through the files of an opened cabinet drawer: he had his back to the door and was inserting pieces of paper into the files. The first the counter clerk knew of the three men was when a shadow fell across his ledger and he looked up to see a heavy pistol pointed straight at his heart.

'This is a stick-up,' cried the man in the soiled raincoat and the brown trilby, loud enough for all to hear. 'Don't anybody move! Do as we say and no one'll get hurt! We want the money and we want it bloody quick. All fivers and quids! No bloody coins!' He pushed a canvas mailbag across the open counter at the young clerk, who, on seeing the gun, had begun to raise his hands as if in surrender.

'Put your bloody hands down and fill that with everything you've got and be quick about it!' the trilby wearer ordered harshly.

At the same time, to his right, the red-haired man had flung up the flap at the end of the counter, rounded the older clerk's desk and flung open the manager's door: as it crashed open, rattling some cups and saucers on a small table just inside, the portly, round-faced, manager, half-rose from his desk. 'Don't you move one bloody inch or you'll get it!' the red-haired man shouted fiercely. Wisely, the portly manager momentarily froze: then slowly, carefully, his eyes fixed all the time on the red-haired man, he lowered himself back into his chair, the fountain pen with which he had been writing still poised in his hand: he did not even blink.

In the corner, the day-dreaming filing clerk, on hearing the commotion, had turned to see what the noise was all about, only to find the red-haired man pointing the gun alternatively at him and then through the doorway at the manager in his office: he gave what amounted to an involuntary whimper and retreated even further into the corner, almost hiding himself behind the filing cabinet.

At the counter, the petrified clerk had lowered his hands, but now began to shake: he seemed to be mesmerised by the gun, staring at it as though he dare not take his eyes from it, especially as it followed his every move. By the door, preventing anyone else from coming in, he had noticed the third man, the flat-faced one with a pudgy nose and a mass of brown wavy hair: he, too, had a gun, but he seemed to be more nervous, more agitated than the other two: he was sweating profusely: the clerk could see the perspiration shining on his brow and he was forever glancing out of the window as though he feared that at any second someone would enter and he would have to deal with them: no one did.

'I don't want anyone doing anything stupid,' the trilby-wearing Sean said quietly to the counter clerk, moving the pistol briefly sideways to point directly at the older clerk, who had remained seated in his chair: the older man was eyeing Sean coldly and seemed unperturbed, even turning his head to look briefly towards the manager's office where the red-haired man was standing with his back against the doorpost, covering both the stunned manager and the white-faced filing clerk.

Sean's gun came back round to point at the petrified counter clerk again. 'Come on, get a move on! We haven't got all bloody day!'

The mesmerised young clerk pulled open a drawer, snatched up three bundles of white fivers and thrust them into the bag: a handful of loose pounds and ten-shilling notes followed.

'That's all the notes I have,' he pleaded, seeing the dissatisfaction and anger in the trilby man's eyes. 'The rest is all coin.'

'You're a bloody liar!' shouted Sean, thrusting the gun forward so that it was only an inch from the man's face, at the same time leaning across the counter to peer into the drawer.

'Open the other drawer, Jenkins!' The command came quietly from the older clerk behind him. 'There's two-hundred pounds in there.'

The trembling clerk moved nervously across to the second drawer, followed by the gun, tugged it open, picked up the wads of notes and pushed them into the bag: then looked up at the man with the gun as if expecting his approval.

'What about the safe? What's in there?'

The counter clerk did not answer, but turned appealingly to his elders behind: it was the portly manager who answered.

'The safe is still time-locked,' he called out from his office, with a nervous gulp, the sweat induced by fear of his own glistening on his brow: somehow, there was something in the eyes of the red-haired man leaning against the doorpost pointing the gun alternately at him and the clerk which frightened him. Was it fear like his own? Craziness? Derangement? He could not tell.

'It's not due to open for another fifteen minutes yet. Not till ten o'clock,' the manager added quickly, as if to exonerate himself. 'We never open it before then. There's never been a need, you see. We're only a small bank. It's only nine-forty-five now – ' He gave a nervous cough as if embarrassed by what he was about to say. ' – We also do it as a precaution – against this sort of thing. You understand?' Another nervous gulp followed: more sweat trickled down his forehead.

'Are you telling me the bloody truth?' Sean demanded loudly, waving the gun wildly at all four of the staff, at the same time drawing the canvas bag back across the counter.

This time it was the older clerk who spoke. 'Yes, he is. It's quite true,' he declared, pulling a large brass watch from the pocket of waistcoat and holding it in the palm of his hand. 'It is time-locked till ten o'clock. The time-lock does not open for another – for another eleven minutes, to be precise.' He said it through the pursed lips of a man who abided by punctiliousness and shrugged as if to say there was nothing he could do about it.

From the flat-faced, pudgy-nosed man by the door came a nervous shout: 'Ah, bloody hell, Sean! Let's get out here! We can't wait. We've got enough.'

'Shut up!' Sean shouted, angrily whirling on him. 'I'll say when we've got enough.' He studied the impassive face of the older clerk still seated at his desk, muttered an oath to himself and then backed away from the counter, still keeping the counter clerk covered with his gun.

'Come on, Liam,' he shouted, loudly. 'We're going. Let's get out of here.'

The man at the door was already holding it open as Sean backed towards it: as they did so, the red-haired Liam came hurrying towards the counter flap. Why he fired, neither Sean nor his companion was exactly sure. They heard him shout angrily, 'I told you not to bloody move, any of you!' and then the explosion reverberated in the small space like a magnified whipcrack: the face of the young counter clerk showed shock at first, then pain and then fear as he slowly crumpled and the red began to stain his shirt. By the time, Liam joined his companions at the door, the young clerk was sitting on the floor, with his back against the counter, crying and holding the wound in his chest: none of the others in the bank had moved so much as an inch.

In the car, as it roared down the High Street, the red-haired Liam was cowering in the back seat: on the same seat, Sean's gun was pressed hard against his temple: in his other hand he held the red-haired man's pistol which he had snatched from him. 'Why did you want to go and shoot the silly bugger for?' he screamed, the spittle at the corners of mouth foaming like the froth of a madman. 'Why, you stupid bastard? Why?'

'He moved!' a terror-stricken Liam screamed back, brushing at the tears rolling down his cheeks. 'We told them not to move. We told them all! He was going for the alarm, I swear it. I swear it. They were warned! You warned them! I warned them! They were all warned!'

'You stupid bastard!' Sean shouted. 'You effing stupid bastard! You know what you've done? You've put a bloody rope around all our necks! If he dies, we'll hang. You arsehole! You bloody arsehole! Idiot! You bloody idiot!'

The car was out of the town by then: green fields, trees and hedgerows were speeding past: the sky was filled by great rain-filled clouds and dark patches of blue: the sun streaming through the windscreen was hot.

Seated now beside the bespectacled driver, Robert Cullen, Olive's husband, leaned back in his seat, cradling his revolver and closed his eyes: he felt no sympathy for his cowering companion: if Sean decided to shoot him there and then, he did not care: he just did not care.

FIFTY-FOUR

AS the car sped out along the Coventry road, Robert suddenly found himself thinking of Olive: where was she? Had she gone back to the village, whatever that was called, 'Glebeland' or something? Wherever that was! Somewhere out in East Anglia, she had said: on the coast. He had never been there: nor had he ever wanted to go: a piddling little place, small and backward, from her description of it. Glad to leave it, she had said. What was she doing at that moment? Sitting talking with her sisters no doubt, the two sisters he had never met, the sisters who had refused to come to their wedding – or who just could not be bothered.

And what were the children doing, Jimmy, Patrick, Jack, the twins, Thomas and John, little Michael and baby Joseph? The three eldest, Jimmy, Patrick and Jack would still be in Thurstone: at school since it was mid-morning, doing their lessons, sitting in the classroom with all their friends: it had been two years since he had last seen them: it would be nice to see them again: but not now, not with the hue and cry Liam's stupidity had stirred up.

And what of the four youngest, the twins and the babies? They would be with their mother, playing somewhere most probably: in a park perhaps? How long had it been since he had last seen them and their mother? Over a year-and-a-half: over a year-and-a-half since he had seen Olive and the boys off on the train to Thurstone: so much had happened to him since then, so much.

From the station, he had gone back to the Rupert Road flat for a sleep and something to eat: it was almost a dare to the police to break in upon him and catch him: if they wanted him, they would have to come and get him! He had slept all day, waking just before five: then he had slipped out of the flat a good half-hour before the sirens began to sound. After first checking the road was clear, he had headed towards the corner, joining the others going early to the shelter, or so it had looked. But, instead of going into the shelter, he had headed for the Underground a good mile away: nothing unusual about that: others were also making for the entrance to the Underground. The shelter at the end of the road was far too risky: if the police thought he was hanging about the area, they would be sure to check there. When he had returned the next morning the house was a pile of rubble, along with those either side, and the road was cordoned off because an unexploded bomb lay amid the debris of one of the houses farther down. Since then, he had seen no one, heard from no one.

He had had to lie low for a couple of days after dodging a suspicious policeman curious about his Irish accent and then had tried to find his sisters-in-law, Martha and Muriel, but their flats had been bombed as well and were empty: worse, both had disappeared. So had Brendan and Gerry, though he guessed where they were: in the army: and, if he knew them, most likely in the Glasshouse at Aldershot. Only he had been able to remain free, dodging the coppers, dodging the red caps, dodging the army, changing his name, not once but three times: Robert Murphy, Robert Logan, Robert O'Neill, each time changing his ID card as well, and his coupons. He had slept at many different addresses, in doss houses, in friends' apartments, sometimes even sleeping rough on station platforms, working here, working there, clearing rubble, even getting a portering job on the railways for a few months through one of his friends: but eventually moving on till one day by chance in a pub he had met his Plymouth friends again: they were laying concrete at one of the new air-fields in the Midlands being built for the Yanks, the United Sates Army Air Forces, to be exact, who were beginning to arrive in the country in increasing numbers.

His friends from Plymouth were still in the same old business 'for the Cause': ostensibly, they worked as labourers alongside thousands of other Irishmen who had flocked to Britain to obtain work, but every now and again they would take the day off to rob the occasional bank or post office, 'for the Cause,' of course, just the small, out-of-the-way ones, little district banks miles and miles away where they could get in quickly and get out quickly and there was unlikely to be a Riley patrol car with its horn wailing chasing after them.

And Robert had joined them: feeling that at last he was doing something 'for the Cause.' Though the bank had been his first robbery, it had been his friends' fourth since the start of the year: quite frankly, it had not been worth the effort, not for two-hundred and fifty quid. The Cause would not see much of that. They would need most of it to live on while they were on the road, for sooner or later they would have to move on: they always did and Robert would have to go with them now: like them, he would have to find new lodgings somewhere else, change his name again, get a new identity card and new food coupons and get another job through other friends from across the water: all of them lying low till things quietened down. Still, it was better than fighting for the bloody British! There was no way they were going to get him to fight for them! If the Germans did come, he would be the first to hang out the bloody flags to greet them! The Irish flag, of course! Or go back to Ireland.

FIFTY-FIVE

OLIVE had spent two harsh winters on the land, exposed to all the elements, hail, sleet, rain, freezing fogs, frost and icy winds streaming off the estuary: in consequence, her hands had become calloused and hard and the dirt ingrained in them: her nails were broken and blackened, her hair often hung lank and disordered over her face: her cheeks were reddened and veined: she no longer bothered to look in the mirror except to wash her face: she made no effort to powder it or to rouge her lips and attempts at combing her hair were half-hearted: it was much easier to jam on her hat to cover it and set off for work.

At the precise moment that Robert was seated in the car speeding away from the West Midlands town, she was working alone in the middle of one of Follenfaunts's sodden fields, leading Betsy, one of the farm's two horses: she was that day shovelling lime from the back of a small, tip-up cart: every twenty yards or so, she would halt the horse, take up a broad shovel, climb up into the cart and toss out the chalky lumps of lime into small piles. As each shovelful left the cart, the blustery wind caught it and blew much of it back at her so that the tattered second-hand coat she wore, her hair, her face, her hands, woollen mittens, stockings and turned-down wellingtons were all covered by the fine chalky powder: she resembled more a ghost than a human.

The coat and the mittens she had obtained from her dead sister Theresa's effects, given to her by Dorothy along with two pairs of shoes, two dresses, a pinafore, two cardigans, a vest, girdle, slip and three pairs of stockings, darned only at the toes: but no money. If Olive felt anything at all as she worked in the keen wind blowing off the estuary, it was a mild thankfulness that she was at least wearing the turned-down pair of third-hand wellingtons: they were too big for her and she had to wear a pair of Patrick's socks and stuff the toes with newspaper, but at least they kept her feet dry: unlike the boots which they had replaced, a discarded pair of Jimmy's which she had had to 'mend' herself with a strip of inner tube rubber for waterproofing and a piece of old bicycle tyre cut off and wired round to form the sole. She had worn them throughout the whole of that first freezing winter and through the length of the following year, right up until the November when in desperation she had paid one-and-six for the wellingtons at a village sale of a deceased couple's effects.

To Olive, shovelling out the small piles of lime to be spread in a wide circle at a later date by either herself or Old Jim, it was just another job to be done, one of a score of different tasks she had done since starting at Follenfaunts and for which the tight-fisted Wakenham still paid her only a miserly thirty-five shillings a week. Eighteen months before, after she and Old Jim had riddled the potatoes in the barn, she had spent the next two weeks cutting kale alone in the November downpours which had begun almost immediately, back-aching work of stooping, pulling and slashing, hour after endless hour, day after day, with clothes soaked through to the skin despite the sack she put over herself as a cowl and the two others she tied front and back about her waist with binder string. After that, she had pulled mangels alone and topped and tailed turnips alone, which caused deep sore cracks on her hands, into which she had to rub Joseph's Vaseline to ease the pain. In the depths of January and February, Old Jim had set her to trimming hedgerows by hand with a billhook and digging out ditches and water courses with a spade, plastering the mud on to the banks to ensure the smooth flow off of the winter rainwater: without wellingtons, her feet had become soaked and frozen, bloodless, as if she had trench foot, and there had been times when she had despaired as the cold and damp had risen up through the holed soles of her boots till her bones ached. One time, her gloveless hands had been so frozen that she could not grasp the handle of the spade properly and she had found herself crying with the cold: but she had worked on and completed it and had not cried since.

When she had finished that task, there were more back-aching days stooping to pick stones off the fields, prising them out from ground hardened by frost or saturated by rain: when the young oats began to push up, she went down between the rows chopping thistles before they got too high, using a paddle, a stick with an inch-long blade because there was nothing more painful to the hands than setting up stooks at harvest time full of prickly thistles: and each evening she picked the thistle barbs out of the palms of her hand as she walked back down the long Follenfaunts driveway towards the village to pick up the twins and the two youngest.

It was not that Old Jim gave her these tasks because he disliked Olive or hated women: he just was not used to having a woman working alongside him with their different ways: their different ways of thinking, their different ways of acting: their lesser strength. He knew what a man, himself, that is, could do: he did not know what a woman could do: so he gave her the tasks which he thought befitted a woman, tolerating her simply as an extra 'hand,' someone to do the more menial work, regarding her, not with disdain, for she worked well and he acknowledged it, but as the older village farmworkers who had spent their lives on the land and knew the seasons in all of nature's moods regarded the three new Land Army Girls who had arrived in the village that summer to lodge at the Chessman and to work on the Godwins' four larger farms. That is, as women, weaker than men, who had squawking voices and squealing temperaments and who seemed to pay more attention to painting their faces, could not lift anything really heavy or push it or haul it and, if they tried, seemed to worry more about breaking their finger nails or getting calluses on their palms than actually moving or lifting the thing.

But each morning as Olive arrived for work in her repaired boots, Theresa's old overcoat, scarf, knitted gloves and plain hat, with the bag containing her sandwiches and her bottle of water or cold tea over her arm, ready to do any task about the farm which he requested of her, Old Jim would look at her with a frown on his face, screw up his gap-tooth mouth, rub his bristly chin and blush with embarrassment at having to talk to her at all: worse, was trying to think of what work he could give her to do next and then having to instruct her how to do it. So he set her to do the more menial labour, the kind given to the less-experienced worker, especially a woman: such as sitting in the draughty barn alone with only her own thoughts for company, sorting potatoes for seed by hand: creosoting the wagon shed till the skin on her cheeks blistered and peeled from the splashes: cleaning out the sty in one corner of the yard to lay down new straw and boiling up the food for the three noisy, squealing, pushing animals who inhabited it: mending the grain sacks with patches and fish glue: or climbing down into the grave-like root pit with crumbling sides behind the wagon shed to fork up the mangels from under the layer of straw before wheeling them on a barrow to the barn and dicing them like chips as feed for the four cows Wakenham also kept.

Olive did all of these without complaint, glad to be earning the money, little as it was: the main work about the farm, the work with the horses, the ploughing, the harrowing, the drilling and the rolling, Old Jim did by himself as if keeping his distance from her: in the mornings sometimes, as she arrived for work, she received no more than a cursory nod from him, not out of any dislike or disrespect for her but simply borne of the man's embarrassment. As she cut the kale, dug out the water courses and prised out the flint stones that first winter, Olive hoped that at some time or other she, too, would be allowed to work with the horses, Betsy and Sam, great shiny-coated, chestnut-coloured beasts which plodded contentedly about the farm from field to field, headland to headland, as if they were born to nothing else. It was the one thing on the farm to which Olive looked forward: ever since going as a young girl into a field with her father when he had worked as the ostler on Old Man Stanson's farm in the centre of the village opposite the school, she had loved horses: she had never been afraid of them, regarding the great, lumbering, docile beasts with an affection which she seemed to have inherited from her father: but those were memories of younger days before her mother had fallen ill and before her father had grown harsher towards her.

Any suggestion, however, that Olive could help Old Jim with the horses on Follenfaunts was met by the old farmworker with one of his peculiarly adamant, yet shy, mutterings, 'No, no, no, thankee, thankee. I can do it meself, thankee all the same! I sees to the horses meself. They 'on't like anybody else botherin' 'em. You jest git on an' do what you've got ter do and I'll see ter they meself,' and he had gone away and done whatever was needed to be done on his own.

The change came unexpectedly one day in the summer as they were harvesting the corn: until then Old Jim would not even have allowed Olive to take hold of the halter and lead them along the headland back to the barn lest on the way she walk them straight into the pond or into a ditch or into a hedgerow. As usual, he had cut the standing corn with a horse-drawn binder and Olive this time, instead of the Bow boy, had walked round the field behind him in the baking sun, stacking the sheaves eight to a stook, four each side to hold each other up in line with the prevailing wind, where they would stand till the corn was ripe and dry. Four days later they returned to gather it in: Olive was following the cart, pitchforking the sheaves up to Old Jim balanced fifteen-feet or so up on top of the four-wheeled wagon, when he had sat down as if dizzy. Olive was not surprised: that lunchtime, the old farmworker had downed a near full bottle of cider and now, in the blazing afternoon sun, he sat atop the load, smiling and blinking at the world in a semi-inebriated state: so it fell to Olive to seize the moment, take the halter of Betsy, harnessed ahead of Sam in the shafts, and lead them over the jolting, uneven ground, back to the yard. She knew it was not without risk: neither Old Jim nor Wakenham would have thanked her if she had sent the load toppling or pitched Old Jim off on to his head: so carefully, watchful of the bumps and hollows, she guided the creaking, groaning wagon across the field, through the gate and along the potholed track for threequarters-of-a-mile to the yard without mishap. Little as such an accomplishment might appear to some, to Olive it was a source of pride: a sense of achievement: better still, when Old Jim awoke from his brief nap and found himself still atop the load and the wagon parked in the yard, with Betsy and Sam contentedly munching on their nosebags, his attitude towards her changed. Until then, she had been just a woman worker: now, before she took her place on top of the load, ready to toss down the sheaves to him so he could build the stack, he had pitchforked the first ones down himself, then climbed down and, motioning for her to stand alongside him, had shown her the secret of how he carefully built up each gable-ended stack from the ground in layers, each layer three sheaves high, the first started with the butt of the sheaves pointing outwards. Then, after two rounds, the sheaves were reversed and placed with the ears outwards: then the middle was filled: after that, another layer was started, continuing to the top. Explaining such intricacies to a woman was the old farmworker's way of praising her for her effort, taking her into his confidence. When the next day the stack was finished and the tarpaulin roped down, Olive felt a sense of accomplishment she had not experienced for a long time: for the first time she felt as though there was a worth to her work.

When the touring threshing gang, three brothers from Budwick, came, driving their chugging steam tractor, which also pulled the elevator and a caravan in which the brothers slept, Old Jim gave her the place atop the stack in front of the drum: and as he and one of the other men pitched the sheaves across the stack to her, she cut the string binding them, tucked it into her belt and carefully and evenly fed the sheaves into the threshing machine, ears first: as old farmworkers knew, it had to be done that way, ears first: they could not just be dropped in any old fashion. From there, the corn went through the drum to the shakers which took it along to where corn and chaff were separated by wind-blown fans: after the corn had been shaken out, the loose straw dropped on to the elevator which lifted it up to the new stack being built of threshed straw by one of the other men. From the side of the thresher, grain ran in a golden river from the drum into sacks and these, when full, were unhooked and carted by the third brother into the barn store.

Wakenham, with a townie's curiosity about country ways, would sometimes waddle up to watch them, leaning on his stick and puffing and blowing with the effort of walking the fifty or sixty yards from the house: he never did anything to help, of course: not even lifting one of the lightweight sacks of chaff which were also bagged from the centre of the machine and could have been lifted by a child. Mostly, he complained about the dust, which in threshing is exceptional and covers everybody and everything, and how it affected his chest and lungs: and, after a quarter-hour, he would clutch at his throat or chest, start coughing and limp away, back to the house and back to his bed or, more likely, the couch in the parlour where he spent much of his time, reclining and immobile, listening to the wireless, which seemed to be his whole life..

The stack-building and the threshing were the beginnings of the change for Olive: a week after the thresher had left, when she arrived for work and went into the barn to collect her machete to go topping and tailing beet, Old Jim had called her over and, again giving one of his more sheepish grins, had motioned for her to follow him into the stable area where he had showed her how to harness both the horses into the shafts of the four-wheeled wagon: it was, Olive discovered, a more complicated task than she had thought. Each of the horses had its own collar, made for it and moulded to fit its chest muscles: Old Jim showed her how to put on the collar upside down, then turn it the right way up to slide it down each animal's neck, before taking out the mane and settling it more carefully. After that, the hames, the two high brass horns, were draped over the collar and tightened at the bottom with short chains. If both horses were going into the shafts, a cart pad was put on each animal's back: attached to the pad was a contraption of thick wide leather straps, called breaches, which dropped over the hindquarters: the belt band was attached to this pad and tightened. Next, the bridle and bit were slipped on and the horses backed into the shafts: a chain fitted to the shafts was thrown over the pad on each horse's back and Olive then slipped round under the neck and fixed each chain on to the shafts the other side at the right height to hook on to the shaft on the other side. On the harness, too, were other short chains on each side called tugs which were fixed to hooks on the shafts: the breaching chain was fixed each side at the back and then the only thing that remained to secure was the thick leather band that went under each horse's belly and stopped the cart from going up in the air if it were loaded too heavily.

That autumn, too, he had allowed her to take a turn at finishing the ploughing while he went off to gather in the cows to start the afternoon milking: admittedly, it was only the last few runs of single-furrow ploughing and Old Jim had already walked some fifteen miles that day in the process of completing the final acre: Olive even imitated his 'Goo on,' to start the horses, his 'Whoa' to stop them, his 'Come by' to make them turn left and 'Way out' to make them go right: at the finish, she had even unhitched them, walked them back, unharnessed them, rubbed them down and fed them.

Now well into her second year at Follenfaunts, she had done the spring harrowing of their single field of root crop on her own, working with Betsy: then she had helped with the spring drilling, preceding Old Jim up and down the field with Betsy pulling the harrow to break up the clods, while he followed with the stronger Sam pulling a fourteen-coulter drill sowing corn: then she and Betsy had light harrowed again after the drilling was done to cover the seed.

Late one afternoon, Old Jim had called Olive into the milking shed where he was about to begin milking the four cows. 'Guv'nor says I hev to teach 'ee how ter milk the cows. Says it's time yer learnt,' was all he said, looking down at the ground and scuffing his boot in the dirt. Then, blushing a deep crimson as he stooped beside her, the shy, stuttering Jim showed her how to keep the milk streaming into the bucket with a steady squeeze and gentle pull on the cow's teats so that the animal let down the milk easily while she ate her corn. Olive could only think that Wakenham had taken pity on her or he had reckoned, being a woman, she would have the milking touch: for, when ten minutes later, Old Jim returned, still red-faced, and went along the line to 'strip,' as he called it, that is, to test whether he could get out more milk from the cows' udders, he could not: for the first time since she had arrived, he mumbled a barely audible 'Y've done well there,' which was all the congratulations he was prepared to give.

The one thing he did not do was have her there when the bull was brought to get on the cows: that would have been too much for the old farmworker to bear, to have a woman present for that!

There was only one job which Old Jim set her to do and for which she did not thank him was helping with the killing of the three pigs: she did it, but reluctantly: she was, she realised, too squeamish for such a gruesomely hideous task as taking a life, in this case, three lives! The necessary authorisation from the Ministry of Food had been obtained and the pig killer, a jovial faced, easy-talking butcher named Albert, from Wivencaster, had arrived on the Wednesday: as Old Jim was that day performing other tasks, Olive found herself directed to assist him: it was the callous brutality of the act which upset her.

As the helper, her first job was to boil hot water in a big, cast-iron cauldron in the yard and keep the fire fed by old pieces of timbering. The mischievous Albert had obviously noted her unease, for, as he laid out an array of razor-sharp knives and cleavers and his wooden mallet on an upturned box, he seemed to take great delight in describing what he was about to do. 'We use this one to slit their throat,' he said with a grin, showing Olive a wicked curved-blade affair, before adding to its sharpness with a few swift strokes along a whetstone. 'You just draw it straight across and bleed them out. Done right, they won't know a thing about it. Has to be done. Man must eat, mustn't he?' Followed by a cackling laugh as Olive shuddered and looked away.

While the water boiled and Albert went across the yard to the sty to get his first victim, Olive was set to preparing the bed of straw on which the first animal would be bled and laid: a minute later Albert returned, a determined grimace on his face as he hauled the violently protesting animal by a rope passed through its nose ring: the poor doomed pig seemed to sense its fate, for it dug in its heels and squealed loud enough to be heard a half-mile away as it struggled to break free. All the time Albert was cursing at the top of his voice and dragging it towards a stake he had driven into the ground in the centre of the straw bed and to which he intended to tie it. 'Yer going whether yer bloody like it or not,' he was shouting. 'Yer going, yer bugger! Yer going!'

Olive had not the stomach to watch the actual moment of butchery and went into the barn to hide, wincing to herself at the very moment the squeals stopped as the knife did its work and the pig died: only after the poor animal had been bled, did she go back out and help lay it on the prepared straw ready for the next task, while Albert went to fetch the second animal. The whole process was repeated as the second animal and then the third were dragged out in turn and dispatched in the same way by the grinning Albert. Finally, with the third laid beside the other two on the straw, it was her task to heap more straw three or more feet high around them and set that on fire to help with the 'skinning.' When the fire had done its work, she and the pig-killer hoisted up the dead animals one by one and spent the whole of the afternoon scraping the singed flesh with sharp knives to take to take off all the hair. After that, they scrubbed each carcass with the boiling water till each was absolutely clean and then, with one swift slash of his sharpest knife, Albert disembowelled them in turn, tumbling the slippery, shining, steaming intestines into the three pails of water which Olive had provided.

That was not the end of the task: the disembowelled pigs were left hanging overnight on hooks in the barn and the next day Albert returned to 'joint 'em up,' with Olive's help again, of course, for it was her job to wrap the cleaved, bloodied meat in greaseproof paper. Finally, it was all done and Olive and the jovial Albert had laid the pieces of the carcasses on the grimy sawdusted floor of his meat van: Wakenham took his share, of course, one of the sides, but the rest, by wartime decree, was taken away to be hung in butcher's shops in Wivencaster, where even the heads were boiled to produce brawn and chops were sliced from the cheeks.

Wakenham's side of pork was put in a trough, the seams of which were lined with pitch, to be salted. Directed by Old Jim, Olive covered the bottom of the trough with a layer of salt and laid the side of pig in it and covered that with more salt: every day she rubbed fresh salt into it and, at the end of three weeks, the bacon was considered salted enough to be cured: then she and Old Jim hung the side from a beam and left it. When Wakenham wanted some bacon, he sent Olive into the barn to lower the side and cut off whatever slice she wanted: it still made her shudder every time she did it, to think she had seen the poor animal dragged across the yard to be killed: but she did it all the same and helped herself as well: just a little slice of pork bacon to be boiled and eaten with some new potatoes from the fields and some fresh peas: the children ate it all, wondering from where their mother had obtained it: Olive did not tell them, but they ate well that night.

Over the next few weeks, her only other task was daily to change the water in which the intestines were soaking: each week, too, she turned them inside out and was glad, finally, when Old Jim came to carry them off to Wakenham's kitchen, where he knitted them like sausages and the fat, breathless, indulgent Wakenham would dripping-fry the chitterlings for his supper or cook them as his main meal along with the best of the vegetables he had kept back from the market.

FIFTY-SIX

BY A STROKE of good fortune, Olive had been able to part-furnish the cottage when an old couple in the village had died within an hour of each other: the old woman, in her early seventies, had died sitting in her chair by the fire, just fallen asleep and died while her husband, who, though seventy-odd, still laboured on the Stanson sisters' farm, sat opposite her resting after his tea. When the neighbours carried her upstairs and laid her out on the bed, the old man followed, climbed on to the bed and lay down beside her: within the hour he was dead himself – of a broken heart, it was said: they had been together fifty years.

As their cottage was tied to the Stanson sisters' farm almost next door, it was taken up by a man named Munson and his wife and child, outsiders from the next county: he had come into the village as the Stansons' next labourer, bringing his own furniture with him on the back of a cart. There being no known relatives of the old couple living, or whom anyone could contact in time, for the whole thing was done in a week, the churchwardens and the parish council, supported by the vicar, decided that their goods and chattels should be auctioned off one Saturday afternoon: it was a tradition whenever old folk died to sell off what their relatives left after they had taken what they wanted: there was always something which someone else wanted and the money benefited the church. People did not bid against one another: they simply walked into the house or yard where the goods were stacked, picked up what they wanted, left a few pence or a shilling or two in a saucer and carted it away: someone, usually a neighbour, would keep a note of what people paid and trusted in their honesty to pay a proper second-hand price.

Olive got there late, so the best furniture was gone: her arrival with her whole brood en train still drew one or two sarcastic comments, thinly disguised as greetings of recognition, from the few village women who were still in the yard.

'I thought it wouldn't be long before you turned up,' snidely, from one woman, wrapping some plates and a fruit bowl in old newspaper.

'Can you afford to pay for things?' asked equally as snidely by another, who was guarding four kitchen chairs she had bought.

'I see you brought some help with you,' more pleasantly from a third, who was carrying away an armful of bedding and tablecloths, but still a sly way of commenting on how many children Olive had!

'I hope you've brought your money with you?' sniffed a fourth, hanging on to a china washstand bowl and pitcher as she dropped her coins on to the plate and made for the gate.

'Anything not taken by this evening, ladies, I'll hev to smash up and burn,' interrupted the new man, Munson, bluntly, seeing Olive bristling up and fearing a row was about to break out between the women.

It was too good an opportunity for Olive to miss. 'I'd take everything that's left if I could get it home,' she said, half laughing as she surveyed the clutter, but meaning it.

'You give me what you can afford and I'll deliver the lot,' said Munson. 'It's better than burning it or smashing it all up. And I've still got to get rid of it then.'

Thus, in that way, Olive was able to acquire a whole host of things for a few shillings: it was still money which she could ill afford, but was too good an opportunity to miss.

Jimmy, Patrick and Jack helped to carry some of the smaller items home, the cups, utensils, two better saucepans and a frying pan and the plates, though they did arrive one plate short when Jack let it slip from his grasp and it smashed on the road: the distraught Jack pleaded that it was the drizzling rain which had caused him to do it: and there was much wailing of injured pride when, as a precaution, Olive took the lot off him and piled them into the pram.

The new man at the Stanson's was as good as his word and later that evening, despite the rain, a loaded farm cart drew to a halt alongside the gap in the hedge: he seemed quite startled when he saw the mound of rubbish which covered the field and the long, low yellow cottage half-buried by an even greater mound and the tarpaulin roof half-sticking out from under it all.

Jimmy, Patrick and Olive were waiting for him to help unload the old couple's death bed and mattress, pillows and blankets, which, curiously no one else had wanted, some more patched blankets, a frayed eiderdown, a rickety black horsehair sofa, a spindly-legged washstand with bowl, china jug and swing mirror and two rugs folded into a tin bath which Olive particularly prized: but best of all was the old couple's square kitchen table: it made quite a pile beside the lane.

Munson looked at them curiously as he stood atop the cart lowering the goods down to the waiting hands below: clearly, he had not expected to make his delivery to such a curious, out-of-the-way place, especially not to a rubbish dump which was home to a whole family: he must have wondered what kind of a family they were: a very desperate one, no doubt, to live in such a place and still be cheerful in their comments.

He even offered to help them carry it all inside the cottage. 'No thanks, we can manage it from here,' Olive replied, perhaps a little too curtly, but the man accepted the remark with a shrug of his shoulders: Olive's pride had got the better of her: she did not want anyone seeing more than they needed to. Even Jimmy and Patrick, struggling with the horsehair sofa, were a little taken aback by her refusal: but then Munson was a youngish man, in his late thirties, and not altogether unhandsome: the two just pulled a face at their mother's foolishness and went back to cursing each other's incompetence in the usual way as they humped the heavy sofa across the cinders.

As it was, it took the rest of the evening for Jimmy, Patrick and Olive to carry it all into the house: the heat of the range fire soon dried out anything which was damp or wet. The big double bed was pushed into one corner cleared of the old brick beds: the new mattress was placed upon it, the pillows added, the blankets laid down and the eiderdown thrown on top: the sofa was set before the range, the kitchen table was placed in the centre of the room, the washstand in another corner: the room was cramped, but no one minded: from having no proper furniture at all, they now had a furnished home! That night, Jimmy, Patrick, Jack and the twins all slept in the big bed, the two eldest at one end, the other three at the other end: Michael and Joseph slept on their old mattress, warm and snug under the new blankets, while Olive slept on the horsehair sofa before the range.

When Olive awoke next morning and looked about her at the slumbering boys, it was with a sense of relief and thankfulness: getting up in the morning would not be so much of an effort and a trial in the future. Over the past eighteen months, she had quite got used to the rigours and disciplines of farm labouring, most of the year rising with the sun, and in winter well ahead of it, to prepare the boys' breakfast, before cutting her own lunchtime sandwiches: then it was a matter of ensuring that faces, necks, ears and knees were washed before shepherding them all down into the village.

Dorothy now looked after only the two youngest, Michael, a boisterous three-and-a-half-year-old, and Joseph, a chubby, thumb-sucking, runny-nosed, red-cheeked two-year-old toddling around in his brother's old trousers and a knitted pale blue cardigan and smiling happily at the world: the five-year-old twins had started school in the autumn and were walked home each day by their brothers.

At the village school, Jack, had proved himself one of the brightest in the infants' class and had been praised for his quick learning by the normally overly critical Mother Mackay: unlike the others who trembled before her harsh criticism, not once had he been called to her desk and ordered to hold out his hand while she rapped his knuckles with a ruler. He had already taken the spelling and arithmetic test and, now eight, was about to join the older boys in the Big Room.

Jimmy, now twelve, and Patrick, eleven, had moved on to the secondary school at Maydun, where Jimmy struggled with his lessons, which was the cause of his sullen attitude each morning when they all set off: several times Olive had to scold him out from under the coats and blankets and threatened once to tip cold water from the pump over him if he did not crawl off his mattress. In London, and Thurstone, Jimmy had been able to sit happily at the back of large classes of thirty-five or more pupils, all of the same age and all being taught the same thing at the same time, and let the others catch the teacher's eye. During his brief sojourn at the village school, being a newcomer of indeterminate ability, Ma Popplewell had placed him on the front row of desks, which meant he could not hide: he had never received such close attention before and was forever being asked questions which he could not answer: it irked him and he did not enjoy school.

Patrick, however, now went eagerly, having happily demonstrated his ability at arithmetic, writing, spelling, reading, history and geography at the village school, much to Ma Popplewell's delight, for she had few pupils with his ability: now he was doing the same in his first year at the senior school: he had even had two of his compositions read out to the class as an example of good work and, in the arithmetic lesson, he was far ahead of his peers, having mastered long division and fractions before he joined his brother.

The two had not entirely given up on their nocturnal activities and still occasionally returned home with their pockets stuffed with peas they had taken from some farmer's field, or apples scrumped from one of Rex Book's orchards, or plums picked in the fruit orchards on Bounds farm. However, they raided the potato and turnip clamps less than before, mainly because Olive herself was bringing home what potatoes and turnips she needed from Wakenham's own clamps, smuggled out in her shopping bag. Old Jim knew she was doing it, or guessed she was doing it, but, since she had helped him to build them, he simply gave her a shy, sideways look and mumbled something to himself.

Both Olive's two eldest had been accepted into the clique of village boys and at playtimes, while Jack played cowboys and Indians with the friends he had made, Jimmy and Patrick both vigorously joined in the usual rough-and-tumble football, chasing a padded sock ball about the playground, charging on to the girls' side of the yard in a mad helter-skelter of swinging arms and kicking feet with the usual disdain boys show for the skipping or hop-scotching girls, before all charging back again towards a goal chalked on the perimeter wall: toecaps were scuffed, knees grazed, shins bruised and occasional punches thrown: but it was all good fun.

They also went swimming with the other village boys in the estuary and, on occasions, hung about the army camp, mixing with the soldiers and joining them for the free film shows in the black hut: the soldiers even let Patrick operate the wheel which turned the searchlight one night and he came home in a highly excitable state

One year later the war was still dragging on and growing in its intensity: though, along the Langwater, the world could seem as pleasant a place as it had always been, especially on a bright and breezy, if chill, summer Saturday morning when Olive set off with the boys along the estuary shore with a special mission in mind. Only the hordes of American planes passing overhead as they went out to bomb Germany distracted them momentarily: as it turned out, it was to be a day which was to alter their lives yet again.

FIFTY-SEVEN

JIMMY saw the parachute first: it came floating down out of the sun about a hundred yards from where he was leading the normal family procession along the top of the meandering estuary seawall some three miles from the village, almost to Cobwycke, in fact. For more than half an hour, Olive and the boys had been staring up at flights of slow-moving, brown aeroplanes, American B-17 Flying Fortresses, coming back from Germany across the lakes of blue between the cavernous clouds. Some flew steadily in groups of eight or ten, still in the same formation as they had gone out: others came along in scatterings of four or five: some struggled along, like they were being nursed home by those about them: others flew singly, like the last one, the one from which the parachute came. It trailed all the others by a good twenty minutes: black smoke was streaming from it in a long trail: one of its engines was stopped and burning, another was feathering: one wing was holed and part of its tail plane had been shot away: even against the blue and the brightness of the sun, the orange-yellow flames could clearly be seen licking at the stopped engine.

For the whole of the morning, the boys and their mother had been out on the vast trenched banks of marran-topped saltings which lie along the northern shore, collecting samphire, an edible seaweed which grew all along the various creeks. Treading barefoot in the black mud, they had spent several hours pulling up the bushy plants, enough to fill three half-sacks before the tide had come swirling back up the creeks, icy cold and sparkling green, forcing them back to the land. Now in the mid-afternoon as the aeroplanes returned they were on their way back to the village, hoping to sell what they had collected to Ma Rowthey at the post office-cum-grocery store before she closed for the day: she would sell it on, just as she did the blackberries and the hips and haws which they picked each September.

Jimmy was hauling the twins on a small pram-wheeled cart: with his head bent into the gusting breeze, strong enough at times to threaten to blow a person right off the top of the seawall, he might never have turned to look back had Michael and Joseph not squealed with fright at that particular moment as the cart, bouncing over the uneven ground, veered dangerously towards the edge of the grassy slope.

'Look,' shouted Jimmy, pointing up, 'a parachute. Someone's baled out!'

They all stopped to stare: Patrick, who had his hands on Michael's shoulders to help push the cart, stood up to squint into the sun, shading his eyes: Jack and the twins, some way back bombing a piece of driftwood with stones prised from the path, also paused to look up as the parachute came seesawing down, allowing the 'German U-boat' to bob away on the waves.

It was Olive, wheeling the loaded pram behind Patrick, who saw the danger. 'He's going into the water!' she cried.

The airman was indeed going into the water: though he had baled out well over the land, the strength of the breeze was taking the parachute back across the seawall and out into the waters of the estuary. The tide that day had been one of the highest, washing a quarter-way up the seawall itself: now, though it was ten minutes into its ebb, in the shelving shallows at the foot of the seawall, where the non-swimmers normally bathed, a man would be out of his depth a mere ten yards from the shore: the airman floating down would splash into the water more than forty or fifty yards out.

Jimmy and Patrick were off and running before Olive could even call out a warning to them to be careful: a heavy, leather-suited airman going into water would need help to crawl ashore and there was no one about to help him except them: and their mother, of course, but then she was a woman and they could not expect much assistance from her! They were quickly followed by Jack and the twins: Michael and Joseph would have done the same had Olive not seized their arms to stop them.

Within a matter of seconds, five boys was standing at the bottom of the seawall slope, right at the water's edge, watching silently as some forty yards out from the shore the airman splashed down into the cold, sparkling green water and the parachute folded over him. That something was wrong became obvious within seconds: they had expected that the man would press the release button and try to swim clear of the rippling silk and tangle of cords, but there was no movement from him: instead, he seemed to be drifting farther out.

'He's trapped under the parachute!' exclaimed Jimmy.

'Maybe he's wounded,' suggested a solemn Patrick.

'He could drown,' declared a frowning Jack.

'He will if we don't do something,' cried Jimmy: he was already hopping on one leg, untying his laces and tugging at his boots.

Taking a cue from his older brother, Patrick did the same. 'The tide's taking him out with it,' he shouted: and in no time at all he and his brother had pulled off their boots and socks, stepped out of their trousers and peeled off their bomber jackets and pullovers, leaving them scattered on the seawall's lower slope.

'You're not going out there after him, are you? You'll drown!' screeched a desperate Olive from the top of the seawall where she was struggling to prevent her two youngest from joining their brothers: she failed in the one and was ignored in the other. Her two youngest gleefully twisted free and joined their brothers at the bottom of the slope, just as the two eldest waded out into the icy water: one moment they were chest deep, the next they were doing a fast crawl towards the stricken airman.

An excited Michael, perhaps not understanding the seriousness of what he was witnessing, shouted up to his mother: 'They think he's drowning, Mum! They're going out to get him in.'

'Come back, you fools! Come back!' a distraught Olive screamed again after the bobbing heads of her two sons, now twenty yards out and splashing through the choppy waves towards the billowing parachute: but she was still atop the seawall, too far off for them to hear and her words were blown away on the breeze. By then the white parachute was some fifty yards from the shore: the air was filling it like a sail: if the boys did not reach the airman quickly, he would be too far out and the main-channel current would sweep him even farther and faster away from them towards the estuary's mouth: if that happened, he would be lost to the open sea.

Jimmy and Patrick were both strong swimmers, as were most boys who lived in villages along the estuary and swam in it as often as time and good weather allowed: redoubling their efforts, they reached the drifting parachute within a couple of minutes or so, almost a hundred yards out. Their first act was to take hold of the billowing white silk and try to drag that aside, but the combination of the choppy water and the stiff breeze defeated them: then, just as they reached the dark, bobbing head, they disappeared from view as the breeze blew the canopy over them all.

Olive's fear was quite real: if her two eldest became entangled in the multiple cords which floated on the surface all around them, they, too, could drown: and, in the space of two years, she would have lost not only her husband but her two eldest sons as well! 'Oh my God, I should never have brought them here,' she wailed inwardly to herself. 'I should never have gone up to Thurstone and brought them back! And I should never have brought them to Gledlang! If it hadn't have been for me, they wouldn't be out there now! I should have left them where they were!'

On the shore, the younger Cullens came scrambling back up the slope to obtain a better view.

Then suddenly the two bobbing heads reappeared, treading water around the ballooning silk: and floating alongside them, with a distinctive yellow mae-west showing up against the dark of his sodden flying suit, was the figure of the airman. Olive could see it was Patrick gathering in the silk of the chute and twisting it and the cords to form a rope, which he was endeavouring to drape over his shoulder: Jimmy, meanwhile, was supporting the dark form in the water, pushing it forwards, keeping the head as high above the surge of the waves as possible: to Olive, all three seemed to be bobbing like corks in the choppy green water.

Slowly, the two boys hauled the downed airman towards the shore: Patrick, restricted by the twisted chute and cords draped over one shoulder, had to do a one-armed sidestroke, while Jimmy drove himself backwards through the water with a series of violent kicks beneath the surface, at the same time holding on to the stricken airman's parachute straps with both hands. It was a struggle to make any headway through the waves and they continually had to shout encouragement to each other as they battled against the fierce undertow of the ebbing tide: both knew that, if one gave up, they and the airman might well all be lost.

To the watching Olive, their progress appeared agonisingly slow: there were times when they seemed not to be moving at all towards the shore, but were drifting farther out: at one point, when the stiff breeze subsided momentarily, she heard Jimmy shout to his brother: 'Keep going, Pat, keep going! We're nearly there, we're nearly there!' It was at that point the fear alone froze Olive's blood.

Then suddenly Patrick was no longer swimming, but was wading ashore, hauling at the parachute with both arms: his face was blue with cold, his teeth were chattering and he was shivering violently, but it meant he was safe: he had reached the shelving and his feet could touch: he was no longer out of his depth: Jimmy, too, was safe. The anxious tears in Olive's eyes were brushed away and without realising it she was slipping and sliding down the slope to help them, to be quickly joined on the small expanse of wet shingle left by the receding tide by her other sons, all open-mouthed with admiration at what their elder brothers had done. So wrapped up in watching their exertions had they been that none had bothered to look after the shoes and coats properly and successive waves had plucked first at the hem of Jimmy's jacket, then at an arm of Patrick's and then at both so that they were floating in the wash of the surf, while nearby almost buried by the shingle and sand lay one of Patrick's discarded shoes. Olive's first action was to push the beaming Jack aside to retrieve them and then move the sodden jackets and their other things back up on to the seawall grass: she could not afford to buy them any more clothing and, besides, she did not have the coupons.

By that time, an exhausted and shivering Patrick, having stumbled ashore with the silk folds of the parachute draped over his shoulders, was on his knees and remained with his head bowed, recovering his strength and his breath, while the waves continued to surge and ebb around him: Jimmy, too, had regained the shelving slope and had paused for breath before gathering himself to make his final effort to drag the rescued airman closer to the shore. Curiously, the man made no effort to help himself: he had remained immobile throughout the whole of the rescue.

'Oh, my God, he must be dead,' thought Olive.

Jimmy corrected her almost as if he were telepathic. 'It's all right, Mum, I think he's still alive,' he shouted into the breeze, at the same time attempting to keep a grip on the man in the buffeting swell. 'He's just unconscious. Come on, Pat, give us a hand. Let's get him in. I'm bloody freezing!'

'So am I!' a shivering Patrick cried angrily through chattering teeth, his shoulders hunched against the chill of the wind and his arms folded futilely across his chest to hug himself: wearily, he climbed to his feet and went splashing back into the waves to help his brother.

Olive, too, casting off her anxieties now that the two boys were safe, went as close to the water's edge as she dared: with an earnest-faced Jack and the sombre-faced twins helping, she took hold of the parachute itself and began pulling: between them, they managed to haul the unconscious man up to the tide line: but efforts to drag him farther were of no avail: Jimmy and Patrick, who did most of the pulling, just did not have the strength and the waves kept plucking at him as if they wanted to pull him back out. It was not so much the man's weight against which they struggled as the fact that he was a dead weight and that, combined with the weight of water in his clothing, his flying leathers and his uniform underneath, made him extremely heavy once he was on dry land. They rested briefly before their next attempt: waves were still washing around their feet and Olive, forgetting to take off her shoes, became aware suddenly of the water swirling in between her toes as a bigger wave flooded up on to the small expanse of shingle: her instinct was to drop the parachute and retreat out of range, but she managed to hold herself in check: then, with all of them pulling together, the airman finally lay silent and motionless on the wet shingle. Around him stood a mortified Olive, fearing even to touch him in case Jimmy had been wrong and he was indeed dead, a curious and unconcerned Jack, vainly waiting for something else to happen, the man to get up perhaps? And opposite them a shivering and dripping Jimmy and Patrick, both vigorously rubbing their bloodless blue hands, arms folded across their chests, shoulders hunched against the coolness of the breeze, were peering down at the prone form as if unsure what to do next.

It was then that the man groaned: an eye flicked open and then closed as the brightness of the sun dazzled him: the eye opened a second time and another groan escaped his lips: when the eye closed again, no more sounds came from him: it was as if he had satisfied himself that he was on land and out of the water: they did not know which. Only then did they take a more careful look at him and saw that his leather suit was split open and horribly charred all down the left side, from the shoulder to the ankle: until that moment, the seawater had prevented them from smelling the charring: one of the man's flying boots was missing as was part of the right leg of his flying suit and the trousers underneath: they had both been cut away and a bandage wrapped inexpertly around a long wound as if done in a great hurry and under great stress. The wound seemed to extend from the top of his thigh all the way down his calf to his ankle as if something had sliced open his leg the way a butcher slices open a pig to gut it: even as they stood there looking down at him, the bandages were turning a darker pink as more blood seeped out and was diluted by the seawater. On that same side, too, the man's arm was tightly strapped across his chest in a crude sling made from a black leather belt and piece of metal piping thrust through the buckle to keep it in place: horribly, too, the man's face was blistered and raw on one side from the jaw to the hairline. The reason he had opened only one eye then became obvious: the eyelids of the other appeared to be fused together as if seared by extreme heat: a sickly smell of charred cloth and burnt flesh was beginning to rise up to greet them.

'What's this?' Jimmy said, puzzled, bending and pulling at a piece of paper rolled tightly and stuck through a small round hole deliberately cut in the man's black leather flying jacket: it was not singed and obviously had been put there by someone else, though, having been immersed in seawater, it was sodden and tore in half as Jimmy pulled it out. In his eagerness, he had failed to notice, or to expect, that one end was pinned inside the airman's flying suit by a small ornamental brooch so that whatever happened it would remain prominent for anyone who came across him, yet fixed whatever happened. They had to unzip the front to retrieve the other half of the paper and the brooch with it: it was not a woman's brooch, but more of a commemorative pin, the kind only a man would wear, about two inches long by one inch high, in the shape of a silver aeroplane, with the unmistakable star and bars of the American airforce on its fuselage and wings, flying across a patch of blue with an enamelled white cloud behind it.

With bloodless fingers, Jimmy unpeeled the two halves of the piece of paper: it was a note: written in large writing were the words: 'USAAF. Please help me. Get me to hospital. Urgent.'

FIFTY-EIGHT

THE MAN was tall and thin, well over six feet, Jimmy reckoned: his face was as blue from the icy waters as were his own and Patrick's: it was a thin face, that of a man of about twenty-three or twenty-four, with a pencil moustache and dark hair: he was bareheaded, having lost whatever cap he had on in the water.

No one bothered to mention that he was an American: that was obvious from his flying suit: just as it was obvious to them all what had happened: the burnt and wounded man had been pushed out of the stricken aeroplane by his comrades, one, probably because they still had a minimum half-hour's flying time back to their base, wherever that was, and, two, because they were on fire with one engine stopped and one feathering, lurching along across the sky and might not make it anyway. Better to get their buddy out and float him down to earth on a parachute as soon as they crossed the coast: that way, they reasoned, people would see him come down and some English farmer, perhaps, would pick him up, read the note, load him on to a truck and drive him to the nearest hospital: you could rely on the English to do that. Except that the nearest farmer had not seen the parachute come down and the nearest hospital was thirteen miles away in Wivencaster. It was just bad fortune for the airman that the wind had veered round from the north east to the north west almost at the moment they had pushed him out and had blown him clear of the dry land and out over the estuary. Had his buddies waited another two or three seconds, he would have fallen on dry land: conversely, had they pushed him out a few seconds earlier he would have splashed into the water too far out for Jimmy and Patrick or anyone else to reach him without a boat: and by the time they got to him in that, the man would have drowned anyway. It was just luck that Olive and the boys were walking back along the top of the seawall so far from the village.

'How do they expect us to do that?' an exasperated Olive asked, taking the flapping note from Jimmy to read.

'Put him on the cart! We haven't got anything else!' Jimmy answered, exasperated that his mother should not think of the obvious.

'Don't be daft,' snapped an irritated Olive, 'It's not long enough. He's a full-grown man. He won't fit on that and we're miles from the village out here.' She was picturing the tall, thin man lying full length on the cart with his head hanging off one end and his feet from the knees down off the other.

'Put him in the pram!' a shivering Patrick cried, anxious to get on with things. 'Jim and I can pull him. It's only about a couple of miles to the road across the fields. We can do it that way.'

Olive thought for a second or so. 'You couldn't pull him all that way on that, could you?' she asked, biting her lip, then adding somewhat irrationally: 'You're soaking wet, the pair of you.'

'Of course, we can,' a defiant Jimmy retorted. 'Me and Pat can do it easily. We'll use the sacks as a cushion. Jack can bring the cart. We'll follow the headlands. It's either that or we leave him here and go and get someone and that could take ages. He could be dead or something by the time we got help.'

There was sense in what he said and Olive had to accept that her eldest was right.

Still shivering with cold, the two hastily dried themselves on their shirts, pulled on their damp clothing and sodden boots, stuffed their wet socks into their pockets and prepared to haul the unconscious American up the slope. It took all of them to drag his dead weight to the top of the seawall, with Jimmy and Patrick grasping his straps and the others, Michael and Joseph included, all pulling on the cords of the parachute. Once at the top, it was a simple matter to extricate him from the parachute harness as every boy knew where to punch the release button, though it did take three tries before Patrick managed it. Then, once the man was free of the silk canopy, they sat him up, folded down the pram's front hood, tipped it up behind him and gently lowered him into the well before righting it to lift him: throughout it all, the burnt and wounded man gave neither groan nor moan.

And that was how they set off, with Jimmy hauling the pram backwards by the handle at as fast a pace as they could go and Patrick pushing from the rear: the man's head and torso rested on the three sacks of samphire, cushioning him from the hard bumping which lay ahead, while his legs dangled down over the folded-down front. Jack, hauling the cart, followed his brothers, followed in turn by the excited twins and Michael and Joseph, skipping along behind. Olive, too, followed, but only after she had folded the silk parachute canopy and thrust it inside her coat where it formed an incongruous pregnant bulge.

The way was rough, for the top of the seawall was embedded with flints and small rocks: had the man not been cushioned by the three sacks, he would have had an extremely jarring ride: but, as it was, he was unconscious and knew nothing of it. After about a mile, they came to the first of the stiles which the farmer – one of the Godwin clan – had erected on top of the seawall, along with barbed wire fencing on both slopes right down to the water's edge itself, to hem in any cattle which might cross the deep delph ditches running parallel to the seawall and which had provided the earth to build it several hundred years before. They managed to negotiate the first fence by the simple expedient of both Jimmy and Patrick kicking down the posts where the wire crossed their path and then easing the pram across.

Eventually, after about a mile and, with the first farmhouse along that God-forsaken stretch still not in sight – it would have been a Godwin farmhouse, anyway – they decided it would be better to follow a cart track leading away from the seawall: that way, they would not have to negotiate any more of the fences as there were three more ahead barring their way back to the village, as well as two stiles: Godwin land or not, it was worth the risk: besides it was a necessity. 'To hell with the Godwins!' was Olive's thought when the boys suggested it to her. 'This could be a matter of life or death!' To the boys, she just said: 'If we have any trouble if we meet someone, you just leave it to me!'

Fortunately, there were no Godwins about that late Saturday afternoon to turn them back or to argue against their trespass: their trickiest moment came in lowering the man and the heavy pram down the steep slope on to the flatter ground at the bottom of the landward side of the seawall, but they managed it without tipping him out. By taking a route along the cart track and the headlands, they knew their way would be more even and they could reach the Salter road more quickly.

Thus was the unconscious airman finally trundled out on to the Salter road halfway between the two villages just forty-five minutes after he was pushed out of the stricken aircraft.

'Anything coming?' Olive asked anxiously as the boys swung open the last five-bar gate and wheeled the creaking rickety pram out on to the road: it had taken them just under half an hour and by then it was late afternoon.

As fate would have it, they were in luck: they had been there no more than five minutes, standing by the verge in the stiff breeze and afternoon sunshine looking up and down the road, when a lorry chugged into view over the brow of the hill: it was the brewery lorry from Wivencaster, with its incongruous gas bag atop the cabin. At midday, it had made an unexpected 'emergency' Saturday delivery of barrels of bitter and mild and crates of pale ale to the Chessman in Gledlang, after soldiers from the searchlight and ack-ack battery on the Park had finally drunk it dry the previous evening. Fortunately, the driver and his mate had stayed to have a pint or two themselves in the comfort and calm of the old village pub, well away from the boisterous town pubs of Wivencaster and the hordes of soldiers and airmen who frequented them. Now, they were serenely wending their way back to Wivencaster, hoping to arrive back at the depot with just enough time to unload their empties, trundle them on the barrow to the sterilising plant, then clock off and go home for their Saturday tea. They should, in fact, have passed that spot long before.

The sight of two boys standing in the middle of the road agitatedly waving their arms, while five smaller children ran along the verge towards them, followed by a distraught woman desperately trying to grab hold of two of the smallest, induced the driver to clamp his foot sharply on the brake and bring the lorry to a smoking stop. It was a big old Leyland, 'a ten-tonner,' as the boys called them, which would have done for both Jimmy and Patrick had it not stopped some twenty feet short in a spray of stones and dust. Olive screamed for the two of them to get out of its path and for the second time that afternoon saw her two eldest blithely ignore her and risk death with no more concern for their own safety than did Hopalong Cassidy or Johnny Mack Brown or Errol Flynn in the films they saw at the army camp with the other village boys. No sooner had the Leyland braked than it was surrounded by seven eagerly shouting children.

'What the bloody hell's the matter?' the driver shouted, sticking his head out of the cab window and glaring down at the children who had run into his path.

'We've got an injured Yank in our pram,' Jimmy shouted up to him above the noise of the engine. 'He came down by parachute. He's unconscious. He was in the river. We dragged him out. He had a note pinned to him.' He held up the torn note to show it to the driver, who squinted at it for a second or so, then turned and said something to his mate. To their credit, the men got briskly out of their cab and approached the pram into which the hapless American was squeezed.

The driver, a portly, white-haired man wearing the heavy leather apron of his trade, turned to his companion. 'Gawd, he don't look too good, do he, Ted?' he said with a shake of the head: just as he bent over the stricken American to take a closer look, the poor man groaned: the sound of men's voices must have stirred him from somewhere deep down in the well of pain and semiconsciousness or wherever it was he had been drifting at that moment.

'He's still alive then?' said the driver's mate, a thin, balding man also wearing a leather apron similar to that of his companion: he bent forward to take a closer look at the airman's burnt face, drew in his breath and declared: 'I reckon we'd best get this poor blighter to hospital, Bert, and the sooner the better. What'd they push him out for? He'd have been better off with his mates, I should have thought.'

'The plane was on fire,' Patrick told them sharply. 'It only had two engines. It might have crashed by now. That's why they pushed him out.'

The two men gave a grunt apiece, as though they accepted, but did not like, Patrick's explanation and then very carefully wheeled the pram round to the side of the lorry: the groaning, now semi-conscious, airman was heaved up on to the open trailer, the two then climbed up beside him, laid out some sacks as a bed, lifted him on to it and rearranged some of the wooden crates to form a low wall around him to prevent him from rolling off.

'Leave him with us now, missus,' said the driver's mate, seating himself on one of the crates. 'We'll see he gets to hospital all right. I'll stay back here with him so he don't fall off.' Then to the boys he added cheerily: 'Don't worry, boys, we'll get him there.'

'He's yours now, just see he gets to hospital,' a curt Olive reminded him, relieved that the responsibility had been passed on.

'Come on, Bert, let's get moving,' Ted shouted to the driver, who was already climbing into the cab: the door slammed shut, the engine revved and the lorry rolled forward and gathered speed in a cloud of blue exhaust fumes: the last Olive and the boys saw of it was with the driver's mate sitting on the wall of crates raising one hand to signal goodbye.

FIFTY-NINE

OLIVE was crossing the lawn on her way to the barn to put away a pitchfork when she saw the movement of the vehicles between the orchard trees: two American jeeps and a small American truck were bumping and bouncing up the drive: and hanging out from under the open canvas hoods of the two jeeps, vigorously waving their arms to attract her attention, were all five of her eldest children!

Jimmy and Patrick were squashed together in the front seat of the first jeep beside a sergeant driver with a colourful round badge on the shoulder of his green serge uniform jacket: as the jeep came to a halt alongside her, Olive found herself being looked at by what were clearly two officers, seated behind: one was a young bespectacled lieutenant in a dark mackintosh with dark black hair and a long face: the other was a captain, slightly older, with a thin, dark moustache: from the wings sewn on their uniforms, Olive knew they were both airforce: United States Army Air Forces, in fact.

The twins and Jack were in the back of the second jeep, which was being driven by a young gum-chewing corporal wearing sunglasses: seated beside him was another older, similarly gum-chewing man, almost too old to be in uniform, Olive thought, with a bulky flash camera balanced on his knees. At the rear, the truck driver, a leather-jacketed, round-faced private, or Pfc, in his early twenties, with a baseball cap stuck on his head and a half-smoked cigar projecting from his mouth, had climbed out of his cab and was staring interestedly about him. In effect, to English eyes, they were 'typical Yanks,' Olive thought: but what were American jeeps doing rolling up to the front door of Follenfaunts? And what were her boys doing in two American jeeps anyway? It could only be about that airman they had pulled from the river three weeks previously: she had almost forgotten about it.

'Mum! Mum! They want to take our photos. They're going to put us in the papers!' An excited Jack jumped out of the second jeep almost before it had stopped and ran across to his astonished mother.

The captain got out followed by the bespectacled lieutenant: the captain was younger than Olive had thought, probably in his mid-twenties, immaculately turned out: his shoes were burnished a rich brown, the buttons on his jacket were polished a bright silver and his olive green uniform jacket and trousers were immaculately pressed: he had a short row of medal ribbons across his chest.

He seemed bemused by the surroundings, as if he were unsure whether he had found the right place, or more likely whether he was addressing the right person: for Olive did not look like the lady of the house he had expected when he had first turned into the drive and saw the Follenfaunts mansion. He had expected someone taller, perhaps in a flowered dress, with a sunhat on her head and a basket under her arm, 'gardening,' as the English called it, like all the older English country women seemed to do. Instead, the woman at whom the children had waved and called 'Mom' – 'Mum' as the English said it – had a dirty face, dirt-ingrained hands, unkempt hair and was wearing a tattered and muddied overcoat and mud-splashed, turned-down wellingtons. He did not know that, when they had driven up, Olive had been on her way back from the stable where she had been forking out the horse bedding and replacing it with new straw: the headscarf which she was in the process of retying when she had seen the vehicles approaching was still in her hand.

'Ma'am,' said the captain, touching the peak of his cap with a leather-gloved hand. 'Ah'm Captain Gelmon. This here is Lieutenant Lutsky –' He pronounced it 'loo-tenant,' of course, rather than the English 'left-tenant' and motioned towards the bespectacled lieutenant, who was lifting out the somewhat sulky twins. Not unexpectedly, they were a little saddened that their jeep ride had come to a quick end and scuttled over to join their mother. 'And this is Sergeant Borowitz, from the *Stars And Stripes* newspaper,' the captain added.

The older, gum-chewing photographer came up alongside the captain and the lieutenant and gave Olive a strange, puzzled smile and then immediately began to fiddle with his camera.

'We're from the United States Army Air Forces base at Marham Broads in Norfolkshire,' went on the captain in a slow Southern drawl. 'We've just come from the village. We waited for your two eldest to come in on the school bus. Am Ah right in thinking, ma'am, that Ah'am addressing Mrs. Olive Cullen, mother of three boys we have here named James, Patrick and Jack Cullen?'

'Yes, that's me,' replied Olive, slightly bemused by the captain's accent. 'What do you want me for?'

'With your permission, ma'am,' the captain said, stiffening slightly with the formality of the occasion, 'we would like to take a photograph of you and your three boys. Word has come to us that, three weeks ago, your boys here, James, Patrick and Jack, were instrumental in helping a badly injured compatriot of ours by pulling him out of the sea when he, unfortunately, parachuted into it. Your boys, we have been told, swam out to him without a thought for their own safety and brought him back into the shore and then were instrumental in helping him to reach the town hospital at Wivencaster, where, I am glad to say, he is now recovering.'

'I'm glad to hear he's all right,' said Olive, a flush of embarrassment colouring her cheeks. 'That's what we were worried about.' Then, feeling an explanation was needed: 'They're good swimmers and he wasn't that far out, just a hundred yards, no more. Jimmy and Patrick went out to him and pulled him in. It was the two men in the lorry who took him to hospital. Brewery men. Draymen. I don't know who they are.'

'It was they who told the hospital doctors about the boys and it was through the hospital that our liaison officer heard about what the boys had done,' said the captain solemnly. 'The injured officer, Captain Buzz Eglington, is a particular friend of mine. He regrets, ma'am, that he cannot be here himself today as he is still in hospital, but he has asked me to do the honours for him and I am pleased to do so. With your permission, ma'am, we should like to take a photograph of your three boys in front of their lovely home – ' He paused to look admiringly at the house. ' – a very fine place you have here, ma'am, a very fine place indeed. King George, is it?'

He meant Georgian, of course: a flummoxed Olive turned to look back at the house. 'Er, yes, yes, I think it is,' she stuttered.

'A mighty fine house,' the captain repeated: then paused a second time, before stiffening himself for the formality of the occasion. 'Ma'am,' he said almost with a polite bow, 'with your permission. Captain Eglington is to be returned Stateside in the next week or so due to his injuries and he has asked me to show his particular appreciation of the bravery of your three boys.'

'What?' Olive was confused: then it dawned upon her. Appreciation! 'We didn't do it for any reward,' she said quickly. 'We did it to help the man. We don't want anything for it.' And 'three boys'? Jimmy and Patrick had rescued the man: were they including Jack?

The captain smiled as if he understood. 'Captain Eglington would be very pleased if you would accept a small token of thanks,' he said: then, turning to his lieutenant, nodded towards the truck as if giving a signal. 'Lieutenant.'

The lieutenant turned smartly and went to the back of the truck, motioning for the sergeant, the corporal and the Pfc truck driver to follow him.

Seconds later, three shining, if second-hand, bicycles, complete with tyres, mudguards, saddles and proper brakes, were being wheeled across the gravel towards a gawping Jimmy, Patrick and Jack. 'Ma'am,' said the captain, touching the peak of his cap again, 'on behalf of Captain Eglington and on behalf of the United States Army Air Forces, we would like you to accept these with our grateful thanks, to you and your boys.'

'We don't expect a reward – ' Olive began in genuine protest: but Jimmy, Patrick and Jack had already rushed forward to take possession of their bicycles, inspecting them with shining eyes and wide disbelieving smiles, almost chortling with happiness: then, all three had mounted them and were pedalling furiously away down the driveway, where they came to a skidding halt in a shower of stones halfway before flying back to perform another skidding halt beside the parked vehicles.

The captain, meanwhile, had turned to his sergeant. 'Sergeant,' he commanded with a nod.

'Sir,' answered the sergeant and, leaning forward into the first jeep, he lifted out a large box, which he handed to the bespectacled lieutenant.

'We would like you personally to accept this hamper as a small token of our thanks for what you and your boys did,' said the captain. 'We know how scarce things are here in England and we brought a few things you might like.'

The lieutenant planted the box firmly on the bonnet of the jeep and opened it up. 'Something for you and something for your younger boys,' he said, taking out four hand-carved model aircraft made of balsa wood and painted silver, with the American stars and bars on their wings and fuselages. Even to Olive's inexperienced eyes they were skilful reproductions, complete with gun turrets and turning propellers, of the aircraft she and the boys had seen so many times crossing their patch of sky during the daylight hours. Sometimes the aeroplanes would be so high in the sky going out over the sea in their formations that they left parallel ice-white vapour trails across the blue: other times they would be coming back, fewer in number, more scattered, often lower in the sky, some trailing black smoke or with engines stopped and holes in their wings and tails: so many at times one wondered how they could still fly.

The twins took theirs with eyes as wide with happiness as had been their brothers moments earlier and the small aircraft were soon droning at arm's length around their mother on some 'bombing mission' of their own to Germany: not that Olive noticed: she was staring equally as astonished at what was below.

'Just a few things for you, ma'am,' said the captain, beginning to take out tin after tin and stack them on the bonnet beside the box. 'Canned peaches, canned apricots, oranges, plum jelly, strawberry jelly – er, jam, that is, ma'am,' he corrected himself, ' – canned pineapple, meatballs, tomatoes, peanut butter, California prunes – dried plums, ma'am. Just stew in water. Oh, and some candy. We know how hard it is to get that here. Hershey bars and for you particularly, ma'am – ' Grinning broadly now, he held up two pairs of nylon stockings. 'All with our grateful thanks, ma'am.'

Poor Olive was overwhelmed by the pile of tins: there must have been twenty-five or more of them on the jeep's bonnet: they would last them for a month! And the nylon stockings! She had not worn stockings of any proper kind for the past two years: her own were woollen, thick and brown and had been darned a half-dozen times. Tears were brimming up in her eyes: she was so taken aback she could only mutter out her thanks, feeling very foolish as the tears welled up in her eyes.

Behind her, up at the window of his bedroom, the wheezing, red-faced figure of Dick Wakenham, having heaved himself out of his bed at the sound of approaching tyres crunching over the gravel, was looking down upon the strange scene being enacted below: three American vehicles were parked on his driveway, with three uniformed Americans standing by them, while Olive Cullen and her children, three of them holding bicycles, stood on his lawn with two American officers in peak caps, being photographed by another American with a flash camera against the obvious backdrop of his house. He would have to ask her about that: he most certainly would have to ask her about that.

Olive's inquest began the moment the waving Americans had departed down the driveway and she and the boys, riding their new bicycles, of course, set off back into the village to pick up Michael and the now toddling Joseph from Dorothy's.

'How did they know it was you three? Someone must have told them if they went to the school looking for the two of you and then waited for Jimmy to come home on the bus?'

'Jack did, bloody daft idiot!' said Jimmy, riding alongside him, but not meaning it: he had Thomas on his crossbar: his aeroplane had been temporarily put aside while he hung on.

'Well, I didn't know!' cried a disconsolate Jack, hanging his head: he genuinely could not see that he had done anything wrong. 'We had to write a composition on doing a good deed. I just wrote that we'd all been down the seawall and we'd pulled a man with a parachute out of the water because he was drowning. Ma Pop didn't believe me. She said I was making it up. I said I wasn't. I said we'd done it, we just hadn't told anyone, that's all. She must have told somebody else because, when they came to the school, Ma Pop called me out straight away. "Here's one of them," she said, and showed them my composition book. The captain and the man with the camera read it and said it was very good.' The latter said with a smile.

Patrick, who was completing circles and figures of eight to the delight of John, on his handlebars, put it in perspective. 'It don't matter, any of it, does it?' he chortled. 'We got our photos took and we got these bikes, didn't we? The bloke who took the photographs said he might even send a picture of us to the London papers after he'd put it in his American paper.' The thought suddenly came to him. 'Hey! We could be famous!'

'We could be in the *Daily Mirror*,' grinned Jimmy.

'Or the *News of the World*!' cried Patrick and they all laughed at that: the boys knew the kinds of stories which the *News Of The World* liked to print, salacious ones about peeping toms spying on women undressing and women in London who were called a funny name and who allowed men to do things to them for money and then robbed them.

'Who told them to come to Follenfaunts to see me?' a puzzled and slightly indignant Olive wanted to know.

'I did,' laughed Patrick. 'They said they wanted to take our photos and needed to ask you first. They asked me where you were, so I told 'em. I said you were up at Follenfaunts House. They said, "Where's that?" and Jim and I and Jack showed 'em.' He smiled again. 'They didn't ask if we lived here, just where were you? So I didn't tell them any different. They just thought we all lived here, that's all! We just didn't tell 'em any different.'

Neither, Olive realised, had she: she was more upset over the fact that she had been forced to smile without protest as her photograph was taken when all the time she was grimly seething because of her dishevelled looks, in her working clothes looking more like a peasant than the supposed owner of Follenfaunts, which the Americans obviously thought she was.

At least, they knew nothing of the precise conditions under which she and her family lived: in a tumbledown, so-called cottage which had two of its walls formed from discarded doors, a leaky tarpaulin for a roof and which was surrounded by mounds of ash, earth, lime, chalk and a mountain of other refuse. No one knew, in fact, not even Ma Popplewell and Mother Mackay: both schoolmistresses knew, of course, that they lived somewhere off the Beckenden road, but neither knew of the cottage itself, nor had they visited it and were never likely to do so.

Though the boys had over time cleared away much of the rubbish surrounding the front gable end of the cottage to give themselves a bigger area in which to play, the end farthest from the road where the walls had fallen in was still half-buried under the great mound: one needed to see it to comprehend its squalor and its awfulness.

It was the same with the villagers: none knew their secret, as yet. 'They live up Beckenden somewhere,' those who were even interested enough to have discussed it once would say on seeing the Cullen children about the village. 'You know, in that cottage where they dumped all that rubbish a few years back, where that other family who come down from the next county lived for a while when they worked at Beckenden hall.'

Then they would laugh and give a shrug to show it was none of their concern: the old aerodrome was too far off the beaten track for them and they seldom had reason to go to Beckenden anyway: the only ones likely to pass that way were children on their way to Beckenden woods to pick bluebells as Olive once had done with her own mother and sisters when they were children together all those years before. There were few cars on the roads then because of the wartime petrol shortage: most, like the brewery lorry, were propelled by gas bags affixed to the roof: besides, the lane along which the aerodrome cottage stood was full of potholes which needed filling-in and overgrown with untrimmed hedgerows which bent right across the road, in places forming tunnels of shade and an ideal place for walkers to shelter from the rain as the boys had discovered at various times: but no one would willingly drive along it: anyone who wanted to get to Beckenden by bicycle or car went by the slightly longer roundabout route, but on a wider metalled road through Tottle.

Annoyed as she was that their secret had almost leaked out, inwardly Olive was thankful as she contemplated the box of tins in the well of the pram: there were more than thirty in all. The glum-faced boys rode well ahead of their mother as they headed for home: they did not even get excited when a flight of the new Typhoons came hedge-hopping up from the estuary where they sometimes practiced on targets on the Othona Flats, which lie at the mouth of the Langwater and were much used for bombing practice, so much so that the villagers had become accustomed to the daily boom of explosions, rather like one can become accustomed to the boom of far-off thunder, knowing by its sound it is too far off to affect you.

SIXTY

HOWEVER, someone did discover their secret soon after: Don Godwin, the very farmer who had evicted them from the bathing hut two years previously. One Sunday evening, he drove slowly up the Beckenden road in a little green van, bumping and bouncing over the potholes, turned into the short lane leading to the aerodrome, parked the van well before the gap and climbed the bank to peer over the hedgerow: what he saw astonished him. Three boys on shining bicycles were tearing up the side of one of the higher mounds and plunging in turn down the reverse slope before executing speedway-style skids on some loose shale and cinders thirty feet away. Nearby, two five-year-olds, obvious twins, with identical basin haircuts, one bespectacled, were holding up model aeroplanes and running backwards and forwards over a plank laid across a large puddle making aircraft noises and simulating explosions as they dropped stones on a balsa wood boat: over near a hedgerow, a three year-old and a four-year-old were taking it in turns to swing across a ditch on a knotted rope tied to the branch of an old oak tree. And watching over them all, was a woman in her mid- or late-thirties, poorly dressed in a patched, flowered pinafore, darned woollen cardigan, legs tanned and bare, feet scrunched inside scuffed and down-at-heel shoes: she was sitting upon a backless white chair in front of a long, low, yellow-walled, tarpaulin-roofed building, itself half-buried at one end by a huge mound of refuse of all kinds.

Don Godwin's arrival at the dump was not by chance: one month previously, the three large pasture meadows to the north, east and south of the small aerodrome field upon which the dump and the cottage stood had been put up for sale by the executors of the late farmer who owned them: the old man, on whose land the aerodrome had been built, had died two months before and all his land was up for sale: and Old Man Godwin, patriarch of the Godwin clan, had made an offer for the four biggest fields, three of which he intended to plough and the fourth of which he proposed to give to his youngest son, Don: it just so happened that the fourth field lay adjacent to the rubbish dump on the aerodrome field.

Don Godwin's own farm, Lowhams, already stretched the mile or so up from the estuary to the Salter road: here was a golden opportunity to extend its already extensive acreage across the Salter road and up on to the Beckenden ridge. However, a small problem did exist with the new land. In Don Godwin's field lay a small disused gravel pit, some forty yards by fifty yards in area and twenty feet deep: it had been dug with machinery by the old farmer and his itinerant labouring family during the lean years just after the First War in an attempt to sell the gravel to the county council for road-mending: but the scheme had been only marginally profitable and had been abandoned after a couple of years. Now all that remained was the water-filled pit, a hazard to ploughing and a waste of land in a time of war when food was scarce and every acre needed to be farmed: just as the rubbish dump also was a waste of valuable land.

Old Man's Godwin's idea was for his youngest son to drain the pit, fill it, flatten it and topsoil it into arable farmland again: it could be done in a matter of weeks, he had said: the old aerodrome dump fifty to sixty yards away, covered in mounds of tainted, earth, clinker, sand and lime, and other refuse tipped there over a number of years, would provide the fill by the wagon-load: the pit would take everything there: and there was nothing else they could use if they wished to do it quickly, which they did. It would be a simple matter to bring in a couple of caterpillar-tracked bulldozers and shove the mounds of ash, lime, earth and clinker and the actual rotting and rusting rubbish the fifty yards or sixty yards straight into the pit itself: after that, they would rake off the cinder hard upon which the old First War aeroplanes used to stand, flatten the remains of the long, low, yellow-painted derelict building on it which had served as the officers' barracks and mess and which was itself derelict and half-smothered by a great mound of rubbish.

The aerodrome had been forgotten, so it seemed, and, since it was an agricultural project, bringing into production some hitherto unploughed acreage, the Government would not mind and might even aid them, providing them with all the diesel, rationed and scarce as it was, they would require to operate the caterpillar bulldozers: they were more likely to be commended than opposed! The Government might even give them a gang of Italian prisoners of war, ten or twenty, say, of those brought back from the mass round-up in North Africa, to help them with the labouring side: after all, there was a camp full of them not twenty miles away on the other side of Wivencaster. With their labour and the bulldozers, and a couple of wagons, they could probably shift the whole lot inside a fortnight, cover it with a layer of top soil, lime it and, with the prisoners cutting any drainage channels required, it could be ready for ploughing, harrowing, drilling and heavy rolling by the early spring, just in time for planting potatoes.

That was the plan, anyway: now he had discovered this bloody woman and her horde of kids were living on it, for God's sake, the same bloody family he had turned out of the bathing huts all those months ago! Gawd, Christ! She had even done up the derelict building and was living in that! What worried Don Godwin was that, if the district council got wind of her living there, it could be the devil's own job to get her off, even if she were a squatter and without rights: the council could be very 'iffy' about such things, mainly because it would first have to find her accommodation and God knows how long that would take: housing was in short supply everywhere, what with the Germans bombing everything flat and the council would not thank anyone presenting them with such an unnecessary problem!

'She's sitting there as large as life as though she hasn't got a care in the world,' he thought to himself, as he quietly turned his van and headed back towards the main road. 'I don't know who the hell she is, but she's got to go, her and her bloody brood! The whole lot of them!'

Whatever Don Godwin did, he knew that he would have to do it alone so that no one would ever know: that would present no problem: he made his own decisions about the farm anyway: he did not ask his father: he was too old and it was a younger man's world now: it was just a matter of how it was to be done and how soon, that was all: at the first opportunity, he decided.

When Don Godwin had turned the woman out of the bathing huts, her and her gaggle of children, he had not expected to see them again: he thought they had left the district, not that he had enquired: so it irritated him that he had come upon her once again. She could not be local, that was for certain, or he would have known her: he knew by sight all the village women who pieceworked for him and his father and brothers on their adjoining farms, the regular yearly bean-pickers, pea-pickers, strawberry-pickers, cabbage cutters and potato-lifters. And, if she were not local, but just some Londoner come down into the country to escape the bombing, as she had said, then it should be all the easier to get rid of her. But how? That was the question. How? It was still puzzling him when he turned the van on to the Salter road and headed up the low hill towards the Lowhams farm chase.

It was not surprising that Don Godwin did not remember Olive: the last time the two had seen each other was in the weeks just before Olive's mother had died and just before Olive left the village for London: having quit the job at the school, Olive had gone pea-picking on Old Man Godwin's farm just to earn some money: it was a dull, overcast June day and she had her head hooded by a sack against the drizzling rain. Don Godwin had been a thirteen-year-old, riding his pony along the headland behind his mother, up on her bay steeplechaser, both heading back towards the dry of the farmhouse. Olive had looked up briefly as they passed: she knew the boy was a Godwin simply by his distinctive blond hair and strangely dark eyebrows, and the lean, almost mournful countenance, which was the family's trademark and which ran through the line of all Josh Godwin's sons: as did the rounded back, which was a characteristic one saw among the older breed of farmworkers who had spent their years humping two-hundredweight sacks of grain about.

Nobody liked the Godwins: you worked for them because men with families had to work somewhere: and, if you did, you obeyed them, took their orders and bit your tongue because you had to. All four brothers took after Old Man Josh in wanting everything done in haste: it was their nature: some said they were just hotheads: others thought they were just plain bloody arrogant! Or ignorant!

Of course, had Don Godwin and his brothers gone to the two-roomed, red-brick village school in Tithe Street along with the district's other children when Olive was working there as a classroom assistant to the infants' teacher, they would all have known her, but none had. From an early age, Don Godwin and his brothers had been taken daily by their mother in her pony and trap to the maypole roundabout in the centre of Salter, where they caught the Bourne Brothers' service bus to Wivencaster to attend a preparatory school: from there, though not gifted academically, they had gone on to the Wivencaster Royal Grammar, all paid for by their father. At sixteen, they had left and begun work on their father's farms, as bosses rather than workers, of course.

Nor were the Godwins good village mixers, so to speak: in fact, so caught up in their farming were they that they were seldom seen about the village: they were landowners first and foremost, having their farms adjacent to each other along the Salter road, two of which had once been neighbouring farms either side of Old Man Josh, which he had shrewdly purchased during the depressed agricultural years of the Twenties when so many farms had lain neglected and unprofitable, when field after field lay fallow, weeds choked the unploughed land, buildings went unrepaired, hedgerows went untrimmed, ditches and drainage channels became choked and farm machinery rusted and rotted in wagon sheds and dilapidated barns.

By the time Olive returned to Gledlang after an absence of fourteen years, the Godwin clan had spread so far eastward along the north shore of the Langwater that they farmed everything east of Gledlang as far as Salter. In less than fifteen years, the family had acquired more than a thousand acres to add to the three hundred and sixty they had already before their expansion began.

'She's got to go!' Don Godwin said aloud to himself as he turned the van into the Lowhams farm chase. 'She's got to go! Her and her bloody kids!'

SIXTY-ONE

THEY were returning from the village when they smelled the petrol: it was dark, well after nine o'clock: overhead, clouds were drifting across the face of the moon, blotting it out one minute, exposing it the next. In the lane, Jimmy and Patrick were leading the usual procession on their bicycles, each with a twin on their crossbar, followed by Jack on his bicycle: they had reached the gap and stopped to allow their mother to catch up, for Olive was pushing the two youngest in the double-hooded pram, all the quicker to get them home to their beds rather than have them flopping down by the side of the road every hundred yards and having to badger them to get up.

'Can you smell something?' It was Patrick who asked the question, sniffing at the night air just as his mother joined them.

Olive wrinkled her nose. 'I can't smell anything,' she said dismissively.

'I can. I can smell something,' declared Jimmy, turning his face into the breeze and sniffing like his brother. 'It could be petrol. It smells like it.'

'Petrol! We don't have any petrol,' retorted his mother. 'Where would anyone get petrol in the middle of a war? You're imagining things, the pair of you. Only farmers get petrol. Ordinary people don't unless they're mixed up in the black market and who round here is mixed up in that?'

'I'm sure I can smell something,' insisted Patrick, raising his head to sniff again: he might have investigated further had not they heard a steady roaring noise overhead, growing louder and louder.

'Lancasters!' Jimmy announced triumphantly, looking up as wave after wave of the four-engined British bombers droned eastwards high in the sky, heading towards the open sea and the Continent. 'Berlin tonight, I bet.'

It was a matter of pride among the three eldest Cullens that they were able to identify most aeroplanes which crossed the sky above them, even those which flew so high they left only ice-white vapour trails: it was one of the bonuses of war: so many aeroplanes in the sky each day. On dark nights, if they could not make out the shape, they did it by the sound of the aeroplanes' engines: the engine of a Spitfire, or more likely a Hurricane, was vastly different to that, say, of a Wellington or a Halifax or a Boston, or the American planes, the B-17 Flying Fortresses, the Liberators, the P-47 Mustang fighters, the Hellcats and others.

That night, most of the bombers were too high and too obscured by the clouds for the elder three boys to try and count them as they sometimes did, more in boyish pride than accuracy: the size of a raid going out was important to them: from that, they would know whether it was one of the much-vaunted 'thousand bomber raids' about which those at school who had battery-operated wirelesses at home had heard from a newsreader with the funny Yorkshire accent. Like all boys of their time, the three were unconcerned by the fact that children the same as themselves, perhaps in Cologne, Hamburg, Bremen, Stuttgart, or somewhere in the Ruhr, even Berlin itself, would that night be subjected to the same terrors to which they themselves had been subjected in London almost three years before. They just assumed that the bombers were heading for Berlin because that was where Hitler and Goering and all the bigwig Germans lived and the hope was that they would be underneath it all: then the war would be over! Such were the times and such were boys' thoughts then.

That evening they had all been to the parish hall in the village for a night's entertainment: a husband-and-wife team, both strangers, had put on a 'puppet and magic lantern show,' supported by two 'counting dogs': posters advertising it had gone up around the village a week before: admittance threepence. At that time, such a show was a welcome diversion from the worries of the war and, for a small village like Gledlang, well off the beaten track, an unexpected excitement. Admittedly, the couple did flit off early the next morning without paying their bed and breakfast bill at Mother Yugo's house, but that was on the morrow: for Olive and the boys, it had been an enjoyable evening's entertainment, the very first to which she had been able to take the boys since their arrival, simply because there had been none and, even if there had been any, she would not have been able to afford it.

Olive was just pleased to see the boys so happy, particularly the four youngest and Jack: they laughed and clapped as loudly as anyone, revelling in the uniqueness of the occasion. By getting to the hall early, they had been able to take the very front row of chairs, the best seats in the place, in fact, right in front of the stage and the little black-curtained puppet theatre, so they were able to see everything clearly. It did not go down well with some behind and there were some audible mutterings, but Olive contented herself with the knowledge that she had paid for her tickets and the seats were empty when they took their places. She just ignored them: just as she had ignored Don Godwin when he had passed them in his little green van as they headed towards the village along the Salter road in the calm of the early evening: had Olive turned to look back instead of putting her nose in the air, she would have noticed the cold-eyed stare he gave them as he went by: she would have seen, too, his van swing abruptly into a gateway, make a rapid three-point turn and speed back down the road and into the chase leading to his own farm.

But she and the boys, they on their bicycles, she walking, were too intent with pressing on: sitting in the parish hall, Olive, in fact, gave him no further thought: she was too caught up in keeping a wary eye on Michael and Joseph, who became so enthralled with the puppets only feet in front of them that several times they left their seats and wandered up to the little black-curtained theatre to peer more closely at them, taking them to be real, if tiny, people. It brought shouts from behind and Olive had to be alert each time to reach forward and pull them back: only the commencement of the magic lantern show finally ended their encroachment as they gazed up at the cutout shadowy figures moving behind the white sheet: everyone cheered as the dastardly squire received his come-uppance and the interval lights went up for tea and biscuits for the adults and orange juice for the children.

The second-half was taken up by the two counting dogs, large, brown and black Alsatians, which appeared on stage with their owners and barked out the answers to sums shouted out by the audience and passed on to them by their mistress, like 'What is three times two?' Or 'Two plus two?' The dogs also barked out 'Yes' and 'No' answers to various questions, also passed on by their mistress, and did various other tricks before the show ended with some amateurish conjuring. Jimmy and Patrick smiled cynically through it all, sarcastically pointing out that the man had craftily tossed the dogs a small tidbit each time they reached the required number so as to stop them barking further and ruining the act: they also knew how he did each of his conjuring tricks, which were not magic at all, but simple sleight of hand for the gullible.

Notwithstanding their gripes, it had been a happy night: made more so by the fact that, on coming out, Olive unexpectedly met her sister Alice walking arm in arm with her soldier boyfriend, John the Cook, who had returned – miraculously, in Olive's view – a fortnight previously and was now stationed at Wivencaster. With both Percy and Hubert away that evening, walking the dark and lonely lanes over near the Tottles somewhere with rifles in their hands, on manoeuvres with the Home Guard, Alice had taken the opportunity to slip out of the house to meet John the Cook, who had driven over with supplies for the searchlight battery still camped on the Park and was combining the trip with a resumption of his courting: poor Alice got out so seldom that had he come in the middle of the night she would have rushed out to meet him – so long as her brothers did not hear her, of course!

Since their father's funeral, the two sisters had spoken with each other regularly – when Percy and Hubert were not there: though, whatever they thought, Olive would not be kept from meeting her remaining sister: she felt that she owed that to the memory of Theresa.

John the Cook was not what Olive would have called an outstanding specimen of manhood, being about thirty-five or thirty-six, no more than five foot, five inches tall, thickset, with plastered-down hair and a broken-toothed smile: but he was cheerful enough and he would do for Alice, she thought, even if he did irritate her from the outset by insisting upon calling her 'Flower' in almost every sentence, and spoke in, what was to Olive as near an unintelligible accent as she had ever heard, worse even than an Irish accent, she thought, full of 'thees' and 'tha's' and 'ba gums!' As in 'Pleased t'meet thee, Flower' when a shy and grinning Alice first introduced her: followed by 'Seven kiddies, Flower! Ba gum, tha's been a busy woman, hassn't thee?' said with a knowing wink when she told him how many children she had, before a final 'Well, goodneet t'thee, Flower, it's bin a pleasure meetin' thee. I look forward to'seein' thee again.'

The plus side was, Olive mused, that John the Cook also still walked with a limp from his own wound: still, he was her sister's boyfriend, if that is what he could be called, and she seemed happy enough with him, clinging tightly to his arm as they limped off together into the darkness, on their way down Shoe Street to some lonely spot along the seawall no doubt: and Olive was pleased enough to grant her that.

The bombers had gone, the twins had dismounted and the three eldest were just riding on to the hard when the bright flash lit the lower reaches of the sky not fifty yards from them: a red-orange fireball mushroomed up thirty feet into the air, expanding as it rose. It came from the far side of the high mound which still obscured the demolished end of the cottage and which had never been cleared because there was just too much of it: at the same time there came a piercing, blood-curdling scream like that of a rabbit caught in the jaws of a stoat.

'Was that a bomb?' a panicking Olive cried as the fireball rolled up into the darkness and evaporated: hurriedly, she turned the pram and headed for the middle of the lane

'That wasn't a bomb,' a puzzled Jimmy quickly decided. 'We'd have heard it whistle and we'd have felt the blast.'

'It could have been an incendiary?' suggested a nervous Olive, ready to retreat further.

'It weren't no incendiary either,' Jimmy said again, equally as surely. 'That was something different.'

At the far end of the cottage, a bright orange glow was beginning to flicker behind the great mound.

'There's only one way to find out,' cried Patrick and he was off and pedalling up the side of the nearest mound intent on taking a circuitous route towards the glow so as to come upon the spot from one side: in no time at all he had disappeared over the top.

Jimmy was just behind him and Jack would have followed had Olive not seized his handlebars and pulled him back. 'No you don't,' she commanded. 'You stay here and keep an eye on the others – just in case.'

Somewhat ungainly, Olive started to follow the two eldest to the top of the first mound herself, climbing with difficulty up the steep path worn over the years by their bicycles, for she had none of the agility of her sons: ahead, she saw them briefly silhouetted against the red-orange glow as they crossed the top of another mound before plunging into darkness of the next valley.

The next time Olive saw her two eldest they were pedalling furiously back towards her: in the brief instant they had been able to look down upon the spot from which the fireball had risen, they had seen something which alarmed them: evidence of a blaze deliberately set: a line of a half-dozen old car tyres carefully laid on the rubbish nearest to the cottage wall. And from the fierce way they were burning, with flames six or seven feet high racing from one to the next, it was clear that they and the rubbish itself had been doused in something highly inflammable: and that could only be the petrol which Patrick had smelled.

'Go back, Mum! Go back!' both boys shouted frantically as they climbed the mound on which their mother stood: behind them, a great roaring and leaping wall of flame had suddenly reared up, fanned by the breeze.

'Some blighter's started this fire on purpose,' an incredulous Jimmy shouted angrily. 'He's trying to burn our bleedin' house down!'

Even as he spoke, the tarpaulin roof burst into flames and disintegrated with a roar: and no sooner had the roof gone than the doors forming the walls caught with a great whoosh and the flames raced along the line faster than a boy can run: obviously petrol had been sprayed upon the cottage as well.

There was nothing for it but for them to retreat to the safety of the road out of range of the smoke and the heat: from there, all they could do was to watch the cottage burn. The speed of the fire astounded them: there was never any hope of saving anything: the fierce flames engulfed everything too quickly and the heat was far too great for any of them even to consider darting inside in an attempt to snatch up clothes or food or even a pair of shoes: to do so would have been tantamount to committing suicide: from fireball to flight had taken no more than a minute.

'Can't we do something?' a despairing Olive wailed. 'Can't we throw water on it or something?'

Her two eldest just looked at each other: they did not like to see their mother in such despair, but they knew that they had to face the reality of the situation. 'The fire's got too good a hold. There's nothing we can do, Mum,' a grim-faced Jimmy told her quietly. 'It's a petrol fire. All we can do is wait till it burns itself out and see if there's anything we can salvage.'

'You have to face it, Mum,' said Patrick, astride his bicycle, watching their home implode in a volcano of sparks and crackling flames, 'some blighter's started this deliberately just to burn us out.' The vehemence was unusual for him.

'Why?' wailed Olive. 'Why would anyone want to do that? Why would any-one want to waste petrol to do that?'

It was a question her two eldest could not answer: they could only stand astride their bicycles and look on as their mother sat down on the verge and buried her face in her hands: the tears were streaming down her cheeks: to the consternation of her sons, her sobbing was audible: she just could not help herself. All the things she had worked for, all the things she had bought, their clothes, their furniture, their food – all were gone, destroyed. Michael and Joseph, taking their cue from their mother, began to cry, too.

The solemn-faced twins looked silently from their weeping mother to the fire, then to their older brothers and back to their mother again: no one spoke: there was not much any of them could say: all they could do was to retreat from the smoke, watch the fire burn and wait for the dawn.

SIXTY-TWO

THE morning broke grey and calm: over the peaceful countryside, a thick column of dark smoke was climbing skywards from the smouldering dump: it was still early, about six o'clock, when Jimmy, Patrick and Jack awoke and began to groan and yawn: they had managed to slip into some form of sleep midway through the night, but it had been short and uncomfortable: the hardness of the ground and the chill damp of the morning air had awakened them.

The twins and Michael and Joseph still slept alongside their mother, two upon either side, the latter somewhat futilely covered by her cardigan. Olive, however, was not asleep, even though her eyes were closed: the same cold and damp which had discomforted her three eldest had precluded her even from dozing. Instead, wrapped inside her overcoat, she had lain upon the grass verge with her back to the burned-out cottage, in a state of utter shock: the fire had taken everything and, now that the morning had come, all she could do was to lie there and wait for the warmth of the sun to revive her.

Eventually, Jimmy, Patrick and Jack climbed stiffly to their feet and ambled still yawning and stretching towards the site of their former home, more in hope than expectancy of finding something among the smoking ruin which might provide them with a breakfast of sorts, for they were all hungry: their bicycles they left by the roadside: there was no sense in risking them.

Nothing remained of the cottage except the ash-grey chunks of concrete from the caved-in walls lying amid a carpet of glowing embers: nor was there any point in attempting to salvage anything: mattresses, sideboard, boxes, chairs, table, their clothes, their food, their blankets, all the furniture they had acquired – all were gone: only the blackened iron frames of the two bedsteads, warped by the heat, and the range itself, blistered and cracked, remained whole.

So they wandered on to the far side of the dump, determined to examine the scene of the fireball: though such was the smoke still pouring from the burning mounds that they had to dart through it with their heads lowered and their mouths masked by their upturned jacket collars, emerging at the other end coughing and spluttering and with eyes watering.

They saw the blackened remains of the green van first, parked directly alongside the mound at the far end of the still-smouldering ruin of the cottage: neither Jimmy nor Patrick had noticed it the previous night when they had retreated from the mound on their bicycles: but then they had had no more than a second in which to stare down at the flames raging up towards them.

Attached to the van, barely recognisable, was what had once been a small bowser, of the kind farmers normally used to carry water to replenish drinking troughs for their cattle in the farthest corners of their land, but which many now used to fetch their monthly supply of precious rationed petrol from those few garages in Maydun and Wivencaster licensed to sell it. It, too, was burnt down to its wheel axles. Though there were no tyremarks on the cinder hard there, it was clear from their positioning that the driver of the van had swung the two around in a semi-circle before parking, for the van faced back towards the road as though ready to be driven quickly out through the gap once the fire had taken.

It was on the other side of the bowser that the three made their grimmest discovery: where the ground was scorched the most was the body of a man: he was lying on his back, with his charred and shrivelled arms raised in a grotesque posture of supplication, as though he were trying to protect his face: except that he no longer had a face: his nose and lips, all of his skin, had been burnt away to leave a grimacing skull. He was not even a proper man any more: the whole front of his torso, from his chest to his knees, was a blackened mass of crinkled flesh: what clothing he had been wearing, shirt, trousers, pullover, jacket, had mostly been burned away: only a few scorched tatters remained, though, incongruously, his socks and shoes were untouched.

'It's that farmer fellah we saw go past last night,' declared Jimmy, peering down at the blackened corpse for a few seconds before pulling a face and turning away. 'You know, the chap who turned Mum and us out of that hut that first night we come. He's the blighter who burned us out! God what a mess!'

'Serve the sod right,' declared a grimacing Patrick fiercely, one hand clamped across his nose and mouth to ward off the sickly sweet smell of burnt flesh.

'Ugh!' was all Jack could manage as he turned away, doubled over and began to retch.

'I suppose we'd better go and tell Mum,' said Jimmy, his face still screwed up, looking sideways at his brothers because he did not want to look at the blackened corpse again.

They briefly inspected the burnt-out bowser, but the smell of it forced them to back away: they also peered into the charred van, though for what purpose other than boys' idle curiosity not one of the three could have said: then they set off back towards the lane.

Various things puzzled them: a man would have to have been motivated by some special force – greed, hate, what? – to do what the dead man had done. He would have had to have taken leave of his senses, they reckoned, even to have thought of it. Had he meant to kill them? All of them? Or had he just wanted to burn them out? To drive them off the dump? Why? For what reason? They were harming nobody. And had the man actually known they were out when he set the blaze? Or had that just been a lucky coincidence? In his demented mind, he could only have been hoping everyone would think that one of them had started the fire while playing on the dump and had then gone off with the rest to the parish hall to watch the puppet show and the 'counting dogs.' It was the kind of thing the police and the fire brigade would suspect: it was the kind of thing boys would do, they would say to themselves. 'And you can trust the Cullen clan to do something and then blame someone else.' People were always willing to believe such things of them, especially of 'the bloody Cullens!'

But somehow, though the boys did not know it – no one did – the man had made a mistake: several, in fact. His first mistake had been to do everything on the spur of the moment when he had seen the family making for the village: haste and delay together had undone him. On his return to his farm, he had had to drive a mile out along the headlands to one of his fields to locate the small bowser: then that had to be towed back to the farm and that had taken him a half-hour or more. A hunt about his house for cash and then the long drive into Wivencaster to fill the bowser with petrol from one of the licensed garages there, using up the whole of one month's allocation of his petrol ration, had also taken up time, as had the return trip: two hours, in fact, during which time a faint, barely discernible breeze had sprung up.

That had been his second mistake: to go ahead when a breeze was blowing, no matter how slight: but then expediency and opportunity must have played their part there and he had either ignored it or not noticed it. All Jimmy and Patrick could assume was that the spray from the petrol must have drifted back over him on the faint breeze as he turned the thin black hose from the bowser on to the tyres, having first doused the tarpaulin roof and the door walls. In the dark, he would not have noticed, perhaps thinking himself safe because he was in the open air and the spray of petrol was away from him: any fumes, he would have reckoned, would have dispersed in the air. A cautious man would have noticed the breeze: tested for it, in fact: a foolhardy man, eager to get the deed done and be gone, would not have bothered. Quite clearly, after retreating from the mound to the vicinity of the bowser, the man had struck a match, probably just to light a rag torch he had made and which he could safely throw on to the mound: instead, he had himself become enveloped in flames: almost simultaneously, the fire had raced to the mound and set that alight as well as the small bowser, which, still with some petrol in it and enveloped in fumes, had exploded in a fireball.

When the three told their mother what they had found, she seemed unable to believe it: she just sat there open-mouthed and stared at them as though she had not heard them correctly. It was perhaps fortunate that at that moment the Maydun fire engine arrived with six bleary-eyed auxiliary firemen upon it: they did not bother to run out their hoses because they had no water anyway: all that night they had been on call elsewhere, to a small port town farther up the coast, and their tank was empty. Some German bombers had sneaked over from Holland under the cover of darkness and bombed the town's docks, which harboured air sea rescue boats and minesweepers: they had been trying to hit a munitions factory, but had missed that and hit an old wool factory making army uniforms. The Maydun brigade had been called to help deal with that fire: even so, it was a six-tender blaze: all the surrounding stations had attended, certainly more important than just an old rubbish dump burning in a field which someone had seen lighting up the horizon and then, in the morning, seeing the column of smoke still rising, had telephoned the fire station: the Maydun tender was just calling out of curiosity on its way back.

Jimmy was the first to greet them. 'We got burnt out,' he said flatly as the leading fireman jumped down. 'Mum's lost everything, house, clothes, furniture, everything. We couldn't do anything to stop it. We didn't even have time to get our stuff out. It was just luck we weren't in there at the time. We would've been if we hadn't been in the village.'

'I didn't know there was a house here,' said the leading fireman, rubbing a grimed hand across a soot-blackened chin. 'I thought this was just an old dump.' Then, addressing Olive, he said: 'Sorry, missus, we couldn't have come any sooner. We've been on call all night.'

'It wouldn't have mattered if you had,' answered the boy, disconsolately. 'You wouldn't have been able to put it out anyway. It was a petrol fire. There was no stopping it once it got going. Me and my brother only just got out of its way or we'd have been gonners. Everything was too dry. It burned like crazy.' He turned and beckoned the leading fireman to follow him as others began to get down. 'You'd better come with me,' he said, 'I've got something to show you.'

Then turning to his mother, he ordered: 'Keep the little ones here, Mum. We don't want them following us.'

Michael and Joseph had finally been awakened by the arrival of the tender and the voices of the firemen: still sleepy-eyed, they were staring goggle-eyed at the dark-uniformed newcomers, regarding them with some trepidation, clinging to their sad mother's coat, hiding. The twins, for some reason, did not seem at all to comprehend the magnitude of what had happened: their eyes were fixed firmly on the red fire engine: they just stood there, scheming, wondering whether they should dare to climb on to it and ask for a ride and perhaps even to ring its bell: such was their small world.

Jimmy led the leading fireman and another soot-faced man round to where the burnt-out green van and bowser were parked and where the blackened body lay still frozen in its grotesque attitude of death, the lips parted and the teeth bared as if in one last snarl at life.

'Good God!' exclaimed the leading fireman, halting a few feet from the body. 'Poor sod! Who is he?'

'Some farmer chap,' Jimmy answered matter-of-factly. 'Mum'll probably know who he was. He was spraying petrol over everything before setting it alight. We were all out at the time. The bugger was trying to burn us out.' He said it in the same emotionless tone as before.

'Are you saying someone started the fire deliberately? On purpose? To burn the house down? Are you sure, sonny?'

'Yeah. Dead sure. Pat, me brother, and me, we both smelled the petrol before it started. We saw the fireball go up.'

Two other firemen came up, peered at the body with the same grim expressions upon their faces and then went over to inspect the blackened bowser, where they found the filler cap among the black ash and sniffed it before nodding together. 'It's petrol all right,' one said. 'One for the police, I reckon.'

Unable to quell her curiosity, Olive came up with Patrick, having left the twins and the two youngest in Jack's care: at that moment, their wishes were being granted: taking sympathy upon them, two of the other firemen were lifting them up on to the tender and allowing them to ring the bell, which was clanging noisily. As soon as she saw the blackened body, Olive wished she had not been so inquisitive: giving a cry of horror, she quickly raised her pinafore to her face with a grimace of disgust and retreated, stopping only when it was hidden from her sight by the height of the thistles and the docks in between.

The leading fireman smiled to himself: he was used to seeing overly inquisitive people recoil in horror and it amused him: a body was just a body no matter what state it was in: and the dead did not know what state they were in, did they?

'Your boy says he was trying to burn you out, missus. Is that right?' the leading fireman asked, putting the emphasis on the 'your.'

'Looks like it,' said Olive cautiously. 'What else would he be doing here. It's the only explanation I can think of. Though why, I don't know. We weren't doing him any harm. We were just living here.' She turned to face the leading fireman squarely. 'Why would he want to do that? You tell me.'

The fireman could not. 'I don't know that I can, missus,' he said with a shrug. 'I truly don't know that I can.'

He paused. 'Your boy here also says you might know who he is.' Despite what he had been told, his voice was tinged with a certain sympathy for the victim.

'If it's who I think it is, his name's Don Godwin,' replied Olive, but without any sympathy. 'It looks like him, what's left of him. That's his van, so it must be him. He's a local farmer. Farms Lowhams. Over there about a mile-and-half. Off the Salter road and down the chase by the wash bridge. You can't miss it. It's signposted.'

The fireman nodded and thanked her. 'Has he got a wife?'

'Yes, poor woman, and a couple of kiddies,' replied Olive. 'Fancy having this happen to him. I wouldn't wish that on anyone.' Olive's sympathy was for the innocent wife and children: not for any Godwin: she had never had any liking for any of them and she was not going to pretend now. 'His family farm all the land between here and Salter. More money than sense, the lot of them!'

'Well, we'll get someone to go over there. The police probably. They can do that. For now, I suggest you and your family get your things together.'

'Why?' Olive turned to face him again. 'We ain't going nowhere.'

'We'll you can't stay here, missus, can you? You ain't got no house now, have you?'

The fireman was trying to be sympathetic, and helpful, but it was difficult in the face of Olive's brusqueness. 'The best thing you can do,' he said, 'is get in touch with the council. They've got places you can go to for a while, anyway. There's a place in Wivencaster, the old orphanage, that takes children from bombed-out families. Your children could go there. They'd take 'em in, I'm sure. There ain't much difference between being bombed out and burned out, is there?'

'My children are not going anywhere near an orphanage,' snorted an angry Olive. 'We'll sort ourselves out, thank you.' Her voice rose and there was sarcasm in it. 'We live here. The boys go to school here. I was born here. I've got work here. We've done enough shifting about. I'll find somewhere myself, thank you very much. We're staying where we are! Go to Wivencaster indeed!'

'Well, it's up to you, missus,' said the fireman, with a shrug. 'So long as you can find somewhere, especially for the kiddies. You have to think of them first, don't you?'

He sighed and began to walk back: the poor woman had just had her house burned down, and her with seven kids, so he was prepared to make allowances: but there was just no helping some people: some people just had too much pride for their own good: a man can only do so much.

It was time to turn to the job in hand. 'We'll, inform the police when we get back to the station,' he told his deputy, a short, chubby fishmonger with a shop in Maydun high street. 'Meanwhile, we'd better get the poor sod covered up. We don't want them youngsters seeing him all black and burnt.'

The four youngest would not have been interested in the body had they even known it was there: Michael and Joseph did briefly trot over to meet their mother and brothers on their return, but then went straight back to the fire engine: they wanted to be lifted up again to sit inside the cab, or at least stand upon the engine and ring the bell once more: that was fun: that was far more important to them than knowing about a body burned to a crisp lying some fifty yards away.

SIXTY-THREE

THE Salter constable, a six-foot-five giant of man named Dawes, came puffing up on his bicycle later that morning: he took off his cycle clips, laid his bicycle on the verge and went off to find the body: when he came back, the ambulance from Maydun was just drawing up: what was left of Don Godwin was placed upon a stretcher covered by a blanket, though it looked more like a tent as they carried him to the vehicle because the dead man's arms were still frozen in the position of supplication in which Jimmy had found him.

By then, however, Olive and the boys were long gone to the village: the boys had to go to school and Olive had work to do: she was not going to wait for him to arrive. No doubt, she thought, as she wheeled the pram out on to the Beckenden road, he would catch up with them later on his creaking bicycle to take a statement from her, Jimmy and Patrick about the fireball and the body: till then, she had other more pressing matters, like finding them somewhere to sleep that night. She would be at Follenfaunts as usual and, if Dawes wanted to speak to them, he could come there: there was really nothing else that she or they could do: the boys were hungry and she needed to provide them with some breakfast.

It was a little after eight-fifteen when she led her weary sons into Gledlang Square: the boys were on their bicycles, Jimmy and Patrick each carrying a twin on their crossbars and Jack wobbling along behind with Michael on his crossbar: Joseph was seated in grand isolation in the pram. Fortunately, what little money Olive had, she had been carrying in her purse so they were able to call at Fred Thorn's bakery to buy two newly baked loaves with her last few pence: the bread was still warm from the oven and they ate one of the loaves there and then, standing in the street, with other village children going past on their way to school, wondering what all the Cullens were doing grouped around their mother while she tore chunks from a loaf and doled it out to their grasping hands. After that, they gathered around the old iron-wheeled pump and Jimmy and Patrick took it in turns to rotate the wheel as each cupped his hands at the lower spout to wash his face and legs and to drink the icy water. At least their immediate hunger and thirst were satisfied: after that, it was a matter of getting Jack and the twins to the village school where they would at least receive a hot school dinner at lunchtime.

The only instruction Olive gave them was to say nothing about the fire and the arrival of the fire brigade. 'You're clean enough and smart enough, so no one need know,' she told them. 'And if that fool of a Salter constable comes poking his nose in, tell him only what you saw. I don't want him knowing anything about my business that he doesn't need to know. I'll find us somewhere for tonight. This is our business, not anyone else's. Understand?' They did and went off.

Jimmy and Patrick, however, did not go to school that day: they cycled up Tithe Street, following their mother to Follenfaunts: she had a task there for them to do. Thus, Patrick was able to speed past the village school with Michael perched on the crossbar of his bicycle, laughing at those in the playground staring back at him and wondering where he was going. Not to be outdone, when the special Bourne Brothers' red-and-white, double-decker bus into Maydun went past, carrying all the twelve-year-olds to fourteen-year-olds from the three other villages along the north bank of the estuary, on their way to the new secondary school at Maydun, to which Jimmy also should have been going that morning, he was able to give the ubiquitous V-sign to all the puzzled faces staring at him out of the windows.

On Follenfaunts, there was a long, low, open-fronted wagon shed, some sixty feet in length, built of brick, with a tiled, sagging roof, divided into three sections by stout oak timber posts: the cart and the wagon took up two of the spaces, with a plough, a harrow and a wide field roller squeezed in between them: but at the farthest end was an area where many of the implements and various items of farm junk were stored. If these could be cleared, then Olive could curtain it off with sacks or something, hung from rope or nails, and create an enclosed area where they could sleep that night, at least, and perhaps for the next couple of nights as well. That was Jimmy's and Patrick's task that day: to clear the area while their mother worked, then to punch holes in a couple of dozen or so grain sacks and tie them together with binder string and hang them from a rope tied to nails to form a crude curtain at the side and the front. It was a measure born of expediency, but it would do for the time being, Olive decided, until she could find somewhere more permanent for them to sleep: though, at the back of her mind, she had not much hope of doing that, not without interference from the busybodies working for the council and she wanted to avoid that. She had had enough of busybodies interfering in her life in London, busybodies like Helen Grogan: they always wanted to know everything that was none of their business: like how they lived, how their health was, what money Robert earned – when he was earning at all – what food she fed the children, whether there was running water in the flat and a proper lavatory, how many bedrooms, what furniture they had, all questions which were of no concern of theirs. It was the prime reason Olive avoided the authorities: except for renewing her ration books and the babies' milk coupons, she kept well away from them, even in Gledlang: in her view, the less others knew of her situation the better. When the 'nit nurse' was due at the village school, she herself checked the hair of those of her sons who went there and she had regularly made them rinse their heads under the cold water pump: and when Dorothy had taken the two youngest to the parish hall to receive their usual ration of orange juice from the district nurse, Olive had always ensured they were clean and washed when they left the house so no one could find fault when they were examined and weighed.

What Olive feared most was that, if there were no accommodation to be had locally, the powers-that-be would insist that she and the boys relocate to some terraced backstreet in a poor part of Wivencaster or, worse, to the orphanage the firemen had mentioned: and she did not want that, not in a thousand years! She had been brought up in the village, the boys had a right to be there and they would damned well go on living there, house or no house, welcome or not, and no damned busybody of a welfare officer or a children's officer was going to stop them: living in poverty or not, the children were happy as they were, and they were healthy. No, Olive said to herself as she turned into the yard with Jimmy and Patrick and the two youngest trailing in her wake, she had managed on her own well enough in the three years since leaving London and she would go on managing on her own.

The only drawback to her continued well-being was that the two youngest, Michael and Joseph, no longer went to their cousin's house: that is why they accompanied her to the farm that morning: the cantankerous Alf had finally put a stop to his daughter acting as a nursemaid –against her wishes, it has to be said. 'Dad wants me to get a proper job with a proper wage,' a sad-faced Dorothy had told Olive in breaking the news four months before: consequently, now sixteen years of age, she cycled the five miles into Maydun daily to work in a fruiterers's on the High Street, a so-called 'proper job' which she detested, and all for a few shillings more than Olive had been giving her. Olive would have paid her more if she could have afforded it, but she could not: so for five days a week, Michael and Joseph now accompanied their mother to Follenfaunts, come rain, hail, gale or shine, whether she went into the fields alongside Old Jim or into the house to do Wakenham's cleaning. There was nothing unusual in it, not in that region then: not in the summer anyway: young children always joined their mothers in the fields when they went picking from May to October, where they would spend up to eight hours a day sometimes wandering happily about all over the fields, creeping along the headlands, hiding in haystacks, wading in the ditches and damning the water courses with sticks and mud or, on rainy days, playing in the straw in the barn: but always knowing when to return for a sandwich and a drink of Tizer or warm tea at lunchtime.

Michael and Joseph liked to follow Old Jim about, especially when he was working with the horses: one day Olive would see them in the distance, standing at the front of the cart, holding the reins or sitting on sacks on the wagon, smiling and laughing as they bounced along with their legs dangling over the side while Old Jim led the horses. He did not seem to mind their presence and, indeed, when he saw them running towards him, he would stop the wagon and lift them on to it. Conversely, the length of the day, whether in the field or in the house, did not seem to concern them so long as they were with their mother: when it rained, they simply scuttled into the barn or into the wagon shed or sheltered under the hedgerow: for them, time passed easily: but winter was coming on...

Old Jim was harnessing the horses into the wagon when Michael and Joseph ran to him: Olive had to tell him her plan, of course, and why she needed that area of the wagon shed to make a makeshift home for that night and possibly for a few more nights after that. Jim commiserated in his usual fashion about her loss of the cottage. 'I – I – I'm sorry to – to h-hear th-that, Olive,' he said, taking off his cap to scratch his head and giving his usual shy, grunting smile as if bemused by it all. 'I d-don't mind what you does s-s-so long as the guv'nor d-don't mind. It's s-s-all right by me.' He looked towards the two children already trying to climb up the wagon wheel on to the wagon bed and added with a shy stutter: 'It'll bring a b-bit of l-life to the place, 'on't it?' Then he was gone, trundling the wagon through the gate and along the headland with Michael and Joseph kneeling at the front and turning a few times to smile back at their mother: they would be back, she knew, when they got hungry. Old Jim was the only person Olive could trust to tell: he spoke so little to anyone else that he was unlikely to blurt it out: it would stay sealed behind his lips for weeks before he would even think to remark upon it again.

SIXTY-FOUR

OLIVE knew she would have to ask Wakenham's permission, of course: but, as the wagon shed lay more than sixty yards from the house and was screened from it by the barn, some trees and a hedgerow, he was, she hoped, unlikely to object. Besides, the open end faced away from the house, so even if Wakenham looked out of his topmost window he would not see them: and he was unlikely to do that for a few days at least, simply because he had been in bed all that week and was likely to remain there for the rest of it – and the week to come, if she read the signs correctly.

Wakenham, then sixty-six years of age, was going through one of his more maudlin and hypochondrial periods. When during the previous week Olive, in doing her normal housework, had gone into his bedroom to drag out the carpet and rug and take them outside to beat the dust out of them as they hung over the linen line, he had lain there wheezing for breath and moaning and groaning about his fate. 'Who will come to my funeral, Olive? Who will come to my funeral?' he had cried. 'I have no relatives in England. My only one living relative is a nephew, Ellis, my late cousin's boy, a captain in the army. He was taken prisoner at Singapore by the Japanese. When I die, who will be there to mourn me, Olive, who will be there to mourn me?'

'You have to go first!' Olive brutally told him as she dragged the heavy rug to the landing and pitched it down the stairs: returning to the room to pick up the rug, she added sarcastically: 'And don't you worry about your funeral, I'll go for one, if only to see you're buried properly. So don't you go worrying about that.' Then her sarcasm gave way to exasperation. 'Good Lord, man! Whyever do you care who's at your funeral? You'll be dead so you won't know anything about it. When you're six feet under, you won't know who's standing above you and who's not, will you? Buck up, man do! You've got years in you yet! Years!'

Wakenham had sunk back on his pillows, wheezing, his head lolling to one side, perspiration shining on his forehead. 'I have no friends in the village,' he continued to whine, more to himself than to Olive. 'There is nobody to care whether I live or die – except Ellis and he is a prisoner of war. He is in a prison camp so he would not be able to come!'

It was all too much for Olive's patience: she had heard it all before, or sentiments like it: eager as she was to get on with her work, she now turned on him and declared, perhaps a touch too waspishly: 'I'd care. I'd care because if you died, I'd be out of a job and out of pocket, too, then what would I do? And so would Old Jim – he'd care because he'd be out of a job, too, and out of pocket as well. So don't go around saying people don't care. They do, even if not for the reasons you want them to!'

In her view, the man could not have made more fuss had he really been dying: there were times when he complained that his asthma and his arthritis were almost too much for him to bear: any asthmatic attack would send him to his bed: his lack of breath and his arthritis meant he struggled at times just to walk about the yard: and for the past few months venturing to the farthest fields to check out his employees' work was beyond him. He still shambled about the house when Olive was not there and she supposed he was able to feed himself and dress himself, judging by the mess of plates and saucepans she found strewn about the kitchen and had to clean each time she went into the house: it was the first task she did when she walked into the kitchen of a morning.

Even when he paid Olive and Old Jim, late each Friday afternoon, Wakenham would receive them in the bedroom or the parlour or the second sitting room, or wherever he was to be found wheezing away with the very effort of breathing, it seemed, and invariably he would give them the same maudlin monologue as he handed each of them the little brown envelope.

Just as Wakenham had always been content to leave the day-to-day running of the farm to Old Jim, knowing and trusting that the old labourer would do all that was expected of him since he had always done it that way, so he would leave Olive to get on with the cleaning about the house while he lay prostrate in his bed or on a couch, which, of course, she did, doing it as she had always done it.

Olive's first task on entering the house over the past few months, as Wakenham's self-pity had grown worse, had been to make him a breakfast of either bacon, egg and sausage or porridge, toast and marmalade, along with a pot of tea: it was no great effort for her to cook him a meal and take it up to him on a tray: it gave her the time to eat some of his food herself: sometimes she would also wrap a few rashers of bacon in some greaseproof paper or tip a couple of cups of porridge oats into a roll of newspaper and slip them into her shopping bag, along with a tin of something from his larder, rice or processed peas or sardines or spam.

No, serving breakfast on a tray to Wakenham sitting up in bed in his Oriental silk dressing gown, breathing like a set of punctured bellows, was no hardship: she feared nothing sexual from him when she went into his bedroom: she had long ago decided that he was not a man who bothered about women. If he had attempted to take hold of her, she had decided long ago that she would just push him away and give him the rough end of her tongue: she did not want any of that funny business: she had had enough of that when Robert had returned briefly before she went up to Thurstone. It had not been a success as they had argued afterwards: now she hardly gave a thought to men: the hard work drained her too much and when she returned to the bungalow, there had always been the children around her: their squabbles, their needs, their care consumed all her energies. What hope did she, a woman with seven children, have, anyway? No man was likely to take her on encumbered by seven children: Olive had got used to that fact and any thoughts of another man she pushed to the back of her mind, even laughing at herself silently whenever they crept to the forefront.

That morning, however, when she went up carrying the tray for Wakenham, she was more tactful: Wakenham must have had a bad night, for he was breathing poorly, struggling for breath almost: Olive set down the tray, but he made no move to eat the fried bread and powdered scrambled egg she had made for him and, instead, contented himself with sipping his tea: his hands were shaking and he appeared to have little strength in them.

Olive took a deep breath and chose that moment to ask about the wagon shed. 'We've had a bit of a fire at the cottage where we live,' she said. 'Most of it's gone, burned down in the night. We've lost most of our furniture, chairs and that, and need a place to stay tonight – somewhere to sleep – just for tonight – in case it rains. The fire brigade have been and put it all out.'

'A fire! Oh my goodness!' Wakenham was aghast: then the horrible possibility struck him of what she might be about to ask: it was the image of seven children running about the old house and the noise and interruption to his tranquility which they would cause which brought a great groan from him: he could just imagine them going up and down the stairs all day, charging along the landing, forever going into or coming out of the two parlours, banging doors, shouting and fighting and disturbing his peace with their tumult. No, no, that would be too much!

'You're not wanting to stay here, are you?' he gasped, throwing up his hands in horror. 'Not in the house? Oh, no, I couldn't. I couldn't possibly have that. Oh, dear me, no. Not with my nerves. Not with my illness. My nerves would never stand it. That is why they did not foist any evacuees on me. I could not have stood it – the noise, the mess! My health is far too delicate, as you know. They wanted to put some in here, but the doctors said it would all be too much for me. They had to send them elsewhere or I would have had a half-dozen of them. Indescribable! The very thought of it makes me ill. Oh dear me, Olive, no, no. I couldn't possibly let you bring your children into the house, I couldn't possibly.'

Olive had expected no other answer: if Wakenham had been amenable to seven children running about his ten-room house, she would have asked him long ago. Maintaining her composure, despite the selfishness of the man's remarks, she said quietly, almost humbly so as not to antagonise him further: 'Not the house – we aren't asking to come in here! No, I was hoping you would let us use the empty space at the far end of the wagon shed where we could camp for a couple of days – just as somewhere to stay – just for now – to put a roof over our heads till I can find somewhere better. I've already spoken to Jim and he says he's not bothered. I'll make sure they won't be any trouble. I'll see they don't get in anybody's way.'

A much relieved Wakenham, who had broken out in a sweat at the very thought of it, groaned his consent: just so long as they were not in his house, he did not really care where his housekeeper-cum-labourer 'camped' with her brood, as if what went on outside the house and about the farm were all too much for him to worry about while he was lying at death's door.

SIXTY-FIVE

WHEN Olive finished her work and walked out of the house at four-thirty as usual, she had a bundle of Wakenham's best blankets under her arm and a shopping bag bulging with enough food to last her and the boys for four or five days: mostly potatoes, some carrots, onions and turnips, some rice, dried egg powder, two tins of spam, two large Bramley cooking apples and some bottled plums: in another bag hanging from her arm, cutlery rattled against fine bone china plates and cups. It was stealing, of course, but Olive felt it was a necessity, especially when she had herself and seven other mouths to feed: and if the old man stayed in bed, he would never know and she could wash and return the blankets and the plates and the cutlery when they moved on: the food would already have been eaten!

The two youngest had returned from their wanderings and were helping Jimmy and Patrick to carry yet more sacks into their new home: they would serve as the mattresses upon which they would sleep that night. On the open ground in front of the sacking curtain, her two eldest had created a small hearth from old bricks and a fire had already been lit: grouped around it in a semi-circle were eight sections of an alder tree, sawn into one-foot lengths the previous winter by Old Jim as firewood for the big house: now they formed the family's seating. Nearby was a pile of other wood, old fence posts, broken branches from the farm's trees, even the bars of a half-rotted gate which Patrick had found about the yard: enough for Olive to cook by and to keep the fire going throughout the evening so that they would be able to warm themselves. It meant that she was able to make a saucepan of tea and a dinner of sorts, though it was frugal fare: potatoes baked in the ashes of the fire till they were as black as soot, then cut down the centre and a dab of Wakenham's margarine spread into the crevice: with them on the plate was added a thick slice of cold spam apiece and some boiled turnip chips and peas, followed by stewed apples which Olive sliced and cooked in the same saucepan in which she had made the tea. The boys did not seem to mind and ate it all without complaint, just as they drank the hot tea from the borrowed cups without complaint: it all filled their bellies: and so long as they were with their mother, nothing mattered: the world could crash down about their ears, but their mother would always see them right: they were safe with her: after all, she was 'Mum.'

The constable duly paid them a visit three days later: unfortunately, Olive did not see him coming and her plan to meet him halfway down the chase between the orchards was thwarted: more than anything, she did she want him to see that they were living in a hovel at one end of a wagon shed, 'the new den,' as the boys called it: plus, of course, there were all the borrowed plates, cups and cutlery lying about waiting to be washed from breakfast. Constable Dawes gave no indication that he had noticed anything unusual as he took a statement from Olive by the wagon shed: peculiarly, he did not seem bothered about what Jimmy and Patrick might have seen, treating it all very matter-of-factly, like he was not too concerned with hearing too much actual evidence from those who had been there.

'How old are your two boys?' he asked with a sniff, leaning across the saddle of his bicycle as he slowly took his notes: and when Olive told him, he just screwed up his face and closed his notebook. 'Well, they're still kids, ain't they?' he said. 'I saw where the body and the rest of it was myself – before they took him away so I can vouch for what you say. And the firemen saw the same so I don't expect we'll be needing any of you for the inquest. If they do, I'll let you know.'

Then he pocketed his notebook, remounted his bicycle and wobbled off back the way he had come. He never did let Olive 'know': to her, it all smacked of a cut-and-dried inquest verdict: Don Godwin's death was going to be recorded as an unfortunate accident by some sympathetic brother magistrate of Old Josh who happened to serve as the coroner as well: the good name of the Godwin family was to be preserved and the youngest son would be buried without a stain on his character.

Not that Olive cared: her concern on the day they buried the remains of Don Godwin in the village churchyard a week later was for Patrick: he had caught a chill when he and Jimmy had been caught in a sudden, drenching shower coming back from the village: both had arrived back at the wagon shed soaked: Jimmy had appeared unaffected, laughing at the experience as they stood stripped and shaking, drying themselves before the fire. That evening, however, Patrick had complained of aching limbs and a feeling of lightheadedness and Olive made him lie down with her own overcoat and two blankets over him: he ate no food, but fell asleep almost immediately, as though he was extremely tired. Towards the morning, however, just as the sun was coming up, he awoke and began to cough up phlegm: he was still spitting it on to the ground when Olive herself awoke: for breakfast, he ate no more than a half slice of buttered bread and then left the crusts.

Olive was concerned, but then children had sudden illnesses from which they quickly recovered: and since their arrival in Gledlang, the boys had had no illnesses whatsoever: the outdoor life suited them all and they were robustly healthy: she kept Jack off school that day and sent a note in with Jimmy. So, as long as Patrick had Jack and the two youngest to keep a bedside vigil, Olive felt she could leave him at least till lunchtime when she would know better how he was: though she took the precaution of ordering Jack to send Michael to fetch her immediately if he felt his brother's condition were worsening. This they both promised to do: but sometime during the morning the two youngest got bored and went off to play in the barn, leaving a forlorn Jack sitting stoically by his sick brother: so when, at lunchtime, Olive returned from her hoeing in one of the distant fields, she found Jack still sitting diligently by his brother's side.

That night, Patrick cried out several times in his sleep and tossed and turned repeatedly: he was shivering and his teeth were chattering: again and again he kicked off the coat and blankets which his mother had draped over him, all the while coughing up more phlegm. Olive herself hardly slept: each cough and moan seemed to bring her awake and each time she felt Patrick's forehead, it was hot and burning.

The next day, before she went off in the morning, she fed him bread and milk and even borrowed an earthenware hot water bottle from Wakenham's cupboard without asking him, which she filled with water boiled in one of the saucepans, in the hope that he would get over his cough and that his fever would abate. Jack remained with him a second day, to help him and to replace the coat and blankets whenever he kicked them off and to keep the fire going so that he would be warm. All that evening, Olive again watched and worried over him and waited: if anything, his coughing and shivering and sweating seemed to be getting worse and she again sat up with him all night, unable to sleep.

It was Jimmy who settled the matter. 'For Christ's sake, Mum, get him to the doctor!' he shouted on the third morning, having again been awakened repeatedly in the night by Patrick's threshing and groaning. 'He's got bloody pneumonia or something! He needs the doctor!'

'Take him to the doctor, Mum, please,' pleaded a bleary-eyed Jack, who had also suffered from having been continually awakened. 'Pat ain't well. You've got to take him, Mum. He's too ill for us to look after him. He needs the doctor and medicine.'

Olive's reluctance was not through a lack of concern: she recognised that Patrick's illness was serious, yet she still hoped she would wake up the in the morning with the sun shining in upon them and find that Patrick's fever had abated, that his coughing had diminished and that he was no longer shivering. It was a foolish hope, but wished for a reason: a doctor would cost money and she had none to spare and no one to borrow it from, except her family and they were unlikely to give her any. In the country then, doctors had to be paid, so a doctor was called only when necessary – one had almost to be at death's door before countryfolk would call a doctor: most of the men in Gledlang paid into the Friendly Society at the Chessman, the Teapot Club, they called it, at sixpence or a shilling a week and were covered, though their wives and children were not: in the nearly four years she had been in Gledlang, Olive had not been able to spare a single sixpence to pay into the Friendly Society.

But on that morning, Patrick was delirious with fever and she knew she had no option: she would have to take him. Instructing Jimmy to tell Old Jim when he arrived, Olive ran down the drive to the Maydun road and, without pausing for breath, ran all the way to her sister's house: her only pause came when she leaned against the doorpost for a few seconds to regain her breath. A sharp rap on the knocker and the bolts were drawn back: unhappily, Percy was the first up and the conversation between him and his sister was brief.

'What do you want at this time of the bloody morning?' he demanded with a sneer at finding his despised sister standing on the doorstep.

'It's Patrick. He's not well. He's got a bad cough and a temperature. He's shivering all the time. I need some money so I can take him to see McFadden. I ain't got any to spare myself.'

'I thought as much,' Percy continued in the same harsh manner. 'Well, you know what you can do. You can bugger off. You only come here when you want something. We ain't got no money to give you. You're earning up at Wakenham's, aren't you? Use your own, we ain't got none to spare.'

'I only need five shillings – ' Olive began, but the door was slammed shut in her face: she waited a few seconds before tearfully turning away, wondering what to do next. It was obvious that she could not just let Patrick lie shivering where he was in the hope that he would get better: she would have to take him to the doctor, money or no money and worry about any payment afterwards: that was the only answer: she would just have to find the money to pay McFadden somehow, but first she needed to get Patrick better.

It was as she walked away that she heard the clink of something hitting the path behind her: turning round, Olive saw a handkerchief, a woman's handkerchief: up at the front bedroom window. Alice was smiling down at her: wrapped in the handkerchief were two half-crown coins, the five shillings she needed. Alice's concern was for her sister and her nephew's well-being: besides, it was Percy's and Hubert's money that she was giving Olive and giving it secretly and in defiance of them made it all the better.

SIXTY-SIX

BACK at the farm, when Olive lifted Patrick up to wash him and to dress him so that he would at least be presentable to the doctor, he was unable to stand and crumpled back on to the sack mattress, coughing and shivering: she knew then that she had waited almost too long: he could not walk the mile-and-a-half into the village and the surgery which McFadden held in the front room of Lil Brown's house at the top of Shoe Street: he would have to be carried and there was only one way of getting him there: in the pram! Aided by Jimmy and Jack, she placed a near delirious, sweating, shivering, moaning Patrick in the pram, all hunched up because of his size, covered him with the children's coats as best she could and then she and Jimmy wheeled him to the village as fast as they could.

A fine rain was falling by the time they reached the house at the top of Shoe Street: McFadden came once-weekly, between ten-thirty and eleven: if no one was there when he arrived, he waited twenty minutes and then left.

Olive got there early and had been waiting well over a half-hour before McFadden pushed open the front door: she had placed Patrick on the black horsehair sofa which stood in one corner of the front room covered by a blanket and which served as an examination couch: on a small table nearby stood a basin and a flowered pitcher of water with a folded white towel and a bar of soap.

Jimmy and his mother both rose out of respect when McFadden entered: he gave them both a quizzical look as if to ask, 'Who are you and why are you here?' Not knowing her, he wondered, of course, who she was: it was his way of a surly introduction: for her part, Olive began her explanation before he had even closed the door.

'My name's Cullen, doctor,' Olive told him. 'I'm new to the village. I'm not on your panel, but I had to bring the boy to see someone. He's coughing and shivering badly. He's been like it for a couple of days. He got soaked coming home from the village. He had to see someone.'

McFadden waved aside her explanation: he was not interested in her exoneration or whether she was new to the village and not on his panel: instead he reached into his bag for his stethoscope, clamped it into his ears and directed the shivering, chattering-teethed Patrick to stand before him, remove his damp coat the two pullovers and pull up his shirt and vest. When Olive was about to speak again, an impatient movement of the doctor's hand signalled for her to keep silent and to take a step backward while he made his examination.

After a few moments, McFadden pulled his stethoscope from his ears and demanded to know: What was his name? How long had he had the cough? When had he got really bad? Had he had any illness like it before? McFadden was a mop-haired Irishman, who spoke with a soft Tipperary brogue which was almost unintelligible to most of the villagers: but Olive, having got used to Irish pronunciations through Robert and his brothers, was able to understand him easily enough and to field his questions without difficulty. As the answer to each question was given, McFadden pursed his lips, or sniffed or made a face: at the same time, he thrust a thermometer into Patrick's mouth, waited for a minute or so, then pulled it out and scrutinised it: this time his face was expressionless.

'He has a temperature of well over a hundred. It's pleurisy, Mrs. Cullen,' McFadden finally announced with a sigh. 'Patrick has pleurisy. He will have to go to hospital right away to ensure he gets the proper treatment.'

'Hospital! I haven't got the money to pay for any hospital!' Olive was aghast. 'What little I earn I need for food. I've got six others to feed, you know. I had to borrow from my sister to pay you.'

McFadden gave a sigh of resignation. 'It's the boy we have to think of and he needs to go to hospital today, Mrs. Cullen,' he said, patiently. 'Pleurisy is not to be taken lightly. Fortunately for your Patrick, his is in the early stages, but nevertheless pleurisy is pleurisy. The lining of his chest is inflamed and that is affecting his lungs and his breathing. He needs to go to a hospital for treatment. Urgently. I insist.'

Sensing Olive's obvious dilemma, he adopted a more conciliatory tone. 'It would be better for him if he were in hospital right now, Mrs. Cullen. I will take him myself if you will allow me. You do not need to worry about the money. I will take him to Wivencaster Cottage Hospital. They will not charge you. It is a voluntary hospital – ' By that, he meant the hospital raised all its funding from donations, bequests, flag days, fetes and balls for the district's more well-to-do: they took in occasional non-payers from the poor and the needy: and, being poor and needy, Olive was more embarrassed than ashamed at being told she would be considered for such help, but McFadden's determination deterred any protest.

'I am doing this for the boy,' he went on firmly. 'Patrick's lungs are infected and, if he does not get the proper treatment, it could become very serious indeed, Mrs. Cullen. If it is not treated properly and immediately, pleurisy can be fatal. If I take the boy, they will accept him from me. Have no fears on that score.'

He was already folding his stethoscope into his bag and snapping shut the clasp: it was quite obvious that he was not going to take 'No' for an answer: and Olive knew she could not refuse. There was no one else waiting to see McFadden, so Patrick was helped by his mother down the steps and on to the back seat of the doctor's car, wrapped in a blanket.

'Wivencaster Cottage Hospital, Mrs. Cullen,' McFadden reminded her. 'You may visit him whenever you wish.'

When McFadden's gas-driven car completed its three-point turn and headed off up Tithe Street towards Salter and Wivencaster beyond, it left an apprehensive Olive and a relieved Jimmy in its wake.

'It's for the best, Mum. It's for the best,' Jimmy said as they walked back. 'You've done the right thing.'

'I hope so, I hope so,' was all Olive could bring herself to mutter.

SIXTY-SEVEN

OLIVE telephoned the hospital twice, on the Friday using Wakenham's phone in the hallway while he lay groaning and wheezing for breath upstairs and on the Saturday from the village phone box: each time she was asked who she was and each time she was put through to the matron, to be told rather curtly that Patrick was doing 'as well as could be expected and it is too early yet to say anything more.' In fact, so abrupt was the matron and so unused to telephoning was Olive that neither conversation lasted more than twenty or thirty seconds.

'Will you be visiting?' the matron demanded during the second call, adding brusquely: 'Visiting begins at two and ends at four.'

'I'm coming tomorrow,' Olive replied, fearful that, were she not to go, she might be excluded by the matron for some unfathomable reason. 'I hope to get there about midday. I can't come till then as I have to work.'

'When you arrive, call at the almoner's office to see the relieving officer, please,' she was ordered. 'There will be some papers for you to sign.' The matron did not say what papers and the receiver was replaced.

Olive took Jimmy with her, as much for his company as to let brother see brother: Jack was left in charge of the four youngest. 'Stay here till we get back,' Jack was ordered. 'And don't you tell anyone where we've gone. I don't want anyone knowing my business.' Jimmy, of course, had already taken a letter into the secondary school.

As no Bourne Brothers' bus ran between Gledlang and Salter on Sundays, Jimmy and his mother had to walk the two-and-a-half miles to catch the sole mid-day bus which ran from Cobwycke via Salter to Wivencaster: and they had to wait for threequarters-of-an-hour at the maypole roundabout in the centre of the village till it came: consequently, it was not until just before two o'clock that they reached the Cottage Hospital.

Patrick was in the children's ward, lying inside a long glass box to which a hose leading from a cylinder was attached: it looked extremely serious.

'Don't look so worried, Mrs. Cullen, it's just oxygen to help him breathe,' the ward sister reassured Olive with a smile when she saw her concern. 'Your Patrick's a fighter. He is not out of danger just yet, but his temperature is down and he is fighting. Once he is better, he will have to stay with us for a week or two, just so that we can build him up a little, you understand... ' Everything, naturally, was said with a positive smile.

To Olive and Jimmy, Patrick still looked as pale and as drained as when he had been seen by McFadden: he was still coughing and, though his fever had abated, his breathing was still laboured and uneven and his forehead creased in pain when he did cough. He managed a weak smile for them when they entered and seemed quite amused at being in the 'glass box' and being fussed over by all the nurses. Apprehensive and alarmed as she was at seeing him there, Olive was at least calmed by the reassurances of the ward sister and so was less agitated when finally she was ushered into the almoner's office an hour later to see the relieving officer and to discuss her application for assistance, which McFadden had made for her: Jimmy preferred to wait outside, seated upon a chair, so he could watch the young nurses going about their business.

It was three o'clock when Olive went to see the relieving officer: she was still answering questions when two cars bumped and bounced their way down the potholed track leading to Follenfaunts, swung right through the gate and came to a halt by the wagon shed: a man and a woman got out of each. The first man was in a suit and carried a briefcase and the woman was in a tartan-patterned fawn coat and was wearing a hat with a curtain of net hanging over her forehead: the second man was in the uniform of the special constabulary with three sergeant's stripes upon his arm and the woman was wearing the mid-blue overall and darker blue cap of a district nurse: they walked slowly to the wagon shed where Jack, John, Thomas, Michael and tiny Joseph were sitting in a half circle in front of the smoking open fire eating a beef paste sandwich apiece which their mother had left them and drinking from a bottle of water.

'Is your mother here?' the police sergeant asked as the woman in the hat and the man with the briefcase gazed sympathetically at the little group for a few moments, then went over to inspect the 'den,' which they did with much headshaking and tut-tutting.

'No, Mum's out,' Jack answered truthfully. 'She's gone somewhere on the bus.'

'Do you know where your mother's gone, young'un?' the sergeant asked next.

'Nope,' Jack lied boldly.

'Do you know when she'll be back?'

'Sometime this evening, she said,' replied Jack with a shrug: it would have been better if she had been there, or Jimmy or Patrick, then there would have been no need for him to answer their questions.

'Poor mites,' said the woman with the hat, giving the man with the briefcase a knowing look: the four youngest children seated upon their log ends were still staring suspiciously up at the four adults.

'That's a long time,' said the woman in the hat, forcing a smile. 'What are you doing now?'

'We're having our dinner'n'tea,' answered Jack, holding up his half-eaten sandwich for them to see, uncaring about his grubby hands and face: he would wash when his mother came home.

The twins and Michael and Joseph were eyeing their older brother: having seen the concern on the faces of the four adults when Jack had shown them his sandwich, they had all paused in their eating as if worried that there was something wrong with their own.

'And you are looking after your brothers on your own, are you?' the woman in the hat asked, still smiling. 'That's very grown-up of you.'

'I've done it before lots of times,' answered Jack, pleased with her praise. 'I often look after the twins and Mike and Joe when Mum's not here.'

More glances passed between the four adults: the man with the briefcase consulted a piece of yellow paper he had pulled out: pinned to it was a small piece of paper upon which someone had written in pencil, 'Family of seven living in a farm shed! Follenfaunts Farm, Gledlang!'

The Salter constable had certainly got his facts right when two days before he had telephoned the department of health at Wivencaster council to leave that message: the family was living in absolute squalor. Goodness gracious! They had found five of them sitting out in the open around a smoking wood fire eating a beef paste sandwich apiece and drinking water from a bottle as their only meal! Their mother was not there and would not be back till the evening, so the eldest had told them. Adding the one already in hospital, that made six children and their mother. Seven! Fancy seven of them all living in 'a tent' made out of sacks tied together with binder string and hung off nails at one end of a wagon shed beside a muddy farm track! And the cooking facilities, if you could call them that! An open fire beside the track, ringed by bricks, and just two old blackened saucepans to cook with lying nearby. And the sleeping facilities! Sacks stuffed with straw and no doubt infested with fleas and mites and lice and goodness knows what else! Good God, it was downright primitive! These children were living like gypsies! In fact, gypsies lived better! What kind of a mother would force her children to live like that? It was disgraceful! There was nothing else for it.

The man consulting his sheet of paper turned to the police sergeant standing alongside him. 'If it's all right with you then, sergeant?'

'Yes, it's all right with me,' the sergeant answered with a shrug. 'I don't see what else we can do, do you?'

The woman in the hat was smiling sweetly now, bending forward and looking directly at the twins and Michael and Joseph. 'Would you like to go for a ride in my car?' she asked. 'All of you. Would you like that?'

Wide smiles lit up the faces of the two youngest: a car ride! They had never been for a car ride before: this was something new, something exciting: they could scarcely believe their ears.

'But first we have to leave something for your mother,' said the man with the briefcase: and, producing a black fountain pen from his top pocket, he carefully wrote upon the sheet of yellow paper, using his briefcase as a rest and occasionally looking about him as if to confirm what he was writing down. It took him several minutes before he finished: after a short search, he eventually found a nail on one of the support posts of the wagon shed on which to spike the paper.

Meanwhile, the five children had already clambered into the two cars and were waiting patiently: even Jack, still feeling somewhat self-conscious at having had to answer questions in front of four strangers, was smiling broadly seated in the back of the first car alongside the two youngest: after all, he had done what his mother had told him.

The man with the briefcase swung the starting handle and the car fired: in no time at all they were bumping and bouncing back down the long drive towards the gate, where they turned left on to the Salter road and headed towards Wivencaster.

The woman in the hat, still smiling serenely, half-turned in her seat to face Jack. 'And where would you like to go then?'

'Can we go to the seaside?' Jack asked, smiling.

'Yes, the seaside, the seaside,' chanted Joseph and Michael, clapping their hands.

'Hmm, I don't know about that,' the woman in the hat said, turning back to face the front. 'We have to call somewhere first. I'll ask then.' She looked across at the man in the driver's seat: he was smiling ruefully.

In the car behind, John and Thomas were seated in the back beside the district nurse, looking out of the window and laughing happily as the trees and hedgerows glided past: it was better than just sitting there and waiting for Mum to return: if they were lucky, they might even see her and Jimmy on their way back.

SIXTY-EIGHT

THEY did not see either their mother or their brother for the simple reason that Olive and Jimmy did not return until the early evening after a long and wearying walk back from Salter: she expected to find the five waiting impatiently for her return, especially as it was well past their normal teatime and they would be hungry. Olive silently cursed herself for not having left them more than just a beef paste sandwich apiece for their lunch, but then she had expected to be back long before: she had not realised that there was no return bus from Wivencaster on a Sunday until after six o'clock. It had taken them an hour to reach Salter and a further hour to walk the three miles back to Follenfaunts: it was almost eight o'clock when they reached the entrance to the driveway. Olive half-expected to find the five youngest waiting at the top of the drive, perhaps seated upon the gate watching for her return: failing that, she would find them moping about the wagon shed, complaining that they were hungry. But there was no one at the gate and no one by the wagon shed: the fire had died and was now nothing but crumbled grey ash: all was silent.

'Where the devil can they have got to?' she wanted to know as she emerged irritated and puzzled from the empty den. 'Where are they, for God's sake? They must be somewhere? We've got to find them before it gets dark?'

'I think I know where they are,' Jimmy called out: he had taken down a sheet of paper pinned on a nail on the support post and was reading it with a grim look upon his face.

'They've been took, Mum,' he said, holding out the paper. 'Someone's come and took 'em. The council at Wivencaster, it says here. Some bloke in the department of health. They've got a number for you to ring.'

Olive snatched the piece of paper from him: it was a carbon copy of a printed typewritten form with an official looking stamp embossed upon it, announcing quite boldly in elaborate typescript that a magistrate at Wivencaster had 'hereby granted Wivencaster council, its servants and its representatives, the right and the authority to take into care any and all children as such to be found at the said place listed and deemed by the said servants and representatives of the said council to be in need of care for the reasons also listed below.' Someone had filled in the blanks 'to be filled in by all officiating officers' with a fountain pen. 'Informant: Not known. Place: Follenfaunts Farm, Gledlang. Name: Cullen. Children? Five there (one in hospital at Wivencaster). Ages: Three years to ten. Mother: Absent – order not served personally. Abode: Farm shed. Running water: None. Bedding: None proper (only straw-filled sacks found). Food: Some, but poorly kept in a box. Sanitation: None visible. Hygiene: Children appeared unwashed. Clothing patched and worn. Reason for removing children: Neglect. Farm shed accommodation deemed unsuitable for small children. One already in hospital with chest infection as result. Parent absent when called upon. Whereabouts not known. Conclusions: Living conditions insanitary. Possible fleas or lice. Lack of general care and hygiene. Insufficient food. Place removed to: Lenden House, Wivencaster. Signed: WJ Webster, chief children's officer, Wivencaster RDC, department of health.' At the bottom of the page Mr. Webster had written his telephone number, Wivencaster 2137, and the words 'Evenings only.'

Jimmy could only watch as his mother's face changed from stupefaction to a shattering anguish: suddenly she seized up both the blackened saucepans standing by the fireside in which he had hoped she would cook them a proper tea and hurled them one after the other against the brick wall at the back of the wagon shed, screaming with fury as she did so: then she stamped back inside the den: after a while, he heard her crying. He would have liked to have comforted her, but he could not bring himself to do it, for he did not know how: rather than listen to his mother crying, he drifted off and went walking about the farm and did not return till late: even then, no words were spoken between him and his mother: it was as if she were grieving silently and any words spoken between them would interrupt that grief.

The following morning Jimmy watched as his mother prepared his breakfast as usual, but in utter silence: she herself ate little, sitting well away from her son as if thinking and not wanting to be disturbed: so when his mother went to work as usual, a bewildered Jimmy went off to catch the Bourne Brothers' double-decker school bus at the junction of the Beckenden road and Salter road without so much as a mention having been made of the others: it was as though they had never been there. Then, in the evening, as he sat by the fire under the lee of the wagon shed, his mother appeared at the flap of sacking curtain, stalked past him and hurried down the driveway towards the village, on her way to make the telephone call. When she returned, her shoulders were slumped and her mouth was a thin, determined line: still she said nothing to Jimmy, but it was evident from her manner that she had had no success: the others would not be coming home. That night, just as she had the previous night, his mother lay on the sack mattress no more than five feet from him, staring up at the roof, still not saying anything, till sleep overcame her: and the following morning she went to work as usual. It was two days before his mother finally spoke: the two of them were sitting under the overhang of the wagon shed eating their tea, when his mother suddenly declared as if awakening from a trance: 'I'm going after them. I'm bloody going after them! They're not taking my kids away from me, not while there's breath left in my body! I'll get them back whatever I do!'

The vehemence in her tone was startling: Olive Cullen had made up her mind to go after her sons because that was the only thing she could do: it was what a mother should do. The following Sunday, she walked to Salter to catch the Bourne Brothers' sole bus to Wivencaster again, visited Patrick first and then called at the home where the others were being held: she would not let Jimmy go with her. He found out why when a police car came bumping down the drive at Follenfaunts, pulled to a halt and his mother climbed out: she did not tell Jimmy what had happened, but something serious must have occurred, otherwise why would the police have brought her the whole thirteen miles back from Wivencaster? When his mother got out, she shook herself free of the policeman's arm and marched proudly off without so much as a backward glance: Jimmy saw it all from the hayloft in the barn where he had run to hide just in case it was the police coming for him, which they never did. Knowing his mother, her temper and her determination, he guessed that she must have been to the home in Lenden where the others were and caused a stir of some kind: if he knew his mother, she had probably banged on the door and shouted out the names of his brothers and told them that she was coming to get them: that she would get them out and home eventually, one way or another: anyone who challenged her just got a verbal earful for their trouble, including the policemen when they arrived.

She did the same thing in the second week: and the third: nothing deterred her: not rain, not wind, not tiredness: so long as she had breath in her body she would visit his brothers and vow each time that sooner or later she would bring them back. No spinster of a care worker or children's welfare officer was going to take her children away from her! 'The bloody cheek of it!' she would say. 'The bloody cheek of it! Damned busybodies! Why don't they mind their own business? Let people get on with their own lives without meddling all the time?'

And each time the police brought her home and dropped her off at the end of the drive.

SIXTY-NINE

THE procession of army lorries had been moving through the village all morning: lorries full of grinning soldiers giving the thumbs-up sign to those standing by the roadside: tanks on long, cumbersome carriers creeping round the high-hedged bends: canvas-hooded jeeps in which impatient, red-faced officers sat: bren-gun carriers with more grinning troops seated on their sides: and behind them yet more lorries towing field guns of every imaginable size: vehicles by the hundred, by the thousand, moving slowly along the Salter road from Wivencaster towards Maydun and beyond: all going south.

'They're going to Burma,' was the consensus of the young village boys who infiltrated the camp on Gledlang Park when Bert the company sergeant-major was not about to chase them off and thus knew all the gossip.

Now there was a delay and the crawling procession had stopped altogether as the vehicles carrying the soldiers from the searchlight and ack-ack battery began nosing out of the gate opposite the thatched cottage to join them.

Olive was standing on the triangle of green at the top of Tithe Street watching with Jimmy when she saw Alice creeping along through the shadows of the tall trees which lined the road there: she was going from lorry to lorry, trying to make it look as though she was just walking past, but carefully looking up into each to see if John the Cook was among the soldiers. As it happened, he was not: he was still back in Wivencaster, deemed unfit for combat and more useful in the cookhouse.

For an instant, when she saw her sister, Alice appeared to be about to turn back: then realising she could not, she waited with downcast eyes at Olive's approach. Olive saw the reason why when she was still ten yards off: Alice had a vivid purple bruise on her cheek and another on her temple: one eye, too, was purpled and there was a long red scratchmark across one of her cheeks.

'What happened to you?' Olive demanded, though she already knew the answer.

'Percy and Hubert,' confirmed Alice, with a shrug. 'A week ago.'

'Why? What for?' demanded Olive.

'They caught me with John,' Alice explained shyly. 'He came over from the camp at Wivencaster and called at the house. I told him not to, but he still came. Said he wanted to see me urgent. They were out at the time, but they came back, unexpected like – ' The faintest of guilty smiles here. ' – We were upstairs at the time. You know. I didn't think they'd be back till later, but they came home early for their tea because they were going on duty with the Home Guard later. John managed to get out the window before they forced open the door, but they must have seen him running away. They wanted to know who he was, so I told them. That's when it started.'

'And they hit you for that?'

'Well, no,' Alice answered with a sheepish grin. 'They got mad because I told them they could get their tea themselves! I said I wasn't going to take orders from them anymore. I was going to see who I pleased when I pleased. I told them to their faces. I told them I was going to keep on seeing John and there was no way they were going to stop me.'

'Which one of them hit you?' an incensed Olive demanded.

Alice turned away as if hiding her face and, for a few seconds, seemed reluctant to answer: then almost shamefacedly, she admitted: 'Percy. Who else?'

'Just him?'

'Yes, just him. Hubert didn't do anything. He just shouted.'

'Right,' said Olive, clenching one hand into a fist: she knew of old how free her brothers were with their fists, especially Percy. 'You stay here,' she ordered Jimmy and, before Alice could stop her, she was striding past the line of slow-moving army vehicles, heading for her brothers' home.

'I'm going to do something I should have done years ago,' she cried to her sister, limping along behind her as fast as her crippled leg would allow. 'I'm going to show those two fat lumps just what I think of them!'

'Don't make trouble, Olive. Don't make trouble, please,' Alice pleaded: but a stern-faced Olive's answer was merely to repeat 'I'm going to do what I should have done years ago!' and to stride on.

The brothers, as they usually did, had left their billhooks outside the back door of the house: Olive seized one and burst into the scullery where she found Hubert barring her path.

'What do you want?' he began, but from the look on his face as he backed away from her, it was clear that he had already guessed

Olive had no fear of Hubert: years of bettering him as a girl in her teens had given her the courage to take him on: and the sight of the billhook deterred him from making any rash move. 'Never you mind, this has nothing to do with you,' cried Olive, giving him a violent push, which was so unexpected that he went stumbling backwards against the copper. 'It's him I've come to see!' she added, pushing open the living room door.

Percy was seated at the table in the parlour eating: the fork was poised halfway to his mouth when Olive entered with the billhook raised before her: a look of terror came into his eyes.

'I'll teach you to hit my sister! You keep your bloody fists to yourself in future!' Olive shouted, bringing the billhook down with a fearful crash on to the table alongside Percy's arm: the wooden top quivered and a mug of tea jumped. As Olive swung the billhook up again, a fearful Percy raised one arm as if to protect himself from the second blow, convinced that only Olive's aim had been at fault: instead, however, she stayed her strike, seized up the plate of half-eaten dinner with her free hand and tipped it upside down upon her brother's head.

'There's your bloody dinner!' she cried as mash, gravy, peas and mince all cascaded down his face and neck: then in a second act, inflamed by the success of the first, she picked up a small bowl of spotted dick and custard standing in the middle of the table. 'And there's your pudding,' she cried, hurling it to the floor.

'Are you bloody mad, woman? That was my dinner!' an angry Percy shouted, leaping to his feet and brushing at the gravy trickling down his cheeks and nose and off his chin. The threat Percy presented was dismissed with a taunting sneer by Olive, who was already on the other side of the table and out of range of any sudden attack. Though Percy remained standing by the table, almost apoplectic with rage, he did not move away from his chair: and nor would he: due consideration for the billhook stopped him. He would hit Alice because she was weaker, but he would not take on Olive because he knew how she could scratch and hit back: she had done it often enough in childhood to make him cautious about starting: and Olive had long ago learned that the way to deal with Percy was to stand up to him and call his bluff.

'You've hit her for the last time,' she declared. 'She's my sister, too, and I'll not have a lout like you thinking you can use her as a punchbag whenever you feel like it. Hit her again and I will come after you, with an axe again if it have to, and next time I'll bloody use it!'

By this time, a goggle-eyed Hubert had followed her into the room: too late to save his brother's dinner or his own spotted dick pudding which lay under the upturned bowl at Percy's feet: meanwhile, a fearful Alice had slunk in through the backdoor.

At last Percy found his voice: he had come to the conclusion that his sister was not at that particular moment going to use the billhook on him or she would have done so by then, though he still kept a wary eye on it: after all, she was unpredictable and half mad at times: better to try and talk to her. 'What happens in this house ain't none of your business,' he tried.

'It is when you start punching my sister,' snapped Olive: again the emphasis was on the 'my.'

A sneer came over Percy's face. 'What's a woman like her doing running around like a twenty-year-old after a soldier she hardly knows anyway?' he asked. 'Letting him shag her like she's a common tart? She ain't going to do that in this house, not while we're here. It's not as if he's going to ask her to marry him, is it? He's probably married already, anyway. They all are. All he came here for was a quick shag and she give it to him.'

'Trust you to make it sound dirty!' retorted Olive, aware that by the doorway Alice was blushing a deep crimson. 'What she does is her business. It isn't any of yours. You're not her father. You're just her brother and a bloody miserable one at that! She's thirty-three years old, for God's sake! She's got a right to a life of her own!'

The two brothers looked at each other and then flopped down on their chairs and began to laugh. 'A life of her own!' jeered Hubert. 'What does she want a life of her own for? There's only one reason a man'd go out with a woman with a leg like she's got and it ain't to marry her! It's to get into her draws, that's all! A quick shag and then "Goodbye, sister".'

'We're going to get married once the war's over,' an unexpectedly bold Alice cried from the doorway. 'We've talked about it and we've agreed, the both of us, once the war's over. I haven't told you because it isn't any of your business either. He's promised me!'

'Promised you?' chortled Percy. 'Promised you?'

'Meanwhile, he's getting in some practice, is he?' laughed Hubert.

They had all reached a point in the confrontation which reminded them of old arguments from their youth: the brothers could see that Olive was not going to back down: she would stand there till doomsday arguing if they let her: eager to end it, they decided to call her bluff.

'Well, if you're planning on leaving this house, you might as well leave now?' a mocking Percy challenged a red-faced Alice by the door.

Before Alice could speak, Olive answered for her. 'We'll do just that,' she cried. 'She can come with me and in future the two of you can cook for yourselves and you can wash and iron for yourselves, too. See how you like that!' Then mockingly she added: 'I hope you two will enjoy cleaning this place on your own for once with no skivvy to give your orders to.'

With a jerk of her head to Alice, she called out: 'Get your things, Alice. You're coming with me. We're leaving this place. I'm taking you out of here. You're not staying here to be punched by them when they think they will!'

His bluff called, Percy leapt to his feet and started round the table as if intent upon seizing Olive and ejecting her by force. 'Is she hell!' he cried. 'The only one who's leaving is you!' But Olive simply raised the billhook. 'Touch me and I'll bloody kill you!' she warned.

There was such vehemence in her voice that Percy stopped: this time she looked as if she meant it: she was standing with her back to the small hallway which led to the stairs: the table was between them and that restricted his field of manoeuvre. If either he or Hubert attempted to grab the billhook, they would be easy targets – that is, if their sister were serious: and he did not want to test the threat and lose an arm.

From experience, both brothers knew that, of their three sisters, a maddened Olive had always been the one most likely to use anything that came to hand to defend herself: once she had even picked up a hoe and hit Hubert with it: another time, Percy had had to jump quickly aside as Olive launched a gardening fork at him: caution was the watchword when dealing with her.

Alice came rushing past her brothers to get behind Olive. 'Get up them stairs. Get your suitcase and get your things. Bring everything you can,' Olive ordered. 'You're finished in this house.'

Alice did as she was bid and packed her things as fast as she could in a brown cardboard suitcase: she shouted only one question down to Olive: 'What about bedding?'

'Throw it out of the window,' Olive shouted back. 'We'll pick it up outside.'

All the time she kept the billhook raised, heavy as it was: the two brothers just simply stood there, glowering at her: the threats continued while Alice packed, but Olive dealt with each of them in turn, such as from Percy: 'If she leaves here, she won't be coming back.'

'She won't want to come back once she's free of this place.'

And from Hubert: 'She'd better not take any of our money.'

'She'll take what's she's owed. You give her the housekeeping, it's hers.'

Another taunt from Percy. 'She'll be back. I give her a fortnight and she'll be crawling back on her hands and knees.'

'Not if I have anything to do with it.'

'If she goes off with that little Yorkshire git, she'd better not let me catch him or he'll get the hard end of my boot up his arse.' That from Percy again.

'She can do what she likes once she's free of you two. And I shouldn't think any man, particularly a proper soldier, is going to be too worried about you two. You're both too fat and too slow to be a threat to a real man.'

It took Alice a matter of two minutes to scoop up all her clothing and toiletries, pile them into the suitcase, pull on her single red coat and black beret: then she was descending the stairs, sliding the suitcase down alongside her legs: for she did not have much strength herself. As Alice reached the small hallway and Olive heard the front door opening, she herself backed out of the living room, the billhook still raised, daring her brothers to follow: then she was hurrying down the path after her sister, leaving the two stupefied men behind her: the last she heard from them that day was the slamming of the door as she tossed the billhook into the hedge.

SEVENTY

THEY had nowhere they could go other than back to Follenfaunts, taking it in turns to carry the suitcase and the bedding and swapping it over every few hundred yards: eventually they reached the end of the long drive, but, instead of going right towards the wagon shed, Olive turned left and made directly for the house. On the way back from Alice's house, she had mulled over the rashness of her action: in a few hot-headed minutes she had deprived her sister of the home in which she had lived for thirty years: how could she now ask her to live in the den with Jimmy and herself!

Olive had grown used to the trials and tribulations she had suffered since returning to Gledlang, but felt embarrassed and guilty that she had now inflicted the same upon her sister: Alice did not have one-quarter the physical and mental strength which Olive possessed. For a start, she weighed barely seven stone in her stockinged feet and, having been the only female in an all-male household dominated by her brothers for seventeen years, was totally unused to making her own decisions: that she should even have stood up to them over the soldier John was, to Olive, remarkable: but then love sometimes breeds unusual courage.

Olive realised that she had to come to a decision, so she did: she had nothing to lose and everything to gain: she would march up to Wakenham's bedroom and propose Alice as his housekeeper, a full-time, permanent, live-in cleaner, cook and general dogsbody to replace herself: it was as simple as that! Just as Olive had done it for two days a week for the past three-and-a-half years, so Alice now would do it for seven days a week, which meant she would be about the place all day and every day doing the same work and be there at night times, too, as company for the old man, a presence to reassure him, especially as he seemed to go to bed each night with a morbid fear that he would not be waking up in the morning.

Strangely, during all the weeks and months she and Jimmy had been living in the den at the end of the wagon shed, Olive had never considered whether they should move into the house permanently: not with him living there: she shuddered at the thought: it was bad enough going into the place twice a week knowing he was there, in the next room, above in the bedroom, smelling him, smelling his bad breath, smelling the results of his incontinence, seeing the evidence of his foul habits, as well as hearing his perpetual wheezing and moaning and having to listen to his never-ending complaints: two days a week of that was more than enough for Olive: seven days a week would have driven her mad. She would have murdered the man to put him out of his misery first, she knew! All the time she had worked the two days in the house, her one reassurance was that, at the end of each day, she could walk away from him into the fresh, untainted air. No, wild horses would not have dragged her into that house to live full-time while Wakenham was still living there! Never! Never!

The only time Alice had commented upon the fact was when she had said of the wagon shed den, 'I don't see how you can go on living there in a place like that,' to which Olive had replied sharply: 'It suits me. We're all right, Jimmy and me. We've got used to it. We've got a roof over our heads no matter what other people might think, which is more than can be said for some. We're in the dry and we've got a fire to cook by. We only use it for sleeping in, anyway. The rest of the time I'm out working.' Which was true.

But now she had Alice on her conscience and she could not ask her to live in the den with them: not in her frail condition: not with a ten-bedroom farmhouse less than a hundred yards away and only one bedroom occupied and that by a man who gave every sign of dying, even if he did not actually do it! Olive needed to know that Alice was not left to brood and to make her own decisions: if she did, she was quite likely to creep back to her brothers' house and ask for their forgiveness and return to the callous, unpaid drudgery from which Olive believed she had just rescued her. No, someone needed to make decisions for her and she was that someone! Who else was there? Besides, she told herself as they reached the front door and pushed it open, she and Old Jim were about to begin the potato-planting and that meant they would often be working late into the evenings: she would feel happier doing that knowing that her sister was safe in the house. So ran Olive's reasoning.

'I'm going to ask Wakenham,' Olive told her sister. 'It's not right a man living alone in a house this size. You could put four families in here and still not fill it. I'd have moved in myself long ago if the man wasn't such a great big kid – ' She was not going to say any more than that. ' – He's afraid of his own shadow half the time I can't go in because of the children – he don't want them in there – but you're by yourself so you can.'

Once in the house, Olive went straight up to Wakenham's bedroom, dragging a reluctant Alice with her: Wakenham was in bed as usual, groaning quietly to himself: too much inactivity had brought on a complaint akin to gout almost to add to his woes of asthma and arthritis and lumbago and a half-dozen other of his real or imagined ailments: one leg was swollen large and he kept his foot encased in a carpet slipper which he had cut across the instep to release the pressure and tied on with a bandage.

Wakenham must have gone downstairs to the kitchen at least once since she had last been in the house, Olive noted, so he could not be all that ill: somehow he had managed to shuffle down in his dressing gown and nightshirt and had made himself a bowl of hot bread and milk sprinkled with sugar and a pot of tea: the evidence was there on the small table beside his bed. 'At least the old fool is not a complete invalid yet,' Olive thought to herself as she entered the bedroom.

'This is my sister,' Olive told Wakenham, pulling the nervous and embarrassed Alice forward. 'She needs somewhere to stay. I'm putting her forward as your live-in housekeeper, taking over from me as of now, so she'll be with you all day and all night. She'll cook and clean instead of me for as long as you wish. She's a good cook and a good cleaner. All she wants is a bedroom to herself where she can sleep and put her things. You've got seven empty bedrooms in this house and two in the attic. She could take one of those. She has no children so there won't be any noise or running about to bother you or disturb your peace and quiet. Don't worry, I'm not moving in. I'm happy where I am, but Alice needs a proper place to sleep and the attic bedrooms are ideal. You'll have to pay her something, though, and she'd want meals and found. You could deduct for them from what you pay her. I'll continue working on the farm, except now I'll be doing it five days a week, six since Jim will be starting the late planting soon and he'll need me and my eldest with him full-time for a couple of weeks so I won't be able to do as much for you, but Alice will. She'll be here night and day.'

If anything, it was this last point which seemed to persuade Wakenham. 'All right, all right, Olive,' he croaked weakly, raising one hand in a gesture of acknowledgement, as though he really were too ill to care. 'There's sense in what you say, I suppose. I could do with someone more permanent. I will take you on if Olive thinks it best. I trust her.' The raised hand fell weakly back upon the counterpane almost as if even that were too much for him: even the sigh which accompanied it seemed an effort.

A nod from Olive and Alice picked up the tray from the bedside table and carried it out: it was her first duty: she was employed. They stayed together for another hour while Olive showed Alice around the house, pointing out her duties and the order in which she herself carried them out. To sleep, Alice chose an attic bedroom with a dormer window looking east so as to get the morning sun and seemed quite pleased by it: the staircase to it, which led directly off the landing opposite Wakenham's bedroom, was closed off by a small door so she was satisfied with that.

'Good God, girl! He's not going to come after you in the night,' laughed Olive as her nervous sister tested the key in the lock. 'He's not that kind. There's not an ounce of red blood in him. Weak as water, he is!'

Even Alice managed a smile at that.

SEVENTY-ONE

THE SUMMER passed: the soldiers invaded France and pushed on towards Germany with the enemy in full retreat: around Gledlang, the first chill mornings of autumn came and the dew glistened ever later on hedgerows hung with sparkling gossamer. Apart from the slackening pace of the war about them, the only excitement was when a doodlebug landed in the river and, although a mile from it, blew down the Godwins' bathing hut!

Alice, meanwhile, had settled into the house, washing, cooking and cleaning for Wakenham, seeming not to mind the smells which had affected Olive, and, with her quiet ways, becoming as near to a domestic mouse as anyone could be: in the evening, the two sisters often sat in the kitchen and talked, for Olive thought it better for her to visit Alice than have her visit the wagon shed.

Old Jim and Olive, with Jimmy's help, gathered in an early harvest, though, and that occupied much of their time: though once that was finished, without the presence of his brothers, Jimmy often became a lone and subdued figure about the farm. He was happy when working with Old Jim and the horses, for that distracted him from brooding too much on their absence: but it was clear to Olive that he missed his brothers, especially Patrick and Jack. No sooner had Olive given him his tea than he would be off, wandering about the headlands as if not knowing what to do with himself, a lost soul waiting for the twilight to deepen into darkness so that he could pass unobserved from place to place. His sleep was often punctuated by mutterings and cries in which he would call out his brother's names, 'Pat! Pat!' or 'Jack! Jack!' In the darkness of the den, Olive could only lie there and wait for him to fall silent again.

So it was with some relief that, in the first week of September, he returned to school, a lonely figure now catching the Bourne Brothers' red-and-white bus by the triangle of green at the top of Tithe Street. Olive missed the children, too, of course, but after the third time she had been brought home in the police car for 'disturbing the peace,' as the officer put it, she had realised how futile was her protest at Lenden House and she had not gone back. She was informed by letter that Patrick had joined his brothers in the home: at least they were all together, Olive consoled herself, and, as there was little she could do, she tried to push it to the back of her mind while she worked: but in the darkness of the den, their images returned to disturb her sleep as much as they did Jimmy's. Sometimes in the morning it was a relief for Olive to get up and realise that she had so much to do in the fields, helping Old Jim with the cultivating, manuring, ploughing and drilling: it kept her mind from dwelling on their absence.

Then, early one morning, as she was heading for the milking shed, she found Alice limping along the track towards her: there had been a ground mist during the night and the sun still had no warmth in its glow to dispel it: the air in the shadows was icy cold. In her hurry, Alice had not even put on her red coat and was visibly shivering as she picked her way between the puddles of mud all around her: she looked tearful and downcast and waited until Olive was within a few feet of her before she spoke.

'It's Wakenham. I think he's dead,' she said simply. 'He was just lying there when I went in this morning with his breakfast. He must have gone in his sleep.'

'Oh Gawd!' exclaimed Olive, following her shivering sister towards the house. 'Are you sure? He's not just sleeping, is he? You couldn't be mistaken, could you?'

Alice shook her head: it was not so much that Olive disbelieved her, it was just that she did not want it to be true: the old man had, in her opinion, exaggerated the seriousness of his illnesses for so long that, just as she had ignored his pitiful whining, so she had never thought he would die so soon. What it would mean, of course, was that both she and Alice probably would now be out of work and also out of a home: she and Jimmy would have to leave the wagon shed – no future employer would allow them to stay there, assuming he even took her on – and poor Alice, as like as not, would have to leave the house if he did not want a live-in cook and housekeeper, which was very unlikely. Olive was not so much bothered for herself, she could always find somewhere, she knew: she was concerned more for Alice: having nowhere to live, there was only one place to which she could return – to her brothers' house! If she did that, it would mean the terrible humiliation of having to beg them to allow her to go back.

'Of all the things to happen!' exploded an exasperated Olive. 'Bloody man! Why couldn't he have held out a little bit longer till you and I had got a bit of money together. Now where will we go? I doubt I'll get work elsewhere and I doubt you will either, girl. And I'm not going into any factory. I am not working in one of them no matter what they say.'

A thought occurred to her. 'Have you told Jim? He needs to know.'

'I haven't seen him,' said Alice, with a shake of the head. 'I expect he's down by the barn with the horses. His bike's there.' She nodded to where Jim's rickety, unoiled, high-handlebar women's bicycle was leaning against the side of the black creosoted barn.

'I suppose we had better make sure he is dead first,' declared Olive, but with no real enthusiasm, as they mounted the stairs.

When they reached the bedroom, Olive found the old man lying stretched out in his bed under the blankets just as if he were asleep: in fact, except for the pallor of his face and hands, one would have thought he was asleep. His lips were blue and his face was an ashen mask tinged with purple and green: mercifully, his eyes were closed so Olive deduced he must have died in his sleep. He had not been dead long, either, about an hour she reckoned, for there was still some warmth to the skin of his cheeks as she touched his forehead, not yet the cold clamminess of death which comes eventually: rigor mortis had not set in either, she noted thankfully as she peeled back the bedclothes to his ankles. Immediately, the stench of death rose to greet her: she let out a cry and, clapping one hand across her mouth, almost gagged with the smell, retreating hurriedly to join her sister who had remained in the doorway, unwilling to enter the room.

'I suppose, we'll have to wash the man and lay him out,' Olive said with a sigh, not the least looking forward to the task. 'It's the least we can do, clean him up and lay him out. We'll have to get some water and a couple of towels to put over our faces. Gawd! He don't half smell!'

It was a quarter-hour later by the time they had washed and cleaned Wakenham's flabby corpse, though, Olive, being more used to men's bodies, did the actual cleansing while Alice, grimacing with disgust and holding a towel in front of her face, kept her head half-turned away and helped only to roll him over upon his side and to steady him while Olive did the distasteful part in pulling off the urine-soaked nightshirt to wipe the discharge from the dead man's rectum and sponge his genitals and thighs where he had ejaculated in death. Because of his bulk, they had difficulty in removing the soiled sheet from under him, but managed to do that after a fashion and replace it with a clean one, at the same time placing a long bath towel under him in case any more fluids should evacuate the body: lastly, while Alice held up each of Wakenham's arms in turn, Olive managed to fit another nightgown over his head, taking it from the chest of drawers inside the door: only when his arms had been folded tidily across his chest were they able to retreat to the kitchen.

It was while they sat drinking tea that Olive managed to persuade her sister the sense of staying in the house. 'I don't want to sleep here with a dead body in the house,' said Alice, biting her lip in trepidation.

'You've got a right to stay for as long as you can,' Olive told her forcefully. 'You are the housekeeper, after all. Whoever takes over will want the place looking clean and tidy, won't they? I expect we shall know soon enough. He mentioned a nephew once, Ellis Wakenham, a captain, I think, in the army, captured at Singapore. It'll go to him, I suppose. If you're here when he comes, girl, he might keep you on.'

The moment Alice had told her of Wakenham's demise, Olive had made her decision: she was almost gleeful when she spoke. 'And you won't be alone either,' she said, smiling. 'Jimmy and I'll move in with you. We don't have to keep the body here. We'll get Charlie Male to take him away in the coffin. He does most people. Puts 'em in his back shed where he keeps his spare coffins. So at least he'll be out of the house. There'll be just you and me and Jimmy. There's no sense in us living where we are, not with a great big house standing empty right on the doorstep. Wakenham's gone so he can't say anything! Don't worry, girl, we can spend a week or two in here till they throw us out. We might as well make use of it while we've got it. So long as we don't pinch anything who is going to know or care? And if we leave now, all that food will go to waste. No, girl, we're staying here. I can take one bedroom, Jimmy can take another. At least, I'll have a decent bed to sleep on for a change. Straw sacks are all right, but you can't beat a nice mattress to lie on. Wakenham wouldn't have the children in here because of his nerves, he said. It's just my bad luck that now he's gone, they aren't here or we could all have moved in together – for a couple of weeks, anyway.'

Out of the window, they saw Old Jim crossing the yard and Olive led the way out to tell him the sad news: when he saw two women bearing down upon him, the old farmworker paused as he always did and bade them good morning in his usual fashion, an almost imperceptible nod of the head, a shy smile of recognition and a greeting mumbled at the earth.

'There's no point in doing anything this morning, Jim,' Olive told him. 'Wakenham's dead. He died in the night. We've just been seeing to him.' She paused for the words to take effect, but Old Jim just stared back at her, as though he did not comprehend how Wakenham's death should interrupt his work or, for that matter, concern him in any way. His eyes did widen fractionally with surprise, followed by a frown and a 'Humph,' which could have been a comment or a statement. Other than that he just lifted his cap to scratch his head and looked bemused: the idea of not doing any work at all clearly worried him: it made him feel redundant, unwanted. 'Can't do that,' he said emphatically, replacing his cap. 'Have to work. Things have got to be done. Someone has to see to the horses, no matter what. It don't matter who dies, they ain't bothered. They still have to be watered and fed and seen to, same as they always is. Same way the cows have to be milked and the chickens fed. We have to feed them and give 'em water, don't we? Don't matter who dies, we can't let the poor things starve, can we? Besides, what else will I do? I ain't got nowhere else to go, except home. So I may as well get on and do what I normally do. I expect we shall get paid somehow. Someone'll pay us. His nephew, I hope. Him what's in the army. I only ever saw him once. I don't care who pays me so long as I get what's owed and the animals don't suffer.'

Alice was more unused to the telephone than Olive and left it to her to telephone McFadden's home at Cobwycke for him to come and to certify death: Alice, meanwhile, had volunteered to hurry as fast as her limp would allow down Tithe Street to the Square to inform the builder, Charlie Male, who acted as the undertaker for all the village's dead as well as plastering ceilings, repairing broken windows, mending roofs if he could find any slates and generally doing any other building job which came along.

Olive went through the operator at Maydun to be connected with McFadden's home at Cobwycke. 'Oh dear,' said the woman's voice at the other end of the telephone, but not with much sympathy for the poor man in whose name she telephoned: Olive presumed it was the doctor's wife. The doctor was out on his rounds, she said, but would be call as soon as possible: Olive just hoped it would be sooner rather than later, as it sometimes was if it were inconvenient for him.

One thing: she did not intend to be around the house when McFadden called: showing him up to the bedroom she would leave to Alice: she still wondered just how much McFadden was to blame for the loss of the boys: on that score, she just did not know. Perhaps, if he had not taken Patrick to hospital, even if it had most probably saved his life, then perhaps the hospital authorities might not have asked the questions they asked of her and the do-gooders would not have descended upon the farm and taken the other children: that is what she thought, anyway. However, as much as it rankled, though, she did not even consider castigating McFadden to his face: after all, he was a doctor and an educated man, someone whom she respected, and it would have been the height of bad manners to have done so: but she still felt he at least must bear some responsibility for alerting the do-gooding authorities to their plight when she would have preferred no one to have known. It never occurred to her that it had been the Salter constable!

SEVENTY-TWO

NONE of the villagers bothered to attend Wakenham's funeral: why should they have done? The man was a relative newcomer to Gledlang: he had lived there only twelve years and, apart from employing Old Jim Borne, he had contributed nothing to its prosperity or taken part in its way of life. He had never attended the village church and had never been seen drinking in either of the village's two pubs, but had kept himself to himself, remaining in his house, complaining to the delivering postman of his asthma and his nerves and other ailments, imagined or otherwise – angina, arthritis, hypertension, rheumatism, bronchitis, pneumonia, shingles, psoriasis and piles – which seemed to attend him all the time. The postman, of course, passed it all on to the postmistress, Ma Rowthey, who in turn passed it on to all who entered the post office-cum-grocery store in the Square, so that the poor man became a laughing stock among the villagers and none cared when he passed away.

There was one mourner: Olive. She at least had made what effort she was able by sewing a diamond of black cloth on the upper arm of her green coat, polishing her shoes as best she could from the shoebox in Wakenham's kitchen and putting on her one and only dark headscarf.

Alice stubbornly refused to go, despite Olive's pleading that she needed someone to accompany her, saying it would bring back sad memories of their mother's funeral, at which she had been so distraught, and also that more recently of her father: nothing Olive could do or say would persuade her. Alice hated funerals for their coldness and their ritual and also, of course, for their utter finality: on the morning of the funeral, she made herself scarce: so when the time came, Olive walked down Tithe Street to the church on her own.

Neither did Old Jim go: not because he feared funerals but because he had the cows to milk, the horses and the chickens to feed and tasks about the farm to be done: besides labourers did not go to governors' funerals: he would feel out of place: and he did not have a suit! He was out working in the field ploughing with Betsy at the precise moment the polished wooden hearse bearing Wakenham's remains was being pulled by Charlie Male's men up the sand and gravel path towards the church door where a stony-faced vicar waited.

So Olive alone of the villagers followed the coffin from the nave to the grave and only she, the two gravediggers and Charlie Male's men saw it lowered into the hole: had anyone placed her hand upon a Bible and asked her to tell the truth, she would have been forced to admit that she attended only in the belief that no one should go to their grave without a single mourner to accompany them to their last resting place and she knew that no one would be there for Wakenham: and, after all, he had given her a job when she had needed it.

There was one other man there, though he could hardly have been called a mourner, for he was not in church when the prayers were said or when the vicar delivered his all-too-brief, eulogy, all three sentences of it: 'We are here today to bury the mortal remains of ... A Londoner by birth and a relative newcomer to the parish, he did not come much into the village and so ... We pray that his soul may find peace in the House of Our Lord. Amen.' Not much of an oration for sixty-six years of life!

The bespectacled man, dressed in a dark suit and a smart black overcoat with a velvet collar, was just entering the gate as Olive walked back down the path and, respectfully, took off his black bowler on seeing her, giving the faintest of smiles as though he were surprised to see anyone there: Olive did not know who he was and so passed him without speaking.

She was walking back past the old smithy when the car came up behind and a polite, educated voice addressed her through the wound-down window: 'May I give you a lift, madam?'

It was the bowler-hatted stranger from the church. 'If you are going back to Follenfaunts House, I am also going there,' he said, smiling as he leaned across the passenger seat and pressed down the handle to open the door. 'Am I right in thinking that you are called Olive? Olive Cullen?'

'Yes. What of it?' answered Olive, genuinely puzzled, first, that the man should offer her a lift and, second, that he should even know her name.

'Please get in, Mrs. Cullen,' the man in the bowler hat said, shifting a briefcase off the passenger seat. 'I am here regarding Mr. Wakenham's estate.'

Olive did as she was bid and he introduced himself as Thomas Wishart, of Wishart and Stebbens, solicitors of London: Wakenham, he said, had telephoned him during one of his illness panics several months before.

'I would have introduced myself before, but I arrived too late for the funeral service,' said Wishart, easing off the handbrake off and pressing on the accelerator. 'I had trouble finding the village and wasted several precious petrol coupons driving fifteen miles in the wrong direction. It was necessary also for me to see the vicar before I drove to the house, to ensure that all was as it should be, you understand?' He smiled as he said it.

'I am pleased I have caught up with you, Mrs. Cullen,' he went on. 'I gather that you were an employee of the late Mr. Wakenham, and that you are still working on Follenfaunts farm, are you not?'

'Yes, I'm still there till I'm told otherwise,' replied Olive, suspiciously. 'I'm owed money. So is Old Jim Borne. And my sister, Alice, his housekeeper. You have to keep going, don't you? You can't just give up on a farm. You have to keep working, don't you?' She hoped the latter remarks would be taken as an example of her diligence.

'Quite, quite,' agreed Wishart, letting out a small sigh. 'That is what I am here to settle.'

'Good,' said Olive and settled back more comfortably in the seat, arms folded: the man offered no other information so no further conversation passed between them before the car braked to a halt on the gravel in front of the main door.

'You have a key to the house?' was all the man asked as they got out: he bade Olive lead the way, taking off his bowler as they crossed the threshold.

The man allowed himself to be conducted into the first of the large drawing rooms where he placed his briefcase upon the table, opened it and took out a sheaf of papers, perhaps twenty in all, and an Ordnance Survey map, which he studied for a few seconds.

'If you would be so kind as to show me around, I should like to tour the house and the farmyard in general, starting here,' he added. 'I need to take an inventory of everything.'

'We haven't taken anything,' an offended Olive declared. 'Everything's still here. We aren't thieves. Not like some people I could name. We'd just like to get what's owed to us, that's all. I'm owed for all of the past week.'

'All in good time, all in good time, Mrs. Cullen,' said Wishart. 'Neither you nor Mr. Borne or the housekeeper have anything to worry about. I am empowered to pay all wages owing up to and including the present until the matter of the estate is settled.' He coughed politely and smiled. 'After I have made my inventory, I shall require your presence and that of Mr. Borne and the housekeeper in the parlour. Shall we say four o'clock?'

Olive was reassured now that knew she was going to get her money: that at least was something: and, if the man from the solicitors was planning to run the estate until the nephew took it over, or it could be disposed of, then both she and Jim might be kept on even longer.

Wishart began a tour of the first room, carefully inspecting the books and the paintings, as well as the ornaments upon the mantelpiece, even the contents of the underside drawer of the dumb waiter beside Wakenham's armchair: all the while, he consulted what Olive soon realised was a complete inventory of the contents of Follenfaunts, from the large bed upon which Wakenham had died right down to the smallest ornament. As he noted each item on his list, the man ticked it off with a gold fountain pen, seemingly oblivious to the fact that Olive was following behind, red-faced with embarrassment and fuming at the same time. Obviously, he was checking to ensure nothing had been stolen!

'You'll find everything's where it should be,' Olive curtly reminded him more than once: though on the day Wakenham had died, while putting back the tea spoons in the drawer of the dumb waiter, she had mused over whether anyone would miss the thirty or so pieces of silverware stored there, spoons, knives and forks of every shape and size, all bearing a hallmark and some still wrapped untouched in tissue paper.

The first room inspected, Olive led Wishart to the second drawing room across the wide hallway where the whole process was repeated at his leisure over the next half hour: after that, she led him to each room in turn, downstairs and upstairs until he had seen the whole of the inside of the house. In the kitchen, a nervous Alice was briefly introduced. 'My sister,' Olive told Wishart. 'She's been working as his live-in housekeeper for the past few months. My son and I have been keeping her company till we can shut the house up.' Wishart merely nodded and wrote it down on one of his sheets of paper.

Outside, they found Old Jim in the barn, cutting up turnips and root vegetables with which to add to the horses' meal: his question was different from Olive's: not whether all wages owing would be paid, but, with a trembling lip, whether Wishart knew if the new owners would be keeping him and Olive on? Working at Follenfaunts was his reason for getting up in the morning: it gave him somewhere to go during the day, somewhere he could be useful. The prospect of not being kept on when the new owners took over weighed more heavily upon him than not being paid the week's money he was owed since he spent very little of what he earned, anyway, except what he needed to pay out for food and rent, his monthly quart of paraffin which he used to light his lamp and the coke he burnt on his fire.

Wishart's reply was disarming. 'That will be for the new owner to decide,' he said with a polite smile. 'I am afraid I cannot give you any guarantee about your work. I am empowered to settle any outstanding wage bill which I shall do today and to make arrangements regarding the continued welfare of the livestock, such as they are. However, I am quite sure that the new owner will require employees and in these trying times I see no reason why they should not offer you a position similar to that which you presently hold.'

It was not an answer which satisfied Jim, for it told him precisely nothing, except that there was to be a new owner, and, after agreeing to wait for his money till four o'clock, he returned to his work mumbling to himself and looking very downcast, while Olive led Wishart around the chicken coops and then along the headlands to the various fields: he ticked off each field in turn upon an Ordnance Survey map, this one fifteen acres, oblong, sown with barley, that one, square, eighteen acres, sown with wheat, the next irregular in shape, twenty acres of potatoes, and so on: it took them till almost teatime. It was as they walked back to the house that, the first and major part of his mission having been accomplished, Wishart allowed himself a satisfied comment. 'All seems well and in good order, Mrs. Cullen.'

'And why shouldn't it be?' said Olive, more sharply than she meant to do, still put out by Wishart's need to consult his sheaf of papers every few minutes and to tick everything, including the plough, the binder, the harrow, and the seed drill, even Betsy and Sam's collars and harnesses. 'I told you, we work here. Why would we want to steal from the place? We'd be cutting our own throats, wouldn't we?'

Wishart reddened slightly, but his only reply was a polite, 'Quite, quite, Mrs. Cullen, but I have to complete the inventory.'

His business around the farm done to his own satisfaction, he finally led the way back to the house, scraping the mud from his black patent leather shoes with a grimace and uttering a mild criticism that the amount of mud and muck to be found upon farms was so unlike the paved and swept streets of London: Old Jim was waiting outside the back door, nervously twisting his cap.

When they entered the main drawing room, a fire was blazing in the grate: Alice had decided to put on a show to counter the grey gloom outside: she had also had the presence of mind to prepare some corned beef sandwiches and to boil a kettle for tea: it was the prospect of a cup of hot tea which detained Olive more than Wishart's plea that she remain: all she wanted was to receive her money and leave.

Wishart seated himself at the polished table and bade Olive, Alice and Old Jim to draw up chairs and to sit opposite him: Olive and Alice did as he requested, rather self-consciously, but Jim, being in his work clothes and unused to being invited to sit in such a well-furnished room, mumbled that he preferred to stand and took up a position by the door: the moment of his demise, he felt, had come.

Wishart took a sip of tea and placed it to one side of the papers he had spread before him. 'I am obliged to tell you,' he said, leafing through the papers as though rereading them, 'that, two months before he died, your late employer, realising that the time of his demise was approaching, sent me an inventory of all his possessions and holdings, from household effects to farm machinery, made soon after he arrived here. It was my duty, as his executor, to ensure that nothing of value was missing from the estate. I am pleased to say that, having toured the property, I find that all is as it should be and, therefore, I am prepared to proceed with the second part of my duties, namely the reading of the will of the late Richard James Wakenham. I should explain that, under the terms of the will, had anything of any value been missing from the estate, I was to enact certain contingencies, namely to sell the whole estate at auction and to deposit the money in a named charity. That not now being necessary, I shall be pleased to read the last will and testament of the late Richard

James Wakenham, owner of the said Follenfaunts Farm, in the said county.' Here he paused, though whether for effect or to give them time to comprehend Olive was not sure.

'To my loyal servant, James Borne, I leave the sum of fifty pounds.'

Olive and Alice looked at each other, dumbfounded. Fifty pounds! Good gracious! Old Jim is rich! The old farmworker tottered a few steps forwards into the room, attempted to speak, but was barely able to stutter.

'Yes, fifty pounds,' repeated Wishart, pausing to look up, unable to understand why the man should be so surprised that such a modest sum had been left to him. 'That is Mr. Wakenham's bequest "for long and loyal service," it says here.'

Wishart paused and looked at Alice, who reddened under his gaze. 'To my housekeeper, Alice Chapman, I leave the sum of five pounds in appreciation of her duties, bearing in mind the length of her service is shorter than that of others.'

Olive could not help herself: in her head she quickly did a mental calculation: if Old Jim were being given fifty pounds and Alice five, then she must receive, accepting that she was mentioned in the will –and why should she not be? – she should at least get ten pounds: maybe even fifteen? Maybe even twenty!

Almost as if knowing what Olive was doing at that moment, Wishart paused for a few seconds and then quietly read on. 'Being cognisant of the fact that I have no issue of my own, and no relatives living since the death of my sole nephew, Captain Ellis Wakenham, was reported to me by the Red Cross seven months ago in a Japanese prisoner of war camp, and that, therefore, I am the last of my line, all others of my family having predeceased me, I, Richard James Wakenham, being the sole and legal owner of Follenfaunts, do hereby bequeath the house and all its contents, together with the lands which surround it, comprising one hundred and fifty-two acres of arable farmland, which forms the said farm of Follenfaunts, in the said parish of Gledlang, plus all my monies, amounting to some three thousand of pounds, to – ' A pause here for effect or just to ensure that they understood the language. ' – to my loyal employee and good servant, Olive Mary Cullen, for her to keep and to have or to dispose of as she sees fit.'

The blood rushed to Olive's face: there seemed to be a roaring in her ears and she felt faint and knew that she was slipping off the chair: she felt the carpet under her and then a mist passed across her eyes: and voices were calling out far off at the end of a long hazy tunnel.

How long she was unconscious, Olive was unsure: when she came to, the flames of the fire were still flickering in the grate and she was lying on the carpet with a cushion under her head: a smiling Alice was bending over her with a cup of water in one hand, trying to get her to drink, cradling her head in one arm, while behind her Wishart hovered, looking concerned to have cause her to faint: even Old Jim was now seated upon one of the chairs, smiling to himself.

'You've been left the house and the farm, Olive,' Alice was saying. 'You've been left everything. You're rich, girl. You don't have to go looking for a place any more. You've got one right here. A great big house, ten bedrooms and a farm to go with it and money. Three thousand pounds! Three thousand! You're rich, girl, you're rich! Hah, ha! Won't those two – ' meaning Percy and Hubert ' – be sore when they hear.'

Olive struggled up on to one elbow, blinking at the brightness of the chandelier which had been switched on: outside the darkness had closed in.

Immediately, Wishart saw that she was recovered, he came forwards, offering his sympathies. 'Oh, dear, Mrs. Cullen, oh dear. I do apologise,' he said: then thrusting a document and his fountain pen at Olive, he added: 'I need you to sign this please, Mrs. Cullen. I must be on my way. I have a long trip back to London to make.'

'What am I signing?' Olive asked, blinking back the tears which had somehow formed in her eyes.

'Why, the receipt for the deeds, Mrs. Cullen, the receipt for the deeds!' exclaimed Wishart.

As Olive looked about her, her eyes met those of Alice, who was laughing. 'Now you can get the children back,' said Alice, laughing and clapping her hands. 'Now you can get the children back!'

SEVENTY-THREE

ALMOST in a daze, Olive wandered first into the drawing room to the right of the entrance hall: it had always been one of her favourite rooms, though she had hated the time when she had spent cleaning it and dusting and polishing there: though that had been for Wakenham: now she would be doing it for herself! The room was spacious, some twenty-five feet by fifteen, with a flower-patterned settee and two armchairs, old, but still very useable, placed on a white polar bearskin rug before a fireplace of grey marble, over which hung an ornate gilt mirror. A black onyx clock with a gold face and gold pillars stood in the centre of the mantelpiece, with two ornate matching pink vases and two matching single-stem silver candlesticks jostling for position at either end: in between, was a scattering of smaller ornaments, a mother-of-pearl snuff box, a silver cigarette casket, a figurine of a blue-trousered boy with a basket of apples and an aproned and becapped rural maid gathering fruit in her hands, which must have cost a large amount of money when they were purchased. The carpet, which Olive had cleaned for so long, rolling it up each time to drag it outside and beat it over the linen line, was hand-woven, patterned in red and, though threadbare in places, still eminently serviceable. A few oil paintings were spread around the walls, mostly of landscapes unknown to Olive: a river scene with some boats and a church spire, a wooded dell with sheep and a cart and a distant view across fields of a church and village. Beside the armchair stood a small rosewood dumb waiter upon which Wakenham had lain his books and upon which, on many afternoons when she had served tea to him, Olive had set down the tray: against one wall just inside the door was a glass-fronted bookcase, its shelves sagging under the weight of Wakenham's treasury of reading. The room was south-facing with a large bay window in which was positioned a settee upon which Wakenham had liked to doze at times: the window overlooked the front lawn and, when the sun was streaming through, it made the room very warm and comfortable: in winter, with a fire burning in the grate, it would be a palace, compared with the draughty den in the wagon shed and the equally draughty destroyed aerodrome cottage.

The second drawing room directly across the entrance hall was equally as large and equally as lavishly furnished as the first, with rose-coloured wallpaper, a large white marble fireplace, more ornaments upon its mantelshelf, a portrait of what she supposed was Wakenham's mother over it, in one corner a grandfather clock ticking away with its pendulum swinging to and fro, a small side table against one wall, four padded bow-legged chairs covered in green silk set either side against the wall, a walnut cabinet to the right of the fireplace with a cut-glass sherry decanter standing in a small tray on top which was where Wakenham kept his gin and whisky: the key was in the lock, but Olive did not bother to open it: she was not one for drinking, much to Robert's chagrin at times. The sudden memory of him sent a sudden shiver through and her heart skipped a beat: she had not thought of him for a long time, such a long time, months, years, and she found the tears welling up in her eyes: what had made her think of him all of a sudden?

The room in shape was very much the same as the first: the same large bay window overlooked the lawn upon which the sun shone and which was streaming through the curtained windows: there was another fine patterned carpet over the parquet floor, a black, horsehair Victorian settee and the three more oils of landscapes hanging upon the walls: Olive was at a loss to consider which room she preferred of the two: the first, she decided, as she closed the white-painted door.

The third of the four large rooms downstairs was the dark-wood-panelled dining room in which stood a long polished table, seating for ten or twelve, but which, since Wakenham had taken over the house, had never seated more than two, himself and his mother: a side bureau upon which the silver service was put and which contained the napkins and cloths filled half of one wall.

Across the hallway was a third small sitting room which had apparently been the retreat of Wakenham's late mother, for, when Olive had first taken up her cleaning duties, she had discovered several balls of wool and items of half-finished knitting there: its floor was laid in a dark parqueting and it was furnished with no more than an armchair, a settee, a rug before the fireplace and a small table such as from which a chair-bound person might take tea in the afternoon: the usual landscape pictures hung upon the walls, which were papered in blue flowers, while a net-curtained window overlooked a side garden upon which the sun still shone till noon.

Room by room, Olive went through the house: it was a dream which she could scarcely comprehend: more than that, it meant, as Alice had said, now that she had a home of her own, she could get the boys back: she posted a letter to Lenden House the very next day and two days later the district nurse and the same woman from the council who had lured away the five youngest – Olive guessed this from the way the silly woman sniffed at her – visited to confirm that she had indeed inherited a house: they were most surprised and most put out by its size and Olive's obvious good fortune: they even addressed her as 'Madam,' though reluctantly.

By the time the boys returned a week later, Olive had taken the main bedroom, the one in which Wakenham had died: in fact, having no other, she kept his bed and slept in that, using his sheets, his blankets and his pillows as well, all laundered first, of course. Alice preferred to remain in her attic bedroom at the top of the short stairs: she still continued her liaison with the Yorkshire cook, John, who visited from time to time: they still intended to marry when the war was over, as it obviously would be sometime. There was no chance of Britain losing it, not now the Allies were in Germany itself: everyone knew that: it was just a matter of time, that was all.

The other bedrooms the boys shared between themselves, Jimmy on his own in the second main bedroom, Patrick and Jack together at one end of the landing, the twins together in the central bedroom beside the bathroom, and Michael and Joseph in the last of them across from Olive's door.

Olive kept Old Jim on, paying him out of the money Wakenham had left, the first time she had ever had a bank account: to know she had so much money thrilled and frightened her, even if it did mean she had to go on the bus each Friday to Maydun and collect the fifteen or twenty pounds she required from the bank: it still seemed an awful lot of money to her. Jim happily came each morning, even Sundays, to see to the horses and the chickens: he was, in effect, her sole employee, although Jimmy and Patrick were quite happy to help him, especially when it meant working with the horses.

SEVENTY-FOUR

THREE COUNTIES distant in the flat fen country of Huntingdonshire, even as Olive marvelled at her good fortune, dark figures in cement-caked boots and cement-spattered clothing were trundling wheelbarrows along board paths up to a line of grating concrete mixers: the barrows were filled almost casually by other men, then trundled off towards where a small army of dark figures stooped and straightened, shovelled and flattened, paused and laboured again.

In the distance, beneath the vast dome of an East Anglian sky, the brown shapes of a hundred or so American Liberator bombers stood silently in rows, stretching into the leaden mid-November murk: small figures moved among them, over them and around them. A small tractor, towing a line of low trucks, each loaded with a single black, glistening, fin-tailed bomb, weaved its way almost nonchalantly towards them: idly perched upon separate trucks, as if they had not a care in the world, were figures in brown overalls and upturned caps. In the far merging distance, the skeletal framework of scaffolding surrounding what would eventually be a huge repair hangar rose up to dominate the flat landscape: various vehicles were grouped in rows before it. The United States Army Air Forces' new, larger Overbury Malting airfield, with its longer runway for the new B-26s, was nearing completion.

In a long, low Nissen hut located in one corner of the airfield, away from the stooping, labouring figures, three men sat huddled for warmth around a pot-bellied, cast-iron stove which was emitting little heat, certainly not enough to dispel the chill coming up off the concrete floor. The hut was a barracks and a mess hall combined: two rows of bunk beds ran down either side, each bed covered by a dark grey blanket, all in various stages of disarray: many were littered with clothing and other personal belongings: four bare trestle tables, upon which a variety of enamel mugs and dirtied plates were spaced, separated the two rows of beds and two untidy rows of fold-up chairs were ranged along them, enough to seat some sixty men at a sitting.

Beside the stove, a lean, dark-haired man wearing a brown trilby and a soiled fawn raincoat was sprawled in a lopsided armchair: Sean, the leader of the bank raid, had taken a two-month-old print-restricted copy of the local evening newspaper from a box of other papers destined to help light the fire the next morning and was casually turning the pages as though searching for something, at the same time idly flicking ash from a cigarette into an ashtray on the arm of his chair.

'It's the right date, but there's nothing about us,' he said with an air of relief.'

The two men facing him were a flat-faced man with a pudgy nose and a shock of brown wavy hair, smoking and idly watching the blue smoke curling up towards the ceiling. 'There is a war on, Sean,' said Robert Cullen: there was sarcasm in his voice and in his manner, but neither of the other two seemed to realise it. 'A bloody post office robbery isn't going to figure too highly when the Yanks and Brits are knocking hell out of the Jerries in Belgium and Holland and the Ruskies are slaughtering them everywhere else.'

'At least, it means they're not on to us, Bob,' said a younger, thin-lipped, bespectacled man in his mid-twenties seated on a hard-backed chair beside him: Charlie, the driver in the same bank raid, was now looking more assured and at ease.

'Maybe,' Robert answered, cocking one eye. 'Maybe. Or perhaps they're waiting for our next little trip out, ready to nab us with the Home Guard setting up road blocks. We only just got through the last one. Two minutes later and they would have had that farm cart across the road.'

'We don't know they were doing it for us,' said Sean. 'It could have been a coincidence. Half-a-dozen old duffers dragging a cart across the lane doesn't constitute a roadblock to me, just a bloody Home Guard manoeuvre. They couldn't have been told that quickly. Besides the Home Guard has been stood down now. They've been disbanded. We don't have to worry about them any more.'

'We don't want to get too cocky just because there's nothing in the papers,' said Robert Cullen, still with a hint of contempt in his voice. 'The police aren't fools, even if they are English police. We have to be careful, that's all I'm saying, or they will be on to us.'

The man in the armchair flicked more ash into the ashtray and tossed the newspaper aside. 'I know, Bob, I know,' he said calmly. 'So long as we keep our heads, we'll be all right. Three Irishmen among two hundred thousand working in this bluidy country, they don't even know who they're looking for, so they're unlikely to come looking for us here, are they, especially as I've made damned sure the jobs we do are miles away?'

The other two laughed: the man in the trilby did not.

'Dublin have asked us to do one more job,' he said with a sigh, 'a special job, something a bit different from the others. I can't tell you too much till I get the word, but it ain't a straight robbery. No bank or post office or anything like that. This time it's not money were after, it's guns. They want us to get some guns and some ammo. We have to be ready for when this war finishes. They're running short over there and they've got guns and ammo stacked all over the place over here, most of it poorly guarded. It's just waiting to be taken. They want us to have a go at a camp armoury, a night job at a small camp near a place called Wivencaster. I had a scout around a couple of weeks ago. It's isolated and no one'll be expecting us so it should be fairly easy. Most of the bluidy British army are in France anyway shooting at the Germans. It's no more than a makeshift camp – some kind of depot – and they've put their guns and ammo in a hut well away from the other huts and only a few feet from the perimeter fence, with only a couple of padlocks to hold it. There's only a couple of sentries at night. It's obvious they're not expecting anyone to have a go at it. It's a couple of weeks off yet. I'll let you know when. We'll be taking another lad with us, a new boy – ' Groans here from the others. ' – Meanwhile, keep your heads down and we'll be all right. As for me, this one will be my last. After this, I'm on my way back to Ireland and you can kiss this bluidy country goodbye. If any of you want to come with me, that's all right by me. We've done enough. Let someone else have a go. I've told Dublin to send someone else over. We three have done our bit.'

They had done enough 'for the Cause': the post office raid two months before had been their seventh 'job' and had netted them just fifty pounds: Robert had had to stick his revolver up against the old man's head before the old woman behind the counter had opened up the drawer: she had shown a lot of pluck that old woman: it was almost a shame to take the money off them.

Sean had asked Robert to carry the other gun and to go in with him, while the thin-faced, bespectacled Charlie waited outside with the car: there were only three of them by then: the red-headed Liam was long dead. As they had driven away from the bank raid in the small Midlands town, they had repeatedly asked him why he had shot the bank clerk and all he had said was that the clerk had moved when he had told him not to move: he had warned him several times, but he had moved as he was leaving: so he had shot him to stop him from moving. He did not say anything after that because Sean had pressed the gun into his ear and pulled the trigger and he had died. A few miles farther on, Robert and the driver had carried the body into a wood, emptied the contents of his pockets, put it into a deep hollow, covered it with earth, leaves and branches and returned to the car: as far as they knew, the body was still there, undiscovered.

After that, they had driven on to Coventry, where they had stayed a week, and after that to Litchfield, for a further week: then Cardiff, Liverpool, Manchester, Leeds and Glasgow. In some places, they had stayed only the week and had left before arousing suspicion: in others, they had stayed two or three months, taking what jobs were available to itinerant labourers: clearing rubble, working on the dockside unloading the American cargo boats, shovelling coal in an iron foundry. In six months in Glasgow, they had worked with a railways repair gang: in Liverpool, they had loaded armaments on to ships: now they were out in the wilds of East Anglia laying concrete for the big new Yank airfield and helping to build the new control tower. Always their names changed: from Sean to George to Kevin to Terence: from Robert to James to Patrick to Jack, John and Thomas: from Charlie to Ciaran, Shamus and Michael; and always there were those willing to provide false identity cards and ration books.

The man in the trilby reached down and picked up a copy of a thicker American newspaper: it was the American forces' newspaper, *Stars And Stripes,* more than a year old: he spent a few minutes smiling to himself as he turned the pages, laughing at their strange bombastic use of language: then his mouth fell open.

'Hey, Bob!' he called. 'There's a picture of some kids here with the same name as yours. Are they your kids? Three of them. Look. Their names are the same as your lads.'

Robert took the paper: there, staring up at him were the unmistakable faces of his three eldest children, Jimmy, Patrick and Jack, each astride a bicycle, grinning and giving the thumbs up sign for the photographer: they all had thatches of fair hair and were all very much older than when he had last seen them: beside them stood Olive, trying to smile, but failing, looking very self-conscious in her headscarf and overcoat: they were all standing on a lawn beside two uniformed American officers with a big Georgian house in the background.

A headline across the top of the picture said in capitals 'US FLYBOYS THANK YOUNG LIMEY RESCUERS' and underneath was a bold story caption: 'When wounded Army Air Forces Captain Buzz Eglington was parachuted unconscious from his stricken Liberator by his crew buddies returning over the English coast, three young country boys, the Cullen brothers, James (12), Patrick (11) and Jack (eight), dived into the sea to pull the stricken flyboy to safety. The quick-thinking boys from a tiny country village, Gledlang, near the town of Wivencaster, East Anglia, just outside London, England, carried the wounded captain to the nearest road and waved down a passing trucker to get him to hospital. Captain Eglington, from Madison, Wisconsin, has now returned Stateside to help speed his recovery. Crewmen at the Marham Heath airbase clubbed together to give each of the three young heroes a roadster bicycle as a special thank you from the Army Air Forces. They are pictured at their home, Follenfaunts House, Gledlang.'

'Where the hell is Gledlang?' asked the man in the trilby.

'God knows!' said Robert, flopping on to a nearby bed, where he spent the next ten minutes gazing at the picture of his wife, his three sons and smiling. Gledlang? Was not that the name of the village of which Olive had often spoken? Near Wivencaster, the big garrison town. That was where Sean had said their next raid was to be. Good gracious he would be only a few miles away from the boys!

SEVENTY-FIVE

THE SENTRY should not have been there: he should have been two hundred yards away at the other end of the wire fence as he usually was at that time, as all the others had been at that time when Sean had observed them, smoking with the other sentry and keeping a wary eye out for any officer making his late night rounds. But this time, he was standing alone under a tree just inside the fence, hidden by the darkness of its drooping branches: either the unexpected sharp shower had deterred him from joining his mate and he was having a smoke by himself or he was by himself for a reason, like he had something to think about.

Sean, Robert, Charlie and a thin youth named Ciaran, the new boy, were already through the fence, crossing the thirty yards of open ground towards the sandbagged entrance of the armoury hut when the sentry's shout rang out: 'Hey, you! What the bloody hell do you think you are doing?'

It was not what a sentry was supposed to call out, but the man seemed to have been startled from some deep reverie: the sudden appearance of four figures crossing the open ground at a half-stooping run no more than forty yards from him took him by surprise. No one was supposed to be there at that time: and it was not any of the lads sneaking back into camp after a night in town: and, if it was not the lads, then who the hell were they? These characters were in civilian clothes: one of them was wearing a trilby and two of the others were wearing workmen's caps: what were they up to, heading for the armoury? And with bloody bolt cutters in their hands! Christ! They were going to rob it! Steal the guns and the ammo! Bloody hell!

Had the four all turned and run at that moment, then what happened next might not have happened, but they did not: instead Sean let out a curse, fumbled inside his raincoat for his pistol and the next thing Robert knew there was a flash and the crack of the gun right beside his head. Almost immediately, a shout of alarm came from the shadows under the tree, followed by a flash and a bang from out of the darkness there: a bullet hummed past Robert's right leg and ploughed into the ground somewhere behind him.

Another shout came from the shadows: 'Halt, or I fire.'

'You already bloody have,' Sean called out to no one in particular and fired two more shots into the shadows. 'Come on, boys,' he cried, turning to run for the gap, 'we've been rumbled. Let's get out of here.'

For a second, Robert, who had been leading the group, paused: suddenly he was alone in the middle of the open ground, holding the heavy bolt-cutters: twenty yards behind him the bespectacled Charlie was already scrambling through the hole they had cut in the wire: Ciaran was just behind him, so hysterical with fear that he was clawing at the other man to get through the gap ahead of him and the two were shouting at each other. It took a sharp kick from Sean and some harsh words before the first two scrambled through: then Sean was through, followed by Robert, minus the heavy bolt-cutters, which he had tossed aside in his sprint for the gap: finally all four were crashing through the brambles, gorse, nettles and long grass, making for the road where they had parked the car.

When the second and third shots from the sentry came, no one seemed to notice Robert fall: he was a good ten yards behind the others, so no one heard him cry out as the pain seared through his side and the impact of the bullet half-spun him round and sent him toppling into the long grass. For a few seconds, he lay there, wondering why he had fallen: but when he tried to get up to follow the others, now some fifty yards ahead of him, racing through the gorse and brambles, he found he did not have the strength and his left leg was not functioning properly. Something had hit him in the small of the back with the force of a sledgehammer: it felt as if his whole side had caved in.

Another two shots buzzed over his head, but they were being fired at the other three fleeing figures: a minute or so later, out on the road, a car engine started up, gears grated, the blocked headlights came on and the car lurched away, gathering speed: then it was gone and Robert lay alone amid the long grass. Finally, after a few seconds, he managed to raise himself up on to his knees, then slowly he crawled away, gasping for breath as he did so, aware that blood was soaking his vest and shirt and seeping down the inside of his trousers.

With an effort, he covered the first hundred yards to an area of bushes: there, hidden by the shadows, he managed to pull up his shirt and inspect the two wounds. The bullet had entered the small of his back halfway up: from the pain and the difficulty he had in breathing, he guessed it must have ricocheted off his ribs, probably breaking a couple: then it had exited through the soft flesh of his left midriff: there, warm, sticky blood was spurting out of a hole big enough to put two fingers into. Robert knew from the amount of blood that it was a bad wound: he knew, too, that really he needed hospital treatment: but he also knew that that was the one thing he could not obtain, not for a gunshot wound, not for a man with an Irish accent, and definitely not after the bank raid and Liam's stupid shooting of the young bank clerk all those months ago. Meanwhile, the best he could do was to remove his jacket, tear out the sleeve lining, tear that again into two long strips, stuff his handkerchief into the gaping wound in his midriff and then wind the sleeve lining strips round his waist in an attempt to bind it in place, all done with effort and pain. He just had to hope that the bullet had not hit anything vital, like a kidney, or torn the membrane between his lungs and his ribcage.

It was good quarter-hour before he could summon enough strength to move off a second time: over by the road, vehicles were pulling up, voices were shouting out orders, torches were splaying over the gorse and bramble heath: that would be the bloody English army reacting to what that bastard of a sentry had reported! The hue and cry was very much on: but when the vehicles began to move off, Robert allowed himself a smile despite the pain: obviously, they did not know about him: they were all setting off to chase the car, thinking they were all in that: no one had spotted him crawling away.

There was nothing else Robert could do but continue to crawl, away from the lights, away from the road, just to put distance between himself and any would-be pursuers. Eventually, he found a sturdy branch to use as a crutch: with this, he was able to stand and to move more freely: the crutch also helped him to keep his balance when he became light-headed, as he seemed to do every few hundred yards or so with the effort of it all, forcing him to rest till his head had cleared. But at least the wound was plugged, he consoled himself: the bleeding had slowed and he was putting distance between himself and the army camp.

It was during one of his many pauses that he suddenly found himself think-ing of Olive and the boys: when Sean had briefed them on the raid a fortnight before, Robert had noted from the map which Sean had shown them that they would be within a few miles of the village where the photograph of the boys had been taken with the Americans. What was the name of that village? Gled-lang? That was it. Gledlang: about thirteen miles due south of Wivencaster, halfway along the north bank of some long estuary, so he could hardly miss it. He pulled the cutting out of his wallet: blood had soaked part of it, but the words were still readable: and what was the name of the house in which they were living? 'Follenfaunts House.' Must be a home of some kind, a big place like that, a children's home, like the ones in Thurstone. A house of that size and style should not be too hard to find in a small village: and who would guess he was there? Certainly not the police: and certainly not the bloody Brit-ish army! Just thirteen miles, if he could make it. Thirteen miles! He would make it. He had covered a couple of miles already! Meanwhile, the bloody British army and the police would be chasing the others: they were all heading back north: no one would guess that he alone of the four had gone south.

What a damned fool mission it had been, trying to break into an armoury of all places to get guns: whoever had thought that one up! What a damned fool mission, even for the Cause!

SEVENTY-SIX

THREE distinct bangs, echoing through the silence of the house, woke Olive: she was still groggy with sleep when she reached the window and looked out: there was no one to be seen: the clock on the mantelpiece showed a quarter past one. It was only when she looked out a second time that she saw something move in the shadows below her window: someone was slumped against the doorframe as if using it as a support. Her first thought was that it must be Alice. 'Good God! What a time to come back!' Olive said to herself.

Alice had left two days previously on a sudden whim. 'I'm going over to Wivencaster to see my John,' she had announced unexpectedly at breakfast. 'I may stay a couple of nights. I need to tell him something. He should have been over to see me last weekend. I don't know why he hasn't come, but, if he won't come to see me, I'm going over there to see him. I'll book into a bed and breakfast.'

'Does he know you're coming?' a sensible Olive had asked.

'No, that's why I'm staying over,' replied Alice. 'It gives me time to get a message to him. If I can, I'll give a message to one of his friends. If, I can't, I'll just have to phone the camp. I need to see him even if it takes a week.'

She had then made herself up, packed a small suitcase, ridden Olive's bicycle to Salter and caught the bus to Wivencaster. Six months previously, she would never have dared to do such a thing, especially if she had been living at home with her brothers: living with Olive had freed her somewhat: now she was far less inhibited.

Olive suspected that there might be another reason other than just love why her sister had rushed off to see John the Cook: she had been acting strangely of late, one minute looking depressed and weepy, the next smiling to herself and still weeping: also, she had been sick in the sink a couple of times: as any woman would have discerned, quite clearly she was pregnant. Olive did not say anything, of course: she would wait till Alice told her: after all, they were sisters: Alice would tell her in time

Three more loud bangs on the knocker: bare feet were already padding along the cold linoleumed landing: from the sound of them, Olive knew it was Jimmy and Patrick.

'There's someone at the door, Mum,' Jimmy called out: he must have sensed rather than heard his mother's movement in the bedroom.

'Hang on, we're coming, we're coming,' a shout from Patrick as the two bounded down the stairs.

As Jimmy swung back the door, the man half-slumped against the doorpost looked up. 'Hullo, boys,' he said with a pained grin: then, seeing Olive descending the stairs behind them, he gasped out in an equally pained manner, still with a smile upon his face: 'Hello, Olive. You've done well for yourself, I see.'

Even in the darkness Olive recognised the voice as that of her 'long dead' husband: such was her shock at hearing him and seeing him there that momentarily she froze on the very last step, unable to take a single step forward.

'I just came to see you and the boys,' said Robert, lurching forward into the hallway and falling to his knees, his face creased with pain. 'I just wanted to make sure you were all right.' As he said it, something metallic fell with a loud clang on to the floor: it was his gun.

Jimmy and Patrick saw the gun and, even in the dark, they could make out the great dark patch on his white shirt: the gun and the stain told them all they needed to know.

'Have you been shot, Dad?' from the eldest Cullen, staring down at his father. mesmerised.

'I have, Jimmy, boy, I have,' answered his father, coughing blood and clutching at his side. 'The bloody English have done for me, I reckon.' He tried to smile, but the words came out hoarsely, punctuated by little gasps.

'Is this your gun?' asked Patrick, bending down to retrieve it.

'Put that thing down!' ordered Olive, her voice harsh as she recovered from her shock: and, rushing forward, she seized the gun from her son and sent it skidding across the gravel outside. 'I don't want any guns in my house!'

Quickly, she slammed shut the door and bolted it: she, too, had spotted the black stain on her husband's shirt: by turning on the light, she could look at it properly. What she saw appalled her: Robert's shirt, his vest, the lining of his jacket, even the tops of his trousers, were black and stiff with congealed blood: worse, fresh blood was seeping from a gaping wound just above his waist: a handkerchief bound round with strips of cloth, themselves black with blood, covered the wound in a crude attempt to staunch the flow: there was another bloody wound in his back

'God almighty! He's bleeding to death!' wailed Olive. 'He needs a doctor!'

'A doctor won't do me any good,' said Robert through gritted teeth, coughing blood again. 'Not now. I've bled too much. It's too late for me, old girl. I only just made it here. If I had got here this morning, I might have been all right, but it's taken me all day to get this far. I had to lie low in a ditch all afternoon because the army and the police were everywhere. I've bled too much, I reckon.'

'Quick, get some cushions from the living room,' Olive ordered her eldest, 'and you, Patrick, get some towels from the airing cupboard. We need to stop the bleeding.'

They both rushed off on their errands and when they were brought, she was able to place one cushion under Robert's head and another under his upper back to ease him up off the cold polished tiles: the towels she pressed against the two wounds in a vain hope of stopping the bleeding.

'How did all this happen?' Olive asked, trying to control the anger in her voice: all she could think was that he must have been doing something stupid again to get himself shot so badly.

'The bloody British army,' said Robert, exhaling breath as he sank back on to the cushion. 'We were doing a job in Wivencaster last night. There were four of us in on it – no names, no pack drill. We were after a few guns, that's all, but it all went wrong. I got shot by some bloody sentry. The silly bugger wasn't where he was supposed to be! He was standing under a tree, having a fag. We had to make a run for it and I got shot. I don't know whether the others got away or not. They went off in the car and left me, the bastards! Maybe they think I'm dead already.'

Olive picked up on the one point which made her heart sink. 'Guns? Whatever do you want guns for?' she demanded, though instinct told her the answer.

'For the boys in Ireland,' Robert confirmed, smiling weakly. 'The boys in Ireland needed some guns. We thought this army camp here would be a soft touch. It had an armoury right near the perimeter fence. We were going to ship them over to Dublin in a fishing boat at night. Plenty of places to land. No bother. It's been done before. It beats robbing banks and post offices!'

'Robbing banks! Is that what you've been doing all this time? Stealing people's hard-earned money for that silly bloody cause of yours?'

Robert waved a weak, dismissive hand. 'I've no time to argue with you, woman,' he said. 'Besides, it was only English money. We were just taking back what they took from us over the years, that's all.'

'With guns! You must be mad, the lot of you!'

'Of course, with guns. How else do you rob a bank? You have to show them a gun or they won't give you the money,' Robert replied, not bothering to conceal his sarcasm despite the pain etched on his face.

'They won't come here looking for you, will they?' It was a repeat of the scene in the flat.

'They've got no reason to,' Robert reassured her. 'No one knows I'm here, so why would they? With luck, they'll be chasing after the others, if they haven't caught them already. No one knows about me and they'll hardly think of looking here, will they? Besides, it won't matter if they do come. Sorry, old girl, but I reckon I'm too far gone. By the time they get here – ' He did not finish the sentence, but raised one eyebrow and adjusted his position on the cushions as if to ease his pain: Olive caught the meaning in his words and felt a cold shiver run through her: it was the same feeling she had had when she stood before the bombed house in Rupert Road four years before.

A grimace and a smile here from Robert and an attempt at jocularity: 'I hope you don't mind me coming, old girl,' he said. 'I just happened to be in the district so I thought I'd come and look you and the kids up. I came across the fields so I'd miss the roadblocks. It just took me too long. Too many bloody soldiers and too many bloody police out looking for me! Or for them. I knew you were in some big house out this way. I saw a picture of it in some Yank army newspaper when we were working at one of their aerodromes. I couldn't believe my eyes. You and the kids in a big house like this!'

'You could hide somewhere if they don't know you're here. We could get you a doctor. There's an Irish doctor at Cobwycke – McFadden. We could get him. He wouldn't say anything.' Olive was desperate now: the colour was draining from Robert's face and he was gasping for breath more and more.

'No,' sighed Robert, trying to smile at her tear-stained face. 'No, it's too late. I just wanted to see you and the kids again.' He looked up at Jimmy and Patrick, standing a little way behind their mother and looking down at their prostrate father, clearly shocked by what they were witnessing: Jack came cautiously down the stairs to join them.

Olive pulled away one of the towels she was pressing against the larger exit wound to see if it had stopped the bleeding: it had not: blood was continuing to seep from it. 'Where the hell have you been all this time?' she asked in exasperation. 'Where were you when the bomb dropped? Four years we've been out here! We thought you were dead. We thought you were in the house. We thought you had been killed when the house was hit.'

A pained laugh through gritted teeth from Robert. 'No, I was elsewhere, meeting a friend. I didn't go back to the house till a fortnight later and it was just a pile of rubble by then. It was several weeks before I heard you'd been seen at the church hall and had left for the country. Well, at least I knew you and the boys were safe.'

'Whyever didn't you come after us?' demanded Olive, brushing at the tears rolling down her cheeks. 'Whyever didn't you write?'

'Where to? I didn't know where you were exactly. I've never been to this place before. You always refused to come here. Besides, I'm not one for writing.'

Above on the landing, the pale and frightened faces of the twins peered down at their father through the banister railings, while on the stairs, an anxious Jack looked on, unsure whether to come down or not. 'Is that the twins up there?' Robert asked, raising himself slightly to take a better look. 'Goodness, they have grown! Hullo, boys. How are you?' He waved his hand, but then fell back on the cushion again.

'Come down here,' Olive called to Thomas and John, but they seemed reluctant, so she turned to Jack. 'Go and fetch them down here,' she said, 'so he can have a better look at them.'

'How's Michael? How's Joseph?' Robert asked, as Jack brought the nervous twins down the stairs.

'They're asleep,' Olive told him: then, realising why he was asking, she said, almost with a sob in her voice: 'Fetch them down. You, Jimmy, Patrick, wake them up and bring them down here. Carry them down if you have to.'

As Jimmy and Patrick raced up the stairs, Thomas and John were presented to their father: they seemed to have forgotten who the man lying in the hallway was and could not understand why they were being taken down to him: nor could they fathom the reason why he smiled at them or why he was covered in so much blood.

After a few minutes, Jimmy and Patrick returned, leading Michael and Joseph by the hand: having been taken from the dark of the bedroom and brought into the harsh light of the hallway, the two youngest blinked and cringed, especially at the sight which met their eyes: rather than go to their mother, who was kneeling beside the figure on the floor, they clung to their brothers instead.

Robert looked at them all in turn, smiling as he did so: then after a while he closed his eyes with a deep sigh: the tears rolled down Olive's cheeks. 'The bloody fool! The bloody fool!' she kept repeating to herself: it was just anger, anger and frustration and loss: Michael, Joseph, John and Thomas just watched, not understanding any of it.

Finally, a blanket was fetched and Olive, Jimmy, Patrick and Jack carried their father upstairs to the main bedroom, where they laid him on Olive's bed and covered him with the eiderdown: then the boys closed the door and left their father and mother together.

After that, Jimmy went back outside to pick up the revolver: it was only a short walk to the manure heap where he buried it: then he fetched a mop and a bucket of water and washed the blood off the steps and the hall tiles and threw the water out on to the gravel.

SEVENTY-SEVEN

THE POLICE and the army came the next morning, as Olive expected they would: they called at the house just before noon: Olive answered the banging at the door to find a sergeant and a constable standing on the step: both were wearing sidearms: behind them by the gate stood four soldiers with rifles shouldered.

Coming to such a large house, the police sergeant touched the peak of his cap out of respect. Pardon him for calling, but they were chasing a fugitive, he said. He was armed and dangerous. A man had been seen crossing a field nearby the previous night and he might just be the fugitive they were looking for. Could they search the outbuildings in case he was hiding in one of them? Nothing to worry about, madam. It was all routine. They just wanted to make sure.

Yes, of course, Olive agreed. 'What's he done?' She tried to sound as casual as possible: it had occurred to her that, if they knew Robert's name was Cullen and that her name was Cullen, too, they might not be just passing by, but on a reconnaissance for a much larger group waiting to rush in and seize him.

'We reckon he might be one of a gang who tried to raid an army camp over at Wivencaster a couple of nights ago,' said the sergeant. 'We reckon there were four of them. We've got three of 'em. We think the fourth may have come this way. It seems they were all working together at one of the Yank aerodromes, extending the runway. Laying concrete. Using that as a cover. False names and identity cards and that. Half of these Irish use false names and false IDs. Helps them avoid paying income tax and the like.' Just like Robert, thought Olive.

'We'd be grateful if you would keep an eye out and call us if you see anything suspicious,' added the sergeant, touching his cap. 'If you wouldn't mind, madam?'

No, Olive did not mind. The two policemen and the soldiers had been up all night, tramping over fields, forcing their way through hedgerows, climbing over gates, poking into ditches, prodding haystacks and creeping through flea-infested outbuildings on other farms: they were cold, bedraggled, hungry and fed-up. They just wanted to search the barn and leave: with luck, somebody else would spot the fugitive miles away and give chase. So after searching the barn, the wagon shed and the milk shed, they left.

Robert Cullen did not see them come or see them go: his eyes were sightless: he had finally died three hours before and lay covered in a sheet on the large double bed in which Olive slept: all night she had lain beside him as his life ebbed to its close: the tears were for the futility of it all, the waste, the stupidity.

That night, as soon as it was dark, Jimmy, Patrick and Jack and their mother carefully carried the body downstairs, placed it on a wheelbarrow and took it to the remotest corner of the farm, well away from any prying eyes. They took it in turns to dig the grave: it took them three hours or more to go down four feet before Olive decided it was deep enough and long enough: then they carefully laid him in the hole: everything was done in silence: the prayers were spoken in their minds rather than aloud: Then they shovelled back the earth and patted it down flat, spreading the excess. Robert Cullen, rebel and supporter of the cause of a united Ireland, had found his last resting place: in English soil: now, too, he would always be near his wife. The four youngest remained at the house, knowing nothing of the burial as they were already abed.

As Olive and the three eldest walked back, there was a drone of bombers high in the sky: the night was clear and stars filled the heavens: another bombing raid was heading for Germany: more women and children would die that night.

Just before they reached the house, Alice and John the Cook came strolling up the driveway in the darkness, arm-in-arm: they were both smiling: Jimmy, Patrick and Jack sloped away, not wishing to meet them or to be seen, and also to put the spades back in the barn.

'I've got some news,' beamed Alice, clinging tightly to John the Cook's arm. 'We're getting married by special licence as soon as we can. We decided today.'

'You're pregnant then, are you?' said Olive, a little sniffily: she neither approved nor disapproved: to her, a pregnant sister was just another fact of life at that moment.

Alice confirmed it with her smile. 'Well, so long as we get married, it won't matter, will it?' she said, hugging John the Cook's arm even tighter, which made him flush with embarrassment.

'I take it, it's all right with you?' queried Olive, giving John a huffy stare.

'Oh aye, it's fine by me,' answered John the Cook, unable to avoid that hangdog look which so marks men at such times. 'We decided on it yesterday. We'd have come over and told thee, but there's been a bit of a flap on at the camp and muggins here – ' meaning himself ' – was right in the middle of it. Some blokes tried to break into the armoury. IRA, we reckon. After the guns, they were. Always said that gun store was too near the fence. Four of them broke through the perimeter fence. It was my bad luck to be on guard duty. When I challenged them, blow me, if one of the blighters didn't fire at me! I was standing under a tree, having a smoke. Bullet hit the trunk inches above my head. Well, I fired back, didn't I? Reckon I hit one of them, too. Couldn't see much in the dark, but I know I hit someone because we found blood. At first, they thought all four had got away, but they caught three of them in a car on the A1, heading for Stamford. They reckon the other one, the one I'd winged, must have crawled off somewhere and hid. Not a sign of him anywhere. They've been searching for him all yesterday and today, but they haven't found anything yet. He must have been a real strong chap not to stop when he'd got a bullet in him. A three-o-three makes big hole in a man when it goes through him. I doubt he got far, though. Couldn't have gone more than three or four miles losing blood the way he was – '

His voice trailed away as though it were disappearing down a tunnel: Olive hooked her arm through her sister's and together they walked back towards the house, John the Cook trailing behind them...